TREASURE SEEKERS

H. BEDFORD-JONES

TREASURE
SEEKERS

H. BEDFORD-JONES

INTERIOR ILLUSTRATIONS BY

MAURICE BOWER

ALTUS PRESS • 2015

© 2015 Altus Press • First Edition—2015

EDITED AND DESIGNED BY
Matthew Moring

PUBLISHING HISTORY

"Carson's Folly" originally appeared in the July, 1945 issue of *Blue Book* magazine (Vol. 81 No. 3).

"One-Legged Dancer " originally appeared in the August, 1945 issue of *Blue Book* magazine (Vol. 81 No. 4).

"Grotto of the Nymphs" originally appeared in the September, 1945 issue of *Blue Book* magazine (Vol. 81 No. 5).

"Wing of the Lion" originally appeared in the October, 1945 issue of *Blue Book* magazine (Vol. 81 No. 6).

"The Sorcerer's Daughter" originally appeared in the November, 1945 issue of *Blue Book* magazine (Vol. 82 No. 1).

"Brittany Treasure" originally appeared in the December, 1945 issue of *Blue Book* magazine (Vol. 82 No. 2).

"The Pledge of Honor" originally appeared in the January, 1946 issue of *Blue Book* magazine (Vol. 82 No. 3).

"Viking Loot" originally appeared in the February, 1946 issue of *Blue Book* magazine (Vol. 82 No. 4).

"The Nobleman and the Ugly Barmaid" originally appeared in the March, 1946 issue of *Blue Book* magazine (Vol. 82 No. 5).

"Death-Trapped Gold" originally appeared in the April, 1946 issue of *Blue Book* magazine (Vol. 82 No. 6).

THANKS TO
Everard P. Digges LaTouche and Gerd Pircher

TABLE OF CONTENTS

I

CARSON'S FOLLY

The first of a fascinating new series.

WHEN THE European war went to pieces under us, Murchison and I were billeted at Lord Iverleigh's huge arms works in Kent—a factory, we would have called it, back home. We had been through Boston Tech together and in the Army together, and were out on loan to the British together.

Murch was a great guy.

"Now we never *will* see Europe, big boy," he said sadly, when we got the news of the twilight of the Hitlerian gods. "We've lent our blooming Allies a lot of good Yankee ingenuity; we've worked out detectors for every damned kind of land-mine the Krauts could think up—and the war's over! We get shipped home, now, and that's all."

"Not for me," I told him. "I've been promising Bill Carson a tour of Europe, and I mean to have it—with or without Frank Murchison. Give me a chance to think."

"That'll be a new experience for you," he retorted. "But go ahead. Count me in."

"Not in the thinking, son. You're merely the executive arm; Bill Carson is the brains. Remember the Frenchman that Headquarters sent to us last week, with the samples of those new Teller and personnel mines?"

"Sure. Some kind of nobleman, but an officer of the Maquis and a go-getter. I liked him," Murchison recalled.

"Well, you go up to London in the morning and find him. Get him here. Then see your brass-hat, red-tab friends—you

"Hello!" exclaimed Murchison.
"Find something?"

know a lot of them—and have them pull wires to get us discharged."

He whistled softly. "So? It'll take a bit of time."

"Mr. Carson's thinking will, too," I told him. "Go on, now; no questions. Either you trust me or you don't. I think we've really struck oil, Murch, if my notion works out; but it's so big that I'm afraid to talk about it yet."

He nodded. "As usual, Mr. Carson, I'll take a chance on you."

Sure enough, when I woke up in the morning he was gone. I went to the lab and got to work, but not on Government jobs. We were all through with the war now.

Our work had dealt with mines—or more properly, with mine-detectors of the newest forms, which we had helped perfect. The *Herrenvolk*, with its usual evil genius, developed

the most infernal types of personnel mines ever known, and the counter-efforts had to keep pace. Plastic containers, for example, made a brand-new type of detector necessary.

In countering this diabolism, we had evolved mine-detectors which went after the thing contained, rather than the container. This effected, we were playing around with some of our own private notions—when the war collapsed and we sat twiddling our thumbs.

Chief among these notions was a gadget which Murchison had dignified with the name of Carson's Folly, although it was our joint product. It was a very neat little portable detector of radionic type, and by shifting about various kinds of tubes in it, different results could be obtained. We thought at first that we had a world-beater here, but changed our minds, for it would not work at any depth less than three feet. Consequently, about the only thing Carson's Folly would *not* detect, was land-mines.

In the course of our experiments, however, we had chanced upon some very singular results. These had given me an idea which I'd mulled over frequently. Another reason our gadget was unsatisfactory was that its waves would not bounce back from a small object like a mine; instead, they slipped around and were lost. The object had to be fairly large. We were not interested in detecting millstones, however.

SO, WHILE Murchison was whanging around London and parts adjacent, I devised new variant tubes for Carson's Folly, and put in fifteen hours a day doing it. The results were in some ways good, in others bad: At less than a three-foot depth it was useless, and the tubes of my invention had an annoying way of blowing out. On the other hand, the recordings on the gauges, which served much as does a radar screen, were highly exact. And what was far more to the point, I found that the wave kick-back varied according to the density of different metals and that this variation also extended to other objects.

This was a discovery of absorbing interest, and I labored on it day and night until I had worked out a chart showing the wave reactions from different substances and according to the nature of the tubes employed. I was getting this chart accurately checked when I had a wire from Murchison that he would be on the morrow and was bringing the Vicomte de Gondy as desired. Murchison had been gone nearly a week.

I was all ready for them when they arrived early next afternoon; in fact, I had had a trench four feet deep dug outside the lab.

Murchison and I had both taken a liking to Gondy. He was lean, dark, vivacious, bubbling over with enthusiasm, and yet he conveyed an air of dependability. He was in his late twenties and had lost his wife during the war. He had traveled all over

Europe and Africa, and had an amazing knowledge of people and places. The war had ruined him; on his previous visit he had told us why.

The three of us got together in the lab, and we were an odd lot, certainly: Gondy, full of life and pep. Me, Bill Carson, built big and heavy and with a cautious slant. Murchison, gray-haired at thirty, a skinny broomstick of a guy. When Murchison laughed he showed all his teeth, and the sparkle in his gray eyes won your heart. He was not your typical scientist, because, like Gondy, he bubbled; he would believe anything plausible, and could spring upon a shocked world some of the darnedest ideas ever heard. Neither he nor I were married, thank heaven.

"Gondy," I began, "when you were here before, you told us about losing all your family wealth during the war. Would you mind going over the story and letting me check it?"

He was puzzled as to why he had been asked here, of course. Now he laughed and relaxed.

"Certainly, if you desire! My father was curator of the Musée des Orfevriers in Paris—the Goldsmiths' Museum, in English. It had examples of fine ancient goldwork from all over the world, you comprehend. He saved the most precious objects of this collection when the Germans came to Paris, taking them to our family home, the Chateau de Gondy, near Orléans. Also, he had there the family wealth. But the Germans were advancing fast, it was impossible to get away, and he barely had time to hide the whole thing, before the flood caught up with him.

"I told you, I think, that he disappeared during the military occupation; whether he's alive or dead, we don't know. The treasure was never found, for the two men who helped him hide it were killed during the fighting. He was responsible for that collection, and the Museum came hard on the family, when France was liberated. We had to settle up for the intrinsic value of the gold. What would you? Some Frenchmen are like that."

He gesticulated, grimaced, smiled.

"We had to sell everything except the chateau and some of

Lucien appeared, then Félice. The suspense hit us hard.

the ground, to make good. Naturally, we exhausted every effort to find the hoard. We knew, in a general way, that it was buried in the garden between the house and the river. We've turned over a good deal of that ground, but the search is hopeless."

"Thank you," I said. "Now, Murch, I wish you'd take the car and run up to the Hall. You remember that whopping big gold salver that Lord Iverleigh had given him by Queen Victoria or the Czar or somebody—the present Lord's grandfather? Well, borrow it off the butler and fetch it back here, like a good chap."

"Say, what the devil are you driving at, anyhow?" demanded Murchison. "And you haven't so much as asked what luck I had getting the discharges."

"All right, consider it asked. What luck?"

"It's going through next week, that's what!" He grinned and sauntered out.

IT WAS only a couple of miles to the Hall, where Iverleigh resided in state. While Murchison was gone, I entertained Gondy with some of our gadgets, trying not to be too joyful. Discharged! Free! It was almost too good to be true.

Murchison came back at last, bringing the big salver in a felt cover. I pointed out the ditch, to him and Gondy, and the two workmen waiting, with spades in their hands.

"Now, boys, this is a demonstration," I said. "I'll stay here out of sight. You take that salver out and bury it somewhere in the ditch. Take out this box of books and bury it. Take out that carton of aluminum parts and bury it. Have the top smoothed over. When you've finished, come back—and don't tell me where any of the stuff has been put."

They were both considerably puzzled, and Murchison said it was a hell of a way to treat Iverleigh's precious gold salver,— which the butler fully worshiped,—but out they went with the stuff. It took the two workmen all of half an hour to get the boxes buried and everything jake. Then Murchison and Gondy said they were ready.

I got out Carson's Folly. This consisted of a big knapsack holding the batteries and so forth, connected with the finder— a light, curved-handle affair, half the size of a vacuum cleaner, and mounted en wheels. It was made of magnesium alloy, and was very light. When he saw it, Murchison guessed what I was up to, and groaned, but I only laughed at him.

"Now, boys, I'll proceed to demonstrate the all-seeing eye of

Carson's Folly," I said, "after which we'll talk business. No tricks. Nothing up my sleeve. The eye is quicker than the hand, so watch carefully! As I know where the trench is, of course, there's no question of hunting around, but the demonstration should be no less impressive."

It was, too; here was where the value of my chart came in. I trundled the detector down the line of the trench. It buzzed. I looked at the gauges, then at the chart.

"At this spot," I said, "is buried the box of books.... Next!"

Next the gold salver showed up, and the chart left no doubt of it; after that, I located the carton of aluminum parts. Gondy's eyes were bugging out when we returned to the lab, and Murchison regarded me with something close to respect—which tickled me.

"Carson, you win," he said. "You hit things on the nail! Eh, Gondy?"

"*Dieu de Dieu,* yes!" bubbled the Frenchman. "It is marvelous! It is like a mine-detector, only a thousand times more wonderful!"

"You're right, it is," I said modestly. "And now we talk business. Vicomte, you're in with us on a three-way split. This machine is not crown property; it belongs to us. With it, we go to your chateau and prove up on our abilities by locating your family hoard of treasure. Half goes to Carson's Folly—which means to us—in a three-way split, the other half to your family or to you. Those are the terms."

We settled down and stayed settled until mess-time, after returning the gold salver to the Hall. I had never realized what our troops in France had to contend with, until I heard Gondy talk. He simply erupted words with every breath. Not that he objected to the deal; quite the contrary, he was all for it.

But he thought up a dozen ways in which Carson's Folly could make our fortunes, and whenever he bogged down, Murchison picked up the ball and thought up a new one. I just sat and pulled at my pipe and shook my head at everything, until

Murch lost his temper and demanded why in God's name I would not listen to reason.

"Because I'm the brains of this outfit, Murch," I told him. "Now look. You fellows are just shooting at the moon. For all you know, I pulled a slick trick on you. This gadget of ours needs to be proven; it must be demonstrated fair and square. Once it proves up—then what? We haven't finished. We haven't even begun! Then I'll show you where Gondy comes in on the deal, and where we go from there. I have things mapped out in my own mind, but I need to play safe. I need to prove this thing to myself in a practical way, and Gondy's treasure-trove will do it. We may strike all kinds of trouble. The thing won't work on anything buried at less than three feet, for instance; there may be other kinks."

GONDY STOOD up, put his arm about my shoulders, and hugged me.

"You're right, Bill," he said. "But how can I be of help to you in future?"

"I'll explain when the time comes," said I. "How about you, Murch?"

He put out his hand. "You win, big boy, as usual. Where are the plans for this vacuum cleaner of yours?"

"In my head," I told him. "And I made the tubes myself and no one else knows what's in 'em."

"Then all's safe," he rejoined with a nod. "Now let's go eat, and get a bottle of champagne from the mess steward, and talk about getting out of uniform."

We celebrated, right enough. Gondy was cutting circles in the moon and could not be drawn down to earth, but Murchison and I talked common sense. Before the evening was over we had considered all our plans, which depended on our discharges coming through. Gondy answered for getting Carson's Folly past the whiskered *douaniers* at the French customs, and everything looked rosy.

We might have known there would be a catch in it somewhere, and there was, but it was slow to develop, and impossible to foresee.

During the next fortnight everything went swimmingly. The British high command, where Murchison had a pull, arranged the details of our discharges and we were mustered out with never a hitch. The gasoline restrictions being lifted, we picked up an old Army car and ferried from Southampton to Havre. Due to breakdowns, it was a two-day trip to Orleans, and that evening, while we stopped in a village inn, Gondy gave us a closer look at his home situation. He was slightly worried about it.

"The chateau was rather knocked about during the occupation," he said, "but a few rooms are habitable and there'll be no difficulty about putting us all up. The uncertainty lies with my brother. He is an older brother, you see."

"Didn't know you had one," I said. "You never mentioned him."

Gondy looked somewhat unhappy. "He is what we call *difficile, très difficile,* my friends—a man of strong passions and convictions; he was a colonel in the Army and a prisoner in Germany for a couple of years. He married a woman who is most remarkable, but not precisely an angel of light. I am glad that she turned me down for him, this Félice!"

"Nice name," commented Murchison. "I used to know a girl named Felicity who sang in the choir, and every time the preacher prayed that we would attain everlasting joy and felicity, we all looked at her and sighed. It brightened the devotional hour wonderfully."

Gondy, who was usually quick on the trigger, speaking English perfectly, missed the joke. He sighed, and looked down at his hands.

"You see, my brother Lucien is older than I, and therefore head of the house in our father's absence," he said. "I have written them, of course, that we are coming, and why, and I do

A voice from outside came to me. I looked out.
Below the windoe stood the girl Olympe.

not look for any trouble, but one never knows. That woman—
well, I am afraid of her, my friends."

Murchison winked at me. "Leave her to Carson," he said.
"That guy came from Kilkenny by way of South Boston, and
anything that wears skirts just eats out of his hand when he
turns on the charm. You should have seen him wangle anything
we wanted out of Lord Iverleigh's daughter—"

"You're a liar!" I said. "She was a lady. All of forty and most
correct."

"The more spinsterish they are, the harder they fall," said
Murch. "Well, never mind, Gondy. We like you in spite of your
folks, and all we're interested in is turning up the treasure, so
forget it."

A knock at the door broke up our conference. The visitor
was an old comrade of Gondy's in the Maquis forces, and the
rest of the evening was devoted to a celebration in which half
the village joined. It was not notable for sobriety.

WE WENT on next morning, and early in the afternoon
reached the Chateau de Gondy, which stood off by itself in
what had once been a magnificent park, with a river at the back.
At least, it was what was called a river, in these parts, but it was
about the size of a backwoods creek at home, and any agile jeep
could have jumped it. My notions of French grandeur shrank
considerably at sight of the place. The buildings were mostly
ruins, many of the big trees had been cut down raggedly, and
in general the chateau looked as though it had been abandoned
to the rats many years ago.

With two scowling servants, Lucien and his wife came out
to meet us, and it was a cordial greeting they gave us. Lucien
was a big bluff hearty man with an air of harsh and indomitable command; he was dark, had a purplish scar across his left
cheek, and his eyes were greedy, but he was making a successful effort to be pleasant. He shook hands with a firm grip and
invited us inside for wine and refreshments; though regretting

that Murchison and I must double up in one room, he said we would find it comfortable.

As for Félice—wow! Gondy, I thought, must have gone stark mad. She was a knockout in any language, cool and trim and beautiful as a dream of spring. To be specific, she was tall and svelte, high-bosomed, exquisitely gowned, with dazzling corntassel hair and deep blue eyes so alive that they fairly sparkled. Except for a too-small mouth, her features were lovely. She had charm, she radiated magnetism; when she wrapped herself around Murchison, so to speak, he fell for her like a busted tank.

But that mouth!

She and Murch strolled into the building; the two brothers followed; the two sour-faced men took our bags and Carson's Folly, and I just tagged along, thinking. It has been my experience to encounter one or two small female mouths, and invariably to my sorrow. I thought better of Gondy's judgment now. Beautiful as it was, that small, tight mouth was an ill omen....

Inside, the chateau was crumbling, furnished in gimcrack French style with a lot of near-gilt furniture and imitation silk rugs, all unattractive. We were taken to two small bedrooms and left to wash up. Murchison glanced at the stone walls, the little window with a bar across it, the two cots and the commode where I was pouring water, and grunted.

"Magnificent, Bill! And athletic, I'll bet."

"Looks more like jail quarters to me," I said, splashing my face.

"I'm talking about her, you burp! Did you notice her walk? And her eyes? And that deep smooth voice like a dove's note?"

"And her mouth, like a steel trap," I added. "Yeah, I did."

"You have no eye for beauty. I could fall for that gal! I think she likes me—"

"You'd better have an eye for husbands," I warned him. "You are an impractical inventor, with your head in the clouds. There's Gondy, so shut up."

Gondy knocked and entered. He was happy as a lark, and had forgotten all his evil prognostications. Lucien and Félice knew why we had come, they were most pleased, and we would have a look at the possible burial-place of the treasure after the collation. Eager speech poured out of him, like steam from a singing kettle.

We went along to the drawing-room and enjoyed wine and cakes and sandwiches as we talked. Lucien expressed himself as delighted that we had come to restore the family fortunes, but asked no questions about how we meant to do it. He had some silver cups in a case, won for riding and boxing. I was no great rider, but I still held an amateur heavyweight title, and he and I discussed topics of mutual interest while Félice chattered with Gondy and Murchison.

No sign, Lucien said, had turned up of the father; they did not have the ghost of an idea what had become of him. As for the treasure, that was equally ghostly. That it had been buried out behind the house was mere supposition. I gathered from Lucien that he had not got on very well with the old man, or Félice had not, though he did not say this openly.

When I suggested that we go look over the ground, everyone assented and we were led through a side door which, like the little window in our bedroom, overlooked the gradual descent to the river a hundred yards away. This was a bleak patch of ground that had once been a garden. Now it showed ample evidence of digging, but nothing else; there were no trees until the river was reached; there a large beech and numerous willows lined the river-banks.

We discussed the treasure. Its value, Lucien said vaguely, ran into millions—meaning francs, of course. I walked along the building with Gondy, leaving the other three chatting, and we tried in vain to pitch upon some likely spot for the hiding-place. There was none. While we talked, a door at the back of the chateau was flung open and out shot a young woman, who came running up to Gondy with a glad cry of recognition.

"*Tiens!* Olympe!" he exclaimed, and shook hands with her, evincing the greatest joy. He introduced me. She was named Olympe Briançon, and was a ruddy-cheeked, bright-eyed young woman—a cook's assistant, her mother being the cook and wife to one of the sourpuss servants; he was her second husband.

What was more important, Olympe had served in the Maquis during the occupation and Gondy, one of its officers, knew her well. After a few moments she left us, and we turned back toward the others.

"To think of finding her here, an assistant cook!" said Gondy, and laughed. "You should have seen her marching with us, rifle on arm and grenades slung around her waist like turnips! She could use them, too—she fought well. A girl of spirit, and she hated the Boches who had murdered her brother.... Well, well—what about the search program?"

The others asked the same thing. The two servants would dig, if we needed them; but to cover this expanse of ground, a good three acres, was going to take time. Carson's Folly was no racehorse. It was finally arranged that Gondy and Murchison and I would have an early breakfast and get started on the job.

THE BROTHERS and I took a long walk over the estate, leaving Murchison and Félice to sit at home and play with the radio. We came back in time for tea, after which, before the cocktail hour and dinner, Murchison and I had a word in private.

"I don't know whether to start on the search," I said. "We'll just have to take turns running the gadget along the ground."

"I've a better notion," he said. "I tried to figure out where I'd hide the gold on a dark night and make sure of finding it again. You know, this is not the first time the Gondy family has been hit by similar bad luck. Gondy says stuff was buried when the Prussians occupied Paris in 1871,—they were all around here,— and farther back, during the Revolution, stuff was hidden and lost."

"Never mind that," I said. "What did you figure out?"

"That the door we used was about in a line with the big beech on the river-bank. A cord run from the tree to the door would make a marker at night; follow it for ten paces, say, and the spot could always be found again."

"Grand! At last you give an indication of brains, Mr. Murchison!" I said. "That really is swell. We'll tackle it, anyhow—following such a line by eye.... Did you have a nice chat while we were so thoughtfully away?"

"Sure. We found mutual friends in London."

"All right. Maybe she has an object. But let me tell you one thing," I said: "When you see a mouth like that, it is never careless, it is never sensual, and you'd damned well better watch your checkbook. Don't think for a minute that you, as a man, are anything except a blind tool in the hands of a designing female—when she's that type—because you're not."

This really got under his skin—so much so that I was sure Félice had made some sort of play for him. This was so far out of character for her that I became suspicious. Murch and I maintained somewhat strained relations for the remainder of the evening.

The dinner was simple but good, the wine was practically divine—Vouvray '29, I remember—and between radio and piano and conversation, we passed a pleasant evening. Murchison had unbent considerably by the time we retired, and all promised well. I was now even more certain that Félice was going far out of her way to get my partner all bemused, and it puzzled me. A woman of that type does nothing without an object; and while her object is usually matrimony, it is rarely infidelity....

Breakfast is never much of anything in French homes, so our breakfast next morning were better passed over in silence. The three of us agreed to take working turns of an hour each. Gondy carried out Carson's Folly. Murchison helped me adjust the knapsack. I took the detector in hand and started at the house door, while with sticks they scratched an irregular line along the dirt toward the beech tree below.

Murchison was indulging in one of his pipe-dreams. What we should really do, he said, was to equip a dozen men with a dozen of these gadgets and then turn them loose to cover all the ground possible. He expatiated on this and Gondy caught the infection and began to elaborate on the idea, until both of them got so interested that they did not hear the buzzer sound.

I kicked over a stone to mark the spot, glanced at the gauges, pushed on till all was normal, and then consulted the chart. According to this, we had struck gold, sure enough; but it was barely thirty feet from the house door, and to me this did not look very logical. The others noticed my halt.

"Hello!" exclaimed Murchison. "Find something?"

AS HE spoke, the buzzer sounded again and the gauge-needles flickered. The men came close, and I showed them the chart figures.

"Either a big rock or a log," I said with truth. "I haven't worked out the differentials, but take your choice. Something solid, anyhow, and not metallic."

About twenty feet farther, well away from the house, we made another strike, and Murchison, who was by this time acquainted with the chart, let out a whoop.

"Got it!" he cried. "Get your picks and shovels, Gondy!"

Gondy went off at a run, but I began to work the detector back and forth. The result puzzled me, because the gauges fluc-tuated.

"Watch it, Murch," I said. "Here, by the chart, we have either gold or silver—the differential there is very delicate. But here, only a foot farther, it changes perceptibly; the waves still kick back but less strongly—indicating books or paper, according to my figures."

"We'll soon see," Murchison said. "You noticed all the digging that's been going on around here. Not very deep; it's a job to put down a three-foot hole! I'll bet they just scratched the ground, while old Gondy, on the other hand, was driven by the fear of Nazis when he put the stuff away, and he probably went deep with it."

This was logical. While we were discussing it, back came Gondy and the two men at a run, carrying picks and spades. I indicated where to dig.

"I'd say there was a metallic box of some sort about four feet long and three wide down here," I told them. "Part of it is packed with gold or silver, the other part with books or papers. The depth, I think, is around ten feet."

The two men began to sweat, and muttered something about magicians, but Gondy set them to digging. He and Murchison were fascinated by the problem of how closely Carson's Folly

The look on Lucien's face was all I needed.
Before he could set down his glass, I
was out of my chair and at him.

would come to the truth; if my conclusions were correct, we really had something in the gadget, and not just a lucky fluke.

While the digging was in progress, Lucien appeared, then Félice. They joined us, nervous and excited; indeed, the suspense hit us all hard. The diggers went down five feet, six feet, and had struck nothing. They were out of sight at the bottom of their pit when one let out a yell. We crowded around, staring down, and watched them clear a bulky object fully nine feet down. Gondy tore off, full tilt, to get ropes.

Half an hour later we were examining a flat metal trunk which we had hauled up. My predictions as to size were confirmed; it was hung with huge padlocks, all badly rusted. It was obviously very old and as obviously was not the hidden hoard of gold. Lucien had it carried into the house and placed in the drawing-room. Leaving the two men to fill in the pit, we gathered around our prize, and Lucien attacked it with hammer and chisel.

Carson's Folly proved absolutely correct. More than half the old trunk contained family plate of heavy silver; the remainder was family papers—old vellum deeds and so forth. Among the plate were numerous *rouleaux* of gold coin. It was the treasure that had been hidden from the Prussians in 1871!

There was wild jubilation. Gondy embraced everyone, we all shook hands, and amid the general excitement I mentioned the prior discovery. Now that I could trust the detector fully, I blurted out about the gold strike closer to the doorway. Gondy rushed out to set the men at it. I went along and indicated the exact spot for them; leaving him in charge, I returned to the others, who were examining the massive pieces of silver plate.

"Well," I said cheerfully, "we're not interested in family relics, so we'll settle for half the gold and leave you the rest. Eh, Murch?"

"Oh, sure!" he assented. Félice spoke under her breath to Lucien and left the room, with her gliding step.

Lucien turned and looked at us.

"Messieurs! Did you say *half* the gold?"

"Yes, we wouldn't want the other stuff," I replied easily. "There's no doubt whatever that they're now digging up the gold your father hid. Half of that, and half of these gold-pieces, will more than reward us."

HE STIFFENED, seeming to freeze all over as he looked at us.

"I think," he said slowly, "there must be some error. True, you have recovered lost property; we are grateful beyond words. But French law is explicit. The finder is entitled to ten per cent."

Murchison caught his breath. I stared at Lucien; he was a changed man, hostile and indomitable, a massive figure of stony resolve.

"You forget," I said, "that we have an agreement with your brother. Half of the find belongs to us."

Lucien waved this away with a lordly gesture.

"My brother is not the head of the family. I am. He has no power to make such an unfair agreement. As to the museum gold, that of course belongs to the Republic, and you can claim none of it. If I decide to reward you with ten per cent of the family property, it will be most equitable."

I was thunderstruck. This was incredible! Murchison burst forth in angry expostulation, and Lucien waved him aside, saying correctly that we had no written agreement. At this, I lost my temper and gave him a piece of my mind. He turned ugly.

"Like all Americans, you are scoundrels and thieves," he broke out in fury. This topped it off, and I went for him. I regret to say that he knocked me flat. As I came to my feet, a cool amused voice broke in:

"What, messieurs! A squabble over filthy gold? For shame! Lucien, apologize to the gentleman, quickly! I demand it!"

There in the doorway stood Félice, radiant and flaming as a flower. We all gaped at her; she dominated everyone by the force of her personality and beauty. Lucien stammered out something, then tendered me a grudging apology. He seemed afraid of her.

"Let us have no more of this nonsense," said Félice, smiling. "Later, we can discuss the problem amicably. This is not the time."

"That's right." Murchison turned to me. We were both smudged with dirt and grime. "Come on, Carson, let's get cleaned up."

"But the gold—"

"Damn the gold! I want to talk with you about this. Come on."

We went off to our own room, and Félice sent a smile after us. I did not like the smile—it was too triumphant, too damned smug—but her intervention had assuredly checked an ugly scene.

In our own room, I poured water into the bowl and mopped my face, and Murchison followed suit. Messing with that trunk had spoiled our morning beauty.

"This is a hell of a note!" I said. "We're in the soup. I forgot that a Frenchman reveres one thing above all else in the world—gold. And a Frenchwoman is more so—"

"Easy, now," said Murch. "Lucien's a bad actor, yes, but I'll warrant Gondy is all right."

"Of course. But Lucien has us by the short hair."

"Our own fault," said Murchison. "He'll bilk us out of all he can, naturally. Do you realize that the plate and other stuff in that trunk is enormously valuable? Ten per cent of that alone will be a huge sum. Suppose the hidden gold is turned up—"

"And he wants to give us ten per cent of the family money alone!"

"By French law, he's right. Even that much will put us on Easy Street."

"Be damned if I'll let anyone bilk me of what's my just due!" I stormed. "Let alone a sore jaw! I can knock hell out of that guy, and all I want is the chance."

Murchison grinned and pulled a chair over to the one little window. He tried to look out on the digging, but the spot was impossible to see.

WE TALKED things over, gradually calming down to acceptance of the inevitable. After all, half of the whole treasure would amount to a tremendous sum; Lucien might well fight for it. We could afford to take our ten per cent and be about our business.

"I had a great scheme in mind," I said bitterly, "for the three of us to exploit Carson's Folly. The contacts could be made by Gondy, who knows everyone and has been all over. He could arrange all the setups of buried and lost treasure; we step in with the detector and do the locating. People aren't going around hollering that they have a buried pot of gold in the back yard, you know. That's where a contact-man is needed."

"Bill! It's a grand idea!" exclaimed Murchison, taking fire instantly. "Why, right now there's buried treasure everywhere in Europe and Africa and Asia—loot of all kinds, too! It's wonderful! We can even make Government contracts—"

He was off on one of his wild dreams, staking out claims in the moon as he often did. "Estates and empires of the moon!" Cyrano de Bergerac's old phrase was certainly true where Frank Murchison was concerned.

A gentle scratch-scratch came at the door. He went to it, stood whispering for a moment, then closed it and came to me excitedly.

"Hey! Madame is here—Félice, you know. She wants me to run along with her and find Gondy. Says she thinks this whole thing can be straightened out amicably. Suit you?"

"Go along and be damned," I said sulkily. "I want no truck with her. She's a bad egg and I distrust her."

"You're nuts," he rejoined. "All right. See you later."

He departed.

I sat where I was, with my pipe for company. I was extremely out of sorts. That crack Lucien had given me had loosened two teeth, and when anything goes haywire with my teeth, I worry. Also, I had a natural desire to give that brute the trimming he deserved. And bitterly did I regret having blurted out about the gold discovery; if I had held my tongue, we could have controlled the situation.

It must have been close to noon when a tap sounded at the door. It proved to be Gondy. He came in and dropped into a chair disconsolately; he was the picture of misery on a monument and I told him so. He spread his hands helplessly.

"I warned you about Lucien. What can I do? Technically, his position is correct. I am powerless. You must think me a cheat, a dishonorable person, a rascal—"

I reassured him as to this, but his remorse and anxiety could not be assuaged. Money meant little to him; I verily believe he thought far less about the lost gold than he did of his tarnished honor. Lucien's argument that the museum gold belonged to the Government was, he said, all bosh—the family had already made good its loss.

"What is more," he said, as we discussed the whole thing, "my brother is a scoundrel but Félice is far worse. I should know; I was once in love with her, and no one is so clearsighted as a disillusioned lover, my friend."

"I've no illusions where she is concerned," I told him. "But she'll back up Lucien, and that's all the harm she can do."

He gave me a startled look. "Yes? Do you know that she has been playing with that machine of yours? She had Murchison show her just how it works. She has brains."

"What of it?"

"My friend, you are in a den of thieves, and it is all my fault," he said earnestly. "You, Murchison, myself—she would get rid of us all if she could, to get that machine. She realizes the possibilities in it. The gold already secured—"

"Oh! Did it turn up?" I asked. He nodded, but showed no elation.

"Two boxes. The same ones my father buried, as the marks show."

"Did you and Murch and Félice come to any agreement?" I asked. I was astonished when he gave me a blank look.

"Agreement? About what?"

"She came here and got Murch, a couple of hours ago. He said they were going to find you and straighten out the thing amicably."

He shook his head. "That's the first I've heard of it. You must be mistaken."

I was not mistaken, but I said no more. I found the whole situation so devious as to be puzzling. Félice might have been flirting with Murchison in order to get an explanation of our detector and its workings; but why get him away from me on a lying pretext? It was all rather odd, and I did not like it by half.

Gondy and I talked over the ten per cent arrangement, and agreed that the best plan was to accept it, get our share, and skip out. He was delighted on learning of my scheme to put him to work as contact-man and to go on a serious hunt for lost treasures; the fact that we liked and trusted him, in spite of what had happened, brought tears to his eyes.

Realizing abruptly that it was well past noon, I suggested getting something to eat, and we went as far as the door—but no farther, for the excellent reason that a bolt had been shot on the outside. We were prisoners, in a true prison cell!

THOSE NEXT hours were hours of savage fury and fruitless effort. Gondy wore his fists into bloody pulp attacking the door and walls and window-bars; both of us settled down, at last, into angry bitterness, as the afternoon passed.

Later, I recollected a highly tempered screwdriver, a favorite tool, which was in my grip. I got it out, and standing on a chair attacked the cross-bar of the window with it. As I worked away, a low voice from outside came to me.

"*Psst!* M. le Vicomte!"

Putting my face against the bar, I looked out. Below the window stood the kitchen-girl, Olympe Briançon, whom I had met the previous afternoon. She was staring up, her features set in desperate anxiety.

"Hello!" I said.

"Is he there?" she repeated.

"Yes."

"Then tell him—be careful, careful!" As she spoke, she slid from the bosom of her dress a long Luger pistol. "They are going to kill you! Give him this—"

An angry voice barked; with a groan, she vanished from my narrow field of vision. A furious outburst sounded, then died away. I jumped down from the chair and told Gondy about it.

He cursed softly.

"She is a true one, that girl of the Maquis! So they intend to kill us, eh? My friend, I warned you; I felt the danger. And to think I got you into this frightful peril! It is terrible."

"It's more terrible that she didn't slip us the Luger," I said. "We've no arms in our bags. We're helpless. This tool won't even loosen the cement around that bar. But—kill us? That's rather absurd, Gondy! It just isn't done, you know."

"You talk like an Englishman," he said gloomily. "Who in all Europe wouldn't wring your neck or put a bullet in you for gold—for the means of obtaining more gold? That machine of yours, and its possibilities, have hypnotized Félice. Doubtless Murchison already is dead. We shall be sent after him. Who will know? They can destroy us, bury us! Lucien will stop at no crime, under her influence. Today gold is the most powerful thing in Europe—"

He rambled on, completely victimized by his fixed idea. I tried to show him how absurd it was; the words of that ignorant kitchen-girl, instead of confirming my suspicions of Félice, had dissipated them—at least, so far as murder was concerned.

Gondy refused to accept my arguments; he was sunk in a despairing self-hypnosis from which I could not budge him an iota. The notion of bad luck and an evil destiny had depressed his usual gay nature to the depths. While we still argued, there came a rapping at the door.

"Come in," I called. "You can open it; we can't."

The door opened to admit Félice, smiling brightly at us.

Gondy leaped to his feet, transfixed by the sight of her. I put down my pipe and rose. She looked at us, met our eyes, and uttered a light, musical little laugh.

"My poor guests! So someone had shot the bolt—a mistake, of course. That stupid *bonne a tout faire*, Marie, must have done it. Well! We were all too excited—we forgot about luncheon! I have come to invite you to join us in a celebration. What the English call high tea, is it not?"

Gondy blinked. "Where—where is Murchison?"

"Your charming friend?" Félice waved her handkerchief. "Oh, he has gone to Orleans in your car, to get a goldsmith to weigh the gold and appraise it! Everything has been settled amicably; you must hear and approve the arrangement, my friends. Come! Lucien awaits us. Poor men, you must be starved!"

It was perfectly done—so perfectly, that I knew it to be false. She went on to deplore the tragic mistake which had locked us in, and that was well done, too. I almost believed her. Far easier to credit her than the poor kitchen-wench with her melo-dramatic warning that we were to be killed. The truth, I thought, lay somewhere between. Félice had some game in mind. She even made Gondy feel silly about his notions, and when she laughed and took his arm, we trailed along to the dining-room where we had supped the previous evening.

This was a rather large room, hung with family portraits and furnished in magnificently carved black oak. The shades had been drawn; light from silver candelabra glimmered on the massive plate we had unearthed, with which the table was now set. Lucien stood at the head of the table, and had donned his most pleasant manner.

"Ah, Monsieur Carson, you must forgive my regrettable scene of the morning!" he said to me. "I was beside myself. Now all has been arranged, subject to your consent—and yours, my brother," he said to Gondy. "When your friend returns with a goldsmith and a notary, the papers will be drawn up. Now sit down, sit down! Here are sandwiches and cakes, and the finest wine in the cellar. We shall celebrate our good fortune!"

Gondy threw off his gloom and went to the other extreme, with a torrent of eager French. Félice took the table's foot; Gondy sat beside me, leaving a place opposite for Murchison. It was very odd, I thought, that Murch had taken the car and gone to Orleans without a word to me—especially since the only keys to the car at this moment reposed in my pocket! This yarn, at least, was a lie.

Being, naturally, quite famished, I reached hastily at the sandwiches before me, taking three and passing them on. Félice handed me another plate of them.

"The finest Strasbourg *foie gras*," she chirped. "A prewar delicacy we've not seen for years—I was saving one tin for some great occasion, and this is it! I made these myself, monsieur. Do not be sparing, I beg of you."

I TOOK a couple, being engaged meantime with those of chicken, and Gondy helped himself. Lucien, patting the wine bucket beside him, beamed at us.

"And the wine—my specialty, messieurs!" he said. "Brother, you remember that excellent Banyuls our father laid in before the war?"

"With the most poignant affection," said Gondy, laughing. "Of proper vintage, that is the rarest and best wine of France!"

"This is it, the last of it," said Lucien, filling beautiful Venetian glasses with the deep ruby wine and passing them. I noted his actions almost subconsciously as I sipped the wine. It was heavy and rich—something like the finest port, only more so.

"You do not like my sandwiches, monsieur?" Félice purred at me. I laughed and bit into one. Gondy, eating ravenously, asserted they were delicious. Then Lucien stood up and lifted his glass.

"A toast to the friendly end of all discord, and good fortune!" said he, then waited, his eye on me. "You are drinking with us, monsieur?"

It had just struck me as a bit singular that no servants were on hand, that we were waiting on ourselves.

"I'd like to ask one question," I said.

Lucien inclined his head.

"Yes? At your service."

"Why," I demanded, "did you fill our glasses and yours from two different bottles?"

A flash leaped across his face—a flash of such utter malignity and virulence that it appalled me.

But, before he could reply, Gondy rose, gripping the table-edge, his face as white as death itself. He wavered on his feet, lost balance, then regained it.

"Poison, *mon ami!*" he gasped. "Poison—"

He lost balance again and fell sideways, so that he came down across the lap of Félice; but I saw his arms go around her and his hands grip her, as they fell to the floor together.

POISON! THEN poor Murch was done for. And we—

The look on Lucien's face was all I needed—that, and the sudden queer feeling inside me, though I had not drunk much of the wine. Before he could set down his glass, I was out of my chair and at him.

There was no monkey-work this time; I was prepared for his tigerish delivery and blocked it. For half a minute or more we let go with all we had, and while naturally he marked me up a bit, I gave him a real working-over, and had a lot of satisfaction doing it. I kept at him as I started, hard and fast, and was going ahead to make a thorough job of it, when the dizziness hit me. I could blame the small amount of wine I had drunk for that.

He was groggy on his feet, but clever and desperate. In the instant that I wavered, he reached out, scooped up a wine-bottle and lammed me over the head with it. I staggered back, got my hands on a plate, and skimmed it at him. It took him across his scarred cheek and knocked him flat. But, with a growl and a yell, the two sourpuss servants came bursting into the doorway behind him and lunged at me.

Luckily, the wine-bucket stood almost beside me. I caught

up a bottle and went at them—breaking it over one head, stabbing with the broken glass at the other—and they broke and ran for it. But that finished me. I was seeing double, a frightful nausea came over me, and I only stayed on my feet by clinging to the table.

I saw Lucien come to his feet, unsteadily, wipe the blood from his face, and fumble a pistol out of his pocket. But I could not move.

"But no! Stop! Stop!"

The voice, thin but clear, came from the other end of the table, by the kitchen doorway. Someone stood there—I could not see who it was, for now everything was blurry. I cursed Lucien, heard him snarl, saw him fling up the pistol at me, with murder in his scarred visage.

The shot exploded; but he was unsteady, and the bullet shrieked past my ear. An oath escaped him. He aimed again— and another shot reëchoed in the room. But it was not his shot. He caught at the air, dropped his gun, and pitched out of my sight. Then I saw who the other person was—the kitchen-girl Olympe of the Maquis, holding her long Luger. Behind her others were flooding in—strangers, men with arms. They were lifting Gondy.

I could barely stand, and slowly, carefully, I let myself down into a chair. The men were crowding about Gondy, the clatter of their tongues filled the room. I looked for Félice, but she had vanished, leaving only some shreds of her gown in Gondy's hands. He had opened his eyes now and was looking around, vaguely.

"A close call, monsieur!" Olympe stood beside me. "Our friends of the Maquis were a trifle slow in arriving; luckily you ate little of the poisoned *foie gras*. The wine was poisoned, also, or perhaps drugged; I am not sure which—"

I did not hear the rest of it—I was horribly sick, and glad of it; the word "poison" scared me.

Some time must have passed; when I woke up, Gondy and

another man were laughing and pulling me up, shoving me into a chair. Gondy embraced me wildly.

"Murchison! He is all right!" he cried delightedly. "They drugged him, locked him in my room—he is asleep, but safe! Do you understand? These are my comrades of the Maquis—it was Olympe who got them here! Oh, holy name of a name of a name!"

He straightened up, his eyes distended, pallor in his face. I looked around to follow his gaze. A sudden silence had fallen. Into the room, up past the table, was walking an old, old man with lined features and white hair and ragged garments. His eyes were vacant, bleared, almost blank, but they dwelt upon Gondy with glad recognition, and the scrawny old arms lifted.

Gondy, bursting into tears, embraced his father wildly, and voices buzzed all around: "M. le Comte has come home again! We found him in the hills—"

That is all I remember, because the ghastly faintness got me again and I keeled over in a dead faint....

Look now to the sunlight of another day, with Frank Murchison sitting beside me in the warm sunlight outside the chateau. I was still a bit shaky, for those sandwiches had been poisoned; the kitchen cat had fed on them and died. Still, I could enjoy my pipe, which was a good sign. Murchison, who had merely been drugged, was quite himself now.

We were alone. Gondy had departed, with his father, to the funeral of Lucien.

"Just think, if the old man had been brought home a day earlier," said Murchison soberly, "we'd have avoided all that mess! He has approved our agreement with Gondy, and we've won a good fat stake. The future looks bright for Carson's Folly, eh?"

I nodded. The old man had not taken Lucien's death very hard.

"No word of Félice?" I asked.

Murch shook his head. It was a sore subject.

"None. She got away with some of the gold coin, and skipped. Gondy says to watch out for her, that she'll be our mortal enemy from now on. I rather believe him."

"Cheer up. Our paths won't cross hers again," I told him.

"I'm not so sure," he said, frowning. "Gondy is really alarmed. He says she had a pistol under her dress—that was why he fell on her and grabbed her. He got it away, but could not hang on to her. He thinks that with our gold-finding machine, as he calls it, in her mind, she'll never let up, and will murder us all if she gets the chance."

"That's bosh!" I said, and talked him out of his bad mood.

WHILE I was at this, a car arrived and Gondy joined us; he had left his father to go on to the cemetery without him. He had a drink with us and launched into one of his gay daydreams.

"My friends! I've just remembered something marvelous! You know, when the American Army landed in North Africa, I was in Algiers. I came back here later and got into the Maquis. Well, there in Africa I learned about a lost treasure—oh, it is a truly superb chance for us! If it would please you to hear about it—"

He turned eager eyes on us. Murchison gave me a glance.

"What say, Carson?"

"Barkis is willing," I replied. "Carson's Folly will work as well in Africa as here. Go on, Gondy, tell us about it!"

He leaned forward and began to bubble happily about the Nazi secret agent and the one-legged dancing-girl—and I knew we were Africa-bound!

I I

ONE-LEGGED DANCER

*The second amazing adventure that befell the
inventor of "Carson's Folly"—a mine-detector that
would not detect most mines, but would detect
treasure or other objects buried deep down.*

MURCHISON AND I sat on the terrace of the St. George, the luxury hotel on the hillside above Algiers, and sipped our cool drinks as we looked down over city and port. Vicomte de Gondy, the third of our party, was somewhere down there establishing contacts.

"Seems funny now," mused Murchison, "but remember how wonderful it seemed when our troops went through here? Actually in Africa!"

"The world has shrunk," I commented.

"Right, Mr. Carson: it has shrunk. And the war's all over. And you and I sit here with our infernal machine, while our partner dates up dancing-girls and houris, yonder! I'm sick of looking at English tourists."

Murchison, a skinny beanpole of a man, scowled at the glorious view and champed on his cigar.

"Why worry?" I said. "We eat well; we sleep well; we enjoy life—"

"Arrgh! You big baby elephant! Just a hunk of laziness. I'm going for a walk," he said, and shooting up from his chair, went striding away.

That was unfair. True. I weigh two-twenty, but none of it is fat; I was just built big. However, Murch and I had been friends since boyhood, in the Army and out of it, so I just chuckled and watched him go.

Carson's Folly, as Murchison had named our joint invention,

after me, reposed in our bedroom—a relic of our war experiences in building mine-detectors. There was nothing wrong
with our baby except that it would not detect mines; it was not
supposed to. Mines were off the market with their Nazi inven-
tors. We were out to make money and see the world, in company
with our partner Gondy, who had been everywhere and knew
everyone.

Gondy, who was outside man for the firm, had brought us
here with an alluring but most improbable story. He had gone
to confirm it and look up old friends, and had been gone two
days, and we were bored. Algiers is interesting but not diverting,
as many a G.I. found to his cost.

Burke went down with a crash and a furious
oath. I got my fingers locked on his throat,
and hung on. His strength was terrific.

I finished my drink, knocked out my pipe, and was thinking about scaring up a tennis match with some of the English tourists here, when one of the Arab hotel guides, a handsome figure in his pastel-hued robes, approached and handed me a card with word that the gentleman was in the lobby. The engraved pasteboard carried the name of *Jeremiah Burke*, followed by several miniature insignia of decorations, in the Continental fashion.

"Don't know him," I told the boy. "Send him out here."

The Arab brought him. Burke was up to my six-feet-two, and broader in the shoulder, built like a fighting man; he wore sun-glasses, and twitched them off to reveal a lusty, cheerful face with twinkling eyes, a heavy cleft chin, gold front teeth and a big nose. He had a hearty, firm grip and a roaring, gusty manner, and was well dressed.

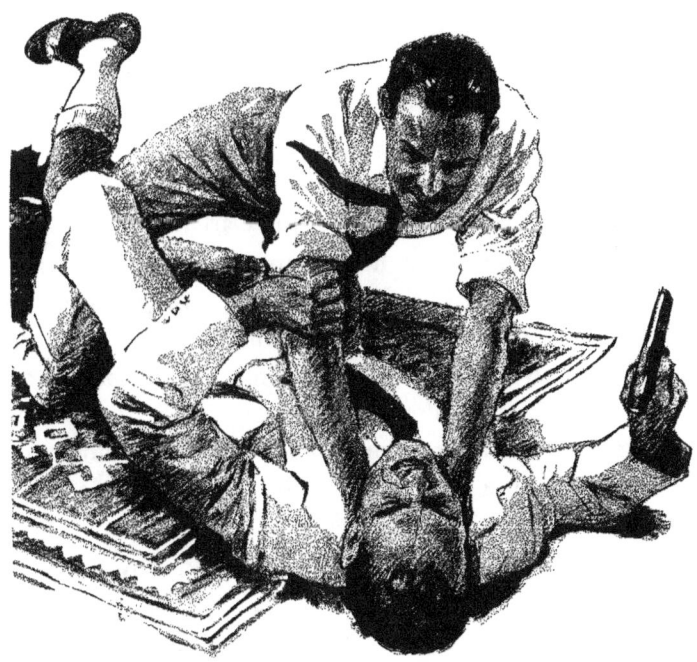

"Delighted to meet you," he said rapidly. "Order some drinks, like a good chap; I'm perishin' of thirst. Ah, it's good to stretch my legs after driving half the day over dusty roads! So you don't know the name of Jeremiah Burke, eh? That's to be expected. I'm the only Irishman in this blessed town—been here most of me life, only I don't live here. I've a villa up the coast, and that's what I came to see you about, because I can't get into it, more's the pity; and I hear your friend Gondy is trying to get hold of it. And I don't want to see you stuck by these damned French lawyers."

UNTIL MENTION of Gondy, I was tempted to think him a madman. As to his being Irish, I reserved my opinion; I am Irish by way of South Boston myself, and he struck me as a phony. So I ordered the drinks, and said I did not understand.

He chuckled lustily; he seemed to meet life with enormous gusto.

"Ha! You'll savvy soon enough, Mr. Carson. The Villa Hermosa—ah, it is truly magnificent! It was built in the old days by the Dey of Algiers, and was finally leased by that abominable Nazi agent Kurt Bremer. You have heard of him?"

"Vaguely," I said. "Wasn't he shot when we were in Algiers—our troops, I mean—at the time of the Darlan affair?"

"The scoundrel was caught and later shot trying to escape, by all accounts," said Burke, smacking his lips. "The villa was confiscated by Government. I've the matter up in the courts now; ultimately it will be restored to me, but you know how these things go in the French courts. In fact, I've been trying to buy it back from Government, damn 'em! I'm willing to do that, of course. The place contains all my family heirlooms—devilish fine furniture and all that."

The drinks arrived. I did not understand why the Villa Hermosa had been confiscated, if Bremer had merely leased it. Burke laid his finger along his nose and winked.

"Graft—plain graft! Death of my life, these bloody French

will do anything for a bit o' siller! But that's not the whole of it. There's Naila. She occupies it now. They won't put her out."

"Who's Naila?" I asked.

"One-legged dancer," he said, and broke into a roar of laughter at my expression. "Come, come! You know, dancing hereabouts isn't what we know at home. Go down to the Kursaal some evening and watch the Arab girls. It's not naughty—merely a matter of using muscles. Throws the natives into spasms, it does! She lost one leg at the knee as a child, but learned dancing, and is or was famous. Bremer installed her as his mistress, savvy? Now she lives there." He winked again. "Friends in Government, of course."

He was garrulous—gave me a whole lecture on Arab dancing, and knew his subject. I had a hard job bringing him down to earth. It developed that, since Gondy wanted to rent Villa Hermosa for a month, he would make no objection, provided we would do him a favor. But his lawyers could object, he said; they could kick up no end of trouble for us.

"What's the favor?" I asked. "I didn't know Gondy wanted to rent the place."

That was a lie; he was moving heaven and earth to get us a month's rental of it.

Well, Burke ran the gamut between tears and roaring laughter. He was so certain of buying back the property, ultimately, that he wanted permission to set out half a dozen trees in the garden, and wanted to spend just two days in the villa as a guest, to inventory the heirlooms, learn what was missing and what was in place, and so forth. Two days.

"Seems fair enough," I said, shrugging. "I'll tell Gondy about it; I have no doubt he'll agree. Suppose you give him or me a ring here, sometime tomorrow—eh?"

He beamed, clapped me on the back, shook hands, thanked me for the drink, and walked away, leaving with me the casual, final and amazing observation that he would gladly pay five thousand francs for the accommodation he asked from us.

A few minutes later Murchison returned from his walk. He was put out at having missed the visitor, and at my not having detained him.

"We've come all the way here on the wild-goose chase of the Villa Hermosa, Carson, and you let this fellow slip away—the one man who seems to have definite, detailed knowledge of the place!"

"He'll be back. And I tell you there's something phony about him—"

I BROKE off. A glittering Mercedes was sweeping up the drive. It halted; there was a burst of laughing voices, and out of the car jumped Gondy. He waved a hand to his friends in farewell, turned and saw us on the terrace, and the car swept away; he waved to us, came striding to join us, and beamed delightedly. He was in his effervescent, bubbling mood, and laughed joyously as he dropped into a chair.

"Where the devil have you been?" demanded Murchison.

"Everywhere! I had to go to Constantine to look up the right people—found them. All is well, my friends!"

"This is a good safe place to talk," I said. "What about a drink?"

He jumped at the idea. We ordered drinks, and he plumped out his news.

"We get the villa for a month's occupancy! The papers will be signed tomorrow!"

He said no more until the drinks arrived and the boy had gone. Naturally we were not shouting our business for all Algiers to hear. Gondy had brought us here on the strength of rumor, gossip and French scuttle butt; now, as he went on to inform us happily, he had proved up everything.

"The villa," he said, "was owned by Kurt Bremer, the chief Nazi agent in North Africa, who lived there in great style. His mistress was the dancer Naila, otherwise Madame Benfar, an Algerienne and a famous beauty. The American invasion caught

Bremer napping, and Naila, turned him in, to Darlan; he attempted to escape and was shot."

He paused for breath, excited color in his cheeks, and then bubbled on:

The buzzer sounded. I looked at the gauges and a thrill shot through me. "There it is, Gondy!" I exclaimed. "Find a stone to mark the spot."

"Treasure stories had always hung around the old villa, but this was the biggest and best authenticated. Bremer was known to have acted as collector for the Nazis, and was supposed to have had a big amount collected from Algiers and Morocco on hand—loot and so forth amounting to millions. It was never found. They say he hid it and was trying to bargain with it for his life, when the end came. Madame Benfar hated him bitterly, it seems; and because she turned him in, she has been allowed to remain in the villa. None of his loot has ever been found. She's quite a remarkable woman, by all accounts."

"Is she clearing out?" I asked.

He nodded. "For a month. Going to visit her people, down south at Sidi-bel-Abbès. I've made an unofficial deal with the Government. If we turn up Bremer's hoard, we turn over half to them and keep the balance. Okay?"

"Okay," said Murchison, and I nodded.

"Why do papers have to be signed?" Murchison asked.

"Rental is a serious business under French law, my friend," said Gondy, chuckling. "Especially when the property has been confiscated. Tomorrow afternoon at four we meet my friends at the Governor's Palace, and sign up. We can take possession next morning, and go to work with Carson's Folly."

We told him about Jeremiah Burke, of whom he had never heard, and he listened with a frown knitting his dark, eager features, then nodded slowly.

"Possibly it is as he says; many property titles here are highly involved," he said slowly. "Our deal with the Government is entirely unofficial; a smart lawyer could spoil everything for us. I would say to give this man the little he wants, and be rid of him. Five thousand francs, eh? A large price for him to pay. It is best to avoid trouble, I think."

WHERE DID the dancer enter the picture? She was meeting us tomorrow; we were renting from her, with Government approval. She would leave us her two Arab servants to run the house—everything was working out beautifully. The

Villa Hermosa lay twenty-odd miles west of the city, past Castiglione, on Highway 11—the coast route. We must rent a car, of course; could do that in the morning.

"But tonight—listen, my friends!" exclaimed Gondy. "You have laughed at the idea of a one-legged dancer becoming famous. Well, we shall go to the Kursaal, on the boulevard past the Arab city, and see some dancers from Biskra—eh? They are famous, these Arab women—rather, Berber women. It will not be exciting, but—well, you shall see!"

We agreed, only too gladly.

I spent an hour, that afternoon, checking over the delicate mechanism of Carson's Folly, in our room, with Murch assisting. It was our pet, our baby, our hope of fortune. Those unseen electronic waves, these tubes of our own invention and make, this radarlike contrivance whose invisible fingers disproved the illusion that earth was a solid substance, had failed utterly in fighting land mines, because it would only begin to work three feet below the earth's surface, and would not report on small objects. However, to our purpose it was, despite certain limitations and faults, superbly adapted.

After dinner that evening we left the hotel, hopped a tram at the nearby Mustapha Superior end of the line, and rode down across the whole city and along the waterfront to the gimcrack Kursaal, to see the most dismal performance of alleged dancing it was ever my misfortune to witness. A dozen Arab women, stunning beauties of obesity, swayed to the music of flutes and drums. They might have been capable of lascivious dancing for tourists, but this was sheer classical Arab art—twitchy posturings.

The audience, French or Arabs, practically went into hysterics over the performance. We did not. Yet some of these dropsical sluts, as Murchison termed them, were the most famous dancers of Algeria; certain of these so-called dances were program numbers renowned throughout North Africa.

However, it gave us an understanding of how a one-legged

*We had heard nothing of Félice; but Gondy persisted
in the belief that her hatred and vicious greed would*

follow us. However, we had forgotten her next morning, when we scouted around downlotnwn.

woman—or one without legs at all—could be a far-famed dancer, at least in Algeria.

Even Gondy, who was usually broad-minded, was disgusted with the show, and we left early and after a few drinks went back to the St. George. We gathered in our bedroom for a nightcap; and Gondy, with a gesture toward Carson's Folly in the corner, imparted advice.

"Except for two officers who are in the secret," he said, "I have not mentioned our real purpose at Villa Hermosa. We must be very careful. Plenty of old Vichy officials are around; like the Nazis, they've gone underground. And have you heard the rumors about many of the Nazis?"

"No end of rumors," I said. "What kind do you mean?"

"That they've employed plastic surgery and false papers by wholesale, to give themselves new identities. This is more fact than fiction, I'm informed. So be careful. Leave the talking to me."

No trouble about that, except for Murchison. He was apt to fly off on the wings of some crazy idea and make it plausible, having that type of mind. We had been pals for twenty years, and I could keep him down to earth, as a rule; but he would bear watching.

"Don't forget," I said, "that there's one person alive who knows us, who has seen Carson's Folly at work and knows all about it, and who hates us the way the devil hates holy-water."

"You mean my former sister-in-law," said Gondy uneasily.

"The charming Félice," added Murchison, with a sigh. "Exactly. But she has disappeared."

"Sure; but she'd give her right arm to do us in and get that machine," I said.

"Bah! We'll never see her again." Gondy lifted his glass. "Well, here's to luck on the morrow, my friends! And a good night's sleep."

I T W A S perhaps an ill-omened mention of Félice. In France proper—it is hard to think of Algiers as being part of France, though it has been so for generations—when we first put Carson's Folly to the test, Gondy's sister-in-law had come within an ace of killing us all and getting away with the gadget, whose possibilities she knew. Since then we had heard nothing of her; but in his moments of depression, to which like all high-strung natures Gondy was subject, he persisted in the belief that her hatred and vicious greed would follow us.

However, we had forgotten her next morning, when we scouted around downtown and at last secured an old but serviceable Panhard. We returned to the hotel for luncheon, and there I was called to the telephone. Burke was on the wire.

"Oh!" I rejoined. "Yes, I spoke of you to my friends."

"Did they consider my request reasonable? And the price?"

"Of course," I said. "We expect to take possession of the villa in a day or two. You may come along whenever you like; I understand it has room and to spare."

"You are very kind," he replied. "Shall we say, then, Saturday?"

"All right. Come to lunch."

"Thank you. Shall you have any need of servants? I'll be glad to supply the need."

"No, thanks. Those now there are remaining."

"Oh! Very well," he said, apparently somewhat disconcerted. "Until Saturday, then."

I told the others of the call. Gondy shrugged, Murchison hoped we would not have the fellow hanging around to eye our discoveries; and then we forgot about him, with our visit to the Governor's Palace coming up.

DRESSED IN our best, we piled into the Panhard; presenting ourselves at four. What with sentries, officers in resplendent uniforms, salutes and red tape, it was hard to believe we were not ambassadors at the very least; the Governor, however, was not bothered by our call, and we ended up in a rather dirty little room with a couple of Gondy's official friends and a notary.

Our chief interest was in Madame Benfar, the one-legged dancer.

She proved to be a swarthy, hawk-faced woman of perhaps thirty, not at all obese, and wearing rather shabby Parisian garments. No glamour, no hint of the artificial leg she wore, no romance—distinctly none—and no dancing; she was just a rather dowdy young woman. But she had character. Her eyes held a subdued blaze as she watched us. A blue cross was tattooed on her forehead. She was unsmiling, severe, strictly business. She arranged to meet us at the villa at ten next morning and turn it over to us, then depart. The papers were signed and our money paid, and she departed. We followed a few moments later.

Gondy remained to joke with his friends, and joined us outside. He handed us a photograph they had given him.

"A keepsake—we might give it to Burke," said he. "A photograph of the late Kurt Bremer. He was quite an accomplished scoundrel, by all accounts."

We regarded it with interest. Bremer was certainly good-looking, in a heavy way, except that he was marked by a broken nose and a couple of missing front teeth. He had lost the teeth when captured.

"Determined-looking guy," said Murchison. "Good thing he's dead, or he might be back and attempt to get his loot."

"Not with the gentle Naila on hand," Gondy rejoined with a laugh. "She fears him, and hates him like poison, or did. She's the only one who never believed him dead."

"What?" I put in sharply. "Is there any doubt of it?"

GONDY SHRUGGED. "Officially, no. It happened in Oran, during the fighting. He was in jail there, and tried to escape when the jail caught fire. There was enough of him left to identify. This picture was taken a couple of days before it happened."

"Hm! And we're counting on recovering his loot," I said.

"May be that he's alive. Maybe he sent and got the loot and split with Naila. Hasn't it been searched for?"

"Repeatedly. She pretty near took the villa apart, and dug up the garden. But you know how these Arabs would dig," said Gondy. "Maybe a couple of feet down. We're gambling that he used the garden and made a good job of it, buried it down deep."

"It's a good gamble," Murchison said, with truth. "We can't expect to go around and just pick gold out of the ground. If we win once in five times, we'll be lucky."

This was understood; we had discussed it often enough not to expect overmuch....

Next morning we upped, breakfasted, packed and were out of the hotel by nine. The old Panhard worked like a charm. To reach Highway 11, we had to go clear across the city and out by Point Pescade, following the seashore closely. Murch and I had Carson's Folly, which was of a magnesium alloy and very light, in the back seat with us. Gondy drove.

It started out gloriously, with the mountains abruptly to the left, and the sea on our right, but it was a nightmare ride all the same. Algeria had plenty of trucks and autos after the war; the drivers, whether Arab or Algerine, were absolute madmen. No one gave a hang for gendarmes—or rather *agents,* since a gendarme is rarely encountered in France outside of books; and every crossroads was a speculation in sudden death. An armored car with a lunatic driver would be a motorist's dream here.

However, we survived, shot through Guyotville and Zeralda, and the hills sank into monotonous vineyards and farms. Castiglione dropped behind; a little farther, we passed some Roman ruins, a fine stretch of forest, and Gondy said we were practically there, with Tipaza just ahead. To the left showed a group of recently built villas, and on the right was the Villa Hermosa—fenced in with stone walls and enormous cactus. We turned into the drive.

This was short; the house was not far back from the road, and outwardly was not distinguished. It was small, of two stories, and a distinct disappointment from the exterior. An old car, heaped with luggage and evidently belonging to Madame Benfar, was at the door. We disembarked. Naila herself came out to meet us, bringing two native servants, husband and wife; she introduced them as Mustapha and Fatima, and took us inside.

There, a gasp broke from us all. It was a fairyland. The ceilings were painted, the floor and walls of tiling in gorgeous colors;

"You look so comfortable in that chair, monsieur!"
Naila said. "It seems to fit you perfectly."

the doorways showed the ancient honeycomb work of painted plaster, now a lost art. The furnishings, the thick Berber rugs, the courtyard with its glorious tiled fountain—everything was magnificent. Arches of marble pillars, a riot of color meeting the eye on every side, and a doorway from the courtyard that opened upon a large walled garden which held a few pomegranate and orange trees. Naila enjoyed the effect produced upon us, and smiled. She spoke excellent French.

"While I am far away in the south, you will be kind to my little house?"

"Madame, you may depend on us." Gondy bent over her hand. He treated her as though she were some great lady. He himself was a very great gentleman. "We do reverence to beauty, whether it be in the flesh or in exquisite surroundings like these, which are worthy of you."

She smiled, liking his flattery. "Once there was a man who did not," she said, and then abruptly made her farewells. We saw her out to her car. An Arab driver appeared, and the old bus chugged away.

"You're the housekeeper, Gondy," I said. "Take the servants in hand, old chap."

Little need; they were perfect. Mustapha was the cook, Fatima the housekeeper. An excellent luncheon was set on a table under an archway, by the central fountain. The two servants were deft, silent, self-effacing; we hardly knew they were around at all. The whole thing was like a page out of "Arabian Nights."

After lunch we moved our bags into the bedrooms, of which there were five, with two baths, and unpacked. We were an hour going over the place, looking at everything, and came near forgetting the hidden treasure in the beauty around us. We decided to go over things carefully now, and start work in the morning, so we took counsel together.

The house itself had been thoroughly examined; it contained nothing hidden. There was no possible hiding-place indoors, as we could plainly see. So we did what others had done—went out into the garden.

This was of some size, a couple of acres. The wall around was high and topped with broken glass. The half-dozen trees made the place look naked and forlorn. Flower-beds had been destroyed by treasure-hunters. Our friend Burke was dead right, I decided: this place needed trees and shrubs. There were six trees and a central well—nothing else.

Each of us figured out what we, had he been Kurt Bremer, would have done with the loot, or rather tribute seized on all sides and collected here. Many Arabs were immensely wealthy and kept their funds in cash; he might well have had millions. Then, the afternoon half gone, we compared our findings. Not knowing the circumstances under which the stuff had been hidden, we were compelled to go blind.

"It's a cinch the well has been examined," I said. "But he needed to hide the hole, and water would be his easiest aid to that. Therefore, I'd say somewhere near the well."

"Nix," said Murchison. "Nobody else in the house, remember, knew about it. He had probably one night to work and no more. My guess is that the spot lies close to the house wall, by the door out of the courtyard. That patio is all intricate tiling—no chance he'd tear that up and have to get it laid afresh."

"We can go over it anyhow, with the machine," I said. "You, Gondy?"

He smiled. "Now that we are actually doing it, the whole thing looks silly and a bit fantastic," he said. "If I were hiding anything here, I'd put it in one of the corner angles of the walls, I think. But I would devise some sort of container that would not make me get blisters on my hands digging."

That was an idea. We went over the whole thing repeatedly and got nowhere.

"All right," I said finally. "Suppose we take two-hour spells with Carson's Folly, begin at the house wall and work back and forth until we've covered the whole place."

MURCHISON GRIMACED. "All right. You and your blessed lawnmower! I used to do that work as a kid, keeping house lawns mowed."

"So did I, around South Boston," I said, "but we get better paid on this job—if we win.… All right, tomorrow morning we start in."

None of us was happily expectant about the matter, I admit. The very look of that garden deadened hopes and put to flight our extravagant fancies.

Next morning—Thursday morning—after the usual meager French breakfast of *croissants* and chocolate, we started work. Rather, Murchison and I did. Gondy took Mustapha to Tipaza in the Panhard, to lay in a stock of supplies; also, he wanted to phone Algiers in regard to Jeremiah Burke. He would be back for lunch and in time to take his two-hour spell at the work.

Out in the garden by ourselves, Murchison strapped on my shoulders the knapsack that contained the batteries and other essentials of Carson's Folly. The long handle of the detector ran down to a flat magnesium disk, on which the gauges were mounted; this, on high wheels, passed over the ground, from which electronic waves bounced back and reported on the gauges. I had compiled a chart, after lengthy experiments, which translated these reports in terms of the substances encountered underground. In effect, our gadget was a sort of radar, and for it we had evolved tubes of varying constituents adapted to the work.

The time passed rapidly. Walking slowly along, pushing the disk across the ground, on lines three feet apart, I forgot how time passed; there was the exciting chance of striking something any minute. Several times, indeed, the buzzer sounded and we had to make computations on the chart. Once we struck a large block of stone at six feet, again a huge tree at ten feet, and then what seemed to be a stone pillar farther down-—Roman remains, possibly. Each such object could be outlined by passing the disk along it, and thus we could chart the underground structure with some accuracy. It was slow work; we figured it would take at least a week to cover the entire garden, working steadily.

My spell ended and Murchison took over. We put a fifteen-foot depth limit on the radionic waves; how far down they would work, we did not know. Murchison got excited over the notion of using the gadget in archaeology, and dilated on this topic until we were practically packed up and headed for Egypt or Greece. He discovered nothing of importance, and had just finished his trick when Gondy showed up.

I knew at once that something had happened. The lean, dark Frenchman was pale and his eyes were burning.

"You have found nothing? I had better—or worse—luck," he said, and with an effort controlled his inner excitement. "I told Mustapha about Burke coming on Saturday. Tomorrow is Friday, you know, the Arab Sunday and holiday. He asked whether, if he and Fatima worked tomorrow, they could lay off Saturday. I said yes. We got to town and he went to make purchases, while I phoned my friends at Algiers about Burke. They looked him up."

"And you found he was a bad egg?" I ventured. He shook his head.

"No, no! He showed up a few months ago as a dealer in agricultural implements at Blidah. They know little about him, but will investigate. Well! I came back to the car. I was standing beside it when another car passed. And seated in that car was—Félice!"

"The devil!" ejaculated Murchison. "Are you sure?"

"Positive, though I had only a glimpse in passing." Gondy, with tragic air, threw out his hands. "You see? She is here. She has followed us. I warned you against her hatred!"

"She did not recognize you?"

"Impossible to say. I was so thunderstruck that I lost my head. I did not even get the car's number."

OVER THE luncheon table we discussed the matter without

result. Gondy was in panic, but Murch and I talked him out of it by degrees. More than likely it was a mistake. Even were Félice here, she could not harm us short of actual assassination, for which she was too clever. But it threw Gondy into the glooms, and even worried Murchison a bit.

We put in four hours that afternoon with the detector, discovered nothing of any interest, and went for a swim, the beach being just below the villa. Tipaza was a town of about five hundred and had no movie, so we had to stay home evenings and listen to the radio and play gin rummy.

I had a room at the corner of the house. Next morning I was up with the sun; I woke and could not sleep. As I was dressing, I saw someone leaving our gate, below. I looked again, and recognized Mustapha. He went across the highway and stopped in at one of the new villas there—the first one. Probably knew someone there, I thought. He went in and stayed quite a time. I would have forgotten it completely except that, later in the day, I noticed that the villa in question bore a big "To Let" sign on the front wall. Curious, but none of my business—and I did forget it, temporarily.

We really worked that day. We had trouble with the gadget, two tubes blowing, and out in the open located something that made us dig, because it seemed like a box with some contents the chart could not determine. Four feet down we found an old moldering chest that held two corpses wrapped in newspapers of 1889. We called it a day and went for another swim. We had worked over a quarter of the garden, however.

On Saturday morning Mustapha and Fatima departed to visit relatives in Cherchell; they left all sorts of food on hand and promised to be back next day. We immediately got to work, having all clear until Burke arrived at noon; then we would do nothing, of course, until he was gone.

The morning wore along; we drew closer to the well, and nothing happened. It was an old-fashioned well with pulley and rope and bucket; an electric motor and pump at the back of the kitchen supplied the house with water. Long bamboo poles lying by the garden wall showed that the well had been tried; we tried it for ourselves and found mud bottom. Only a fool would have hidden anything there.

Toward noon, Gondy and I took the final trick, Murchison leaving us to await the arrival Jeremiah Burke. Before quitting, I had a notion to circle the well with our gadget, and did so. I was some six feet from the well, on the side opposite the house, when the buzzer sounded. I looked at the gauges, and a thrill shot through me; the chart confirmed my findings—metal, papers, and still deeper, gold! The whole thing lying six to eight feet below the surface, but in small compass.

"There it is, Gondy!" I exclaimed. "Find a stone to mark the spot—no chance now to dig. We must wait till Burke has gone, tomorrow evening."

Jubilant, he ran to give Murchison the news, after marking the spot, while I dismantled Carson's Folly and carried it to my room. We had no chance to discuss our luck; before I descended, Burke had arrived in an old but serviceable Renault. I had only a moment with Murchison, on the stairs.

"Is it true?" he demanded. "Are you positive?"

"Dead certain," I told him. "I don't quite understand it; apparently some metal I couldn't figure out, papers,—perhaps paper money,—and gold at bottom."

He clapped me on the shoulder exultantly.

After that, the boisterous, booming verbosity of Burke was upon everything like a cloak. He was in whites and looked prosperous. He must have seen that we were in high spirits, but made no comment. He had fetched along a champagne magnum which he insisted on opening at luncheon, and seemed bent upon making a good impression. He did so, too—we were all in ebullient mood over our discovery.

Over our Nosi Bé coffee—the house was well stocked with this delicacy, so popular in Algiers—Burke laid out five lavender thousand-franc notes.

"There are your five thousand *balles,* and with my heartiest good wishes!" he exclaimed. "With your permission, I've taken the liberty to have two gardeners arrive later in the afternoon, the blessed cool of the day, to put in the trees I mentioned!"

We refused the money; we could do no less. Then Burke took us over the house, which he admitted he had not seen in years. The ivory-inlaid rifles on the walls, the Arab weapons, the rugs, the furniture—everything had a history. He knew the story of every heirloom, and the stories were fascinating as he told them. When we came into the small writing-room, he stopped short at sight of the picture Gondy had put in a niche in the wall—the photograph of Bremer.

"Well, well, well!" he exclaimed. "Look at him—ugly as life, the rascal! Where the devil did that spring from?"

"Part of the furnishings," Murchison said with some mendacity. "Who is it?"

"Why, that blackguard Kurt Bremer himself!" Burke rejoined. He began to tell some yarns about Bremer's activities as a Nazi agent, disclosing the unlamented Kurt as a rapacious, utterly heartless devil.

Gondy disappeared to take out the dishes. After a time he came back and caught my eye. Our guest knew that our servants had taken a day off, so I excused myself to help with the work. In the kitchen, Gondy turned and caught my arm, staring at me.

"Bill! I'm certain of it! His car is the same one!"

"What are you talking about?"

"That Renault—his car! It is the one I saw Félice in yesterday!"

"You have Félice on the brain," I said. "It's not certain you did see her. And all Renaults look alike, especially old ones."

THIS WAS true, and it shook him. I asked what he thought of Burke. He shrugged.

"How can I tell? These Irish are different. He is not my kind. There is something, I know not what—it rings false."

"My impression exactly," I said. "Now, forget about Félice. If your fancies are true, something dirty is up; but they're not true. Surely you must see as much."

He admitted it, and we started in with the dishes. Burke appeared to lend a hand in his bluff, hearty way. Murchison, who was a coffee fiend, began to make some more of the brew, then went to answer the hammering call of the front door-knocker. He came back with a gray-blue telegraph form, which he handed to Gondy.

"For you," he said laconically.

Gondy opened and read the message. His face changed, and he looked up at us.

"It is from Colonel Duperre," he said, mentioning the officer who had handled the rental of the villa for us, and to whom he had phoned for data on Burke. "He is at Cherchell for the day, visiting a friend, and wants us to come over this afternoon. He has important information for us."

"Don't hesitate on my account," said Burke genially. "It's only twenty-five kilometers, a gorgeous drive, and you'll see some magnificent Roman ruins!"

"You fellows go if you like," I said. "Too hot for me to go gallivanting."

The others understood that I had no intention of leaving Burke alone here. Duperre was to be found, it seemed, at his friend's house; Gondy gave a number in the Rue Cavagnac, and Burke burst forth:

"A fine street, that! You'll have no trouble finding it. Go straight into town and turn at the Nicolas Hotel, and the Rue Sidi Braham takes you right to it. Used to live in Cherchell myself. A neat town, I call it!"

He pressed cigars on us—fat, juicy Havanas. Gondy and Murchison decided to get off, because the afternoon was half gone now; and they wasted no time about it. We went out to see them off in the Panhard. Burke looked at his watch; it was half-past three. His gardeners would not be here with the trees, he said, until another hour or more.

"Do you mind looking into the garden with me?" he asked. "I'd like your approval of where I think of planting them."

I was at his service, and said so. We went into the garden; he shook his head at sight of the rather desolate place. Water should be piped from the well to irrigate the whole place, he said, and was right about it. There should be a tree by the well, too—it was the place for a fig that would grow mightily. He pictured that monster, far-spreading fig-tree with the gusto of an artist. It must be placed just so, that it might be abundantly watered yet not overhang the mouth of the well; it must face toward the house and to the south, for the proper ripening of its luscious fruit. In short, there was one and only one possible place for it—

And he put his foot on the stone that marked my discovery point.

I agreed with him heartily, of course, while inwardly cursing the coincidence. He launched into a discourse on figs of various sorts and their pollenizing; he was very glad to see that we had a couple of spades in readiness for his gardeners. In short, he was enjoying himself hugely, as we walked back to the house.

Murchison's coffee was ready. I suggested a cup, and Burke agreed delightedly.

"Shall we have it in the writing-room?" he asked. "It is a delightful place, with those exquisite pillars and arches cutting it off from the other rooms, and the floor is a step lower—an admirable idea!"

I PUT the coffee cups and so forth on a tray, and we went in to the writing-room. I put the tray on the table and we got settled. Burke rubbed his hands zestfully.

"There is something I must discuss with you over the coffee, my dear Carson—"

He broke off as the door-knocker pounded. I excused myself, rose, and went to the front door. I opened it and was amazed to see Madame Benfar standing there, bare-headed, a light gauzy wrap about her shoulders; and behind her, of all people, Mustapha!

"May I come in?" she asked, as though intending to enter whether or not.

"But of course!" I swung the door wide. "I thought you were far away—and you, Mustapha, in Cherchell!"

She gave me a look from those eyes of hers that fairly scorched me.

"As far away as the villa across the road, monsieur," she said. Her black hair was knotted about her head and a scarlet hibiscus flower glimmered in it. "You have guests?"

"A guest, madame, in the writing-room. If you will join us—"

"Your friends have gone away?"

"To Cherchell only, madame."

We entered the house, Mustapha vanished; and if I had been amazed by the appearance of Naila, Burke was simply thunderstruck when we walked into the writing-room and I introduced him. He had doffed his sun-glasses; now he put them on again.

The villa across the road? I remembered Mustapha having gone there. But why, in heaven's name? I sank more and more into the utmost perplexity, for now Naila became gayly talkative—indeed, she showed herself a different person, sparkling and laughing radiantly and as chipper as a bird. Burke lost his bluff hardiness and became taciturn.

"I'm glad you're here," I said. "We've given M. Burke permission to plant a few trees in the garden—I trust you'll not object, madame? It seems that he has some hope of ultimately obtaining the villa from the Government. His gardeners and trees will arrive in an hour or so."

She broke into laughter that seemed to me almost hysterical, yet it was unfeigned. I failed to see the joke. So did Burke, apparently.

"I'm sure Mustapha will welcome your gardeners and make

them feel at home," she said. She seemed ten years younger; that hawk-face of hers was all dimples when she laughed, but her eyes remained glittering and unsmiling and alive. Burke had ensconced himself in a mammoth overstuffed leather chair in one corner.

"You look so comfortable in that chair, monsieur!" she said. We were speaking French, of course. "It seems to fit you perfectly. Coffee? Thank you, M. Carson."

I poured coffee. She lit a cigarette. Burke bit into a cigar, one of his fat Havanas. I saw Naila start slightly; it was the first time, I think, she had taken her eyes off Burke. She was looking at the photograph in the niche.

"Where did that come from?" she demanded in a queer, hard voice. "May I see it?"

I handed it to her in silence. She looked at it for a moment, then put it on the table, against the sugar-bowl.

"If that man ever came back here," she said to me, with a casual air, "do you think that he could disguise himself from me?"

"No, madame, I fancy not," I said, smiling.

"You are right; he could not. That is why I have waited here, month after month, year after year; I knew that he would come, that he must come. Like the beasts whom he served, he truly loved only one thing in the whole world—gold."

"Madame, permit me," said Burke. He seemed to find some difficulty in speaking. "I think that you are wrong in saying so. I have heard of this man. I believe that he was passionately devoted to you—"

"Don't be absurd," she broke in coldly, "He loved no one but himself. He was cruel, heartless, despicable—a murderer. I was his victim, not his beloved. He killed the one man I ever loved, in front of me."

Burke sat back, puffing hard at his cigar. The dark glasses veiled his eyes. Naila uttered a sudden sharp little laugh that sounded like glass breaking.

A surge of relief shot through me at hearing a car come into the drive and halt beside the entrance. Gondy and Murchison back—so soon? Anything that could break this growing tension would be blessed, I thought. I had half risen when Mustapha appeared in the arched entrance of the room and spoke.

"A light truck, madame, with two men and a woman. They are, I think, natives."

"Oh, yes! My gardeners!" Burke lunged forward and came to his feet. "Excuse me. I had better go and direct them—"

Swift as a flash, Naila jerked up her skirt. I had a glimpse of her leg to the knee, a metallic, mechanical leg. Her hand caught something that was fastened to it, and whipped it up—a pistol, almost touching Burke's side. He froze.

From her lips came swift Arabic. Mustapha vanished. She rose, holding the weapon against Burke's side.

"Look at that picture, M. Carson," she said. "Imagine how that man would look if his nose were straightened, his brows changed, his mouth slightly altered, and the missing teeth replaced by two gold ones—"

Burke moved like a flash of lightning. He had taken the cigar from his mouth; he dashed it against her hand, knocking it aside, one foot swept out with vicious force and kicked her good ankle; as she fell, he recovered balance and grappled me.

I was caught off guard—quite naturally. He had me, whirled me around, and flung me straight at her as she was rising. I smashed against her and we both went down. I rammed my head against a marble pillar and the concussion knocked me momentarily silly.

AN AUTOMATIC had leaped into Burke's hand. He faced us, faced the room beyond; he had whipped off his dark glasses, and fury had purpled his features.

"Quiet!" he barked. "Don't move, you fool! Must I kill you?"

Madame Benfar lay face down, arms extended—his words were meant for me. She was evidently knocked senseless, and

I was next thing to it. I sat up, put a hand to my head, and groaned. A snarl came from Burke.

"If you'd gone with the others, you'd have been safely put away—you had to stay here, you damned American swine-dog—well, you'll pay for it! You out there—come in, come in!"

There was a scuffle of feet in the room beyond, a frightened squawk from Mustapha, and I had a glimpse of figures there. Two Arabs, holding Mustapha. An Arab woman, in the ugly white robe that cover all Arab women from head to feet, leaving only a hole for one eye to peer through.

But as I looked, she reached up her arms and twisted clear of the robe. My heart leaped as her features came into sight—Félice, by all the gods! Félice, working hand in glove with this disguised Nazi devil!

If I had hesitated then, heaven only knows what would have happened. Luckily, I did not. With another groan, I let myself fall forward. Burke was standing on one end of a small Berber rug. As I fell, my hands gripped the other end. I jerked. The rug slid out from under him on the slippery tiles—he went down with a crash and a furious oath.

Wrenching myself across the intervening distance, I had him—got my fingers locked in his fleshy throat, and hung on as he thrashed. His strength was terrific. He flung me around like a doll.

The explosion of a pistol rang deafeningly in our ears. Naila was on her feet, her weapon smoking; the automatic exploded again and again. A woman's shriek burst out—not hers. Everything was blurred with motion now, as Burke fought me. He broke my hold, flung me aside and came to one knee, a pistol in his hand—

Another shot. I saw him crumple up, almost above me, then sink down in an inert heap. I caught at his pistol, and his limp fingers let it go. Everything had fallen silent; I struggled to my feet and stared around. Naila stood looking at me; there was no one else in sight.

The roar of a car's engine came from outside, and lessened. Mustapha came with a gasp and a run, babbling something; Naila shut him up. Turning, I looked down at Burke. He—or Kurt Bremer—would not return again.

"Your head is bleeding, monsieur," said Naila. "Sit down and let me attend to the hurt."

No doubt the reaction took hold of me. I remember uttering an hysteric laugh, fumbling around for a chair—and that was all....

When I wakened, it was to find myself in the same chair, my head tied up. Someone was holding brandy to my lips. I swallowed, and a wrench of astonishment seized me—the glass was held by Murchison! He was beside me. Gondy stood watching us, bandages swathing him to the eyes—the sparkling, laughing eyes.

"What the devil!" I exclaimed. "Where is she?"

The room was darkening in twilight. Burke's body was gone—Naila, too.

Murchison laughed.

"Apparently Félice got away," said he. "It's all over, old chap. We damned near got finished on that mountain road—a car crowded us off. The Panhard's done for, but we escaped with some bruises. Got back here just now, in time to clear things up with your friend Naila. Sit back and take it easy. Don't worry."

"The treasure!" I gulped. "He—Kurt Bremer—"

"We know all about it," he said. "Time enough tomorrow for the treasure-hunt. Today we're just glad to be alive. Naila told us the whole thing; she's taken Bremer's body to turn him over to the police. Colonel Duperre will be here tomorrow."

I frowned, puzzled. "But he wired you today from Cherchell—that was why—"

"All a delusion and a snare," broke in Gondy, snapping his fingers. "A snare set by that charming Félice, damn her! They crowded us off the road and meant to finish us—were shooting at us when other cars came along and scared 'em off. She came on here expecting to get Carson's Folly for herself—and came within an ace of getting it, too!"

I sank back in the chair—Kurt Bremer's fine leather chair into which Jeremiah Burke had fitted so snugly—and Murch poured more brandy.

On the morrow Colonel Duperre arrived. It was he who had charge of our private agreement with the Government, about the treasure. He joined us in laboring by the well in the garden, and we labored to good purpose. I had been right in thinking that Kurt Bremer must have hidden the stuff close to the well, since water would be amply available to hide the traces of his work.

From the hole we took out two Standard Oil gasoline tins with the tops cut off; each was packed with gold-pieces on the bottom, and hard fat packets of American dollar bills and British sterling notes above. When our first enthusiastic and voluble excitement had calmed, Colonel Duperre packed the tins out to his car, where an orderly waited. We were sure enough of our share, later.

"Oh, I forgot!" Gondy suddenly turned to us. "Murchison, remember that garage man who helped pull us out of the wrecked car yesterday, and who lent us a car to return here with?"

"Yes. What about him?" said Murchison absently.

"He was an Italian. The Fascisti had chased him out of Italy; he went back with the Allied troops and then returned to his garage business here when the war ended—"

"What the devil are you driving at?" I broke in.

Gondy gesticulated excitedly.

"He told me the most amazing story! Mussolini's private hoard of gold, that was hidden and lost when Italy was invaded! This man's sister saw it cached in the grotto of the nymphs at Griffiti. The Black-shirt officer in charge killed the two men helping him, and an hour later was run down by a truck and wiped out—"

For once, Murchison did not take fire at a spark of moonlight. Instead, he stood looking thoughtfully at nothing.

"Talk about it later," he murmured. "Look here, if you chaps agree, I think we ought to cut in the one-legged dancer on our share?"

We agreed, and gladly. None the less, I had the conviction that one of these days we were going to visit Italy—if not sooner.

III

GROTTO OF THE NYMPHS

Carson's contraption failed as a mine-detector,
but it would locate some sorts of buried
treasure. When they tried for Mussolini's cache,
they got more than they'd bargained for.

I WAS ALONE with Carson's Folly, and unsuspicious; in short, a blasted fool.

Actually, I was taking my ease in the vine-clad arbor outside the little tavern of Astisi, among the Umbrian hills. The war was long over, having passed this village lightly and afar. The unmourned Benito had long since been slung up by his heels like a dead steer in the public square of Milan, along with his die-hard lieutenants; but Italy was learning to her cost, many a clever blackshirt had gone underground and stayed there.

Here in Astisi the peasants gleaned their sheaves, pressed their oil and wine, and went their daily rounds in ancient fashion. Fewer of them, yes.

Four of us had started hither. In Naples, my old pal Murchison—who named Carson's Folly for me, though he was equally responsible for the gadget—collided with a truck. He sustained a few light contusions and a ravishingly pretty nurse, and remained there to follow us in a few days.

In Rome, our contact-man Gondy had a wire that his father was dying in France, and hopped the first train, to rejoin us later. Marco and that fool Bill Carson, who spoke enough bastard Italian to get along, went on alone. It was really because of Marco that we had come. He had been born here at Astisi. The Fascisti had chased him out. He had been an interpreter with Mark Clark's Army, speaking a Mulberry Street sort of English. Like his sister Elena, he was tough, athletic, hard-boned—the regular peasant type.

And now I sat in the afternoon shade with my pipe and bottle of wine. Marco had taken our rattly old bus and gone to visit his sister on the farm, a few miles outside Astisi. Carson's Folly sat in my room, and Bill Carson sat here sipping wine, like a fool. Why is it that we never know when the wings of death are close upon us?

Not a soul except Marco, of course, dreamed why we were here; or so I thought.

The innkeeper, a lusty mustachioed bandit, came and sat with me, bringing more wine. He showed fine white teeth in frequent raillery at my Sicilian dialect, appreciated my American tobacco, and chattered in a hill dialect that was almost incomprehensible.

We were in Italy strictly on business. Murchison and I'd been confined to laboratories until the war's end—hush-hush work, devising novel detectors to counter the ever-changing types of land mines produced by the infernal Kraut ingenuity. Among other things, we dreamed up Carson's Folly, our biggest failure.

This was an electronic gadget based on the type used by oil prospectors—only it was no good for oil; and so far as mines went it was a perfect bust, because it was apt to ignore such small objects, and would work at no depth less than three feet. Otherwise, it was grand.

War's end gave us a choice—either go back home to South Boston and maybe open a radio-repair shop, or else go see the world with Carson's Folly in hand. We picked the world and

Elena pointed out where digging had been done. If
we found treasure, we would bring it to the farm.

took it for our oyster. By virtue of elaborating on our useless
gadget, and altering its electronic properties by tubes of various
sorts, we began to prove that the old oyster held some rich
pickings.

Our friend the Vicomte de Gondy came along on a three-
way split, because he was a good egg (though given to rhap-
sodic dreams like Murchison) and he knew everyone and could
develop projects for us. Projects? Yes, treasure-hunting projects.
He had turned up this affair of Marco's.

So now I sat here with the innkeeper, waiting for Marco to return.

Mine host jabbered on—something about a Signore Botti who spoke English, a politician, who would be here this evening. A grain-buyer for the district, as nearly as I could make out, whose sister was coming with him; this was accompanied by a leering wink, whose significance I missed. Signore Botti had once been a big-shot among the accursed Fascisti, but now, like others, he had reformed.

The hell with him, I thought; and in acute relief welcomed the return of Marco, who came striding in upon us and put mine host to flight. It was close to sunset. Marco, swigging the wine, leaned across the table and declaimed in a mixture of French, English and Italian, his hard brown features flushed, his eyes alight. He had talked with his sister Elena, who now owned the family farm, and everything was well.

This Elena, it proved, was really something. Her husband had died in Tripoli. She was left a widow with two offspring, and was now rapidly aging, being close to thirty. After Marco skipped out for his health, she took over the family farm; he had deeded it to her, and she ran it ably. What was more to the point, she had witnessed all that passed in the Grotto of the Nymphs, which was on the farm—all except the most essential thing, of course. Marco recapitulated with many gestures.

A high Fascist officer and two blackshirts had come in a grand big car, which by its decorations belonged to Il Duce himself—this was just before the Chin blew up. Elena, hidden among the hillside brush, watched it stop before the Grotto, which was a cave famous in local story. The three had carried in two small chests, with tools and shovels. They had worked a long time; then two shots sounded. The officer came out alone and drove away. An hour later, reaching the main highway, he hit an Army truck and was killed. Sometime afterward, patriots had come down from the hills, and on hearing Elena's story searched the cave. They found the two blackshirt corpses, but not the treasure—obviously, said the excited Marco, the private treasure of Il Duce himself.

SUCH, IN brief, was the tale that had brought us here, and was now confirmed.

In my highly practical way, I made Marco savvy that treasure could not be hidden in the rocky floor of a cavern. He waved his hands.

"But, signore, it is no floor of rock! *Regardez*—a grotto *antichissimo,* of the most ancient times, from the days of the giants! Fulla da fine dirt, signore, and marble gods, and da vampires liva there, you bet! *Per Dio,* I tella you—"

Being a peasant, he had vampires and hermits all mixed up with centaurs and giants and gods; the point being that the cave had an earthen floor, and in ancient times had been called the Grotto of the Nymphs. Further, he said Elena expected us to come tomorrow and dig up Mussolini's hoard of gold, and we could keep half what we found. We need not wait for my friends. Marco and I could do the job, and welcome.

I smoked over that, and told him I would decide in the morning. He swigged some more wine, hugged me, and departed to spend the evening with old friends, saying he would be here with the car at nine. Like the fool I was, I let him go and sat thinking.

How much of this yarn was goose-feathers, how much was true, we did not know. Something, probably, had been hidden in the grotto, and the man who hid it had died quickly thereafter, and the secret was lost with him—presumably. Murchison and Gondy and I would have a lot of fun running down the facts; and if anything had been buried, Carson's Folly would locate it.

On the other hand: Gondy might be gone for weeks; Murch was enjoying his hurts and his pretty nurse; and I was already fed up with this squalid little hill village. Why not settle the matter while I had the chance? Further, these peasants were

*"Now," I told him, "the detecting
waves should operate—:*

notional. This Elena gal might welcome us tomorrow, kick us
out the next day.

The sun sank in the west; the wine-jug was empty; and
Signore Botti arrived with *la Principessa.* His sister, the innkeeper had said, but I had not interpreted his wink aright. *La
Principessa* indeed! I had a glimpse of the alleged princess as
she got out of Botti's big car. Her face was half-swathed in a
dust-veil, but her figure—divine! Her clothes were admirable.

Two figures stepped into the light.
They held German pistols.

Just as well Murch was not here. He would have gone off into some rhapsody about Italian princesses, whereas practical old Bill Carson knew that she was just Botti's mistress, and scratched her off.

It was odd, though. Botti got not a room but several rooms, and called her "Princess," and treated her with the greatest respect. Botti himself was big and bony, with an angular jaw and agate-hard eyes, and his pockets were apparently filled with big black cigars. They would be here for several days, someone said.

Nor did Botti follow her and the luggage upstairs. He put the car away, then fell into talk with mine host, and I gathered that they were discussing me. I had to hang around to escape the fleas in my room and await dinner while my insecticide worked; and although the dinner was something special, it was plenty late—as usual in Italy.

Presently Botti came over, clicked his heels and smiled at me.

"Your pardon—I am Angelo Botti, and I understand you're an American. Will you honor me by joining me in some rather good wine? That rascal keeps it hidden for me."

I gave my name. His fluent English astonished me; he had been in charge of English prisoners during the war, he said, though he had learned the language earlier. The wine was indeed excellent. Botti was a politician, he avowed. His cigars were better than they looked. He talked a blue streak—liked to hear himself talk English—but not about himself. About Italy and her future. He was not a bit disheartened over the war damage.

"National pride, my friend, will restore us!" he affirmed. "Fascism, yes, under some other name. You'll see; Italy will expand before anyone realizes it. The plans are all made. Even now we have begun to infiltrate into Ethiopia; we'll get an economic hold on that country. Tunisia will be annexed to Sicily—"

THIS AND more of the same came out by degrees, until I sat there swallowing hard and pinching myself to see if it was real. It was. Botti hated the British like poison and said so, but loved Americans or pretended that he did. He had absolutely no hesitation in pouring out boasts about the coming Italian revival.

And he made it real. The man was remarkably shrewd, intelligent, able. As he painted it, his dream impressed me. I asked how he dared pour it all out to an utter stranger, a foreigner, and he broke into a laugh.

"But you're an American—that's different! Americans are our friends. Besides, they do not matter in European affairs."

So he thought, anyhow. Gradually I perceived that he was entirely sincere, neither drunk nor insane, but under the influence of a tremendous mental excitement—possessed by a swirling riot of ideas that had gone to his head. He just had to talk them out, and figured an American as being safer than an Italian to talk with.

This was no ordinary experience. This man was no fool but little short of great; his visions had a scope, a grandeur, that took my breath. He was what Mussolini, at his best, had dreamed of being: a statesman, an empire builder, and a powerful one.

Yes, he was like a man hopped to the gills with dope. This terrific thing, this bold conception, was all the while growing inside of him, and I was getting the overflow. It just had to explode somewhere. Therefore, I figured, it must have freshly taken hold of him. How? Whence? Had he devised it all himself?

The answer came little by little—a word here, another there. He had driven from Genoa today; a long drive. La Principessa was an old family friend, *en route* to Rome; he had given her a lift. When he spoke of her, his eyes lighted up. He might be crazy about her, and he was, but also he was deeply respectful. She was assuredly not his mistress, as I had first thought. Her name? He evaded that.

So it came to me—perhaps telepathically, from his brain—that she was the source of this political inspiration which had so totally gripped and enthralled him.

"What are you going to do without money?" I asked him. "You know as well as I do that Italy is broke. These things can't be done without financial security."

Instantly he closed up. Did you ever touch a clam, open to

the waters, and have it contract at the touch into a baffling mass of shell? That was the way he reacted.

"That," he said, "is all arranged. It is settled."

He said not a word more, except to make his farewells. He went upstairs; supper for him and the princess was sent up. I ate mine down below and enjoyed it, but I was still in an electric thrill from Botti's words. If his predictions came true—and he was the man to make them come true—he was the coming master of Italy. Not so bizarre as it might sound. This nation, distracted and broken as it was, could be welded into a new unity by such a political scheme as he sketched.

I was still sitting there, finishing the cigar Signore Botti had given me, when in came Marco, glanced around, and hastily joined me. Fear was in his muttering voice:

"I cannot stay, Signore Carson. *J'ai grand peur*—they hava come, they hava come!"

"Who and what?" I demanded, astonished.

"Fascisti, blackshirts. Three or four of them, at farms somewhere around here. They have asked questions about my sister, about me!" He abandoned his jargon and spoke in pure Italian,

Félice leaned forward, oblivious of me. Signal?
She had never intended making me any!

and terror glinted in his eyes. "And about the treasure stories, the grotto!"

"Nonsense," I said. "Those days are gone forever, Marco."

I SAID this, but I knew better myself. Except in the northern socialist districts, Fascism had just gone underground; it had not been stamped out at all, and most of the big-shots were doing business as usual under Allied occupation. Marco knew it too, and his toughness had turned to shivery ice.

"We finish da job tomorrow quick," he said. "They have come for Il Duce's treasure. We grab it first and run. Nine o'clock, signore."

He slipped out and was gone—scared and no mistake, but in true peasant fashion resolved to hang on to the treasure.

Blackshirts? If they monkeyed with an American, it would be just too bad for them. I had an automatic and could use it. This hint of possible frustration made me resolve to go through with the thing—fast, as Marco wanted it.

I went to my room and turned in. The insecticide had worked; the fleas were gone. I got to sleep and later wished I had not, because I dreamed. And in my dream moved a rarely beautiful—and terrible—woman: Gondy's former sister-in-law.

WHEN THE three of us started to oysterize the world with Carson's Folly, we operated first on the buried family treasure at the Gondy chateau in France. It turned up the treasure, all right, and it also turned up blood and passion and the fury of greed. We came close to death there, all of us. Gondy's brother did die. And his wife was the cause of it all—she knew about Carson's Folly, knew vaguely how it worked, wanted it for herself and damned near got away with it. She had brains, beauty and was bad clear through.

Bad? Not in my dreams this night. Félice de Gondy filled them with loveliness. She was tall, high-bosomed, with deep blue eyes all alive and spun gold hair, and her personal charm was sheer magic. When she turned on the power a man was lost—any man. In my dreams I was madly in love with her, just as Murchison had been. Madly!

It had been different in real life. She had a small, tight mouth, showing greed and cruel purpose, and this had revealed her actual character clearly enough to Bill Carson.

I woke up, sweating, and sat bolt upright, fancying that she was there beside me. It was just a shaft of moonlight, striking in through the window. Instead of Félice, there was Carson's Folly beside the bed—the gadget itself in its carton, the long handle in its careful wrapping. I rubbed my eyes in relief—then looked again. The two sections were not side by side as I had left them, but at a little distance from each other. Somebody had been in the room!

I was in that half-awake, half-dream state following heavy slumber when the brain imagines all sorts of queer nonsense. I came out of it with a grunt of disgust, and could have kicked myself. I had moved the gadget, of course, in opening the window on retiring.

"You're a blithering idiot, Bill Carson," I muttered, dropping back on the pillow. "Just because that woman has followed us and Gondy's in deadly fear of her, you imagine the damnedest things—and even dream of her. Forget it and go to sleep! She's not within a thousand miles of here. Signore Botti and his ravings must have knocked you off balance."

I went back to sleep and dreamed no more....

Wakening early, I shaved and got downstairs and breakfasted with the swarthy innkeeper. He was cheerful and jolly, asked if I had slept well, cracked a joke about La Principessa that would not bear repetition, and then took my breath away.

"So you have come to find Il Duce's treasure, eh?"

He chortled with mirth at my expression, waved his hands at me, yet was half serious. Oh, it was no secret! Everyone knew that Mussolini had sent his private loot here, had buried it somewhere; the whole district knew it. And what else would an American be here for? Marco had babbled about magic powers and electric eyes that could see through the earth.

Marco had babbled, then; I was relieved. The whole district was agog with stories and rumors of Il Duce's buried treasure; everyone was ready to jump at any sort of conclusion. Some former blackshirts had turned up—they had come for Mussolini's loot. An American turned up—he had come for Mussolini's loot. A wonder they did not say La Principessa and Signore Botti had come for it! Perhaps they did.

This decided me to go with Marco, get the thing settled at once, and clear out, before complications with excited peasants led to riot and mob trouble.

It was close to nine, so I carried down Carson's Folly—it was made chiefly of magnesium and weighed little—to be ready for Marco's arrival. Signore Botti appeared, big and powerful and gaunt, with a cheery greeting and a black cigar in his teeth. He looked curiously at the carton. A new spraying device for vineyards, I said, and he nodded.

"Yes. You Americans have done marvels here with such things," he observed. "You have changed the agricultural customs of our people, with your powders and sprays. I buy twice as much grain in this district as formerly, thanks to American innovations."

Marco rattled up in his old car and I loaded in the gadget, then we bounced away. Marco was more cheerful this morning, but still uneasy. Elena, he said, awaited us.

WE HAD a three-mile drive among hills to the farm, a tiny whitewashed house where two bambinos stared at us and Elena got in. She was of harder fiber than Marco—pleasant enough but bitter tough with hard peasant labor, and her black eyes held a deep fire that his lacked. She would be an old woman at forty, no doubt.

A short half-mile on to the Grotto of the Nymphs, following a winding track. Here was a bit of hillside vineyard, long abandoned and grown high with brush, with an opening eight feet high in the hillside. Walls and roof were of natural rock; a few scattered blocks of marble, and holes where metal clamps had been, showed that in ancient years it had boasted a marble façade, now gone.

We left the car standing, and went in, with a lantern and my flashlight. I was much impressed by Elena's matter-of-fact way; she was all business. She gave me neither smiles nor suspicion; she accepted me because Marco said so. She pointed out where the two murdered blackshirts had been found, where digging had been done vainly, then said she must get home. She had work to do. If we found treasure, we would bring it to the farm.

"Certainly," I assured her. "We may find nothing."

"Americans never fail; it is impossible," she said, and departed afoot, leaving us alone. I was not sorry. Those implacable, deep, glowing eyes of hers made me nervous.

The cave was an empty hole in the earth; no nymphs, no writing on the walls, no romance, no nothing. Murchison, who was given to such nonsense, would have peopled it with the ghosts of Greek goddesses; he had made an angel out of Félice, too, and she had made a proper fool out of him. It did have a dirt floor, which confirmed Marco's accounts. It ran straight into the hill for thirty feet, being twenty-one wide by my pacing, then made an elbow turn, narrowed, and after another twenty feet shrank to a foxhole and was gone. The dirt and accumulation of centuries probably covered a rock floor, I figured, at some depth.

"Well, we've all day before us and it's nice and cool in here," I said to Marco. "Where do you think anything would have been buried—where, if you were doing it?"

He laughed, gesticulated, and finally said around the elbow turn. I nodded, getting my pipe alight.

"I agree; the inner cave, by all means. Come on and get the stuff."

We fetched in Carson's Folly, which looked not unlike an outsize vacuum cleaner on big wheels, with its high handle. I put it together and connected the dry batteries, which were carried in a knapsack that went over my shoulders. Then I changed tubes from the box of extras, because I had to allow for the rock floor that must exist, and different impulses were necessary.

Murchison and I figured on going home some day and putting the thing to commercial uses, but not yet. This model machine was a unique and even wonderful thing; the tubes, in particular, I had made myself. No duplicate existed. We carried the entire plans in our heads, and already I was thinking of various improvements. I had devised a chart, and as the supersonic waves kicked back from any obstacle and registered on the gauges, the chart translated these and told what the underground substance was. It was far from perfect, of course.

We were at work in the inner turn of the cave, with the lantern giving us light. Marco was absorbed in the gadget, which I explained in part as I worked; both of us forgot that time was passing. I removed the knapsack, placed it on the floor, and showed how the radionic waves bounced back from the rock below and registered. The gauges told correctly that there was rock under our feet, about four yards down, as I figured. This required some rather precise adjustments which I made.

"Now," I told him, "the detecting waves should operate at a depth of between five and ten feet, but I may have to adjust—"

SHADOWS MOVED. Two figures stepped into the dim circle of lantern-light; they held long German Luger pistols. They wore black shirts and the Fascist insigne. A gasp broke from Marco, squatting beside me. He went up in the air like a jack-in-the-box and stood with arms raised. A third man showed himself. He spoke in Italian.

"Outside, you two. *Sbrigati*—move fast!"

Marco burst into terrorized appeals. I said nothing, could do nothing; my automatic was in my bag at the tavern. The three frisked us swiftly and then shoved us toward the outer grotto, one of them taking along the lantern and setting it down outside. The stabbing finger of a flashlight touched us and swept around.

*Elena was alone. "That woman!" she
demanded. "Did she shoot you? I could have
killed her easily. And I let her go!"*

Two other figures were there, passing us without a word or a look, heading for the inner cavern. One was Signore Botti, who held the flashlight. The other was his veiled princess. We stood beside the lantern, the Lugers trained on us.

Even then, even when Botti and his princess went past and disappeared around the elbow bend whither we had come, no inkling of the truth occurred to that poor dumb nitwit of a Bill Carson. I merely stood and gawked. It was all a fantastic and unpleasant interruption—a mishap of the first water, but nothing more.

Marco, undoubtedly, knew into what bloody hands we had fallen, or guessed. His impassioned appeal became a frantic, almost hysterical harangue in furious Italian. All the while he was craftily edging away from me, turning first to one Fascist then to another, wringing his hands as he held them up. Then, suddenly, he gave the man next him a shove, knocked him against another of the three, and made a break for it. And, by the gods, he came within an ace of getting clear!

One Fascist blazed away wildly, the shot roaring in multitudinous echoes. I kicked one in the shins and he began to hop around. But the third man leveled his Luger and fired twice, just as Marco reached the entrance to the grotto, and brought him down like a running deer. Then he whirled about to fire at me, but the voice of Signore Botti checked him.

Powder fumes swirled around us; the echoes roared and re-roared; excited voices were quelled to nothing, and poor Marco lay outside the entrance with blood pooling around his body. The three blackshirts glowered at me while Botti addressed them sharply and kept fingering their guns after he disappeared. At any rate, I had to thank him for my life; yet, although my knees were shaking with the near touch of death, inwardly I was in a fury of rage and grief and horror. I had liked Marco.

The three murderous rats lighted cigarettes, spoke among themselves, and kept a close eye on me as though they were hoping I would make a break as Marco had done.

"You dirty bastards," I told them in my choicest Italian, "you'll pay for this!"

They grinned nastily. "We've killed Americans before this, and shall again," said one coolly, and the others assented. They meant it, with ghastly cold-blooded complacency. Marco gave a sudden convulsive kick, and relaxed; he was dead.

I sat down on a chunk of rock by the lantern and got out my pipe—not as a gesture, but to calm my shattered nerves. As the moments passed, I realized how completely this gang had me in their power. No one knew where I was, no one cared. Later in the day, of course, Marco's sister might come to investigate— small hope there.

Then, catching a tiny whir of sound, I pricked up my ears, incredulous. What the devil! Carson's Folly was at work, no doubt of it! Signore Botti was in the farther cavern, and La Principessa with him. Surely they did not know how to work it? They might be experimenting, of course, but not a soul knew how to work the gadget except ourselves; not a living soul, except—except—

The woman I had dreamed about: Félice de Gondy! She knew, vaguely.

IT WAS here that an inkling of the truth grew upon me. Oh, fantastic nonsense! It was impossible, out of the question. And—yet and yet, could it be that I had dreamed about her because her vital and electric-charged presence had been some-where close? Could that woman be Botti's princess?

Absurd. No, Bill Carson, not absurd at all, you half-witted oaf! She was on your trail. She knew you were alone here. Perhaps she had made sure you would come here alone with Marco—perhaps Gondy's father was not dying at all—perhaps Gondy had been drawn away by a ruse, deliberately!

Signore Botti and his great schemes for the Italian revival— had Félice inspired those schemes of his? She was entirely capable of it; she could inspire the Sphinx itself with devilish ambitions. She scintillated with sparkling ideas, plans, possibilities; she was alive with energy, she radiated force and glittering dreams. That woman with the tight little steel-trap mouth and the glorious eyes—she who dressed so exquisitely, whose beauty could captivate any man! Félice, with her inordinate greed for gold—

Despite the coolness of the grotto, I began to sweat as I sat there, thinking of her, picturing her mentally. A slight sound came to me with startling force, a tiny sound yet ringing in my ears like Gabriel's horn; it was the buzzer of the detector, announcing that something had been located. Silence ensued. They guessed, then, what it meant. Félice knew nothing about reading the gauges or what they signified, but she would have sense enough to know what the signal meant.

And I was correct. A moment later Botti appeared with his flashlight. His grimly powerful features were back into the inner cave, a flashlight in his hand. He was talking to her as they went, and his voice filled the grotto with redundant roaring echoes ringing with exultant triumph. "Two boxes"—that was all I could make of it. Marco's sister had said that two chests were carried in and hidden. So he had found them—or Félice had!

SINKING DOWN again on my rock by the lantern, I sucked my empty pipe and waited. What sort of a role was Félice playing? Certainly I had never made love to her in the past, but she had my pulses pounding now. She had not brought Signore Botti here merely in order to trick him; that was nonsense. Did she really want her old position back with the Gondy family? Of course not. She had done her best to kill all three of us before this. Such were the facts—but how sure of them was I? With the thought of my hand upon her throbbing heart, I was sure of nothing, and that is the honest truth.

They had brought up the two chests; the air was racked by resounding echoes of blows on metal, of rending, splintering assault, of confused voices. A silence fell; they had burst open one chest and were at the other one, as the furious sounds testified. Again the echoes lessened into silence.

It was broken by a heavy tread. Botti appeared, flushed and lowering, his flashlight holding upon me.

"Here! Come here, you!" he spat out, with a resounding Italian oath. I obeyed word and gesture. He shoved me ahead of him and started back around the elbow-turn.

The scene came into view, another of the men holding a second light. Beside the excavation they had dug stood the two men and Félice; she was stooping, leaning over the two splintered and smashed chests, examining their contents.

"Lies, lies, lies!" burst forth Botti's resonant tones. "The treasure of Il Duce! The hoard of Fascismo! There it is—look at it!"

The two boxes were filled with papers, and nothing else.

No wonder Botti was prey to a savage fury. I stared down at the boxes, enmity forgotten, even the murder of Marco forgotten, in the incredible fact before me. For this we had all wagered life and death—for nothing except paper. All of us alike had been duped and tricked by rumor and and story and wild surmise—

"Wait, *wait!*"

Félice came to her full height, springing up, clutching a handful of the papers from one box. She swung around to Botti and thrust them at him.

"Look at these!" she cried. "Do you see what they are? A treasure greater than any gold! The secret reports and archives of Il Duce himself! Letters, records—"

"Paper!" ejaculated Botti in scorn. "Not gold, but paper!"

"Paper that will hang a thousand men!" she corrected him. "Paper that will bring down the mighty, paper that will expose and lay bare those who sit in safety! Paper more potent than any gold—paper worth millions of lire to whomever holds it—"

Botti's powerful face changed, as his light played on the papers he held. A low, astounded exclamation broke from him.

"*Per Dio!* You speak the truth, Principessa!"

For an instant he stood silent, overcome; as well he might. The secret records of the Grand Council—treaties, agreements, reports, letters—a weapon to make any politician in Italy supreme, a treasure of more worth than this grotto filled with gold! Then he came to life, in a burst of furious energy and thrust his flashlight at one of the two blackshirts.

"Here! Take this box out, put it in the car, and come back for the other one. Your light, Principessa!"

She gave him the electric torch, as they called it, which she had been holding. The two men stooped, lifted one of the broken chests, and marched off with it. Signore Botti fell on one knee and began rummaging among the papers in the second chest, playing the light upon them. Félice leaned forward, peering over his shoulder eagerly, quite oblivious of me. Signal? She had never intended making me any signal!

I shifted my weight, balanced—and kicked out.

Both of them, no doubt, had completely forgotten about Bill Carson; of the gun Félice had promised, there was no sign. My toe caught Botti under the chin and sent him sprawling back on his hands and hams. The flashlight hit the floor and went out, and we were in pitch blackness.

As I kicked, I spun around with the intention of getting out of there quick, and risking bullets. My foot caught in the splintered box-lid, and down I went. In that dense darkness I hit the edge of nothing and went on over—and in blind panic landed with a shock that knocked the wind out of me, very luckily, or I might have yelled for help. I thought I had gone into some unseen chasm.

I had fallen into the excavation from which the chests had been taken, and it was only six feet deep; not as deep as the sea, but it served.

Botti cursed in lurid Italian. Félice added some very shocking French phrases; I gathered that she had barked her shins on the open box of papers. I lay quiet, gasping for air. Then a match flared.

"Gone!" barked Botti. "He kicked me over and ran for it—"

"Never mind. Your men will get him as he comes out," said Félice, "unless he's hiding in the outer grotto."

The match went out; Botti cursed.

"Light another," she told him. "I have torn my dress."

After an instant, another yellow flare danced up. With it, Botti burst forth in a wild screaming cry:

"What are you doing with that—stop it, *stop* it—"

A pistol-shot roared in reverberant echoes. Darkness fell, and silence.

I KNEW instantly what had happened. Standing in the darkness, I clawed at the edge of the hole, pulled myself up and over, and got to my feet. My own flashlight was still in my pocket. I got it out and ventured to press the button.

The ray fell upon the body of Signore Botti, almost at my feet. She had shot him through the head, then had run for it. My blood chilled. Calmly telling him to strike another match, grabbing out her gun—and murdering him as the match flared!

I pocketed the light, having got my bearings, and struck out after her.

Only a little, a very little, time had passed since those two blackshirts carried out the first chest. In the outer and larger grotto, the lantern still burned feebly. Halfway to the daylight of the entrance was the shrouded figure of Félice. She had come to a halt, was peering at something outside.

The body of Marco lay there in the sunlight beyond the entrance. Farther still, the three blackshirts came into view. They had evidently put the box into the car of Botti, and were now coming back for the second chest. The sight of them put me suddenly in mind of my own peril. I must get that gun from Félice and—

Everything seemed to stop dead.

Félice was crouching; I could see her outlined against the daylight, pistol ready. She meant to open fire on the three when they came—but they were not coming. They, too, had come to a halt. They were staring, not at the grotto entrance, but at something or someone among the bushes just above it.

The quick, ringing crack of a carbine sounded. The first black-shirt caught at his chest and doubled up. Another shot. The second man fell, winged. The third slid out a pistol and threw it up—but the carbine cracked again and he spun around; another shot dropped him. The wounded man was crying out something desperately and trying to rise.

Once more the carbine cracked, and he dropped in the dust almost beside Marco.

The cause? I could not tell; at all events, it meant safety and rescue. I started forward. Félice was moving toward the entrance, was almost at it, when I stopped her.

"Félice! Wait!"

SHE WHIRLED like a cat. She saw me approaching. Surprise, startled alarm, hatred, flashed across her features.

"You!" she cried out. "You!"

Her pistol jerked up and she began to fire. Desperate, I leaped for her. The first two bullets missed completely. The third dropped me—I felt the impact as it struck, lost balance, and came down on hands and knees. Still another bullet whistled over me and ricocheted whangingly from the rock walls. Then she turned, picked up her skirts, and ran, dropping the pistol. She passed the three dead blackshirts, and was beyond my range of vision. Gone.

I was hurt, dizzy, faint, and wanted only to drop completely and lie quiet. The sudden whirring roar of a car engine roused me and spurred me into effort. She must have reached Botti's car, I thought, and dragged myself upright. The roar rose into a thrum and then lessened. The car was gone, and Félice, with half the loot.

Feeling, barely able to keep my feet, I staggered out into the sunlight and it blinded me. A voice said something, and I turned. There, among the brush just above the cave entrance, was a figure, coming down toward me. I recognized the shape of Marco's sister, Elena; she was alone, and over her arm was a carbine. That tough, hard-lined peasant's face of hers was grimly set. Her dark eyes burned luridly.

"That woman!" she demanded. "Did she shoot you? Too bad. I could have killed her easily if I had known. And I let her go! Where is the other—the big man?"

"Inside," I gasped, jerking my thumb at the entrance.

She took the carbine in both hands, walked past me, and vanished into the grotto. I tried to call her back, to explain, and could not utter a word. Well, she would find Signore Botti all right, if she went far enough; her carbine was not needed. The thought made me laugh crazily—and then I must have dropped, for that was my last memory.

I came to myself in semi-darkness. I was lying in bed, in my room at the tavern. A candle burned on the table and a man sat beside it reading. Gondy, for the love of heaven!

At my exclamation, he dropped his book and fell on his knees beside the bed, catching my hand and staring at me.

"Carson! You—you've come around! Thank God!" he breathed.

"Must be dreaming," I said. "Are you real? How'd you get here?"

"I arrived too late," he said mournfully. "The telegram—it was false, a decoy. It was that accursed woman; my father is perfectly well. Yes, I know she was here. I know everything. It has kicked up a terrific mess, my friend."

I pressed his hand; he was real. A cigarette? He gave me one.

"I saw Murchison in Naples and hurried on here to join you," he said. "Quiet, now. Your ribs deflected the bullet at some cost to themselves; it's a nasty wound. But there's a good surgeon here, an Army man. I have a car and I'll take you back to Rome in a couple of days, and we'll join Murchison there. Everything's all right."

"But it's not!" I said. "First, that damned imitation treasure—"

Gondy broke into a laugh. "Oh, I know about that too! I went over it with Elena; and don't kid yourself. Even if Félice got away with some of it, the remainder is big-time stuff. Elena confided it to me; we'll take it to the United States Commissioner at Rome, and you'll see some mighty sick ex-Fascisti when it gets publicized! Say, that girl Elena is good! She was hanging around keeping an eye on the place, when they shot Marco. She just went home for her carbine and got down to work. Too bad she missed potting Félice—if that's who the Principessa really was."

"That's who, all right," I grunted. "Grotto of the Nymphs— all kinds of nymphs, too. Hot babies and killers. But say! Where's the detector? And where's Carson's Folly?"

"Packed up and under the bed." Gondy smiled at me. Then his lean hawk-face lit up and his dark eyes widened. "And, Carson! I was able to phone my father at Genoa—that's how I discovered the fraud. But who do you think I ran into there?"

"Another nymph?"

"Hell, no—my old pal the Marchese Grimani! A Venetian, one of the old families; he gave me the grandest story you ever heard, too!"

HE BECAME vivacious, eager; he bubbled away about Grimani and was all lit up with enthusiasm.

"A most remarkable thing, Carson! You know the winged lion of St. Mark that stands before the Doge's Palace in Venice, on a pillar? It was shattered to pieces after Napoleon took Venice and ended the ancient Republic. Later it was put together again—some of it, not all. Grimani has a piece of the original at his suburban villa."

"What of it?" I demanded, not half impressed by his enthusiasm.

"Oh!" He gestured frantically. "I began at the wrong end. When the Nazis were rampaging through northern Italy and Venice, before V–E Day, and looting everything in sight—gad! What a story! The dead gondolier and the ghostly treasure of St. Mark—"

"Lay off, will you?" I broke in. "We've struck one ghostly treasure already, and it went sour on us."

"But this is real!" he cried. "It's at Grimani's place—he gave me a letter to his steward! We have his full permission to occupy the villa and search all we like, and I tell you Carson's Folly can turn it up!"

I sighed and relaxed; no use trying to combat his wild eagerness. Then and there I knew in my heart that as soon as we were reunited and able to travel, we were heading north to Venice on the trail of the ghostly treasure and the dead gondolier—ouch! More of these goose-feathers—

However, time proved me wrong about it; we did not go to Venice.

IV

WING OF THE LION

As a marvel mine-detector it was a flop, and
they called it Carson's Folly. But it could and
did locate certain other foreign objects buried
deep—as witness this drama of an old Italian
garden and what was hidden beneath it.

"YOU KNOW the winged Lion of St. Mark, on its pillar in the Piazzetta in Venice?" said Murchison, his thin, bony features dreamy. "After Napoleon extinguished the Republic, that Lion was smashed into ninety-two pieces."

"And glued together again? What the hell do I care?" I grunted comfortably.

"It has something to do with our being here, Bill Carson; be reverent!" he chided me.

"Well, I'll bite, Murch," I said. "What has it to do with us?"

"I don't know yet." He rubbed his bluish jaw softly. "Gondy has gone to Venice to gather full details—"

"Forget it," I said. "We're occupying the villa of the Marchese Grimani, in the lap of luxury, and he's made us absolute masters of the place, so relax and enjoy life. I'm not going to hunt for any damned treasure till I get good and ready."

He sighed, extinguished his cigarette, and took a header into the blue-tiled pool beside us. I stayed put. I had two bullet-sore ribs that still hurt me.

With our pal the Vicomte de Gondy, we had coaxed our somewhat ancient Fiat across Italy to Padua, and on down the Fusina road along the Brenta River to here. Beyond lay the shore, the old dead lagoons, and the chain of islands on which Venice was built. Here along the Brenta were the decayed villas of ancient Venetian nobility, mostly gone to rack and ruin. This Grimani villa was far otherwise. It was new, modern, up to the

Everywhere she went, Corona toted her
parcel as though it were gold and gems.

minute, with a fine farm and stables for the Grimani polo string
stretched out behind. The war had finished the ponies, but
otherwise the place was scrumptious.

The country was well built up, and flat as a pancake; from
the garden wall, we could see the campaniles or bell-towers of
half a dozen villages, the river with its crumbling villas on either
shore, and the lagoons with the roofs of Venice far away. The
Marchese Grimani was in the diplomatic service, and wealthy.
He had given Gondy letters to his *ministro* or steward, a one-
armed war veteran named Giovanni, putting the place entirely at our service; we could root it up or burn it down as we
liked. In short, we were—most unaccustomedly—in clover.

Murchison crawled out of the pool and flopped his skinny
length beside me.

"It seems queer, Carson, to think how you and I had a hand
in a war and helped our men in their march to victory! Or do
you ever reflect on such matters, you big hunk of cheese? Do
you ever reflect on anything except Bill Carson?"

I regarded him amiably and puffed at my pipe. We had been pals since schooldays in South Boston.

"You needn't envy me a well-upholstered frame, Murch. Look out these people don't grab you and plant you as a bean-pole."

"They don't grow beans here," he rejoined. "They grow squash and grain. Say, Bill! You know, the yarn that brought us here is a regular story out of the Middle Ages? A dead gondolier, the ghostly treasure of St. Mark—and close by, at Vincenza, our folks have unearthed a whole cache of Nazi loot!"

"Forget it," I told him. "Ghostly treasure, my eye! I'm interested in the earthly kind that Carson's Folly can detect—the kind, my boy, that we can spend."

"Well, look around you," said he. "It's here some place in this garden, or else the Marchese is a liar. Fifty per cent goes to him if we locate it, mind."

Gondy had wangled the deal with the Marchese. Gondy had an unholy gift for learning where to go for buried treasure; he could smell it afar. And being a grand gentleman and a good scout, he stood in with all the European nobility who grew legends of hidden gold in their back yards.

This garden before us was a garden, and no mistake. Over the walls lifted a few poplars stripped to bare poles and feathery tufts at the crest. A marble fountain composed of three indecently clad girls jetted water that ran by clipped hedges and trim flower-beds. The paths were neatly graveled.

"It'll break Giovanni's heart if we go to digging here," I said. "But since the story is probably no more than a hopped-up legend, maybe Carson's Folly will stay in its carton. We'll know more about it when Gondy gets back."

"Yankee skeptic!" grunted Murchison. "If the Lion of St. Mark can grow wings, can't you believe in buried treasure?"

"You show me one of the wings, and maybe I will," said I, and that ended it.

The end of Europe's war had got us discharged from our labors, on loan, in British radionic laboratories. Mine detectors was our specialty. Not the old magnetic kind, but a seeing-eye type that would pick up a plastic mine or even smell a booby trap out of thin air. The work being still strictly hush-hush, I can say no more.

One of our failures was the gadget with which we were now working. With his usual veneration for his partner, Murchison had tagged it Carson's Folly. As regarded mines, it was a complete bust, and we were welcome to it. But with our optimistic ingenuity, we had adapted it to the great universal dream of suffering humanity—finding buried treasure. You may laugh—but it worked! It worked so well that our lives had been in constant danger ever since; hence the bullet-wound, from which I was now practically recovered.

We had tested the thing on Gondy's family treasure-trove, turned it up, and with it turned up peril. One person too many now knew about it. Félice de Gondy, our pal's former sister-in-law, had trailed us ever since, with a vicious greed and a more vicious hatred, had lately come within an ace of killing me, and was still somewhere at large. We could feel reasonably safe from her here, though.

G O N D Y H A D driven on to Fusina, there taking boat for Venice. He returned just in time for a cocktail before dinner, and we sat at a table on the garden terrace.

"I'm going to make you happy, my friends!" he declared, beaming at us, his thin hawk-face all aglow. "First, there's a definite treasure, and it's here."

"Ghostly?" I interjected.

He shrugged. "Perhaps. Alfred Rosenberg, Nazi minister of civil administration and official looter for Hitler and Goering, occupied this house for a time, after the Nazis took over Italy. He looted Venice from here—churches, museums, private collections—and Padua, with other inland places, and got plenty. Giovanni was not here then as steward. The Strilone family, old retainers of the Grimani, were here; the father, two sons and a daughter, Corona. She will be here tomorrow, by the way, to assist us."

With this preamble, Gondy started on the story he had verified:

Rosenberg was called away very suddenly—he left by airplane from the field near Venice, without warning, in the middle of his last "confiscating" trip to the city. Some of his loot was at the villa: two private collections of gold coins, ancient and modern, the finest in Italy, of immense value; and with these, the shroud of St. Mark. What this was, no one seemed to know exactly—a relic of some sort stolen from the cathedral, Gondy thought.

Old Strilone, who had been a gondolier, and his two sons were at the villa when word came that Rosenberg had de-

I hit that guy, and laid him out. The dog came for me;
another man flashed a knife. Corona was shrieking.

parted. It was in the evening. They fell to frantic work, packed
the coin and the relic very hurriedly, and buried them somewhere in the garden; Corona had gone to visit relatives at
Fusina, overnight, and was thus away. She returned next day,
to find her father and two brothers lying in the gardens. Rosenberg had sent after the loot, and the S.S. men, unable to find
it, had shot the three. They searched in vain and departed.

Others had searched since then, too, finding nothing. The only thing that saved Corona from the killers—and Gondy gave us an odd look as he spoke—was the Wing of the Lion.

"What does that mean?" Murchison demanded.

Gondy shook his head. "When she arrives, ask her, my friend. You may believe her."

"Well, let's be practical," I suggested. I am somewhat hard-headed, as Murchison alleges, his word for *sensible*. "As for the relic, which I take to be your ghostly treasure, we can scratch that off. And the gold coin wouldn't belong to us, or to Grimani, if we did turn it up. So what are we doing here?"

Gondy turned to me, gesticulating. "But it would, Carson! That's the point! They got the law down on Grimani because his people had hidden the stuff. Italian law is queer, and he was in a jam and knew it. So he compromised and paid up. The authorities were coming down on him about the relic, too, and he skipped out and stayed gone. There's a fat reward if the thing is ever found, but the gold does belong to him now. He'll be tickled pink to settle for fifty per cent with us, if we find it."

"Okay, then," I assented. "I suppose plenty have looked?"

The whole garden had been dug up by all concerned, with no result. Old Strilone, before they shot him, scrawled on a bit of paper that the treasure was buried in the garden; the paper was found afterward, in his clothes. Where, he did not say. Since nothing was ever turned up, the conclusion was that he had lied about it.

"Uncertain, unsatisfactory and unpromising," I said, when Giovanni summoned us to dinner. "This gal Corona has hyp-notized Gondy. But if you guys say the word, we'll have a go at it."

They were all for it, so the thing was settled....

That evening Giovanni came to us, practically on his knees, with tears and gestures. He knew we had come to look for the treasure. Everyone in the vicinity knew it; else, why were we here at all? He begged us to spare his beautiful garden. He had worked like a dog for the Marchese, getting that poor dug-over garden into shape, and if we dug it up all over again, he would positively die of grief and chagrin and despair.

"Giovanni," I told him, "we're not going to dig up your garden. We're going to look for the gold with a machine powered by the evil eye; the devil himself is in it. We're not going to touch a spade until the machine finds the treasure. So be reassured."

Giovanni crossed himself, gaped at us, and went off half convinced that we were in league with Satan himself. He did not care, so long as we spared his garden.

There was no hurry; we agreed to interview Corona on the morrow, which was Sunday, and start work on Monday. Despite my croaking, I knew the gold might be here. Others had searched, yes; but that was an old story. Frantic men hiding loot from the Nazis would go deep with it. Treasure-hunters would merely scratch the surface—they never relish the expenditure of elbow-grease. That's why they are treasure-hunters....

Corona showed up next afternoon, guarded by two relatives.

Murchison is an impractical chaser of rainbows; Gondy is a gentleman; I am pretty dumb, but know my way around; yet inside of five minutes that girl had us all eating out of her hand. Why? If I knew, I could tell you.

She wore a simple white dress and carried a package wrapped in old newspaper. She had dark eyes and hair and singularly transparent features, as though there were a light somewhere behind them. I have no recollection of her height or her figure; all I recall is her face. It was not pretty—just regular features, no makeup; but you felt she was at peace within herself. Utter simplicity in every line; yet a vivid intelligence lay in her eyes, a faintly smiling grace touched her lips. She was unworried, serene, unquestioning.

I HAVE said all this about her, yet have told nothing. Out of her eyes something looked at us—quiet, sure, steady. I scarcely heard as Gondy questioned her, and she repeated her story about finding the bodies of her father and brothers, and showed us a hurried scrawl, in phonetic Italian, about the treasure; she had kept it. I was trying to figure what it was about her that so impressed us. She was not a mere negligible innocent. She was extremely positive. There was some sort of a force within her—oh, I cannot put it into words at all. We were simply children before her.

"No, I was not harmed in the least," she said. "That was quite impossible."

"Why was it?" Murchison demanded. "Since when did the Nazis spare women?"

She looked at him. "Signore, I had the Wing of the Lion with me; I was bringing it to my father, from home. If he had had it here with him, he would not have been harmed."

Superstitious people, these Venetians. A trifle amused, I asked what she meant by the Wing of the Lion. Her gaze shifted to me. I ceased to feel amused. The clear light in those eyes of hers left me baffled and uneasy and frustrated.

"I think, signore, you will learn more about it one of these days, though not from me," she said quietly. "The Lion of St. Mark, the figure that has stood for a thousand years in the Piazzetta, was broken when Napoleon took our city, or a little after. It was broken into many pieces. One of those pieces was never found, and was reproduced; but later my great-grandfather found it, and it was kept in our family as a sacred relic, and it has protected us. It protects whoever keeps it. I carry it with me always, now. No harm can come to one thus protected from evil."

WITH A gesture, she indicated the paper parcel. Gondy asked respectfully if we might see the relic. She assented, untied the string, and opening the paper, took out a piece of stone, nearly flat, yet oddly curved and chiseled and weathered with the years.

Describe it? Well, it looked like nothing at all; it might have been part of a wing, or anything else. A dim tracery of feathers was discernible on one side. A flat, pointed piece of stone, six inches wide and more than that in length—uninteresting, very. But to this simple child—she worked in the lace factories at Burano, it proved—the thing was more than a relic; it had a sacred power of protection.

Further, she had an idea that we were in need of this protection. Her family had served that of Grimani for many generations; her father and brothers had died here in this service, and she knew perfectly well that we had come here to search for the lost treasure.

"I should like to stay and help," she said. "I shall not be in the way, I do not need much to eat, and I can help with the kitchen work, signori. The Striloni have always been servants of the Grimani. Also, it would please my father if he knew that the Wing of the Lion was here, protecting you."

She rambled on. It appeared that to her superstitious mind this little old relic of hers was somehow tied up with the shroud of St. Mark, whatever that mysterious bit of loot might be. If the Wing of the Lion were here, our search would succeed and her menfolk would not have perished in vain. I could not quite get it all through my head and did not try. I took for granted that Gondy would get rid of her at once.

But to my astonishment, he called in Giovanni and his wife, and seriously discussed adding Corona to the household as she desired. I got Murchison aside in protest.

"See here, Murch, we don't want this gal hanging around. She'd only complicate things tremendously—"

He gave me an injured look and cut me off.

"Lay off the grouch, Bill. She's something special; you know it as well as I do. I don't take any stock in her superstitious notions, of course; but—well, maybe she has something on the ball, at that—"

"All right," I grunted. "If that's the way you feel about it, it suits me."

So Corona moved in.

*Corona held the lantern. We managed to get the
larger one up, but it took a heave and no mistake.*

She helped in the kitchen; but she was everywhere, underfoot
all the time, sitting around with her sewing, making fun of my
Sicilian dialect and teaching me the Venetian, loafing about the
garden and so forth. Murchison made an effort to get her into
the swimming-pool, but this seemed somewhat repugnant to
her, so he desisted.

And everywhere she went, that old relic of hers went—in

the garden, down by the river, off buying provisions. She toted her newspaper parcel as though it were gold and gems. I was tempted to make fun of her about it, but did not.

Actually, her presence grew upon all before we knew it, and I do not mean physically. She was a spirit and not a body, if you get what I mean: a sort of blessed peace seemed to be wherever she was; yet she was no silly little prig. She never spouted religion; she had plenty of quiet humor, and could laugh like a silver bell. Just the same, I could understand why a touch of awe came into Giovanni's face whenever he looked at her. As Murchison said, she had something—and it was not of this world.

However, it is not to be supposed that we just sat around drooling over an ignorant chit of a girl and her superstitious fancies; we had work to do, and with Monday we got down to business.

Pushing Carson's Folly all over that garden looked like a hopeless task, because the gadget could not be hurried, and we had to avoid doing too much damage to Giovanni's flowerbeds. There was bound to be a good deal of scattered brick and stone underneath, the house being built upon the site of an ancient Grimani villa of the Fourteenth Century, which had gone to ruin like so many others up and down the Brenta.

So we unpacked our pet and put it together. It was extremely light, being made of a magnesium alloy, and in appearance was not unlike an outsize vacuum cleaner on high wheels, being connected by wires from the long handle to dry batteries carried by the operator in a knapsack. We were figuring on making an entirely new model in less awkward form, this being the only one in existence and developed as a mine detector. In fact, Murchison and I had the plans in our heads for a perambulator-type detector with which we could get around better.

We had often wondered whether the thing would work through water, and put it to the test on the springboard over the swimming-pool, in which we sank an old iron chest that ornamented the loggia. I tried to explain to Corona how the electronic principles worked, and to my real surprise found that she knew all about it. One of her dead brothers had been in charge of the radar aboard an Italian warship, when Il Duce had a navy, and she had absorbed the idea from him.

Well, the gadget worked. The waves picked up the iron chest and reported, showing that we had something really unusual— radar dislikes obstacles, particularly water. In no time at all Murchison was off on one of his moon-chases, talking about sunken galleons and sea treasure, while Gondy took fire and began to bubble about the Mediterranean being shallow and filled with sunken ships, ancient and modern, for the picking.

I became disgusted with both of them, and took the detector over to the garden and went to work at my stint; we were to take two-hour spells, and Giovanni was to be called in for any spade-work if necessary. I began at the house, working down toward the bottom of the garden. We calculated, correctly, that to cover the entire garden would take us some days.

BEFORE I had been at work an hour, the buzzer sounded to indicate a strike, and everybody gathered around us excitedly. Even Giovanni, who had been furtively watching us, came on the run, managing with his one arm both to hold a spade and to cross himself as protection against the evil eye or the devil, or both.

I had worked out a chart to cover the figures on the various gauges. According to this, we could tell with pretty fair accuracy the depth of the buried substance and even what it was. I had adjusted the instrument for a maximum depth of ten feet, and it seemed that we had now struck something no farther down than four. Its nature puzzled me, because the figures on the dials corresponded with nothing on the chart.

Giovanni, who had followed the profession of gravedigger before the Army got him, suggested a corpse. I checked this off; we already had figures charted on corpses, from previous work. So we resolved to determine what the find was, and Giovanni set to work.

We turned up two enormous pottery jars.

Corona discouraged our laughter. These, she said, were something special. Grimani's father had brought home two gigantic Etruscan jars, of which he was very proud. They had vanished ten years ago, when this house replaced the tumbledown old villa, and these must be the same ones. She knew all details of the family history over a long period.

THE JARS were put on the loggia to be washed. I went on with the work, but found nothing else. Gondy replaced me, breaking off for luncheon; he located some brick and stone and rubble, which required no digging.

Murchison took over in the afternoon while I was taking a nap. He found something, but did not want to wake me. He completely misread the chart, and Giovanni wasted a lot of work digging up an old log.

Communications in Italy being restored, after a fashion, Gondy hopped off in the car for Fusina, after supper, to wire the Marchese about finding his father's Etruscan jars. When he returned, Murch and I were playing gin rummy while Corona sat over her sewing and listened to the radio. Already she was more like a guest in the house than a servant. She had the odd dignity of a family retainer, and took it quite as a matter of course that we liked having her around.

Gondy was disturbed about something, I could see, but said nothing. Next morning before breakfast he joined me for a dip in the pool, and as we clung to the chrome railing at the deep end, he turned worried eyes to me.

"I wired Grimani last evening, you know. And, Carson, I met a chap I knew and went with him to the boat; it was just leaving for Venice. And I could take my oath that I saw someone in the crowd that was aboard the boat—someone whom we know."

"Naturally, you—eh?" His meaning jumped into my mind. "Not Félice, again?"

He nodded. "Of course I could not be certain; it was only a glimpse."

"You've got that dame on the brain; forget it!"

"I was in love with her once, or thought I was. No, my friend, it was no mistake. She is somewhere around here. She has trailed us. We shall have trouble. These people hereabouts know or guess we've come for the treasure; they are all gossiping about it."

"Well, be sensible! What of it?" I growled at him. "There are villas up and down the river; we're not off in some lonely spot. Even if she's here, what can she do? Not a thing. She's quite harmless."

"That woman is never harmless, Carson," he replied. "She hates you and me, in particular, with a vicious hatred. She'd give anything on earth to get her hands on the detector. She knows how to use it; she knows what it can disclose. Keep a close watch!"

He made me uneasy, for a time, but we said nothing to Murchison about it. Gradually the feeling departed. It was impossible that Félice could do us any harm here. She might be spending the season in Venice. Why not?

A strange thing happened that day. I do not want to have it appear that Corona made any pretense to being occult or gifted with second-sight; most emphatically, she did not. When she made a statement, she expressed a simple fact and that ended it. When she said that the evil eye—in which all Italians have devoutly believed for centuries—was watching the house, and that she could feel it, she was not putting on an act. She was just stating something that she believed—probably without knowing why or how, as when a child says there is a lion just around the corner. Maybe there is, and only the child sees it.

So with Corona. When she sat sewing in the garden and watching us at work, she had her sacred relic right in the chair with her. When she spoke of the evil eye, Gondy gave me a significant glance, which I ignored. I am not superstitious. I liked and respected Corona for the sweet child she was, but I was not going out of my way because of her childish notions.

This day, Tuesday, we turned up some queer stuff, but nothing queerer than the cockeyed notion Gondy imparted to me as we sat watching Murchison slowly pushing the detector around.

"Bill," he said, "this proves that I saw Félice, that she is somewhere near."

"What does?" I asked.

"Corona's talk about the evil eye; she's sensitive, and she can

feel it. The evil eye is a fact, you know. The human eye does give off emanations or frequencies; it's a scientific discovery. Those vibrations, from an evil person, can—"

"Look!" I pointed to the ten-foot garden wall, the nodding trees showing above it, the blue sky beyond. "Where is she? Not there. Not here. Probably getting a hairdo, in Venice. Forget your nonsense, will you? Pretty soon you'll have a fixed idea, and then they'll lock you up in a straitjacket."

Murchison's yell interrupted us, and we gathered around.

There was a rush of figures, and one woman's voice in French that froze me. "It's he!" she cried. "C'est lui, lui!"

He had struck something, sure enough, and a tube had blown out. That was immaterial; we had some spare tubes, which we had made ourselves. The chart, however, showed that the detector had come upon wood and metal at a ten-foot depth. We summoned Giovanni, and gave him a hand with the job, which ruined a bed of imported tulips. I got no gold reaction from the find, but none the less excitement ran high. Giovanni and his wife were practically in hysterics; even Corona became vivacious, eager, wildly expectant.

The build-up was terrific—and digging down ten feet, let me add, to excavate a box, is no joke. It was nearly noon when we got it up: an old, moldy, rotted box. I smashed it open with a spade—and disclosed twenty-odd copper cooking vessels, such as crowd the kitchen of any Continental house.

Our chagrin was acute. Giovanni triumphantly bore off the stuff to grace the kitchen of the villa. Corona laughed and laughed. We had to fill in the damned hole; after which we took a dip in the pool, Corona retiring. She would not hang around, even though we wore trunks, when we were swimming. It was not from any false prudery—as was proved later that afternoon; I think she just disliked the general idea.

AT LUNCHEON we were a disgusted lot. We had not yet covered a third of the garden, for unearthing our discoveries took a good deal of time. Giovanni waved his arm and chuckled; we were doing well by the Marchese, said he. After lunch I replaced the blown tube and went on with the job with Gondy to help me, while the others went inside to take a siesta.

Toward the end of my stint, I located a big stone, according to the chart, but the dials fluttered oddly, the size was peculiar, and the thing was not deep, so we dug to see what it was. It proved to be an earth-stained, incrusted marble statue of a girl, life-size and intact except for her missing clothes. Undoubtedly an antique, said Gondy, either Greek or Roman.

"Another memento for the Marchese, and the hell with it!"

I said. "Come on, we'll fill the hole, and then you can take over. I'm going for a walk."

Corona wanted to go for a walk too, so we went. She kept her newspaper package under her arm, of course. The roads were dusty and unpleasant, the crumbling villas were uninteresting. Some were new, however. Many were rented out for the summer, the old Venetian aristocracy having largely perished. Corona did not stalk along like a sedate nun; far from it. She was like a butterfly—now darting off to exchange gossip with peasant women, now volleying repartee with a group of laborers, again branching away to investigate a flower-bed that took her fancy and returning with a handful of blossoms. She always caught up with me, and I let her roam without hindrance.

We were on our way back, and somewhere up the line of river-bank villas, when it happened. A number of men were gathered in a noisy group about the gateway of a villa ahead. I paid no attention whatever to them, until I heard Corona utter an indignant cry, and saw her go running at the group and plunge right into their midst.

Then I followed at a run—for a burst of furious voices arose, and with it a savage snarling sound that froze the blood. When I got there, two men were trying to hang on to Corona; she had her arms around a fuzzy yellow dog; another dog was jumping at her, blood was all over her white dress—and one of the men yanked her away and then tripped her.

I hit that guy with all of my two hundred pounds and laid him out. The dog came for me and I kicked him under the jaw and sent him howling away, shaking his head. Another man flashed a knife, and I let him have it under the belt, and that settled him. Corona was shrieking something at me about the Wing of the Lion—she had dropped her precious package. I scooped it up and slammed a man across the face with it, and the group broke up. Two of the men stood scowling at me; the others scattered; and I turned to Corona.

She was a sight—her hair down, her dress bloody and half

ripped away, and the dog still in her arms. The poor mutt was ripped and shivering and bloody; it seemed the gang had been kicking him around for their dog to finish. Italy has produced a lot of saints, but they are all dead; and Italians in general are sometimes a cruel lot.

She would not let go of the dog, but pulled up her skirt to show a long gash on her thigh; so I took her and dog and newspaper package up in my arms and carried her on home. The two scowling Italians, who were probably occupants of the villa, sent curses after us, but I could afford to ignore their hot air; I think one of the two had got his nose broken. Corona did not want me to carry her, but she weighed practically nothing. All the way, she kept talking about the evil eye—meaning, I suppose, that we had struck a bad gang.

There was excitement and to spare when we got home. Gondy was all for streaking off to Venice for a doctor and Pasteur treatment, but Corona forbade it positively, while we were getting the long gash on her thigh washed and bandaged.

"Nothing will develop," she said positively. "That dog was not mad. Besides, I was holding the Wing of the Lion, and therefore it will be all right."

In fact, she was not at all concerned about herself—her legs, her looks, her torn dress and what it exposed. All her thought was for the injured dog. Leone, she called it, after St. Mark's Lion.

The poor mutt was in a bad way, but we took care of him. Leone belonged to a peculiar breed of yellow, vicious curs who infested boats from Forli, or some such place. He repaid our kindness with snarling affection of a sort, but a worse pet would have been hard to find, even after his excitement died out. Murchison got a shot of painkiller into him while Corona held him, and then we sewed up his ripped hide and left him to lick his hurts well.

That finished all work for the day. Giovanni's wife put Corona to bed, with the Wing of the Lion on her bedside table, and we got cleaned up for supper. Giovanni said that the villa in question had just been occupied by strangers and they might get the law on me for assaulting them, and this made me laugh. Gondy was all for going up there at once and cleaning them out—and later I wished we had—but compromised on taking the radio to Corona's room, where she had Leone in a basket, and talking with her.

NEXT MORNING, Murchison and I sweated in the garden; Gondy went to town and sent the Marchese another wire about the pots and pans and the statue, and Grimani sent back a ribald reply in regard to the marble Venus, which were better left unrecorded.

We made no finds that morning. Corona appeared as usual; the gash was giving no trouble, thanks to the protection of the Lion. As for Leone, nobody came for him, and he had apparently decided to adopt us. The garden had a large gate of iron grill-work in the side wall, and by this Leone took his place, so that he could see everything outside as well as in. Possibly also, as I suggested, that he might be near the garbage can. Like myself, he was a very practical sort of fellow.

Beginning with afternoon, we began to pick up the damnedest lot of junk ever seen. Probably this garden had been a big fill when the house was built on the villa site; nothing else could explain the stuff. As little of it registered with accuracy on the chart, we had to dig more: than we had figured on, which slowed work. We found a rotted old boat, part of a cistern roofed with lead sheeting, and a barrel tightly packed with old clothes, which ended our labor for the day. Carson's Folly was certainly justifying its name.

At all events, we had covered a full half of the garden....

As might have been expected, people hung about the gateway from morning to night, to gape. It did them no good because, like most such Continental gates, the iron grille was covered on the inside with rusted sheet-iron. The holes at the bottom were all right for Leone but no good for curious peasants or boys, and the wall was too high to be climbed, so we wasted no worry on this angle of the treasure-hunt.

The following day proved unexciting. Corona reposed near the fountain in a deck-chair under a big beach umbrella, with her sewing—and, of course, her newspaper parcel. She was quite positive that under the influence of the Lion's Wing, we would turn up the sacred shroud of St. Mark. It was singular about this name; we could not discover what it meant. There had never been any such relic as the saint's shroud, so far as we could learn, in Venice, and nobody was sure just what sort of stuff Rosenberg had got away with, or why he bothered with any such thing at all unless it were for the reliquary and not the contents. Murchison made some disgraceful jokes about Hitler and the saint's shroud. Well, we could afford now to laugh at the Nazi rats, but nobody had done any laughing when they were going strong.

We made no finds all morning, and were covering ground with more speed. Gondy had another wire ready for the Marchese, detailing the junk we had uncovered, but waited to see what the afternoon would bring forth, before sending it. With his misplaced sense of humor, he was hoping he could add the three words: "*also the treasure.*" A tiny detail; how much it was going to mean! Also, Giovanni and his wife wanted the evening off, to go to Fusina and see the cinema. An American film, only four years old, was showing there, and everybody was nuts about it. So we promised them they could go, if no treasure showed up; Corona said she would clean up the kitchen after dinner anyhow, and all was happy.

Her gash on the thigh was healing in first-rate order; Leone was hobbling around snarling at everyone; and Murchison, I remember, was developing a toothache that spoiled his disposition. In the middle of the afternoon Murch, who was running the detector, picked up a slab of stone ten feet down, and we let it alone. Nothing else had been uncovered, when I took over from him for the last stint of the day, to end at five with cocktails.

When five o'clock neared, I was working along the wall beyond the garden gate, and not a solitary thing had rewarded my patience. Murchison glanced at his watch.

"Ten to five. I'll run along and fix the drinks—a grenadine for you, Corona? On the terrace in ten minutes, folks."

He took the orders and departed. Corona followed, with her confounded parcel and her sewing; Gondy, the telegram to Grimani on his mind, slipped off to write it. I was left to finish my job, with Leone sniffing at my heels and giving me sour looks in return for kind words.

JUST THEN the buzzer sounded under my hand. I paused, gave the dials a glance, then fumbled out the chart with a heart-leap. Gold! Clear as anything, there it stood. I checked back a yell and went on. The buzzer again—gold! Over a space three feet long, the signals came distinctly as could be. There was not a shadow of doubt that I had struck the treasure. Next instant, the detector went completely dead.

I marked the spot with a stick, then trundled Carson's Folly back toward the gate and left it, by the wall, and examined it. Two of the tubes had blown out. I gave Leone a pat, and he bared his teeth. I laughed, went up to the house, and got cleaned up, saying nothing to anyone.

Gondy and Murchison were gathered around the drinks when I came out. Corona had not yet appeared. I joined them, sat down, and shook my head.

"Highballs! Nothing doing. Save 'em for dinner, Murch. Didn't I see a bottle of champagne in the liquor cabinet?"

"Hell's bells! You said a Scotch highball, didn't you?" growled Murchison.

"That was then. This is now. Go on, get the bubble-water and bring four glasses. I mean it. Not iced? Then bring ice, and we'll make champagne cups."

"Are you nuts?" demanded Murchison.

Gondy gave me a queer eager look.

"*Mon ami,* what is it that you have?" he asked, meaning the same thing.

"Did you write that telegram?" I asked, and he nodded.

"Yes. I'll run Giovanni and his wife to town after supper, and send it—"

"Then you can add three words to it," I told him. "Good idea to get Giovanni out of the way, too—"

They caught on, then, and there was a joyous explosion that lasted until Corona appeared, bringing her grenadine.

"Not a word to her!" exclaimed Murchison. "That is, till later. Good idea to leave Giovanni out of it entirely—if you're sure, Bill."

"Dead certain," I said, and rose to hold Corona's chair. Gondy grabbed her grenadine and took it in with the other drinks, and Murchison went for the champagne. Corona gave me a wondering look.

"We've just discovered that it's my birthday," I said, "so they're getting champagne, and you are going to join us in a celebration, little one."

That satisfied her, and she laughed prettily, saying that I must put the Wing of the Lion under my pillow tonight, and it would bring me luck for the coming year. When she said this and looked at me, I felt ashamed of the lie and almost blurted out the truth. That shows what the girl had done to us.

The celebration was held; the lie was sustained, and we sent Giovanni and his wife a glass of bubbles each. They were chagrined that they had known nothing of the birthday, and apologized for the dinner; it was excellent, however, and all of us had a hard job keeping down our jubilation. Corona, I think, did suspect something.

We did not linger over that meal; twilight was upon us ere it ended. We arranged that Gondy was to take the couple to town, send his wire, and return; and meantime Murchison and I would start the job. The indications were that it was eight feet deep, so there was no hurry about his return.

He got off with them, finally, and then we told Corona the big news. She clapped her hands with the glee of a child on hearing that we meant to dig up the gold ourselves.

"Good! I'll hold a lantern for you. And we'll put the Wing of the Lion there too, so all will go well, and the shroud of St. Mark will be safe."

"The saint's shroud protected by the wing of the saint's lion?" I asked. "Nonsense! Why don't you be your age and show some sense?"

She gave me a sudden, hurt look. "But, signore! You make me dreadfully afraid that the saint may teach you why!"

I was in no mood for that sort of thing and said so, and we got to work. Corona fetched a lantern from the kitchen—and her newspaper parcel; and we went out into the garden with spades. The night was pitch black, with cloud and wind. I had marked the spot with a stick; we put the lantern against the wall, pulled up a chair for Corona, and went at the job.

We had a respectable hole dug when Gondy returned. He put the car in the garage, and burst in upon us excitedly. I yielded my spade to him; he tore off his coat and flew at it. The light soft earth needed no pick. As the hole deepened, Corona put down her package beside it, and held the lantern at the edge, while Leone sniffed around and made a nuisance of himself as usual.

Deeper and deeper.... I spelled Murchison, and was down a good six feet. Hoisting out that dirt was a real job, for it had to be thrown clear. It was Gondy who made the strike and broke into excited, gasping words as he wrestled with a small stout box. There was another and larger one beside it, and both were heavy as lead—or gold.

WE GOT the small one out first, enlarged the hole, and managed to get the larger one up; but it took a heave and no mistake.

"Better get 'em in the house," said Murchison, "and open them up there. If this is really the goods, we'll want to keep the stuff under cover. We can close the hole later, or let Giovanni do it."

First we toted in the little box, setting it in the living-room, while Corona, all in a dither, flew around to find tools. With the larger box we had real trouble, for the weight was really something. It fell, out on the terrace, and smashed open one end—it had been hastily and carelessly nailed together. At last we got it inside and set it down with a bang.

Corona, eyes alight and color in her cheeks, showed up with a hammer and chisel, and I attacked the already broken larger box. We wrenched the boards away, and disclosed what looked like old clothes and curtains. Corona gave an excited cry.

"My father's old clothes, signori! And look—the curtains were from the windows yonder—"

Something was wrapped up in them, something heavy and big. We got it out into the light at last, and stood staring at it. A metal chest of some sort—blackened silver, it looked like, heavily carven and chased. It came open to Gondy's hand, and then—well, we were speechless. Corona stood with her eyes bulging at the glitter of gold and gems. Plates or sheets of solid gold and silver, set with blazing jewels, magnificently chased—

"The shroud of the saint!" cried Corona. "But no, it is not—"

Gondy broke in upon her. "I know what it is! The *pallium*—the *pal' d'oro!*" he said softly, reverently, as he stared. "The frontal piece for St. Mark's altar that Doge Orseolo had made in Byzantium a thousand years ago—the greatest treasure of the cathedral! They've never dared breathe that it was gone, understand? They've kept a close mouth about it. Someone said that Rosenberg had the shroud of St. Mark—just a name—"

"The *pal' d'oro!*" breathed Corona. She knew of it, naturally, but had never seen it before. She fell on her knees, touching the gold and gems with her fingertips.

"That smaller box," said Murchison, "probably holds the coin collections. Well, boys, there'll be a fat reward for this glittering bauble, as we know. I expect we'd better box it up again. And that lantern is smelling—put it out, Bill, will you?" Suddenly Corona leaped to her feet. "The Wing of the Lion!" she exclaimed in consternation. "I left it outside by the hole. Some dirt fell on it, and then I forgot it—"

"Well, forget it now," I said, picking up the lantern. "I'll go after it, Corona."

"And take that blasted pup out—leave him in the garden awhile," said Murchison. "He got excited yesterday and made a mess in the hall, and Giovanni had a fit over it."

Leone came, whisked out the open door past me, and we headed for the garden and the excavation. He broke into a furious barking; I paid no attention, for barking at nothing was the best thing that mutt did, but bore on toward the hole and the dirt-pile.

There, I had to set down the lantern and hunt. Sure enough, dirt from the hole had covered up the newspaper package, but after a moment I located it and lifted the heavy stone and stood up, wondering how Corona could endure to carry such a weight around with her all the time. I was just going to pick up the lantern, when a crashing noise made me swing around—something was happening at the gate. Another crash, and it flew inward. Rays from flashlights stabbed around and one blinded me.

Next thing I knew there was a rush of figures, a burst of excited Italian voices, and one woman's voice in French that froze me.

"It's he!" she cried. "*C'est lui, lui!*"

Félice!

I had no time even to move. They were all around me; one figure threw up a big revolver, almost in my face, and the explosion blasted me. Again! The double concussion knocked me off my feet. I had a dim vision of Leone hurling himself into the group, teeth and claws going like mad in snarling fury—then I keeled over on the dirt-pile by the lantern, a wrench of agony going through my body.

I kept my senses, however. Yells went up. Murchison and Gondy came bursting out of the house on the run, but there was no opposition. The intruders had scattered and were gone in the darkness. Leone came to me and licked my face, and I brushed him off as the others came up.

"What happened?" cried Murchison.

"Félice," I said, gasping. "She was here—pointed me out— they shot me twice—"

Suddenly they were pushed aside, and there was Corona. She fell on her knees beside me.

"Oh, signore, signore—I warned you!" she exclaimed. "Look at him, signori! The Wing of the Lion! I told you it was a protection—look!"

I WAS still clutching that parcel. Gondy leaned over, took it from me. The newspaper wrapping was torn and shredded. Both bullets had struck it squarely, had been deflected by the stone, and while the concussion had knocked the wind out of me and hurt my tender ribs, I was undamaged.

But Carson's Folly was gone....

We gathered in the living-room by the treasure boxes, after leaving Leone to guard the gate, which Gondy had chained up. The occasion called for a drink, and we had it.

"You were just an accident, an incident, Bill," said Murchison. "They broke in to get the machine; that's what she was after. They thought you were done for, and skipped out with it."

"Won't do her any good," I grunted. "Two tubes were blown out when this gold was located. Nobody else can replace those tubes. Nobody but us knows about them."

"That's right!" exclaimed Murchison, brightening. "And, say! We can go to work and make an entirely new model, now—the perambulator thing we've already figured out, with all the improvements!"

"Good enough!" said Gondy. "By the way, there's something I forgot—"

Corona shoved past him, clutching her precious package, and her wide, bright eyes were fastened on me.

"Signore," she said quietly, "you will not laugh at me any more now? You have seen for yourself. If the Wing of the Lion had not protected you, now you would be dead. But it did protect you, and it put those evil persons to flight."

There was a little silence, Gondy and Murch giving me a queer look. However, Bill Carson knows when he is licked.

"Corona, my sweet child, God bless you!" I said. "No, I'll not laugh at your notions any more. I respect them, and you too, believe me. You're right. I admit it freely."

Joy flooded over her face. She caught my hand, kissed it, and then whisked away—she was going to make a prayer to the saint, she said.

"Well, Bill, you ought to do the same thing," said Murchison, with his sardonic grin. "You ought to make a thank-offering to St. Mark—say, your share of the reward for this altar thing."

"You think so?" I asked seriously.

"Sure. It's the thing to do, even for a hard-headed beggar like you."

"All right, then," I said. "You take charge of the matter. You get me a receipt signed by St. Mark and I'll hand over the money. Now give me a drink and let's have no more foolishness—"

"Wait!" cried Gondy. "I forgot to tell you. When I sent the Marchese that wire, I picked up one that had just come in from him. It was a long one. About a famous buried treasure that we should look into—somewhere near Genoa—and it's something concerning the doll's house and the sorcerer's daughter—oh, now I can't find the blasted telegram anywhere! Must have left it in the car. But Grimani says the treasure is absolutely authentic, my friends!"

MURCHISON WAS kindling; I knew the sparkle in his eye.

"The Doll's House—and the Sorcerer's Daughter!" he murmured. "It certainly does sound attractive!"

"You and your moonlit pathways! All right, we'll go to Genoa," I said. "But first we must collect on our job here. Then we'll have to build another detector, Murch. And this time we'll name it for you—Murchison's pram! How's that?"

Gondy gave us a puzzled look. "Pram? What is that—pram?"

"British dialect for perambulator. In American, baby-carriage," I told him. "It'll be built something like one, anyhow."

We could all joke about going to Genoa and so forth, yet each one of us had the same identical feeling. Whether or not we shared the superstitious notions of Corona Strilone, it was going to be something of a wrench to part with her and her precious package, not to mention the mutt Leone.... Well, I suppose she married a fat butcher and has eleven children now. As usual.

V

THE SORCERER'S DAUGHTER

A strange treasure quest made possible by a war-time invention that failed as a mine-detector but would locate objects buried deeper.

MURCHISON AND I left Genoa with the Baby, as we decided to call it, in our rattling old Fiat. Our pal the Vicomte de Gondy had gone ahead to line up the project and obtain quarters in Alassio, on what used to be Mussolini's Italian Riviera. Now French troops were in possession, and although the war was well over, tourists had not yet begun to clutter up the landscape.

As yet we knew little about our quest for the Dolls' House and the sorcerer's daughter; Gondy would attend to all that. We had been busy with the Baby.

Murchison and I had served during the war in radionic laboratories, devising mine detectors that would offset the infernal Kraut ingenuity. Once discharged, we roped in Gondy as our contact man and set forth to make our fortune. Gondy was impulsive, charming, handsome and reliable. Murchison was skinny, often grouchy and apt to be flighty, but a fine technician. With me, Bill Carson, to act as brains and ballast, we got on beautifully.

The Baby resulted from one of our laboratory failures. It started out as an electronic detector of mines, which it decidedly was not; it was like hunting quail with a Boston bull. So, with our usual Yankee ingenuity, we turned it to detecting other things, and by electronics out of radar, so to speak, we got something good. We had tubes of our own devising, and into the Baby put our best brains, vastly improving it over our original detector. We were, in brief, after buried treasure—and we had proved that we could get it.

Now, aside from legends, people do not stand on street-corners and holler that they have buried treasure in their back yards. Locating such deposits takes finesse. Gondy had this, and he knew everyone worth knowing on the Continent, spoke half a dozen languages, and was a good scout. He had turned up our present job, about which as yet we knew little.

"Well, the Baby works, that's sure. Never saw anything sweeter," said Murchison, as I piloted the old Fiat along the endless series of railroad tunnels and crossings that marked the Riviera road north of Genoa. "She really works, Carson! And they say this Alassio place is the biggest resort on the coast, outside of San Remo, filled with English tourists before the war. Looks like a cushy little job for us and pur magnesium Baby."

"We were lucky to get our hands on that magnesium," I replied. "But don't expect any cushy job extracting gold from Mother Europe, Murch. Especially from Italians. We take our lives in our hands when we try it."

"Tell me something new," he grunted. "Hi! There's Alassio, I bet."

SO IT was—a glaring, Fascist-perfect resort of boulevards and modernistic houses crowded inside Cape Santa Croce. This entire coast, where the Alps ran down to the sea and left a thin

strip of beach between narrow valleys, had been improved out of recognition by Mussolini's regime, but we could glimpse a glorious five-mile stretch of open *plage* beyond that ran to the next little town, the hills rich with grayish olive groves and pricked out with vineyards.

We rolled into the town and found the Grand Alassio where Gondy was to meet us. And there he was, sipping a drink on the terrace, springing up eagerly when he caught sight of us and darting out to the curb.

"Hurray!" he exclaimed, pumping our hands. "All well? Hi! Don't get out here. We aren't staying."

"What?" We stared at him. "Not staying?"

He waved his hand at the *plage*. "No. We'll go right on to the next town, Laigueglia. They don't like Beppo here. I'll get my bag and Beppo, and be right out. Besides, Laigueglia is closer to our objective—a road goes right up from there.... Back in a minute!"

He popped off into the hotel, and reappeared with a porter, who carried his bag and something covered with a cloth.

"Beppo! What the devil is Beppo?" exclaimed Murchison. Then we saw that the covered object was a cage, and a voice came from it.

"Beppo, damn your eyes! *Schweinhund! Je m'en foutre—zat, alors! Corpo di Bacco,* give me a drink!"

EVEN THE porter winced, as the cage erupted a torrent of the most scandalous German, French and English ever heard on the open street. Some passing French soldiers grinned and added a few choice expressions. Gondy climbed in and took the cage.

"Beppo is a parrot," he said unnecessarily. "And it belongs to the sorcerer's daughter, *mes amis,* so control yourselves. The thing was sick, and I brought it to town and got it doctored. It has no shame. Beppo! Be quiet!"

"Go to hell, you bastard!" said the voice, followed by a scream of rage.

"For God's sake, get going," pleaded Gondy, as a crowd began to form. I threw in the gears and we got away. Gondy was sweating, and Murchison cackling delightedly. "I've got a place engaged at Laigueglia, a cottage of our own, and a couple to take care of it. They won't mind the cussing—but no hotel would take us in."

He jerked the cover off the cage, and there was Beppo cocking a wary eye at us. He was the most devilish and beautiful thing I ever saw—a solid, bright, iridescent green except for vivid scarlet markings about his eyes and crest.

"He's fifty years old, from Brazil, and has spent all his fifty years learning filthy language," said Gondy. "And yet, my friends, he is also a saintly bird, actually! He knows a lot of Scripture and beautiful poetry and noble sentiments—and around Marina he never utters a bad word."

"Who, if one may ask, is Marina?" demanded Murchison.

"The sorcerer's daughter," said Gondy. "Since her father died, she has reeducated this beast of the devil."

"Marina! Marina!" squawked out Beppo. "Gentle Marina loves poor Beppo! Marina is an angel, you damned fools!"

A diabolic ingenuity was in the bird. No wonder Italians crossed themselves at the sight of him—and did it again in a hurry when he talked. Murchison was tickled pink, and I did not mind a bit, but poor Gondy had suffered and now he was fed up.

We covered the five miles of open road along the wide *plage,* and Laigueglia opened before us—another crowded little town at the base of the steep hillside, with a white stucco church, narrow streets, and houses mostly in glaring bright colors. Gondy guided us and we came to rest before a pink house under high trees, where an old couple appeared, to welcome us and make us at home.

This, said Gondy, was it. So it was: A pleasant house with a shady patio, and well stocked with everything; we liked it. For the next half-hour we unloaded and got unpacked, then settled down in the patio around a drink before luncheon. Explanations were needed, and Gondy gave them.

Donna Marina Borno was the sorcerer's daughter, so-called. She lived in the valley up above, at Andora, or where Andora used to be. Plague and wars and earthquakes had gradually laid

Andora waste; and in the great earthquake of 1887 that destroyed so much of this coast, Andora had finally perished.

"That earthquake is important," Gondy said. "That is why we're here. The Borno family owned much of the valley; the old chap must have been quite a boy. He was a chemist and had a laboratory—hence the local name of sorcerer. Donna Marina is, I fancy, about thirty-five, and gifted in her own way. She has some country cousins who have made life hell for her and still do. They live in the hills somewhere nearby, fought in the Partisans against the Nazis, and are a tough lot. Beppo is one protection against them—a sort of watchdog. Last time they came to raid her house, she peppered them with a shotgun and has not been troubled since. Oh, Marina is strictly all right, I assure you!"

"In spite of Beppo?" I asked. Gondy nodded, his high-boned features and bright eyes all excited. I could see that he liked Donna Marina.

Murchison struck in quickly:

"Well, what about treasure? That's what brought me here, my good vicomte."

"Gold!" screamed Beppo. "Gold! *Que le grand diable l'emporte!* On your knees and pray, my friends. On your knees! Gold will steal your souls."

"Shut up," snapped Gondy testily. "That brings us back to the 1887 earthquake, Murchison. A land boom was on; the government was building the railroad and tunnels that pierce the hill-shoulders above the shore. Borno—the grandfather of Marina—had a bank in Andora, a sort of country bank. A big shipment of government gold was sent up from Rome, to pay the contractors and workmen and soldiers; it was in Borno's bank, when the earthquake happened. The destruction was terrific."

He paused to finish his drink, and proceeded:

"All communications were cut off. Bandits came down from the hills. Borno took the gold home, took everything he had in

Unaware of Beppo, I got a bad start on hearing from the tree above me part of the Gospel of St. John in a priestly voice... The bird could imitate anyone.

the ruined bank with it, and buried it. Two of his servants did the work. All they could say, afterward, was that the gold was buried ten feet from a eucalyptus tree—they did it by night. Practically every tree in that place has been dug around a dozen times; no soap. Borno, I should explain, had a stroke the next day and never spoke again; he died without having revealed the secret. His son, the sorcerer, never found the treasure. The Marchese Grimani, at Genoa, gave me letters to Donna Marina, and consequently she's been most agreeable. We may search when we please; half of what is found, belongs to us."

BUT WHY have our headquarters here in Laigueglia, we asked—and a dozen more queries.

Gondy sketched a map on the table for us, patiently. Some miles along the shore, around Cape Mele, was the present railroad station and resort of Andora-on-the-Sea. The original Andora lay up the valley of the Merula River; the valley angled sharply back, so that to the old site from this place, Laigueglia, was only two or three miles—right over the hill, by mule-back or shank's mare.

"She has no place there for us," he went on. "Grandfather Borno, the banker, had his stroke because his grand house went to pieces after the earthquake. Now Marina lives in a small wooden house built on the grounds. You can see better than I can tell; mules will be here in the morning for us. It's a stiff climb, but we can come back afoot. And Carson needs exercise. He looks fat and puffy."

"The hell with you!" I said. "What about this Dolls' House thing?"

"That is where Donna Marina lives," Gondy said. "Wait. You'll understand when we get there, Bill. Now tell me about the detector—"

We prattled about the Baby, Beppo cursed and prayed, and then our delayed luncheon was ready, and we decided to spend the afternoon on the *plage*.

The whole thing looked rather hopeless to me. Mules! Country cousins and a feud! A woman running the place—I should have told Gondy never to have business dealings with a woman. I did not like the looks of the setup at all, but refrained from saying so. Murch felt about the same way, I could tell that. Further, Gondy's manner hinted at surprises ahead, and I do not like surprises.

Next morning, early, half a dozen mules and muleteers appeared. We loaded aboard the Baby, which had more bulk than weight due to its magnesium construction. Gondy was condemned to carry Beppo, naturally, and he shrieked curses at us in three tongues as we got off.

So began this day of surprises, of which our road or track was the first. It was steep, and in part was paved with rough cobbles, but huge olives shaded it and very beautiful we found it, as we mounted above the blue Mediterranean.

It was a pleasant climb—a short two miles, till we came out above the valley of the Merula, a gentle descent ahead and an outspread view which started Gondy bubbling, in his eager way, to explain.

From the stony valley rose an isolated hill crowned with ruins—the former town of Andora, with its castle, now consisting of two or three cottages, heaps of rubble, and a restored little church attached to the castle debris. The river, down below, was a stony expanse broken by a bare trickle of water and a few pools, and crossed by a magnificent ancient stone bridge. A Roman work, said Gondy; the Via Aurelia, now forgotten, ran here.

Everything, from the stones and gravel running toward the sea, to the lifting hills in the background, was desolate and empty of life. Not a peasant wagon, not a living creature, broke the dead landscape, but patches of color appeared—the dusty green of olives by the bridge, the vivid white and scarlet of oleanders along the river pools, and on beyond, Gondy pointed to a clump of eucalyptus trees adjoining the olives.

"There's the Borno house—now it is the Dolls' House. Let's get going."

We got into motion again, Beppo squawking indignantly and profanely.

The group of eucalyptus trees towered over us as we drew near; they were old, huge, massive trees, their berries dropping over everything—but they grew inside the wall. An old wall,

Damming out the water, we got the hole dug.
We dumped in the box, neat as a pin.

likewise massive, a wall ten feet high and cruelly topped with broken glass. Walls in Italy mean you come in at the gate or stay out.

The gate, too, was huge and massive, made of openwork iron an inch thick. Through it appeared eucalypti, the ruins of a stone house surrounded by other trees and an unused entrance drive. Beside the gate hung a bell-pull, which Gondy jerked hard. In answer, a man appeared hobbling along the drive—a gray-headed man, holding an enormous key which he waved at us.

He came to the gate, looked us over, exchanged greetings with the muleteers, then uttered an exclamation at sight of Gondy, whom he recognized.

"Yes, Donna Marina said to bring you, if it was you," he said, and swung the gate open. "You know the way, signore." Bright little old eyes in his weathered face glittered at us as we entered. Gondy paid the muleteers, saying we would walk back to Laigueglia and they might go, after unpacking the loads. Beppo must have recognized the sights and sounds, for he set up a delighted screeching that must have carried a mile.

Within the walls was a large space of ground, most of the huge eucalypti being at the back. We passed the tumbled ruins of the stone building, and sighted, ahead, a cottage of stained but unpainted wood. I noticed nothing unusual until I saw the muleteers staring and crossing themselves; then, upon closer view, the oddity appeared.

That little house was covered, up to a certain height, with tiny figures like dolls or puppets; but they were carved from the wood itself, not merely slapped on. Not only were they exquisitely carven, but each one was an individual. Apparently they were portraits. Some were grotesque, many were really beautiful; but all were filled with an impish gayety, like elfin laughter, and I found that closer inspection heightened this quality.

"I'D BETTER warn you that Donna Marina speaks English," Gondy said in a low voice.

Why warn us? There was no chance to question him, however; we halted, our packed-up Baby was disembarked, the muleteers and mules departed, and Gondy, with Beppo's cage in hand, went to the door. There were no steps; the house was on ground level. We saw why, as the door swung open and Donna Marina appeared to greet us.

"Good morning, gentlemen!" she said brightly, even gayly. "You are welcome, more welcome than I can tell you. And Beppo too! M. de Gondy, you have my warmest thanks—"

Beppo cawed and screeched in wild delight; Gondy bent over her hand, Murchison and I looked every which way and inwardly cursed him for not telling us, as we were introduced. Donna Marina was only a face, a torso garbed in a gay silk blouse, with long arms and strong, muscular hands attached. The rest of her was hidden under a shawl; she was in a wheel-chair.

The vivid strength of her grip astonished me, my handshake astonished her and made her laugh; we made no pretence of imitating Gondy and kissing her fingers. I liked her laugh, and I liked her.

She had rich silky hair of dark brown. She wore dangling gold earrings. Her hazel eyes had the challenging look of one who meets the world chin up; her features were aquiline and perfect, yet she was not beautiful but rather, like the carven puppets on the walls, betrayed an impish, gleeful wisdom, as though she knew all secret things. The character in this face, its sheer force of personality, was something remarkable. She took instant charge of the situation, her bright, alert eyes studying each of us.

"Well, gentlemen, don't look embarrassed," she said, not mockingly but cheerily. "You behold a creature who has not walked since a horse threw her, twenty years ago; the sorcerer's daughter, my neighbors call me. This is the Dolls' House, as they call my handiwork, my sole amusement and occupation. They believe these carven figures are possessed of Satan, and no doubt extend the compliment to me also. But I assure you that within these walls is no satanic power, but quiet peace. This is my home, where you are also at home. Shall we go into the garden? Yes, M. le Vicomte, you may guide my chair, although I am quite capable of doing it myself, but it is pleasant to be attended like a lady."

We left our stuff lying. Gondy took her chair and manipulated it; though, as a rule, her fierce independence refused any such help, she liked his perfect courtesy. As we passed along the house, she pointed out certain figures and told who they were; as I had thought, they were portraits. Some of them pictured the Borno country cousins up in the hills, and these were brutal, savage fellows. Like the originals, she said; Alessandro and Timoteo Borno were brigands even now.

The gardens had once been beautiful—a small, formerly sunken garden adjoining the little house, dotted with antique statuary, was now sadly dilapidated. Beyond lay a less formal expanse within the high walls. Gigantic eucalypti and high cypresses waved and dapple-shadowed the ground so that little grass grew, and here she halted us.

"Now let us speak of treasure, gentlemen," said she. "It is here, somewhere; enough gold to put us all on our feet, including me! I' have no hope that you will find it; that old grandfather of mine was a clever fellow. But it is here, within these walls. Often men have dug for it. Once my pleasant cousins came, locked me in the house, and worked for three days turning up the ground; in vain. The last time they came, I used a shotgun—they were looting my house, breaking my carven figures. I peppered them well, and they ran."

WE TALKED for a time. She had no idea where the gold was hidden, except that it was ten feet from one of the big trees. This meant little; a dozen of those trees were scattered about. At one corner was a pool of water twenty feet across; it came from a spring, she said, and seeped away under the wall. The water was shallow but it was always fresh and clear.

Murchison and Gondy went to get the Baby, and left me alone with Donna Marina. I asked permission to light my pipe, and she laughed.

"Do, Mr. Carson, do! My, but you're a big, strong man! I used to be tall like you."

I obeyed.

"I think you're taller than I am now, Donna Marina," I told her. "There's a genius in those carven figures of yours that I'll never attain, in my own work. You have a great gift; it would be recognized, in America."

Her sharp eyes met mine, and softened. She smiled.

"That's kind of you. America! I have a greater reason for wanting to go there. Some of your soldiers were here during the war. One was a surgeon. He said that if I went to surgeons in America, I might be cured and might walk again. That's why I hope you can find the gold."

"Then perhaps we shall find it," I said. "There could be no better reason. You hope against hope, is that it?"

She nodded, and glanced at her hands.

"I hope, without belief; that expresses it. These hands are strong, they keep busy, they can do things, Mr. Carson. A gift? Yes; in compensation for what I have lost, perhaps. I am grateful that I have no bitterness or anger."

"No. You've had an outlet, in the work you found to do."

Her eyes flashed suddenly. "But I warn you! Alessandro and Timoteo, the cousins, are brutal men. They'll know of your search here; probably they know now. They have friends in the coast towns who keep them informed of everything. They would think nothing of killing me and you alike, were the treasure to be found."

She was so terribly in earnest about it that I smiled.

"They're not the only ones. Take Gondy's sister-in-law, Félice, a beautiful but savage young woman. She's tried to do us in more than once, and has come close to effecting it. She hates

us consumingly, has followed us about, and would pounce suddenly."

The hazel eyes widened on me. "A woman? And hates you?"

I told her about Félice, more to get her mind off her own
troubles and to amuse her, than for any other reason. All three
of us fervently hoped we had seen the last of Félice.

Jealousy, greed for gold, hatred of us because she had failed
to injure us—what motives moved Félice de Gondy? Perhaps
all. She had succeeded in getting away with our first detector,
though it was ruined and useless to her; she knew all about it
and coveted it fiercely, being well aware of its possibilities.

"That woman should be locked up," said Donna Marina
firmly.

I laughed. "You're telling me? However, she's not around
here, I trust."

"So I thought about those precious .cousins of mine," she
rejoined. "Yet they come, when least expected. They seem to
know all that goes on here. One cannot prevent leaks."

MURCHISON AND Gondy now appeared. They had
delayed to put the Baby together, and now came pushing it
gayly along.

We had secured, while in Genoa, a light wicker perambulator frame in which to house the batteries and instrument; it
was high off the ground, but for our purposes this mattered not
at all. Our detector used no magnetic principle. We had a practical and extremely mobile affair now, eminently suited to our
projects.

Donna Marina was delighted with everything, as we showed
her how the gadget worked and put it through its paces for her.
We had not built it for depths; the electronic rays had a limit
of forty feet, farther than we ever proposed to dig.

But as we worked it for our hostess, explaining how, on radar
principles, the waves kicked back and registered on the dials
when encountering obstacles, and how we had charted these
results, which varied with the substance encountered, so that

we could tell with fair accuracy what the obstacle was, the tiny buzzer rang. Something had been struck. We read the dials, consulted the chart, and found that rock had been encountered at thirty-two feet.

"Right!" cried Donna Marina, clapping her hands. "There is solid rock under us, my friends—the soil goes down for only thirty feet! Your *enfant du diable* is proven right!"

"Child of the devil, sure enough!" growled Murchison. "Now

*They must have stolen in very quietly. We were
caught, with no possible evasion or escape.*

we'll have to do some adjusting, Bill Carson. Use the weaker
set of tubes, eh?"

"Right," I said. "A fifteen-foot depth is all we need here."

We accompanied Donna Marina in to luncheon. She was
sadly frail, it appeared; if she worked or moved about during
the morning, her injured back became very painful and she had
to remain in bed for the rest of the day, so the meal was her
farewell to us.

The interior of her house was charming, simple, rich with all
sorts of wood-carving, and arranged for her convenience. There
was little elegance; she said frankly that money was scarce
hereabouts. Bookcases were everywhere, low ones which she
could reach herself. Aside from the manservant who had met
us, two women kept house for her.

So, the meal over, we made our farewells for the day. We were remaining to work, of course, and were made entirely free of the place to follow our own devices. These were simple. We went back to the garden, got the Baby adjusted, and went to work.

Sunset found us walking home over the hill trail, with nothing discovered.

Thus began a round of pleasant, fruitless days which we enjoyed enormously. Sometimes we went to work over the hill trail, other times we walked the *plage* and around the cape to Andora-on-the-Sea, and up the stony Merula valley with its pools and oleanders. We left the Baby in charge of Donna Marina, at night; the walk back and forth was excellent for us all.

Usually we lunched with Donna Marina, and to this end carried delicacies, staples or wine to eke out her table. She would bring Beppo into the garden and sit talking with us, or we would separate and sit indoors with her, where Beppo's scandalous conversation was limited to Scriptural passages and prayers; he never swore in the house, thanks to her training, and out of it never did anything else.

Sometimes she would turn the bird loose in the garden. He would flash among the trees like a radiant green streak; and once, unaware of him, I got a bad start on hearing from the tree above me part of the Gospel of St. John in a priestly voice. The bird could imitate anyone, and one day at luncheon Gondy was horrified to hear his own voice outside the window telling a scandalous story in French.

Donna Marina, however, laughed, until she cried.

A S F O R finding gold, we got no "forrarder." Yet the lack of success did not worry us, fantastic as the statement may sound. We were living an ideal life in our quiet cottage, with plenty of sea-bathing; and each day the excursion up the valley of the Merula to the Borno house was like a new adventure into un-guessed possibilities. Here I must speak chiefly for myself. Although we all shared the feeling, I think mine was the strongest—a sense of attachment, even of affection, for our hostess there.

An intimacy upgrew between us. We had got on well from the very start; this crippled woman was an amazing creature, all brain and intuition and gentle fantasy. She had no bitterness, except toward those cousins of hers. Her mind was like a poised, darting, flashing hummingbird, flitting in all directions, balanced upon wings invisible though reaching out with delicate surety of touch. She, who knew so little of life, yet knew everything. I found myself, in our talks, baring my inmost self to her, my personal problems, the little things in my life which were hidden. Why? Because she could explain them all to me, as one explains the perplexities of life to a child.

I swear she had an insight, a perceptive wisdom, not of this world. She would take some incident of my career, perhaps of my family life or my schooldays, and hold it up and twist it until every facet flashed with reflected light; and it would be understood. Why this habit arose, or that friendship died, and so forth. Little unimportant things of enormous influence. She would have made a marvelous psychiatrist—and it was all mere intuition, an inner wisdom. Or she would wheel her chair around the house-walls and pointing to each of the carven puppets, tell who they were and their life-history—not the external life-and-death, but the inward character and failure and success, and why.

She liked Gondy for his courtly manners and his fineness of quality. When Murchison spent an hour or two with her, he came away a different man, all his sarcasm hushed. How she could scratch away the top-soil and reach down to the true sub-stratum of values in anyone! She was no Pollyanna, though. She showed me how she had tucked that shotgun under her arm with its stock against the wall, so she could fire it without being shattered by the recoil; and she laughed heartily over the way she had peppered the country cousins.

As she had said at our first meeting, within these walls existed only a happy peace. She, who suffered daily, created happiness all around her; it was remarkable.

I am dilating on these things, because they had a vital bearing on what happened later. You will recall how, after the war, the French occupied this frontier strip of Italy; Washington and London were trying to crowd them out, especially after the trouble in Syria. Consequently, things here were a bit uncertain. A lot of Italian patriots, like the cousins, had taken to the hills, gone clear off the reservation, and were raising hell from time to time.

Naturally, among ourselves we frequently discussed Donna Marina. We had done pretty well for ourselves with our invention; we had come away from Venice, for example, with a whacking lot of gold coin, our share of the work in those parts, and while the Baby had been an expensive luxury, like all babies, we had plenty of loot on hand and were not sure how we would get it safely out of the country or turned into bank balances.

O N E   E V E N I N G at supper, after another day's fruitless search, Gondy spoke up.

"I'd like to ask you chaps about something," he said, with an oddly awkward hesitation. "The chances are looking slimmer and slimmer for that Borno gold. If this project proves to be a failure, what's going to happen?"

"We'll worry along," I rejoined cheerfully. "We've got plenty in the bag."

"I wasn't thinking of us," he said, "but of Donna Marina."

"Oh, her!" said Murchison, and avoided my eye. "Hm! I've been kind of dreading, myself, the idea of going away and leaving her empty-handed. I suppose, Bill, to a practical guy like you, it sounds silly."

"The hell with you and how it sounds," I told him. "All that the future holds for this gal is the possibility of rolling into Johns Hopkins or the Mayos and walking out on her own two feet. And you goddamned nuts may laugh, but I asked her yesterday if—if she'd let me send her to the United States—and she wouldn't."

"No, of course; pride," said Gondy. "She wouldn't."

"Hell, Bill, we're not laughing," growled Murchison, squinting at me. "No, we're not laughing at all. Don't get us wrong, you big bear-cub."

"Look, boys," spoke up Gondy, very cheerfully now, "I have a suggestion, a perfect one, I think. Why not take the gold coin we have on hand, which is unsafe anyhow, knocking around with us, and box it up, and—discover it? Of course, her pride would make us take half the loot, according to agreement, so we'd have to figure carefully—"

"Holy smoke, you've hit it!" I exclaimed. "Eh, Murch? What d'you say?"

He nodded, his thin features brightening. "It's a go, you bet!"

We discussed it. The scheme was flawless from any angle. Donna Marina, of course, would fiercely resent anything that hinted at pity or at charity, so we had to do the job with great care.

First, for the money; we found there was ample in our treasury. Gondy was deputed to scout around town, get the proper kind of a box, age it with acids, and pack the gold.

"I'll do that tomorrow," he said. "It'll weigh like the devil. How'll you manage to bury it without her knowing?"

"We'll do that next day," Murchison said. "Carry it up there in the car and leave it. She always takes a nap after lunch. Tote it in then and bury it in that shallow pond. It'll be a quick job."

"Will the Baby work through water?" queried Gondy. "Radar waves don't, I understand."

"Our first model did; remember, we tested it?" I put in. "Besides, that won't matter a hang. She won't know enough about it to raise the question. But what about the bottom of that pond? We don't want to lose the box in the mud."

"It's not mud, but sand," said Murchison. "Old man Borno made the artificial pond because of the spring in that corner;

she said he was a clever old guy, and he was. There's a pipe under the wall that'll carry off the water, with a lever to open it. She told me about it the other day. But we can't drain off the water before planting the gold."

"Speaking of the pond," I spoke up. "We've covered nearly all the place except that. Hadn't we better search it first, with the Baby?"

"And then go back and find our plant? Not much," Murchison objected. "That would look phony to her. Still, we ought to search it."

"Suppose I get the box fixed up tomorrow," said Gondy. "Next day, we'll get it planted, in the afternoon. That'll be Saturday. On Sunday, if she doesn't object to our working then, we can go wading with the Baby and search the area thoroughly before turning up our salted mine—strike it the last thing. Eh?"

We already knew Donna Marina had no objection to Sunday labor, of our variety, so this settled everything satisfactorily.

In the morning, Murchison and I went up over the hill trail, leaving Gondy to make his preparations. When we came to the crest and paused to get our wind, looking down over the empty, stony valley, Murchison cackled out a laugh.

"You're a funny guy, Bill! You know, I figured you'd be the obstacle to this fake business. Instead, you're all for it."

"And I thought you'd be the one to crab about any such charitable use of our loot," I said. We looked at each other and grinned. Murch was a great guy, actually.

THAT NIGHT Gondy had it fixed up—a beautiful job; he had even disinterred an ancient box rotten with mold, and had packed the gold in half-rotted sacking. We chucked it in the Fiat on Saturday morning and went by what Murch called "the large way." He liked to show off how much he had picked up in London, during our war stay there; that was the expression used in 17th Century London to denote going home by way of the river, or some such nonsense.

We tooled the car up the shore road to the new Andora, then

around and up the Merula valley to the ancient town ruins, and so to the Borno place. All morning we snooped around the garden with the Baby, cleaning up places we had missed while Donna Marina looked on and Beppo, who was in a pious mood, sat on a branch near her chair and intoned Gregorian chants and snatches of Latin prayers. When I joined her, she gave me a radiant smile.

"Well, it doesn't look as though we were going to discover any treasure, does it?"

"Never say die till the last dog's hung, Donna Marina," I replied cheerfully.

"I'll be very sorry for your sake, if we fail," she said. "You boys have put a lot of effort into this search."

"We'll be sorry for your sake, which makes it even and does none of us any particular good," I said, and she laughed softly. "We haven't touched that lower corner of the garden, where the pool is. We'll tackle that tomorrow."

"Say, tomorrow afternoon, then," she said. "I'll rest in the morning. Come to lunch, and we'll make an afternoon of it together."

"And meet failure with a smile. Eh?"

"Of course." Her brown, impish features were alight. "What else?"

"*Orate, fratres!*" croaked that green devil from his perch on a branch overhead. "*Orate, fratres! Pax vobiscum!*"

"Shut up," I snapped. "Shut up, Beppo!"

"Go to hell," he rejoined, with some additions in French.

Donna Marina chuckled.

"You're spoiling my poor bird, Mr. Carson! If I go to America, what shall I do with him?"

"Take him to Hollywood and you'll be rich," I told her. "He'll support you in luxury there."

"Don't you want to let the water drain out of that pond before you search it?" she asked, with sudden remembrance. "It can be done easily."

"Not unless we find something. We can wade around with the Baby—the water's only a foot deep at most."

I never saw her more cheerful and gay, even though she must have felt in her heart that we would have no luck. We lunched as usual, and she trundled off in her chair for her nap. We had a smoke, to give her time to get asleep; then Gondy and I fetched in the box from the car and Murchison joined us at the pool.

To bury it under the water, was more of a job than we had figured, but one spot was a natural for the purpose. The water came in a little bay to the foot of a big chunk of lava weathered into fantastic shapes, and we could get at the water from two sides; so we fell to work there. Damming out the water with sand and mud, we worked fast and got the hole dug—just a shallow one, naturally. We dumped in the box, scraped sand over it, and let in the water anew, and everything was neat as a pin again.

THAT AFTERNOON we finished with the garden; we had combed every square foot of ground, even around the trees. There was still the chance that we would turn up the Borne treasure in the pool, of course, but none of us had much hope. It was a good bet that old Borno had not buried his gold there at all, but somewhere else.

We drove home to our Laigueglia cottage and a supper of *fecchini* and "red ink," and there Gondy found a letter awaiting him. It was from his father, in France, and it had news of his sister-in-law, Félice—the infernal female who had stolen our first model and skipped out, unaware that it was useless. She had shown up near Lyons to hunt with it for a supposed treasure there, had got into trouble with the police, and had disappeared, leaving the gadget behind.

"Now she'll probably trail us once more," Murchison said gloomily. "She hates us like poison. She'll probably guess why we let her have the no-good gadget."

"Well, we should worry!" cried Gondy, laughing. "She's not

here; that's certain. If she shows up later on, we can thumb our noses at her. So forget her! Good riddance, and well gone."

"Where do we go from here?" I asked him. "This job is about washed up and we'd better be looking ahead. Have you anything in mind?"

Gondy nodded brightly. "Several things. I've been trying to get in touch with one or two friends—may get a wire any day."

He was a religious soul, by spells, and went to church next morning. Murchison and I spent the morning on the *plage*. About noon we climbed into the old Fiat and went chugging around the cape and up the little valley to the Dolls' House.

LUNCHEON WAS notable. Marco, the wiry old servant, waited on table; he and the two women who took care of the house were going visiting for the afternoon. We would have the place to ourselves.

After the meal, Gondy took Donna Marina's chair out to the garden, while I followed with the Baby. I noticed that the wicker top was pulled down over the body of the thing, but paid it no attention. We assembled at the lower end of the garden, near the pool; the high eucalypti made wavy patterns of shade and sunlight around us and their fragrance was pleasant.

Donna Marina swept us all with a twinkling glance.

"Well, gentlemen! I have a small parting gift; it is all I can offer you. Why not take a look at that Baby of yours?"

I pulled back the wicker cover, and we stood staring.

Over the batteries and mechanism had been neatly tucked a white knitted cover. And on this cover lay three of Donna Marina's precious puppets, each one exquisitely fashioned. There was Gondy, slim and mustached and smiling, to the very life. There was Murchison, skinny and rather sardonic, a speaking likeness; and there was Bill Carson, clumsy and heavy-set with even his missing front tooth showing.

These were not just toys. They represented long stolen hours of the most delicate work imaginable. They held great artistry, a merry and elfin genius; love had gone into their making, as we realized full well. She could have given us no gift that meant more. For a moment or two we were pretty awkward in expressing our thanks—until suddenly old Murch stooped down over her chair and kissed her smack on the lips. Then he stood up, scarlet, stammering, confused—and we all roared with laughter; then Gondy and I followed his example, by invitation.

After that we took off shoes and sox, turned up our trousers, and went at the shallow pond with the Baby by turns. Beppo, who had been turned loose, flitted about like a radiant green flame in the sunlight, losing himself for an hour or two at a time in the trees or squawking insults at other birds. I took the first trick, then let Murchison take over and went back and sat with Donna Marina.

"Silly fellows!" she said, her eyes dancing. "To waste kisses on a useless creature in a wheel-chair!"

"You're beautiful," I said. "Beauty isn't looks; life isn't a cinema. Beauty is harmony and peace, a rhythmic unity. These carvings of yours express it, like music. They have a perfect unity, with no discordant note. That's what Murch was trying to say."

"I like the compliment, even if it doesn't say much for your morals."

"I believe with Huxley that morals were invented by man. They're unknown in nature."

"You have a glib tongue," she said lightly, but I saw she was pleased.

We had left the knitted coverlet and the three dolls in the carriage; they did not interfere with the gadget. Time passed; the area under water was being thoroughly searched, and nothing had turned up. Gondy took over; we had agreed that he was to find the cache.

Donna Marina kept up her vivacious air, but with an effort. She knew that this was our last day together; the search had failed. But, if her disappointment were acute, she gave no sign of it. We watched Gondy coming closer to the little bay. At length he rolled the Baby slap over it and halted, getting out his cigarettes and starting to speak.

The buzzer sounded. He jumped a foot. Murchison was on his feet with a yell. I ran forward to examine the dials, pulling up the white coverlet to look at them—mere pretense, of course.

"We've got it! We've got it!" I cried, and looked up at Donna Marina. She had pulled herself up in the chair and was leaning forward, her brown merry features alive with excitement.

We marked the spot, pushed the Baby back, and grabbed for the spades at hand. We put on a splendid act, if I do say it, getting in each other's way and scrabbling at the sand, until Donna Marina told us to dam back the water out of the bay. So we did, and then went at the digging furiously, laughing and chattering.

We got up the rotten box, and smashed it open with a spade, and poured handfuls of gold coins into Donna Marina's lap. She laughed and cried, embraced each of us, and if we needed any reward for our fakery, we had it then and there from her glorious happiness. America? She was going just as quickly as she could make arrangements! Then she insisted on dividing the gold into the agreed amounts—and while we were doing this, the country cousins arrived! We were, naturally, concentrated wholly on what we were doing.

They must have stolen in very quietly, having found the gate unlocked. The first we knew of their presence was when Alessandro, a mop-headed giant, burst into a laugh. He and Timoteo, another mop-head, held German Lugers trained on us. Half a dozen more ragged bandits, armed with all sorts of weapons, had spread out around us. We were caught, with no possible evasion or escape.

"Hands up!" roared Alessandro. "You with the others, witch!"

He meant Donna Marina. She was not afraid of him; she flew into a fury, and the garden rang with a flood of Italian like drumming rain. Not a word of the dialect could we understand. Gondy, no less excitable, flung himself into the argument and got knocked senseless for his pains. Donna Marina screamed, and fainted.

Well, our gold was gone. Alessandro and Timoteo were scooping it into their pockets and while Murchison knelt over Gondy, I talked to the precious pair. They could savvy my Italian, and in a way were not such bad eggs. They agreed to let us take Donna Marina and Gondy into the house, and to leave it untouched; possession of the gold had put them into high good humor. Timoteo even agreed to help with Gondy, whose scalp had been badly cut, and picked him up in his arms. This was not pure charity; he wanted that shotgun Donna Marina owned, and this cut the last faint hope out from under me. I had meant to get my hands on that gun myself.

I TOOK Donna Marina's chair, Murchison helping. Timoteo followed with Gondy, and I was thankful poor Donna Marina remained unconscious. We were a pretty glum lot.

We got into the house. Donna Marina's room was at the far end, overlooking the garden, and I pushed her chair there and left her; she was better off as she was. Timoteo followed with Gondy and laid him on the bed, and demanded the shotgun. Murchison found and gave it to him, and with a grin he stamped out.

"This is a hell of a note!" growled Murch. "Leave Gondy be; he'll come around. What are they doing?"

A squabble of voices resounded. I went to the big window and he joined me. The whole gang were around Alessandro and Timoteo, screaming for a division of the loot. For a moment we thought hopefully trouble would develop, but the two Bornos grinned and began to hand out money. *Our* money, dammit! We both cursed in heartfelt agony.

Suddenly Murch grabbed my arm and erupted in fresh profanity. One of those muggs let out a yelp and a laugh, went to the Baby, and began to push the buggy. Others gathered around and halted him.

"My Lord, they'll ruin it!" gasped Murch.

"They can't hurt it," I told him. "They have no idea what it is—good God, Murch! What's happened?"

Something had happened; for a moment we could not discover what. The whole group of men froze; fear and terror leaped into their faces. Then they began to cross themselves.

"Sorcery! Sorcery!" cried out one of them in a voice of horror. "It is her doing! She will do it to us too—it is sorcery!"

AT THIS moment a shrill yell pealed out above them:

"The police! The *carabinieri!* Run, you bastards—run! The police!"

A vivid green streak shot through the air, but none of them saw it. Already scared stiff, they let out a chorus of howls and broke. Timoteo dropped the shotgun and led the rout, still crossing himself, for the gates.

"Good for Beppo!" grunted Murchison. "Hey, Bill! They'll catch on pretty quick—hop out and get that shotgun—I'll try to lock the gates—"

The window was open, and of course, this being Italy, was unscreened. I jumped out and legged it to where the shotgun lay. It was loaded. I scooped it up and then turned and put after the gang. Murchison was not even out of the house yet when I came past, and going by our Fiat, sprinted down the drive. The whole gang were at the gates, fighting to get out. I ducked behind a tree and let them have both barrels. A chorus of screams went up, and those bandits evaporated like nobody's business. Murchison came along, we got the gates shut and locked, then stood looking at each other and panting.

"But the gold went with 'em," mourned Murch. "Let's go get the Baby safe, then look after our hospital cases. What started the gang off on that sorcery business?"

"Search me," I said. We hiked back down to the lower garden. The Baby still stood where it had been halted, over the hole we had dug in the sand. I stopped dead.

"Murch! Look! That explains it—"

Even in this bitter moment, we could not restrain a laugh. The cover of the carriage had been pushed back, and there on the white coverlet lay the three little replicas of me and Murch and Gondy. Sorcery, indeed! Those nitwits had taken for granted that we had been bewitched and changed into dolls—and Beppo had done the rest.

Suddenly Murchison froze. "Bill! Do you hear what I hear?"

I listened, and jumped forward. We had not thought to switch off the Baby, which in consequence was still running. And the buzzer was sounding repeatedly, over and over!

"What does it mean?" Murch gaped at me. "Has the thing gone nuts?"

"My gosh, man!" I exclaimed, pointing. "Don't you see? This is the best place we found to plant that gold. It was the best place old Borno found, likewise. Look at the dials! Let's see if they register gold—"

They did. Gold, ten feet down, deeper than we had put our box....

We reloaded the shotgun, revived Gondy, and put him in charge. Donna Marina we dared not touch; she was apparently all right, except for the fainting, so we left her and while Gondy stood watch at the gates, Murch and I went to digging. We stripped to the waist and worked like fools, forgetful of everything else.

Beppo came and perched on the Baby and did some fancy cursing. We got deeper and deeper. At last we struck a box and tugged it out of the hole; there was another beneath it. They were stout, iron-bound chests, three in all. When we got them out in the westering sunlight, we were so completely fagged out that we just dropped.

"Well, aren't you going to look at them?" asked a voice.

"Go to hell!" I gasped. "That damned parrot is imitating Donna Marina now."

"It's a damned good imitation," she said, laughing. We looked up, and there she was in her wheel-chair. Then Gondy came, reporting that the last he had seen of the gang they had broken up and gone every which way. He was struck dumb at sight of the boxes, then seized a spade and went at one, and got it smashed open.

And once more, that afternoon, there was a flood of gold coin in the sunlight, and it revived us completely.

"Well, gentlemen, this is more like it," said Donna Marina, fingering the coins we had dumped in her lap. She was quite all right; she had come around by herself, and had come out to find us. "Yes, this is much more like it."

"Like what?" I asked.

Her eyes twinkled at us and she broke into a laugh.

"More like the money that my grandfather buried in 1887. I meant to ask you," she said, "when we were interrupted by those bandits, how it happened that the first box we discovered contained modern money. Did you forget that all gold coins are dated?"

We looked at her, then at each other; and then—well, we were too confused even to lie gracefully. We just confessed everything.

THAT NIGHT when we got home it was late. A telegram was awaiting Gondy. He read it and looked up, his eyes dancing.

"Boys! Here's something good! It's from an old friend of mine, one of the chaps I was trying to reach. He's at a place near Penmarch, on the coast south of Brest. Strange people there—the Bigoudins, a race older than the Bretons or Celts—older than the Druids, even!"

"The hell with it," said Murchison. "I'm thinking about saying good-by to Donna Marina."

I nodded. "Right. So am I. And I move that we stick with her until we see her safe aboard a boat for America!"

We did, too.

VI

BRITTANY TREASURE

A strange people dwell in Brittany, survivors of a prehistoric race with a language and superstitions of their own. And it was a strange adventure that our mine-detector treasure-seekers encountered among these Bigoudins.

WE WERE rolling down to Brittany in heavenly summer weather, pushing our disreputable old Fiat across the roads of France and having a grand time, with a blind faith in our cicerone and contact man, the Vicomte de Gondy. That title of his could get us by with murder in this country, where his family was old and famous.

Not until we neared our destination did we get curious about the job ahead, because Gondy was really showing us *la belle* France and we liked it. However, we got him down to brass tacks at last.

"We're going to a place near Pen-march, on the coast south of Brest," said he. "I've fixed it up through a friend of mine whose great-uncle will entertain us. His name is Keradoc. He's an old man, a famous antiquarian or scholar, and he's mad as a March hare."

This was encouraging. All three of us were, from normal viewpoints, more or less cockeyed. You have to be a bit screwy to devote your life to treasure hunts. Our pal Gondy was a Frenchman and that explained him. Murchison and I, after seeing the war from the inside of laboratories in England, where we had developed mine detectors and other scientific G.I. marvels, were touring Europe with Gondy and the Baby.

We had done our bit for V-E and V-J days; and with more luck than most, we were now profiting by it in the piping times of peace. We had developed the Baby from one of our less successful—distinctly so—laboratory discoveries. It was intended to be a radionic mine detector operating on radar principles. It did not work. We turned it into a gadget that did detect underground metals and other substances.

We took in Gondy and set out to make out fortune. We were doing all right, too, but made the odd discovery that the war had been too big for us. We could not get away from it. We ran into its effects everywhere, effects moral and physical. Human nature had been twisted, civilization itself had been warped, by those years of war, massacre and rapine. People grinned nastily at conventions, at balanced values, at moral values. In the war-

The flashlight beam dazzled her.... She knew she was caught and put her hands up to shield her eyes. "Come here," I ordered. "Do you speak English?"

ravaged lands, mankind had gone back a thousand years. America was untouched, but Europe was living in a caveman's dream.

"We're in Brittany, aren't we?" I asked. "The old Celtic land of Druids, of giant stone menhirs and cromlecs and fishermen and queer costumes."

"Worse," said Gondy. "Penmarch once rivaled Nantes, commercially, but tidal waves and a sinking coast knocked it out. Keradoc's family is ancient, has occupied its place for centuries, and the old boy has grubbed in traditions and legends until he's

nuts, I gather. But there seems to be a definite treasure, so I thought it'd interest you."

"Interesting folk, these Bretons," observed Murchison.

Gondy held up a finger.

"But these aren't Bretons, though most people call them so. Actually, this district is occupied by Bigoudins—a race older than the Bretons or Celts, older than the Druids, older than any other, the remnant of Europe's first prehistoric people. Pre-Christian beliefs linger among them. They firmly believe in wizardry and sorcery and so on."

"You're taking us into a nice mess, aren't you?" I asked.

He chuckled.

"We're seeing things, *mes amis!* It's worth while. I've sent on letters from my friends; old Keradoc is expecting us. He has plenty of room in his ancient stone house by the sea—I can't answer for its comfort, though. He's a famous ethnologist, belongs to all the learned societies of Europe, and the treasure is a family affair, authentic."

"How did you learn about this treasure?" I asked idly, little dreaming what horrible importance was to attach to this same question, later.

Gondy chuckled.

"A newspaper clipping about it came in the mail—oh, weeks ago! I never learned who had sent it. I followed it up, found that I knew old Keradoc's nephew, and that was that. Shall we have another bottle of wine?"

"Two," replied Murchison....

We came to Penmarch, a little old town of fishermen, through the most desolate and picturesque district of France, where before the war tourists and artists had flocked daily by thousands. Everything was stone. On all sides were enormous pointed rocks set on end in Druid times; the houses were stone; the shores and fields were stone.

Huge districts were sunken marshland, or moors empty of life. People had congregated in the towns.

HERE AND there castles crowned the hills, bits of old buildings poked up from nowhere, chapels or churches occupied lonely nooks. As Murchison said, all of Europe would be like this—after the next war; people congregated in little huddles, the country all depopulated and empty, hunting and fishing and weaving the only occupations, cities non-existent.

"All England would be like this right now," he added, "if the Nazis hadn't been stopped in their tracks, as they were. Damned picturesque—but good for nothing."

He was right. Wars, almost continual wars, had done this to the Bigoudin country.

From Penmarch, we had to feel our way along the coast; there was no railroad, the highway ran inland, and we had to end our journey by a country road no better than a stony sheep-track that ran down to the sea and the House of Tristan, as the Keradoc place was called. What a grim spot!

It loomed against the sunset, an enormous stone box, half of it in ruins. Below was the shore, swept by Atlantic surges; half a dozen little huts were crowded into a cove. People lived there, happy in the life of their fathers, knowing nothing better. Old Keradoc was the lord of desolation, right enough. Buried treasure in such a place? The very thought seemed absurd.

"I see where we're going to live on fish for a while," I said.

"Stop thinking about your belly, Bill Carson," snapped Murch. "It's too big already. What you need to do is some climbing among these huge rocks."

This was unhappily true, but I only grinned in a sickly way. Murchison and I had been pals since boyhood days in South Boston.

OUR ARRIVAL was a notable event. Keradoc and the four family servants who took care of his joint came to receive us. The four were gnarled, brown, highly costumed museum pieces from the hamlet below; they spoke no French. All the names in these parts were queer and outlandish, it proved.

Keradoc was different. At first we took him for one of our

People lived there, knowing nothing better.
Old Keradoc was the lord of desolation, right

own kind. He was immensely tall, thin, white-haired and hawk-faced; he looked like a cross between Don Quixote and Sir Aubrey Smith. He had jet-black eyes, and they were alive, young, vigorous. He was a handsome old chap, courteous and extremely pleasant, and put us at ease immediately.

But—over the stone doorway of the house was carved a big swastika.

That should have warned us; the Nazi emblem has shadowed the world in grief and horror. However, this house outdated any Nazis by centuries.... Our stuff was unloaded, then the Fiat was run under shelter of a wall and covered with a tarpaulin, and we went in. See our rooms, said Keradoc, have an *apéritif,* then come out and see the view in the sunset.

The house was massive, dark with few windows and old black oak, solid as a rock, primitive in its furnishings, and overload-

enough. Better treasure in such a place?
The very thought seemed absurd.

ed with books and desks for them. Big, mammoth books bound
in vellum; new books, old books. There were oil lamps, hurricane
lamps, ship lamps. An enormous fireplace, with the swastika,
again, carved over it. Cupboards, or rather armoires, that held
queer things. Weaving and embroidery of the country relieved
the bare bleakness. Our beds were massive, spring-less, fairly
comfortable. Our rooms were little stone cells off a corridor
that was blocked up just beyond—we were among the ruins, it
proved. Each cell had a window and was just large enough to
turn around in.

WE SAT with our host in the big central room; he studied
us, we studied him. I liked him; he was honest. If he uttered
some damned singular sentiments, it was not for effect; he
meant them. If he had strange beliefs, they were real beliefs and
not put on for show. We all liked him, even if he could put a

shiver into us with some of his notions. Not that he tried for effect—they just overflowed, as it were.

When we mentioned the war and its effects, he nodded quietly at us.

"In the old days," he said, "Penmarch furnished men-at-arms in the thousands, and almost a thousand boats lay at her quays. It was a rich land here. Now it is a region of *ankou.*"

"I don't know the word," said Gondy with interest.

"Death. *Ankou* is death personified—not a god, but a force. It is everywhere here. Our people have second sight. Mystery is part of daily life. But come out, and see our heritage for yourselves! The best and richest of it lies straight out from shore, here."

We went with him to the big entrance doors, and out to the naked rock that gave a view of the whole coast and sea in the reddened sunset. He waved a hand westward.

"There is Ultima Thule, the Isle de Sein, island of the dead, where the Druids were buried—the strangest place in Europe. This country itself is a land of the lost. Gigantic reefs fringe the shore out yonder, guarding the coast. We suffer for the sins of our fathers, who were pirates and filibusters in the Middle Ages."

"You spoke of a heritage out there," I said, squinting at the glittering sea. "I see nothing. Not even islands."

"That is it," he said gravely. "Lost. Sunken Armorica! Gone is the land of Alata, far is the dream of Altair! It sank under the sea, at many periods. It was the home of the Druid gods, of the pre-Aryan people, of whom these Bigoudins are the descendants. Ainan was the sun-god. The sea-god was Mainen, who ate the land and the sun; he was the beginning and the end of Alata, the blessed land."

"How do you know all this?" said Murchison, turning to him. "From books?"

"No," replied Keradoc. "From the dead, who speak to me and tell me of it." A smile came to his keen, alert features in their blowing white frame. "An old man's fancies, my friends! No harm done; I have studied traditions and legends and occult things—"

"Well, now, be explicit," Murchison broke in, almost rudely. "Do you go in for occult stuff—ghosts and spirits and so forth?"

"Yes and no," Keradoc replied. "At times I have such fancies; this whole region is under the spell of the occult, you know. I have a pupil now, staying in the hamlet below because she is a woman, who studies such matters with me. But ghosts? No, of course not."

"Okay, then," said Murch, relieved. "I don't want to monkey with such things, that's all. Don't believe in 'em anyhow." He spoke in English, but Keradoc understood and smiled thinly. "What's that swastika," he went on, "carved into your house? A relic of the Nazis?"

Keradoc chuckled as he looked at us. "No, my friend. I'll explain it to you—shall we say, tomorrow? We must go to dinner now, and afterward I must go to my pupil, but tomorrow I am free. And we have treasure to discuss, over our dinner,"

True enough. We went in to dinner. I do not like fish, except scrod and Boston chowder, but this was something to remember; it was cooked by people whose folks had cooked fish for generations, and it was better than a New England shore dinner, even. Over the meal, Keradoc spoke of our errand here. He was very matter-of-fact about it.

"One of my ancestors was a freebooter, like everyone else around here. He brought home a rich haul from one cruise, and buried it, to avoid giving up the King's share. He was killed shortly afterward, and had only time to tell his son where it was buried, when he died. It is in a cave down there by the water, not far from here."

"So?" I said skeptically. "Why wasn't it dug up?"

"Many tried; it could never be found," Keradoc said simply. "The cave is ancient. Ankou, or death, lives there according to local belief; it is a strange place, geologically. Not natural but

"I promised to explain this," Keradoc said. "It
is called the Vajra. *Together with the cross and*

swastika, it is one of the earliest religious symbols."

artificial, made by the same forgotten race who raised these granite monoliths you see all over our country—the prehistoric people. Oh, perhaps nature had something to do with the origin; no one has been sure."

I frowned. "Does it have a rock bottom?"

"Stone and earth. The strata are not horizontal but vertical. They were leveled off in ancient days, making ridges of stone with earth between. The covering, the roof, was artificial. It is hard to picture," he added apologetically. "You'll see it in the morning. None of our people dares to go near it, these days. Perhaps the Druids buried their dead in it, before the Romans came. Voices have hinted at this to me."

Him and his voices! "More of your occult second sight, eh?" said Murchison.

"I am sorry; I cannot explain," Keradoc said gently. "I am not an occultist, if that is what you mean, one who has to do with the other world—ah, medium is the word! I am no such thing. People of education and culture seldom are; these things are reserved for ignorant, earthy people strong in brute vitality. Why? No one knows, but so it is."

Dinner was over. He put on a wide Breton hat, hooked a cloak about his tall spindly frame—he was even skinnier than Murchison, who is a human bean-pole—and after lighting a lamp and apologizing to us, went off to visit with his pupil.

AFTER FINDING some shells to serve as ash-trays, we lit up, and looked at one another.

"You do not like it, this place?" Gondy asked us.

"I do not," said Murchison with emphasis. "The old boy's all right, but he's goofy. So is everything about the place. This poppycock about Ankou, or death, for one thing—"

"Wait," I said, trying to be practical about it all. "Fishermen like these who live with the sea and get their living by the sea, are always close to death. It's natural for them to personify death, to be superstitious about it; quite a common thing, in fact, especially if they're half pagan."

"You don't fall for this occult stuff, Bill?" snapped Murchison bitterly.

"No, but a lot of it is far from absurd," I retorted. "It's true that all the old coast-line of Brittany and Normandy has sunk under the sea in ancient times. People who live here have inherited all sorts of wild legends and believe 'em. Now, what if this place *is* cockeyed and gives you a shiver and isn't a bit promising? So much the more reason for us to conquer our feelings. What would life be without obstacles? We don't like 'em, so we've got to fight 'em down. We're not quitters. We don't grow by going somewhere else whenever the trail gets bad. If buried gold was easy to find, others would have it already. There are problems to solve—"

"All right, all right, scratch the sermon, will you?" growled Murchison. "But the place gives me the creeps just the same."

"Carson's right," said Gondy quietly, "Me, I do not like the setup here, now that we are here; but do we quit for that reason? We're not children, *mes amis*. The odd thing is that Keradoc, with his wide hat and white hair and thin body, is the image of Ankou or death as these Bretons personify it. I remember, now, hearing stories in my youth."

"Vote on it," I said. "If two want to clear out, we'll go. I vote to stay."

"I'm no more a quitter than you are," snapped Murchison. "So it's settled."

We saw no more of Keradoc that night. We were tired, and we turned in early, before our host returned. I had bad dreams, but said nothing about it in the morning.

Sunlight and sea and brisk salt air made the world look different. With morning, we were ashamed of our childishness. We had brought our own coffee along, being in France, and Gondy taught the wrinkled old hags in the kitchen how to make it, so everything was cheerful when we started out with Keradoc after breakfast to visit the cave.

It was not far—perhaps three hundred yards up the rocky

*I heard it again. "Bill! Hurry up, Bill!" It was
Murchison's voice. We all heard it but could see
nothing of him. I went for the pool in a hurry.*

shore from the hamlet, and a path went there, under the cliffs, which were broken and heavily weathered. We needed no guide; there was the thing above high watermark, secure from the highest seas. It looked something like an open-ended cradle, over which enormous slabs of granite bad been tipped to make a rough roof. The floor of the cave was twenty feet across—I paced it—and went straight back for a hundred feet or a little over.

It was not a very level floor. The strata or ridges were irregular, the layers of earth between them were wide and thin by turns, sand was drifted everywhere; it looked hopeless to think of working here with the Baby, and to search those endless seams of earth by hand was a job for fools. It would have required an army, and it was easy to see why the treasure had never been located.

We sat down there and then with old Keradoc and explained the difficulties. Our detector, which was made of a magnesium alloy and very light, was mounted in a wicker baby-buggy for easier manipulation. It could be pushed around here all right. But the supersonic rays or waves, which would reflect back from any buried substance and indicate its position, would get all balled up with the rock strata. To me it looked quite hopeless and I said so, but Murchison, who had taken my sermon of the previous night to heart, turned stubborn.

"Hold on, now," he barked. "We've made those waves diverge, in order to cover more ground as we go along; so we can narrow them down again, can't we?"

"Yes," I agreed. He nodded triumphantly.

"Okay. Then suppose we all work at it. One pushes the Baby. The other two, with shovels, locate the widest seams of earth and mark them by stretching cord. If anything worth while was buried here, it was stowed away in the widest and deepest seams, you bet! We can work the Baby between the ridges, savvy?"

"Might work," I admitted. "But I doubt it."

"Well, I'm not looking over the place and then walking away without a try—"

Gondy chuckled at me, and I had to admit that Murchison had me there. We would try it, at least. But we had to get cord and tools, and fetch down the Baby. There was no danger of any local inhabitants bothering us or even entering the cave; we could safely leave our machine here over night, said Keradoc.

TO GET ready took us most of the morning. After lunch we came back to the cave and started to work, with Keradoc, looking like an old magician's ghost, watching us with vivid interest. We lined up a couple of wide earth-seams and found they ran to a depth of thirty feet, which was surprising. Luckily, we could limit the force and penetration of the radionic waves, so when we had them set for a maximum depth of fifteen feet, the Baby would work.

It was damned discouraging labor: the rock everywhere interfered, to keep within the seam of earth was difficult, and the Baby was buzzing away and reporting on rock below half the time. Yet we found that it could actually be accomplished, after a fashion. So open was the cave, with the sky showing through the crevices between the rocks above, that there was no sense of being shut in.

After an hour of it I took a breather and walked outside with Keradoc, who smoked a vile old clay pipe. We stood looking along the shore; it was savage naked rocks, without a trace of sand-beach. We sat down and chatted, out of the wind, and I caught sight of a figure at some distance—a woman's figure and an interesting one. Keradoc smiled.

"That is my pupil," he said. "She is a great lady from Paris, and young and beautiful; but because of the war, like so many others, her life has been saddened and wrecked, and she has turned to occult studies and such things. I asked her to meet you gentlemen, but she refused. She wishes to be alone and solitary. She even wears immense black sun-glasses, as tourists do."

"Gondy might charm her out of her sorrow," I said. "He's quite a lady-killer."

"He is a splendid gentleman," said old Keradoc. "No, you must not interfere with my pupil. We are doing serious work; I do not wish her disturbed."

"Magic?" I suggested. He gave me a smile.

"No, my friend; enlightenment, understanding. We shall write together a book on the Breton legends, with explanations of them, which has never been done."

"I get it. She's one of these cultists, eh? Well, you're more than welcome," I said.

None the less, I still liked the old boy. He was jam-packed with curious knowledge of all kinds—useless, of course. About prehistoric Europe and the round-headed people and the long-headed tribes, or something of the sort. He could reel off Greek and Latin by the yard, but did not know how deep the reefs lay out in the bay before his eyes. He could tell with horrible detail how the Druidic sacrifices were performed, yet would not hurt a fly; he was a tender soul, in spite of his hawk-face and hypnotic black eyes. But he did have some very odd beliefs, and was superstitious to the backbone.

We put in a good afternoon's work and found that with infinite patience we could get ahead with the Baby. We left the machine in the cave for the night, though I carefully removed the tubes; these, with the spares, I kept under my bed, for they were the essential heart of the gadget and were of our own invention.

Keradoc's mysterious pupil came to the house that evening. He let her in and took her straight into his own study. Murchison sniffed perfume, but we saw only her tightly wrapped turban and tweed coat and the cheaters that hid her face. The house was never locked, it seemed, and she or anyone could come or go at any hour, and did.

I doubt whether any of us took much stock in the treasure story, but next morning as we worked toward the back of the cave the Baby buzzed and indicated iron at six feet down. We got Keradoc; he stood, trembly and shaky, while we explained.

I was astonished by his emotion; he was no stone-face after all!
Well, to be brief, we dug up a small iron chest that contained
badly molded clothes, a spyglass, a bundle of French Revolu-
tionary assignats, and half a dozen English sovereigns. Nothing
else. Nothing to tell its history.

This was something like; it proved that the Baby was doing
all right. Having been digging hard, I knocked off for a smoke,
went outside, and found old Keradoc standing there looking at
the sea, with tears on his cheeks. He beamed at me.

"Tears of joy, my friend," he said. "Success will mean so much
to me! Now I must see the people yonder,"—he nodded at the
hamlet,—"and get them to take me to Penmarch this afternoon,
on errands. I'll be back tomorrow."

"One of us can take you in the Fiat," I said. "It'll save no end
of time."

He assented gladly. After lunch Gondy set off with him in
the car. Murchison and I kept going with the work, encouraged
by our morning's luck; but we found nothing more. Keradoc
had taken the sovereigns, which meant a small fortune on the
black-money market, but we made no objections.

That afternoon the wind had fallen; evening came on sultry,
with thunderheads in the south and heat-lightning flickering
over the horizon. Murchison and I had a dip and turned in
early. Later, I was wakened by a choking cry from his room. I
went in on the jump. A flash of lightning showed him lying
naked on his bed.

"What's wrong, Murch?"

"Hey, were you in here just now?"

"No, you woke me up."

"Well, somebody's prowling around here! I was having the
damnedest dreams, and came wide awake to find a hand touching me—fact!"

"You're nuts," I said. "Drank too much cognac after supper."

I WENT back to bed, but could not get to sleep for a long

time. I lay tossing and finally dozed off—and all of a sudden came wide awake. Someone or something was leaning over me and fumbling under my pillow. I reached out, grabbed a bare arm, felt a naked body—a woman's body—and then it was gone. Lightning flared across the sky, and showed the room empty. An odor lingered, to prove it was no hallucination.

Next morning at breakfast I told Murch about it. He gave me a queer look.

"I smelled her too, Bill. You know, these French dames do seldom wash! Maybe it was the cook, maybe some fisherman's wife—"

Nix, I told him. These Bretons wear enough clothes to outfit an army; even the men, in their *bragou-braz* or baggy breeches, are swathed and rolled in clothes galore. Naked females just ain't, in this region. We argued pro and con, and finally went to work. We entered the cave and Murchison halted, pointing to the Baby.

"Look! That's not the way I left it, Bill! I had just finished going over that wide seam of earth. Now it's clear across the ridge of stone, in the next seam!"

The explanation flashed on me. Somebody had been at the Baby, sure, and that same somebody had been in our rooms, looking for—what? The tubes, of course! Without tubes it would not work.

"If you ask me, it's the Paris dame, old Keradoc's pupil," said Murchison. "I'll fetch a blanket down here and keep watch tonight."

"You're not to be trusted," I told him, "with any gal in that kind of costume!"

We indulged in the usual joshing. Of course, in the light of retrospect, it would seem that we should have guessed the truth instantly, yet it occurred to neither of us. So long a time had elapsed since danger had crossed our path, that we did not recognize it.

LATE IN the morning our absent ones returned. Keradoc

came in, looking very happy, heard we had discovered nothing
new, and went off; he was giving his pupil a lesson right now,
also bringing her some mail. Rather deftly, I thought, I got him
to produce her mail. It was addressed to Madame St. Escoffier.

"I could have told you her name, if you had asked," he said
to me, and went out with a chuckle.

Gondy showed up, breathless and bubbling with news.

"Well! I've discovered everything about Keradoc," he announced. "Who'd have guessed? You know why the money
means so much to him, why he's giving this woman lessons,
why he'd sell his soul to the devil if he could get money for it?"

Naturally, we did not; but Gondy had uncovered the secret:
Keradoc, in World War I, had lost two sons. Both were aboard
a troopship that was torpedoed after leaving Brest, and went
down in these very waters, practically before his eyes. Since
then, he had devoted himself to the support of two homes for
children whose fathers had been lost at sea, one at Penmarch,
the other up the coast at Audierne. Clients never lacked in these
parts, but money did.

The Nazi occupation had left both homes on the rocks, and
crowded with kids. Keradoc kept them going. He had sold
everything of value he owned, had borrowed heavily when his
farms were gone, and had just raised a loan on this home of his.
Every franc he could get, went into the two homes; a memo-
rial to his two sons, I gathered.

This, of course, made us view the old boy in a different light—
also his superstitions. With his two sons lost in the waters out
yonder, it was no wonder that he went in for legends and more
or less occult stuff, and believed the local yarns. We could forgive
him practically anything, after learning this.

MURCHISON AND I were slow to tell Gondy about
our night's adventure. It looked silly in the sunlight—a screw-
ball story, sure enough. However, we did tell him as we went
to a late luncheon. It made him look grave, but we had no
chance to discuss it since we wanted to keep it from Keradoc

for the present. The old chap had finished his lesson and we all made the most of a lobster banquet that was nothing short of divine. Then Keradoc beckoned us into the big room, and pointed to the swastika over the fireplace.

"I promised to explain this to you," he said, getting some of his relics together. "First, look at this. It is called the *Vajra*, and has been used from the earliest ages in Hindu and pre-Hindu worship. Together with the cross and the swastika, it is one of the earliest religious symbols we have. It represents the thunderbolts of Indra."

He handed us a heavy bronze object, five-pointed, explaining that it represented five darts or spears, the central one protruding slightly. He spoke of the earliest caveman, crouching in his shelter as the lightning struck—thunderbolts hurled by the god Indra. Hence this symbol. I mentioned that the swastika was usually thought to be an emblem of sun- or fire-worship and he shook his head.

"No. Now watch." Picking up the Vajra, he brought down the points on a sheet of paper. "Here we have five points," he said, and caught up a pencil. "Connect these points with lines and what have we? Why, a cross! Put a tag to the right at the end of each line, and there is your swastika; turn the tag to the left, and you have the swastika reversed—or one capital Z laid across another. The Z has always, to primitive artists and others, represented the jagged flash of lightning; in ancient China, even, the name of the swastika was *lei wen*, or thunder-scroll. You see?"

"No," said Murchison. "What do we see?"

Keradoc turned with a smile. "Why, that the swastika, from earliest times, is simply a protective charm against being struck by lightning!"

"It didn't help the Nazis against the U.S.A. kind of lightning," I commented, and there was a general laugh.

Keradoc, still babbling away about primitive symbols, went out with us to the cave, for his absorption in the work was complete. We were working at the back of the cave; the seams of earth there were much wider, and it was also the likeliest place for any treasure to have been buried. Gondy went in with him. I paused outside with Murchison, watching a couple of red-sailed fishing-boats far out at sea.

Suddenly Murchison uttered an exclamation.

"Eh? What is it?" I demanded. He gave me an odd impish look.

"Go along, Bill. I'm going to do a bit of first-hand investigating—I'll be along pretty soon."

With this, he started down toward the shore. No one was in sight; I could not savvy his abrupt departure, but he must have seen something or someone. He was heading for a pool among the rocks where we had taken a dip the day before, off to the right, so I concluded that he was on the same errand now. It was a warm afternoon. With a shrug, I went on into the cave.

For perhaps an hour we inched the Baby along the seams, finding nothing at all. Then Gondy asked where Murch was. I told him Murch had apparently seen something on the shore, but was probably taking a dip.

"He should not have done that!" exclaimed Keradoc sharply. "There is always danger among the rocks—one should never go bathing alone! Come, we'd better go look for him."

We refused to share his worry; but he insisted, so we bore him company. There was no sign of Murchison anywhere, and we started down for the shore rocks. It was along there, I recollected, that Keradoc and I, a couple of days previously, had seen the figure of his pupil, Mme. St. Escoffier, walking. I wondered whether Murch might have caught sight of her now—anything was possible with that guy.

The shore was empty, when we reached it; nowhere within sight was anything. We went toward the pool. I halted abruptly.

"What's that? Listen!"

I heard it again. "Bill! Hurry up, Bill!" It was Murchison's voice. We all heard it but could see nothing of him. His voice, but very faint and weak; it did not come again.

I went for the pool in a hurry—and then, when I was right in the water, caught sight of him lying almost under me, floating against the rock. He must have been clinging there; later we found his fingers badly cut up. Now he was face down, and the back of his head was a red mass.

For once, size told. Frantically, I got him out, and Gondy helped get him up above. He was unconscious, and very nearly drowned, but old Keradoc took charge like a good one and emptied his lungs, then knelt above him and pumped. Color came back into his face; he coughed and breathed, but remained senseless. The back of his head was almost bashed in.

"He fell, struck his head, was knocked into the water, and would have drowned there had the tide taken him out. Luckily, it's coming in," said Keradoc. "Such accidents are frequent when people clamber alone on these cliffs. Can you carry him?"

Gondy and I could manage him easily. We got him up to the house and Keradoc bandaged his head; it was badly gashed. Either he had hit a rock or a rock had hit him. We put him to bed; the hurt was bad, but nothing to cause anxiety. We hung around, hoping he would wake up and tell us what had happened, but he did not; he went off into a deep sleep.

ALL THIS had taken time; the afternoon was past, so we decided to resume the job with morning. We were talking over a drink with Keradoc, when Gondy asked abruptly:

"This pupil of yours, monsieur, this Madame St. Escoffier—she is a blonde?"

Keradoc's black eyes twinkled at him. "Not at all, my dear fellow. She has blue-black raven hair and brows. Did you find a golden hair in the water?"

Gondy relaxed. "No. I was thinking of my—my sister-in-law, Félice de Gondy. Just a passing fear—"

What with the drink and all, we broke down and told Keradoc about that gal of the tight little mouth—how she had caused her husband's death, had tried more than once to kill us, had actually gotten away with our first model of the Baby only to find it quite useless, and how she had followed us in vicious hatred and more vicious greed.

I told him about the experience Murchison and I had enjoyed during the night, and it was evident that he did not believe a word of it. He puffed away at his pipe and fingered a tiny "magic bag" sewed to his coat, in Breton fashion—a charm against witches.

"Perhaps it was the Druid priestess who comes from the Ile de Sein of nights," he said seriously. "Evidently it was not your Félice, or she would have killed you."

"Unless she was looking for something—" I began, then broke off at a glance from Gondy.

Later, when we were alone, Gondy scowled at me.

"I got a bad turn, thinking Félice might be around here," he said. "She knows how to work the machine; she might have been looking for the tubes, last night. And the way I heard of this treasure—the clipping that came in the mail! A trap set for us, eh?"

"Far-fetched but possible," I replied. "However, Keradoc's pupil is a brunette, so she's not Félice."

"Did you bring the tubes from the Baby?" he asked suddenly.

I had not; the affair of Murchison had made me forget it.

"Doesn't matter. I'm going to take blankets and sleep down there tonight," I told him. "And a flashlight. Ghosts don't get along with flashlights, by report."

Dinner passed, and Murchison was still sound asleep.

Later, Gondy went down to the cave with me. I had found a spot against one wall, halfway down to where the Baby stood. One of the rock strips stuck up, with a three-foot seam of sand between it and the wall, and I stretched my blankets there. With the night air sweeping in, it was a cool and delicious spot.

"I'm uneasy," Gondy said. "Félice knows about the Baby, and

can work it. Her prime object is money—she'd sooner have some treasure we dug up than anything else, but in default of that, she'd damned well like to kill us, as we know to our cost. So far as my family is aware, she has disappeared completely."

"Leave her there, then," I told him. "Don't get to thinking about her or she might show up. You know how it is—if you're worried about a disease, you're apt to get it, and so on."

He laughed and said he guessed she would not show up here at any rate, and presently took his departure. I sat up for a long while smoking, watching the stars and sea, then turned in, with a string running from one wheel of the Baby's carriage to my finger. I was asleep before I knew it.

THE STRING tugging at my finger woke me up. It tugged harder, and broke.

My first feeling was of panic; a ghostly terror shot through me as I saw someone in white moving about—the woman from the sea whom Keradoc had mentioned! Then, of course, I knew better. There was a dim light; it came from a lantern set on the floor. I looked at the white figure again—it had vanished. My first panic returned, and I lay there frozen and not daring to breathe.

Until I heard the faint whirring hum of the Baby at work. No ghost, then! I took another and steadier look. The figure was there, all right; it was shrouded from neck to heels in a big black cloak or coat, and when this fell aside it showed white. A woman in white underthings!

She had come in with the lantern, whose dim light had not disclosed me at the side. She was pushing the carriage along the seam of earth we had marked with a cord. I sat up; try as I might, I could not see her face. The tide, crashing surf on the shore below, filled the cave with noise, but I could hear the whirr of the machine steadily going. The woman was at the rear of the cave, the lantern was between us. I had her trapped—maybe!

So this was our nocturnal visitant, and I had mistaken her

hot-weather attire for nudity, a pardonable error for a bachelor to make.

I sat, uncertain what to do. After all, this unknown woman had done us no harm—but how had she known how to operate the Baby? Félice, undoubtedly, must have sent her here, I thought—like a fool. Well, give her a scare, chase her out and be rid of her! I got out my flashlight with one hand, with the other reached for my shoe.

And just then the detector's buzzer started to sound, and the machine went dead. A tube had blown. My heart leaped; I knew this was apt to happen if something underground were encountered. The woman did not know it; a gasp, then an exclamation of dismay broke from her. No better time—I shied the shoe straight at the lantern.

It struck squarely, shattered it, knocked it over.

She screamed slightly; then the flashlight beam caught her and dazzled her. She pulled the cloak together. Long black hair fell down about her face. She knew she was caught and put her hands up to shield her eyes from the blinding ray.

"Come here," I ordered, and she approached. "Do you speak English?"

"Yes," she faltered. "A little. Not much."

"Well, sit down, Madame St. Escoffier, and let's talk it over. I suppose Félice de Gondy sent you here?"

A moan escaped her. She swayed, put out a hand to the wall for support, then sank down close to me.

"Yes, yes, I admit it," she said, speaking with a thick accent. "Please—that light! My eyes are very weak; it blinds me. Put it out. I will tell everything."

Tears were in her voice. I switched off the light. The oil from the lantern had caught fire and burned with a bluish, flickering flare, enough to see by dimly.

"I suppose she told you how to work the machine?"

"Yes. I meant no harm, monsieur! It was to find the treasure—"

"Where's Félice now?"

"In Penmarch. She was to come here tomorrow," she answered. Suddenly a sob burst from her. She leaned forward, caught my hand convulsively, kissed it. "Please, please!" she sobbed gaspingly. "You will not be harsh, you will be kind, forgive? Americans are kind—"

What I have to tell is humiliating enough without evading the truth. I have noticed that all explorers and travelers are splendid he-men who never, never fall for any temptations offered by beautiful damsels. Whenever I hear that kind of yarn I have my doubts, and I bet you do too.

A breath of perfume reached me—pleasant surprise! She was close; she was warm; she was young and beautiful—according to Keradoc—and she had suffered greatly. Also, she was holding my hand. I was feeling rather good over having trapped her, and I had no intention whatever of repulsing any temptations that might arise, if you want the truth.

"Cheer up, baby," I said comfortingly. "It's true that you've done nobody any harm, but you're going to answer a few questions just the same."

"Anything you want, monsieur," she replied meekly, "I will tell you."

"Hold up your face and shut your eyes. I want to switch on the light and see what you look like without those cheaters you were—"

I was still speaking, when I heard something—a clop and clatter of boots outside the cave.

Then came Gondy's voice:

"Bill! Hey, Bill, are you there? Wake up! I've got news— Murch has told me—"

The woman beside me caught her breath, moved, twisted, about; something smashed me between the eyes and knocked my head back against the wall, and I went out in a shower of sparks and stars.

I WAS out, probably, only a few minutes. Wakening came, with a badly throbbing head, to find the cave full of light from a flashlight that was switched on in a steady beam. My hands were tied in front of me, and securely tied; they hurt.

Also, my misery had company. Two persons were working at the Baby, and the buzzing whirr told me the machine was going and had again struck something. Then a voice spoke.

"Thank you, monsieur. Now sit down with your friend."

Gondy stumbled over toward me and sat down, cursing vividly under his breath. The Baby was switched off and the lady approached. She held a large and efficient-looking pistol, which we knew that she could use very handily.

"Awake?" said Gondy to me.

"Yes, dammit," I replied. "How did you start the gadget?"

"You had a couple of spare tubes packed in, remember. No use refusing."

The woman laughed. "None whatever, my friends. So the good M. Murchison did not drown after all?"

"Not your fault, Félice," snapped Gondy. "He told me how you hit him with a rock and left him to perish."

"You Americans are hard-headed," she commented, with a trill of mirth.

Félice! In this one word, Gondy had told me everything. This woman, whom I had taken for an accomplice, was Félice herself! Chagrin, shame, humiliation, beat upon me like waves as I sat there and listened to her silvery laughter. The laugh vanished in a whiplike word.

"*Allos, mes enfants,* get up!" she snapped. "Both of you—up! I have no desire to kill you—I prefer to profit. But I'll do so at the first excuse, as you well know. Take the spades and dig. Set your friend free, my dear Gondy. Put his mighty strength to better use than holding a lady's hand in the dark."

Mockery, cruel mockery—she had the whip-hand and knew it. She poured it on thick, told us to shout all we liked, no one could hear; threatened to shoot Gondy through the foot if we balked, swore to do us no harm if we dug up the treasure for her.

Because we knew full well her vicious nature, because we knew her threats were not idle, we did it. Two of us, enslaved by this one devil of a woman! The dials on the Baby indicated metal of some kind at eight feet down. We took the pick and spades and fell to work, I am ashamed to say.

She spared us nothing; she was in high fettle, and taunted us, hatred in her voice. She told how she had set the trap for Gondy with that clipping, how she had wormed herself into Keradoc's graces as a pupil of the mysteries, paying him high prices for lessons, how she had dyed her blaze of golden hair a deep black. While we labored away, she amused herself and vented her real hatred of us.

Murchison had glimpsed her on the shore that afternoon, had caught up with her, and had recognized her as they talked; so she had done for him on the spot, or thought she had. She made no secret of it. Well, I suppose she had something to be proud of, after all. She had certainly euchred the three of us, she had made fools of us most efficiently. She had intended to find the treasure herself by working the machine of nights, but without the tubes could not do so—until tonight. And then, at the very first effort, she had chanced on the treasure!

Whether treasure or not, she had certainly found something, and we could not deny it. The farther down we dug the hole, of course, the more completely we were at her mercy. When we were at the bottom of that narrow excavated seam, she needed only a club to keep us in order, for we were helpless.

"How the devil do you expect to get away with the loot?" I growled at her. She gave another of her silvery trills of mirth.

"Oh, my poor dumb American! In your own car, of course. M. de Gondy has the keys, no?"

He did, for a fact.

EIGHT FEET down we struck something metallic, and then slaved away at the damned thing getting it freed and up to the cave floor. It proved to be a massive iron chest, not large but heavy as lead. Félice, keeping at a safe distance from us, told us to smash it open with the pick.

We did so. The flashlight began to dim out; the batteries were exhausted. But Gondy had brought one with him, and she took it and held the beam on the smashed chest as it disgorged loot over the cave floor. It was like a fantastic dream. Loot in money, in gold coin, in cups and jewels and rotted fabrics; and now it was hers, not ours.

She stepped back to the rear of the cave, picked up a bundle, removed her cloak, and buttoned a dress around her. Then, pistol in hand, she returned to us and threw down the cloak.

"Wrap it all in that," she said. "And, if you please, the car keys!"

Gondy swore, and threw the keys at her; she caught them deftly. I raked the stuff all into the cloak and made a bundle— stout, heavy, too heavy for her, I thought. I should have known that this tigress could handle anything, heavy or not.

"Into the hole, now—quickly!" She jerked the pistol at me. "See if there is not something more. Move!"

I obeyed. She ordered Gondy to join me—and when he hesitated, slapped him across the face with the pistol, practically knocking him down on top of me, raging and cursing. Then she stood on the brink, and threw the dazzling beam down at us, and laughed.

"You fools! You two silly fools!" she taunted us. "Do you think I'd go away and leave this precious machine, which can find all the lost gold on earth? But I shall leave you, my friends—leave you here in the cave of Ankou, of death! In the grave you so obligingly have dug for yourselves, to tell no tales—"

Sweating and filthy, we looked up. She meant her words. The flashlight beam touched her pistol hand; I could see her reach up and throw off the safety catch. But, as she did so, there came a scrape and thud of hob-nailed boots, and a voice.

"Not yet, vile woman! It is for you that Ankou has come—for you! I have heard everything—"

A cry slipped from her. She twisted around. It was the voice of Keradoc. I leaped and tried to pull myself up from the hole, and had a glimpse of him as the light swept around and struck his tall figure with the flying white hair. He was coming straight for her. She took a step backward, another—

I could not get out of the hole, but was at the edge. The second step brought her feet within my reach. I lunged forward and caught her ankle, just as she fired. A wild scream burst from her. With her weight as leverage, I was able to get up and over the edge. She tottered and fell. Keradoc was upon her at the same instant. Again she fired, and the blast of flame seared my cheek. The light had fallen; everything was as black as a dungeon.

For a moment there was a furious, deadly scramble. I was underneath, and tried to get her by the throat. Instead, I got her pistol arm and twisted savagely as I lay. She screamed again, and the pistol came away in my hand. Keradoc was thrashing about and cursing, and his boot must have hit my sore head. It knocked me clear of the mêlée.

As I scrambled about, I came upon the fallen flashlight, came to my feet, and turned on the beam. It struck the staring features of Gondy, emerging from the hole. It touched old Keradoc, lying at one side and moving feebly—but unluckily I did not see the blood. I was looking for Félice, and I found her.

She was halfway to the cave entrance, stooped, dragging behind her the bundle in the cloak, which she could not lift. I shouted, started after her—and she ran for it, dropping the bundle. Not all of it. A stream of yellow objects trailed from her as she fled—she must have filled her bosom with the treasure, scooping it out of the bundle. I should have shot her and could have done it—but after all, she was a woman. I fired one shot, purposely wild; the bullet struck the floor and ricocheting, went screaming out to sea.

Then she was gone, and I let her go. Gondy's voice was

ripping at me in fear and horror, and I caught his words and turned.

As the light struck back at them, I saw that Keradoc had come to one knee and was holding his side. She had shot him in her first blind rage and panic.

I gave Gondy a hand up, and we both rushed to Keradoc's side and laid bare the wound. The bullet had ripped his skinny old chest; we both thought him dead. Gondy gave me a savage snarl.

"Get her, get her! Leave the light—I'll take care of him! Get her—'"

Barefoot as I was, or rather without shoes, I dropped the flashlight and sprinted. I came out into the cool, starry night, cursing my squeamishness in not shooting her when I had the chance. I heard the cough of an engine, turned, and went charging up the path for the house. The car-keys—the car!

No qualms this time. I meant to get her without pity—and when I reached the turn below the house, saw the headlights of the car. I fired, fired again; the pistol was empty but the hammer clicked on until I threw the useless thing away. The headlights moved, swept off in an arc, and were gone.

She had escaped....

Those shots out in the open aroused everyone, both in the house and in the hamlet down below. Gondy and I carried Keradoc outside the cave and waited there; others came and lifted him on up to the house. Murchison showed up, bandaged and trousered, and everyone crowded about the old man in the big central room of the house.

Keradoc was not dead. The bullet had struck across his chest, breaking a couple of ribs as it went; at his age, the hurt was not trivial, but it was far from mortal.

In the morning we gathered at his bedside, heaping over his woven Breton coverlet the gold coin, the rings and ancient jewelry and a couple of silver cups we had retrieved from the cave. How much Félice had got away with, we could not tell.

But there was plenty here—plenty for everyone, orphanages and all. Keradoc clasped our hands and tears came on his cheeks; he was very happy.

So, I might add, were we.

NEXT DAY came word that the Fiat had been found near Penmarch, abandoned. We went into town to claim it, Gondy and I, and when we saw it we looked at one another silently. On the seat was a stain of blood. My bullets had not gone altogether astray—and I had no remorse about being glad, either. Nothing whatever had been found of Félice; she got clear away. The devil looks after his own, as Keradoc said.

"You'd better glance at this letter," Gondy told me, as we were driving back to the house, and gave me a letter he had picked up at Penmarch. "Sounds interesting, this yarn about the British nobleman and the farmer's daughter."

"Oh!" I said. "Was he a traveling salesman?"

"No," replied Gondy innocently. "A paratrooper—a cross-eyed paratrooper. You'd better read it."

I did, and whistled softly; I knew where we were going next, you bet!

VII

THE PLEDGE OF HONOR

*Exploring France for buried treasure with
a mine detector, a former American officer
stumbles into startling situations.*

W E W E R E heading north from Cabourg; along the coast ahead lay little Norman towns—Villers, Houlgate, Deauville and so forth—built up with villas in between, the *plages* still studded with anti-invasion blocks and wrecks of many a landing-craft and tank, though the war was long over.

"It was here, my good Murchison, that our mine-detectors helped win the war," I said.

"Right, my good Carson, right," he assented, barely avoiding a smash with a Caen bus, and keeping our rattly old Fiat to the road. "We provide the genius to save the Army; the generals get the glory; and the dogfaces never give us a thought. They don't even know that Nazi mines would have blown them all to glory, except for you and me."

"Well, practically so," I agreed. "Where's the place that we pick up Gondy?"

"Use your eyes, blind boy! See those real-estate signs? Dead ahead, they say, lies the beautiful Beaulieu-sur-Mer—probably a lot of jerry-built rat-traps with pottery cats on the roofs and surrounded by brummagem summer villas."

We abused each other and the French landscape impartially, being old friends from boyhood days in Boston, and very happy. We would be still happier when we picked up our pal Gondy—the Vicomte de Gondy—whom we had not seen for a week past.

W A R ' S E N D had found us in England, dodging buzz-bombs and slaving in laboratories to invent mine-detectors that would outwit the newest land mines of the Jerries. We did it, or helped to do it, and wangled a discharge and set out to see Europe and make our fortune. As a means to this end, we took along our cherished invention, the Baby, which had flopped as a mine detector, but whose radionic waves would pick buried treasure out of the ground like nobody's business.

We took in Gondy because we liked him. Also, he was the contact man we needed. He knew Europe like a book, and everyone in it, and was apt at locating lost or buried treasure for us to unearth. What sort of job we had here on the Norman coast we did not yet know; he had gone ahead to make arrange-

ments. Murchison and I did not get along too blissfully with the French lads, to be frank about it.

Beaulieu proved to be a crossroads with a liquor shop, a post office and a summer hotel perched above the beach. We went into the liquor shop and found Gondy; and after a hilarious greeting perched at his table. He had located a bottle of Scotch, and when we had approved his judgment we got down to business.

"A mile from here," he said, "home awaits us. I have rented a summer villa, complete with a *bonne a tout faire,* or maid-of-all-work. Does that please you?"

"Whatever you do suits us," I replied with cautious gal-

lantry. "However, I recall that the lure which brought us here said something about buried treasure."

Gondy waved his hand. "Later, Carson, later! Here we shall repose like the fabled lotus-eaters, knowing no one, with nobody knowing or caring about our business, and nobody to split with if we recover anything."

"Is there anything to recover?" demanded Murchison warily.

"You'll be surprised, *mon ami!* Come, let us be on our way."

We all headed north in the old Fiat. Now, we knew that Gondy had his head in the clouds and might get us into some screwy situation quite innocently; but whatever was done, was done. We could not let him down. He was our kind of guy, and on the level.

Beaulieu was practically nothing except a lot of villas running along the flank of a long hill. The villas lay on the left of the road, their grounds extending to the beach below. On the right were other villas, the hillside running steeply up behind them. Some of the houses were occupied; some had been bombed or burned during the war.

Gondy halted us at an open gate, and we turned down into our new domain, which sloped gently seaward, and we were pleased as Punch with it. The house was small, two-storied, simply furnished and beautifully clean. During the Nazi occupation it had sheltered a Vichy collaborator named Forain, a thorough rascal .who happily had since been shot.

The servant, Yvonne, was dark and clumpy and mustached, with rough, heavy hands and vacant eyes. As Gondy laconically explained, she had been shipped off with a lot of local people as labor slaves by the Nazis, and her mind had been slightly affected by their cruelty. She was just pleasantly amiable and dumb, and saluted us in the startling but unconcerned manner of French peasants seeking to be friendly, when we shook hands.

"I am enchanted, messieurs," she said. "*Je suis vierge encore— c'est très rare,* I assure you, in this district. You will find me very honest."

Murchison swallowed hard. To her, the fact that she was a virgin was merely a good indication of her character, a recommendation to cause some pride. But his expression made me and Gondy chuckle.

The grounds were large, dotted with trees, and completely fenced in by most efficient French fences, a gate in the lower fence giving access directly on the beach. Trees hid the adjoining villas and the road; we were absolutely out of the world here, entirely private. Just below the house, was a rough square of concrete—a gun emplacement installed by the Germans to help fight off invasion.

YVONNE, WHO lived in a dark little room off the kitchen—our rooms were upstairs—had lunch ready for us.

The meal ended, we climbed into bathing-suits and went down to the beach. Thanks to the war, mines, Nazi obstructions and so forth, we had it to ourselves; normally, said Gondy, it would be crowded with tourists in summer. Deauville was not far off, and whenever we wanted a touch of fun, it would not be hard to find. From the beach we could see up along the coast and across the Seine estuary to Le Havre, which was still practically a heap of ruins.

"Before getting to the situation," Gondy began, "I should say that at the Beaulieu hotel an Englishman is stopping who would much like to rent one of our rooms and make this place his headquarters. He would not be here much; he spends most of his time running about the back-country in a vest-pocket Austin car. He's a war veteran, and a trifle balmy."

"Good God, man! Are you starting a lunatic asylum?" exploded Murchison. "First that cook, and now a goofy Britisher!"

There were moments when Gondy could become very French, and this was one of them.

"My country, Murch, has an axiom that all English are mad," he said stiffly. "That does not mean insane, but just a bit off. Let me explain: Lord Arthur Buckleden was in the commandos, later became a paratrooper. He was dropped somewhere around here in advance of D Day—the invasion. He was hurt. A farmer's daughter saved him, took care of him and later brought him to safety. He became—ah—amorous of her, and now is trying to find her again. He inherited enormous wealth; that is, as much wealth as any Englishman has these days."

"What does this Lord Buckledown want with our place?" growled Murchison.

"He is lonely," said Gondy, "and in love, hopeless love."

"The hell with him—"began Murch, then met my eye and sniffed. "Well, we'd better meet him and size him up before we say yes or no. Is he a real lord?"

"Oh, quite!" said Gondy. "I knew him during the war. I was liaison officer with his corps. He did not tell anyone then that he was a lord; Wemyss, was the name he used."

"Weems!" repeated Murchison, sourly wrinkling up his features. "I thought we were done with all those English words they call names. Well, never mind; get along with it. Where does the treasure come in?"

I knew why Buck was in love. She had dignity, pride, tenderness.

Gondy brightened. "Ah! I am coming to that. Well, this collaborator, this Forain who lived in our house, was taken by surprise on D Day, like the Krauts themselves. He had been an art dealer and was a connoisseur. Regard, now! While living here, he made trips to the south of France, everywhere, taking choice pictures."

"Oh!" I said. "Looting museums?"

"No, no; he left that to his Nazi friends. He took only the finest things in private collections, and occasionally from churches—the choicest art of the past few centuries. Nothing large, you comprehend; often the finest in art is in smallest compass, like triptychs or altar-pieces. Nearly all these things were privately owned. If found, they do not have to be handed over to any commission."

"But they belong to somebody, not to us," I objected.

Gondy assented vigorously.

"Just so. A group of dealers in Paris, representing the owners, have already offered three million francs for the recovery of the Forain loot—that is, the new francs, not the old Vichy money! Let us say, in dollars, a hundred thousand—I think we can get them up to that figure. Not bad, eh?"

Not bad, indeed; half of that sum would be very handsome if we earned it. We had already learned that buried treasure, contrary to fallacious popular belief, very seldom runs into any big money. A wrecked vessel with bullion aboard, perhaps might do better. As a rule the results, although eminently satisfactory to us, were intrinsically not large. Yet they were large enough to keep us on Easy Street, always with hopes of striking something big lying just over the horizon. And meantime, the zest of the game was keen.

"All right," Murchison said abruptly. "Where's the stuff hidden?"

Gondy inspected him with half-quizzical amusement.

"Somewhere in our garden, Murch. I doubt whether the machine could react from a mere bunch of canvases; but they'd be well packed. Forain had little warning, no time to get his stuff away, when the American forces broke through at St. Lo, and the German rout began. He did not even get himself away; the partisans caught him and shot him, a couple of days later. It's common local gossip that the stuff was buried here. Germans were all the time digging along this hillside, installing guns and emplacements."

"Surely you have something more definite than that?" I demanded.

"No." He spread out his hands, helplessly. "It should be enough. We need a rest. It is pleasant here. The local people do not guess our objective. I can name you some of the pictures Forain seized; many are famous."

O U R   S E N S E of loyalty kept us silent. Neither Murchison nor I cared for this job. Pictures! We were after cash. And this Lord Buckleden did not attract us; we wanted privacy. The whole set-up was cockeyed, I thought. So we arranged to have His Lordship over for dinner, if possible, and Gondy went to get hold of him.

Murchison and I went into the water. There were signs up forbidding it, and quoting rather hysterically the danger from mines and so forth; this section of the *plage* had not yet been cleared, for lack of manpower. Some of the local pussyfoots got excited, and two police agents came along and whistled. We had a good swim and did not come in until we got ready; but it was no joke when we did come. It was pretty near a riot, because Gondy was not on hand to do his stuff, and Murchison took the stand that if we wanted to get blown up, that was our business and the police be damned.

We ended up down the beach at the *mairie* and paid a twenty-franc fine each—or rather Yvonne, who was doing her marketing at the time, paid for us, and we went home. When Gondy came along with word that Buckl'en, as it was pronounced, would be over for dinner, having just got in from one of his back-country trips, it made a fitting end to a perfectly frabjous day, as we declared bitterly.

And what fools we were! We were having a drink when Buckleden showed up with a bottle of real Scotch and a big package—steaks he had fetched home from a farm inland. He was a rather short but strapping chap with no haw-haw accent—in fact, he had spent some years in Canada; instead of being cross-eyed he just had a cast in one eye; and as long as we did not talk about the war, he had a good grin and knew how to tell a story. He was dark, strong in the face, and a right guy. Inside of twenty minutes he was "Buck" to us all and we were on the best of terms, and he agreed to move over in the morning.

An odd thing took place that same evening: Buck turned to us with a quiet word, as Yvonne was serving coffee in the sitting-room; she seemed to think it should be served in there.

After talking what would have settled half a dozen ordinary mortals, big Michel folded.

"Do you mind if I ask your maid something?"

"Why should we mind? Of course not," said Murchison, who was not very much on the European politeness.

Buck, who spoke fluent French, beckoned Yvonne.

"Will you let me look at that little cross you're wearing, if you please?"

Yvonne's hand went to her throat, where she wore, on a white ribbon, a tiny gold cross. Her dull features remained unchanged. She slipped off the ribbon and handed it to him.

As he looked at the cross, I saw an extraordinary change in his dark features. They became darker, under a rush of blood. His eyes dilated; for an instant I thought he would leap to his feet. Then he relaxed and nodded at the girl.

"Will you take a thousand francs for this little cross? No? Five thousand?"

I thought he had gone mad, sure enough; the thing was not worth a dollar. Then I was astounded when Yvonne refused point-blank. A sullen fear shone in her eyes, and she held out her hand for the thing back. Buck handed it to her.

"Where did you get it?" he asked.

She shook her head. "I don't remember, m'sieur. It brought me safe home out of the hands of the Boches."

She went away, indifferently. Buck looked excited, then repressed his emotions.

"What's that girl's history? Do you chaps know?" he asked.

"She was swept up with a lot of other slave labor from around here, by the Krauts," said Gondy, "and was freed when they went to pieces, and somehow got home. I understand she suffered a good deal and it affected her wits. She came from a farm somewhere near by. I can give you the name, if you care for it."

Buck nodded, and wrote it down. "I thought that I recognized the cross," he said apologetically. "It's like a million others, of course."

We asked no questions, understanding that it probably had some connection with his curious search.

NEXT MORNING he showed up in his tiny Austin, put his stuff in our spare room, chugged off and was gone for two days. That brought us up to Saturday night; and we all went up to Deauville and hit the tables and drank too much, and later were sorry we put in so many dances with the gold-diggers from Paris....

On Sunday morning Buck routed us up early and made us all go to church at Villers. That we did it indicates what we thought of him by this time. And that afternoon, sunning ourselves on the *plage,* we got confidential with him. We told him about the Baby, and he told us about his search. He was not a damned bit sentimental about it, either.

"This lass, Jeanne Duchesne, lived on her father's farm, but she was not the peasant type like your Yvonne," he said. "I've established that she and her father were rounded up with others for a labor battalion by the Nazis close to D Day—this must have been just after she saved my life. No word has come from them; nobody knows what became of them, though others have filtered back home since the war. She may be all right; she may be in some desperate situation and badly needing help. I can't let her down, of course. Sure to strike someone, if I keep at it, who knew her or what became of her. More of the poor devils are coming home all the time."

He did not mention romance; nor, of course, did we. When we told of our business here and explained what the Baby was, he was a bit incredulous at first, then considered us a trifle weak in the head—good fellows and all that, but gently touched. He really took little interest in the whole thing. He was wrapped up in his own affairs, naturally.

Monday morning he got off in the Austin for another trip, somewhere back of the Caen ruins, where he had heard some D.P.'s were getting repatriated. That dark face of his held a grave determination.

Meantime we had not neglected our own affair, though we had not worked very hard at it, either. We pushed the Baby around one part of the garden, and we got results—the kind of results that made us curse our job and think about going in for honest work. We had to do our own digging, remember. We located a handsome big sea mine, unexploded; a packing-case filled with Teller mines, ditto; and on top of these nerve racking experiences, we brought up another packing-case marked "Cognac" and completely filled with a Nazi officer who must have been killed about D Day and buried hastily. After this we seriously considered ditching the job entirely. Instead, we divided up the garden into three parts, each took a part, and worked as we felt like it—each one digging up his own finds. Naturally, nothing was found. I made one strike, which the dials reported as metal of some kind at six feet down. I left it alone and went right on. No more metal, thanks!

Murchison, who had a bad tooth, located a retired English dentist at Cabourg and got it pulled; then domestic trouble arose to conclude an unfruitful week. Yvonne wanted to leave us; why? She liked us; she liked the job; she had no complaints; but people were talking, and her folks were suspicious. The town was full of wild stories about these Americans who had brought a baby to beautiful Beaulieu—someone had seen us pushing a perambulator around.

If we had been keeping the house full of mistresses, nobody would have thought twice about it; but three bachelors and a baby got the French Mme. Grundy well het up! Gondy had to pull his title for all it was worth. Just then Buck showed up, and he had some influence. We got the mayor, two priests, two police agents and the postmaster together and showed them that the Baby was an electrical invention on which we were working; and after pulling a lot of corks, we were declared brave fellows and perfectly harmless, and Yvonne stayed on the job, much to our satisfaction.

BUCK REPORTED no luck on his trip. He kept on trying to make Yvonne talk about her Nazi experiences, but she remained dumb. Then one afternoon he showed up with a litre

*"My children, you must explain all this to
me," the old priest said quietly. "Monsieur,
who are you, if you please?"*

bottle of the cheapest sort of peasant wine, and at sight of it
she cooed with delight. He settled down in the kitchen with
her. Murchison had gone to Cabourg to get his tooth-wound
treated for infection. Gondy was running the Baby in the
garden. I just loafed around and after a while came into the
kitchen.

The bottle was half empty; Yvonne was giggling; Buck was jabbering at her, trying to get a spark of remembrance awake in her addled brain.

"A fine spectacle," I said. "I can imagine Parliament discussing it: A noble lord swigging *vin ordinaire* with a kitchen slavey! Gimme a shot."

He grinned and obeyed. The stuff was like vinegar.

"Carson, I'm positive that little gold cross belonged to Jeanne," he said. "Hers had a scratch where I tried to scratch my initials for her and could not. This one has the same scratch, 'pon my word!"

"More power to you," I said. "Feed her another slug of that poison."

He did so. Yvonne gulped it down, giggled again, and touched the cross at her neck.

"This got me safe home," she said. "Jeanne said it would, and it did."

The words hit Buck like an electric shock. But the glow faded from Yvonne's eyes. She did not even remember what she had just said. Jeanne? Never heard of any Jeanne.

"If we let her ramble under the influence of this rat-poison, we may learn something," I said. "No use trying to make her talk; she just gets confused and scared. You run down to the crossroads and get another bottle of the stuff."

"Then you'll not get any dinner," he said, with a critical glance at Yvonne.

"Get your information, and we'll dine at Deauville and make a night of it, in celebration. You should worry! This skirt is our grief, not yours. Better get two bottles."

He departed at speed in the Austin. I refilled Yvonne's glass.

Gondy came in, calling me. He had found something and could not be sure what it was, and wanted to know. I explained the situation and left him to entertain Yvonne and keep her thirsty.

Out in the garden, I investigated. Sure enough, Gondy had struck something. I studied the dials and gauges which registered the kickback of the radionic waves. We had worked out a regular chart which gave the reactions of various substances, but the present figures did not fit in.

The depth was easy; seven feet. But the substance buried there puzzled me. According to the reaction, it might be either wood or paper. The waves had a weakness in their rebound, suggesting that it lacked solidity. The area of the find, too, was surprising. By careful experiment, I set it down as seven by seven feet square. I came back to the kitchen, just as our friend Lord Arthur Buckleden popped in—not with two more litres of the acidulated red ink, but with three!

"Thought I'd best play it on the safe side," he said.

I discussed the find with Gondy. "As far as I can guess, old pal, a crate of wallboard might be buried there, flat side down."

He looked startled. "Or—canvas?"

I nodded. "Exactly. Or corpses. Or mine-wire or explosives. Or some other product of damned Kraut ingenuity. You go dig it; blessed if I will! I have bad dreams every time I think how we dug up those Teller mines. Consult Murch about it when he comes back; let him diagnose the Baby's reports for himself, and see."

When Murchison got back with the Fiat, however, he was doing no diagnosing or digging either; he was going to need a guardian for a day or two. That jaw of his had become infected, and the dentist had stuffed the wound full of sulfa; he was coming to repeat the operation tomorrow. Poor Murch, who was inclined to be flighty at best, would now be wandering around the empires of the moon sure enough; the only safe place for him while the sulfa worked was in bed. He agreed, dolefully, and Gondy took him off upstairs.

Yvonne was now steadily working her way through the second bottle of painkiller and blissfully enjoying it; in fact, she was prattling away nobly of this and that. Although any Norman peasant can handle enough *vin du pais* for a corporal's squad, she was getting very nicely lit up. Still, we got nowhere. Buck could sling the local patois, and I was trying Army French on her, and the only result was more giggles.

Then Gondy came back, and after listening a moment, brushed us off. He started in with his elegant Touraine French and put on his best *grand seigneur* manner; and Yvonne, her eyes bulging at him, reacted beautifully. At length he touched the cross and drew her attention to it.

"Oh, yes, m'sieur!" she said, with a hiccup. "Jeanne gave it to me when she got off the train. She said it would protect me, and the good God knows it did!"

Buck leaned forward, his eyes eager, but Gondy motioned him back.

"So she got off the train. At Rennes, I suppose?"

"Oh, no, m'sieur! That was at Aulain, after her face was so badly hurt. The Boches let her go. M. le Maire took care of her."

"A mayor? On the train?"

"Now, m'sieur, you make fun of me!" said Yvonne. "The Mayor of Aulain, naturally. *Zut, alors!* She dared to do that and spoil her pretty face, but I did not. What spirit, that Jeanne! And how terrible it was, with all of us crying—"

She began to boo-hoo in sympathy. Buck, his hand shaking, refilled her glass, and her tears were drowned. So, unhappily, was her recollection. We got not another word out of her, though we sat and pumped that arsenical red ink into her until the third bottle was gone and her back teeth must have been afloat. No soap. Finally she got sleepy, and we knew the session was over.

GONDY AND I were now almost as interested in Buck's search as he was himself. After dumping Yvonne on her bed, the three of us took quick counsel.

"Aulain!" exclaimed Buck. "That's the other side of Rennes; I was there last week. A day's drive from here, the roads being what they now are. Well, we've discovered one thing! Jeanne never went to Germany! She got off the train. The mayor of the place took charge of her. But nothing in these parts has been heard of her since; and she was hurt, somehow. Apparently by intention."

His eyes flickered at us, one at me, one at Gondy. His voice died. His thought was only too clear. She was probably not alive now.

"I'll have to clear it up," he muttered. "Now we have a straight clue, at least."

"You're going to Aulain?" I asked.

"Of course."

"Too late in the day to get off now. Would your British hauteur take offense at the idea of a companion?"

Buck started slightly, then grinned.

"Carson, I'd be tickled pink!"

"Fine. That leaves Gondy to look after Yvonne and Murch, and me to cook dinner. How does it stack up with M. le Vicomte?"

"Swell," said Gondy. He wanted to dig up Forain's cache of art, anyhow.

NEXT MORNING Yvonne was again as dumb as ever, and not only was unable to add anything to her story, but recalled none of it. So I crowded into the pint-sized Austin beside Buck, and away we went.

He had only one reference to Yvonne's story, just after we got off.

"You know Bill, Jeanne was a tremendously pretty girl. I suppose you did not miss the implication in Yvonne's words— that she had done something to her face. Probably to save herself from being put into an army brothel by those filthy Huns."

"I got it," I said; and he nodded. That closed the subject for us.

"Y' know, I've never regretted for an instant my commando work," he observed. "The idea that I was able to send some of those damned beasts out of this world has always made me happy—good deed and that sort of thing.... Have you a road map?"

"Hell, no," I said. "Do you need one?"

"Of course not," he said, chuckling. We did not refer to Jeanne again.

Except for the main pipe-lines to Paris, the French roads were very much out of kilter and would be for a long time, since there was little vehicular traffic to demand their repair. Consequently our jaunt across Normandy was not rapid, though Buck drove like a fiend when he could.

We got into Aulain late in the afternoon. It was a small town beside a stream, and carried no scars whatever of the war, though it was on the main railway line. We located the *mairie* and went in to find out who had been mayor about the time of D Day.

It was more of a trick than you would imagine. The Norman in his native habitat is a crabbed soul, and endures foreigners, meaning anyone outside his own district, only for the sake of their money. As for giving them information, that just goes against the grain. However, everyone had heard plenty about displaced persons; and when they learned it was a question of a D. P., we got some grudging replies. The mayor at that period had been an *avocat*, a distinguished gentleman of the village, whom we would now find at home enjoying his old age in leisure.

We located his home, and there located him. Did he remember the girl of whom he had taken charge, when she had been put off a train because of a hurt face? He did not. He did his best to brush us off completely. Threats on Buck's part got us nowhere. It was not until I went into the full story, told how Buck had been a paratrooper and so forth, and pulled all the stops on the romance involved, that the whiskered old rascal thawed a bit and remembered—vaguely.

The young woman, he said, had been treated by a local doctor, and had then been taken in charge by the brothers Dornay. These were descendants of the renowned poet of Rouen, of whom the whole world had heard; they had a farm some kilometers from town, and were substantial citizens. They had given the young woman a refuge at their farm; what had become of her after that, the *avocat* had no idea whatever. Only the brothers Dornay could tell.

By this time it was too late to pursue our search further. We got quarters for the night in the local hotel, and spent the evening making a tour of all the bistros in town. Buck wanted to get a line on the Dornay brothers, and got plenty. They had been leaders of the Resistance movement against the Nazis in this district; both were men over thirty; they lived with their families in a big double farmhouse, and they were good men to let alone.

Of Jeanne Duchesne, and whether she were alive or dead, Buck could learn nothing. He was drawn into a knot with suspense, that evening. In his phlegmatic English way he gave no hint of emotion, but he had the shakes and put away enough cognac to float a ship. I was alarmed for him, but in the morning he showed up clear-headed and cool. We got away in good time, and a little past nine sighted the Dornay farm.

It was a big, substantial place, marked by a rusting Mark IV tank which one of the brothers had himself knocked out during the war, and now placed here for a memento of the past. I took for granted that if Buck found his dame, they would throw their arms around each other and go into a clinch on the spot. That shows how dumb about it I really was.

The house was an old stone one shaped like the letter E, with the usual whopping manure-pile in place of the central bar. This was a Thursday, as it chanced—the weekly holiday in French schools. Quite a number of youngsters were playing around when we came, indicating that the Dornays had sizable families; they vanished, as we climbed out of the Austin, and two men approached us from the house.

The average Norman peasant is apt to be rough and tough, and independent as a hog on ice; obviously these Dornays ran true to form. The larger, who was the older brother Michel, was about my size, six foot two; he was solid and hairy, with huge rounded shoulders telling of tremendous strength, and his whiskers surrounded two vicious little eyes. The younger and smaller, Aristide, had a clean-shaven mug seamed with lines, none of them good ones, and looked like a bundle of steel wire. So he was, too.

They came to a halt, staring at us. Buck addressed them politely.

"We are seeking, messieurs, to speak with the brothers Dornay—"

The big fellow cut in on him, without a smile.

"Yes, we know all about it. You are a mad Englishman. You were a paratrooper. You have been sneaking about this district for weeks past. Well! I am Michel Dornay; this is my brother Aristide. We know how you were questioning people about us in town last night."

Buck was taken aback. "You're well informed, M. Dornay."

"Naturally." Michel scowled. "We do not like Englishmen. What do you want with us?"

"Information in regard to one Jeanne Duchesne."

"I understand that too," growled Michel. "I know of no such person."

"You brothers undertook to give her a refuge," said Buck. "Come, my friends! You did good work during the war; so did I. We're not the kind of men who need to lie and cheat one another. I'd be ashamed to lie to a comrade who helped me fight the Boche. So would you, eh? Let us talk like old soldiers."

It was a good approach, and for a moment I thought it would do the work. Then Aristide snarled something under his breath, and the big fellow drew himself up.

"Comrades? No accursed Englishman is a comrade of mine," he said savagely. "But I am no liar. The young woman you seek wants none of you, so clear out."

"Not on your word for it, my friend," said Buck. "If she says as much, well and good. I don't propose to clear out until I see her, and that's flat."

MICHEL DOUBLED up his fists as though he could use them. This was an extreme gesture—your Frenchman will grab for a knife or pistol and think nothing of it, but any show of fists brings cries of horror from a crowd. I judged it was high time to intervene.

"Pardon me," I cut in. "Being American, not English, I cannot see any great sense in these proceedings, messieurs. My friend owes the lady a debt of gratitude and wishes to pay it. Why should you stand between? What business is it of yours?"

"American? Yes, your tongue proves that," said Michel, turning to me. "Well, it is our business because we are her protectors. She does not wish to see this English milord; therefore it is settled. We have plenty of weapons in the house yonder, if you wish trouble."

"Then, being men of sense," I told him, "suppose you let her tell my friend her wishes. You admit she is here."

"No! We admit nothing," snapped Aristide. "You're on our property. Get off."

Buck laughed, and I knew what that laugh of his meant.

Michel spoke first, however.

"That is the truth," he said. "I am no liar. She is not here."

"I believe you," said Buck. "But you know where she's to be found."

"Certainly," assented the big fellow. "And I shall prevent you from troubling her. It is the truth, likewise, that she does not wish to see you or anyone else from her past life. She has said so."

BUCK WAS sweating, and his eyes were dangerous.

"Very well," I struck in anew. "My friend will write two words or perhaps three on his card, and give it to you. You will show it to Mile. Duchesne. She will write either 'Yes' or 'No' on the card, and we shall be guided accordingly. We can return in a day or two for her answer, since we must push on to Rouen today. Eh?"

Michel's scowl cleared away. "Why not? Admirable! Americans have brains, certainly!"

"Give me the card. She shall have it when she—"

"You can take it to her," intervened Aristide, kicking Michel's ankle.

"Oh, of course!" assented Michel. "I'll take it to her myself."

Buck gave me an angry look, but complied; getting out a card and scribbling a few words, he handed it to Michel, then turned on his heel and went back to the car. I paused to shake hands with the brothers, merely as a gesture.

"Will you kindly direct us how to reach the Rouen highway from here?" I asked.

"Straight ahead on this road," said Aristide. "Five kilometers on, at the crossroads where the White Horse stands, take the turn to the left; that will put you on the highway."

I thanked them, joined Buck, and sent the Fiat rattling away. He swore viciously.

"Will you please explain this nonsense, Carson? In another thirty seconds I'd have taught those dunghill cocks the lesson they need."

"That's what you think," I said cheerfully. "Brother Aristide had a pistol up his sleeve, ready to drop into his hand. And somebody with a rifle was standing at the nearest window. Those guys were all ready for us; they had word last night from Aulain about our errand. Is that enough, or shall I continue?"

"If there's any more, let's have it, Yank," he said, losing his frown.

"Plenty! Michel spoke truth; she's not at the house—but she's returning. Why? I don't know, but I know how to find out. There's a tavern at the next crossroads; every other tavern in Normandy is named the Cheval Blanc. We'll stop there for an hour or two, and gossip and drink Calvados, and get some answers. Is that enough?"

"No, dammit," he said.

"Okay, then. We'll depart, presumably for Rouen, and we'll come back without any warning of our arrival preceding us—probably Sunday morning. These Normans are either good Catholics or rank Communists. Michel wore a cross or something around his neck. If he's a good Catholic, he'll be going to church. We'll find out where these people go to church. We'll go too. Your gal had a cross and made use of it, so she'll—"

"Oh, I'm an utter damned ass!" he broke out. "Carson, you've more brains in your little finger than I have in my whole carcass. Forgive me." Anxiety twisted him. "I'm on edge. I can't understand it. Why wouldn't she want me to find her?"

"I no savvy neither," I replied. "But they know you're an English milord, not just a cross—I mean," I caught myself up hurriedly, "not just a paratrooper named Wemyss."

"Cross-eyed paratrooper," he said, and hit me on the knee and grinned. "Oh, boy! You're all right. Carry on with the show and I'll be your batman, damn you for a smart Yankee! I don't deserve to black your boots, even." After a moment he added: "Y'know, I was afraid of that chap Aristide. The smaller they are, the more dangerous. If we have a mess with those lads, you take Michel. He's your size."

"Agreed," I told him. "Being one of these commando killers, you can probably look after your own small self better than I can. But if you tangle with Aristide, you'll need everything you've got, milord. And at the White Horse, keep your trap shut; don't let 'em know you're a Britisher. We don't want to start another war. We want information."

Buck grinned all over and clapped me again on the knee. He certainly was a right guy.

WE GOT to the White Horse—at one side of the crossroads with a little stone church at the other, and a blacksmith shop between. We went into the tavern and I planted Buck solicitously in one corner with a bottle of apple brandy; then I circulated among the half dozen farmers who were liquidating the noonday heat. I spoke of my sick friend and of how I was an American writing a book and needed to learn about a few of the old customs of Normandy, and they ate it up.

As soon as we got to clinking glasses, I knew all was well; that is a Norman custom only when the guy is okay. When I began to make notes, everyone laughed and pitched in to fatten my pile. We ate bread and cheese and sent some to Buck, and kept on talking. A word here, an allusion there, and I got what

I most wanted to know. The church had a long name I never did understand, but the country for miles around worshiped here, even the school-teacher. What school-teacher? I asked, with sudden premonition.

"Oh, La Balafré," began one, when another cut him off and said something in patois, about the war; whereat he looked sheepish and said no more.

We had another drink; then I remembered my sick friend and after a handshake all around, went back to him. In another five minutes Buck and I were heading north.

"All the luck in the world, Buck!" I told him. "She's known hereabouts as La Balafre, or the Scarred Lady; it's a name of respect, and connected with the war—easy enough to guess what. Also, she teaches the country school somewhere around here. Also the mass usually attended by everyone at the church behind us is at eight o'clock."

Buck groaned. "Must we wait till Sunday?" he pleaded.

"If I'm running the show, yes. That's our best chance to escape being murdered by the Dornay gang. Look, my noble friend! The Dornays happen to be church members in high standing. Most of their crowd belong to the Communist wing, and you can bet will not be found at the crossroads church."

"I see. You're right again," he admitted. "I suppose you've figured everything out to the last detail, General Ike."

"Penultimate detail," I corrected him. "We be at the church at seven-thirty if not earlier. The Dornay party have some little distance to come and will probably arrive at the last minute. We want to be back in the last dark corner when they walk in, so we can catch our party when they leave. I expect we can look for plenty trouble, but hardly for shooting—not around a church. Satisfied?"

"No, but I will be," he said, and his face cleared. "This is Thursday: What do we do meantime?"

"Go back home, roundabout—Trouville-Deauville tonight, hit the tables, drown our sorrows, fight off the sparrows from

Paris, and drift home early in the morning or after breakfast, and stay there until Saturday evening, when we start out and drive all night in order to get to church early. We'll come in the Fiat, not in this bus."

"Why the Fiat?" he asked.

"More room. You don't suppose Gondy and Murch are going to let us run off to battle by ourselves, do you? Also, it won't be recognized as yours."

We hauled out a road-map and worked around to Deauville in time for the evening's fun. The Monte Carlo evening-attire restrictions did not pertain here, most of the Normandy casinos being a bit on the cheap side, so we made a night of it.

I stuck to the galloping bones, and all they did was lead me in a funeral march. But not Buck. He headed for the baccarat rooms. He had plenty of coin, was furiously reckless whether he won or lost, and was down on the world generally; consequently, after I lost my shirt I looked him up and found him sitting in a regular foxhole of thousand-franc notes, and more rolling in fast.

Some English nobility were on hand, and they knew him. The Greek and French plungers said he had the evil eye, on account of his cast, and had lost their nerve. He just took everybody in sight. He gave bales of banknotes to every *cocotte* who tipped him the eye, ordered champagne like a lord, and about four in the morning the manager came around with tears in his whiskers to say the bank was broke.

Buck introduced me to a couple of dukes who were cadging drinks; then we loaded the loot into the Austin and drove down the coast highway and got home about dawn. We sneaked in and went to bed, leaving three or four hundred thousand francs out in the seat of the Austin, and did not wake up until the middle of the afternoon.

EVEN THEN Buck refused to be wakened; he still had another day to kill, he said. I bathed, shaved, dressed and found Gondy slaving away in the garden while Murchison lolled in a beach chair at the edge of the hole and encouraged him. Poor Gondy was done up, and had not yet reached the cache, whatever it was.

We had a pleasant reunion. Murchison's tooth was now in good shape and he had recovered from his sulfa spree, but he would not touch a spade.

"No thanks, boys," he said. "I'll fill in the hole afterward, but I've had my fill of mines and corpses. Come on with the yarn, Bill Carson! Did Buck find his dame?"

I felt sorry for Gondy; vicomtes are not brought up to spade work. After we had talked over my story, Gondy and Murchison agreed we must all go along with Buck. Then Yvonne came and tied up Gondy's blistered hands and I took over the spade. As a matter of fact, he had almost reached the cache.

With careful approach, I reached it and started to dig around it, having established that it was nothing worse than another packing-case. It was only a foot deep, but seven feet on each side, as I had previously discovered—and that meant a lot of digging. Sunset came and brought Buck to join us, and I had only uncovered half the damned thing.

"You Yanks are brilliant guys," said Buck critically. "Scientists or something, aren't you?"

"What the hell's on your Yorkshire-pudding mind?" I demanded ungraciously.

He grinned. "Why don't you open the exposed end, pull out what's inside, and leave the container buried?" he asked.

We looked at one another; it was the obvious thing, naturally.

"That's exactly what we propose to do," I replied. "But with darkness coming on, we'll wait till morning, thanks. Might be a couple guys inside that got run over and pressed flat by a tank. Anything's possible in this little garden of paradise."

"More truth than poetry in that," said Gondy, and we quit.

Buck tossed all his bales of thousand-franc notes into the back of the Austin, intimating that if everything went well, it would go for honeymoon expenses, and if things went wrong, what the hell did anything matter? Gondy, with whom I canvassed the business, privately, regarded it as serious in the extreme.

"The girl Jeanne probably slashed or damaged her face and is permanently scarred," he said. "Among her own people it would be regarded as a proud badge; not so elsewhere. And if she has discovered that this man is a British milord, you can see why she would never want him to see her again."

"Maybe you can, but I can't," I told him. "If she fell in love with him—"

"That's the very reason, Bill! You've never been in love and—"

"I've been in love a dozen times," I said indignantly.

Gondy sighed. "Sure. Your kind of love. This is the real thing, if it exists at all."

I gave up. He was incurably romantic and nobody can savvy a romantic Frenchman....

In the morning, we attacked the exposed end of the packing-case and tore it apart. From it we extracted picture after picture—we had struck Forain's cache and no mistake this time! Some were little ones, some large. Some were framed, most were not. Gondy had a partial list of the stolen pictures, and they checked up. Most were old pictures and some were scandalous. We stacked them all in the house; it was Gondy's job to contact the Paris dealers and get the reward. Murchison and I filled in the hole and then packed up the Baby.

Buck did not even take a look at them. He was busy showing himself off around town and was tight with nervous tension again.

A LITTLE after seven next morning, Sunday, we parked the Fiat outside that White Horse crossroads and filed into the church. Activities were under way already—farmers, old women in white lace caps, and younger folks filtering in and out, but no sign of our party. We got a back seat and had a hard time keeping awake; then just as the candles were being lighted, in came the Dornay delegation.

Big Michel marched in, Aristide at his heels, both of them dolled up in their Sunday clothes; then came the women and children, and they were certainly a swarm to behold. We had eyes for only one of them, however, a slender, pale girl in white. As she went past, we could see only the left side of her face, and we knew then, or I did, why Buck was in love. She was not just pretty; she was an angel. She had everything: serene dignity, pride, a brave tenderness. No, not everything either—she was not happy. When she got down on her knees and hid her face in her hands, she was absorbed in earnest prayer to the exclusion of everything else.

Then, when everyone stood up, we could see the right side of her face. I stole a glance at Buck and looked away quickly; his own face was a study in emotions. No wonder. The right side of that girl's face was a red, poorly healed scar—a bad one. In America, she would have worn a heavy veil, but not here, of course. In France, such things are not hidden; they are met and conquered, because everyone knows about them.

All through the service, we had to sit there looking at that poor scarred half-face of hers. The minute it was over, we scrambled to get out among the first, and Murchison, at my shoulder, gave me a murmured word.

"What's our play, Bill?"

"Interference," I said. "If it gets messy, I'll take on that big fellow, Michel."

They came streaming out. We waited at the gate of the churchyard. Michel and Aristide came out. They saw us, exchanged a startled word, stared at us, then came forward. Aristide gave Buck a nod.

"Here is the card for you, monsieur," he said, and extended the card.

Buck took it, tore it in two, and started forward as Jeanne Duchesne appeared.

"Get out of the way," he said. Aristide blocked him.

"Impossible, Englishman. You have had her reply; we cannot permit—"

Something happened to Aristide right there. He did land one crack that brought blood to Buck's face—then he learned about commando tactics. Buck actually moved too fast to follow; I just heard Aristide groan, saw him collapse, saw Buck throw him aside like a sack of meal—and then Michel was moving in on Buck. I stepped between.

For a while that was about the liveliest churchyard in all France. Women screamed. Buck was approaching Jeanne, who stood like a white statue staring at him, I had my hands full and Murchison and Gondy stood fending off the buzzing farmers—the fact that Gondy was a Frenchman, gave them pause.

Nothing gave *me* pause. Michel was doing his best to paralyze me. I am not one of these clever guys who can knock out a bruiser with a mere jerk of the finger. The only way I could handle big Michel was to hit him under the belt, and I did it—without effect. I had to keep on doing it, and did. After taking what would have settled half a dozen ordinary mortals, he folded.

Right then, the crowd started moving in on us from all directions—only to come to a dead halt. The priest appeared, an old, white-haired man, and with a word he stopped everything. Next instant he stopped too, as Buck stood in front of Jeanne. What they said was public property, but they did not care.

"Jeanne Duchesne?" said Buck. "Are you Jeanne?"

"Of course, monsieur," she responded coldly. "Can't you see?"

"No," he said, with a vague gesture. "My eyes, you know—not so far away. Come closer. I must see you, Jeanne."

He was only a foot away, but he craned closer, until he was almost touching her, puckering up his face and staring. Then he put out his hand to hers, and smiled.

"Oh! You are, you are!" he exclaimed. "Jeanne, my dear! I told you that I'd come back and find you—"

If he gave her a shock that left her white and gasping, you can imagine what he did to us. Murchison spoke at my ear.

"The damned little lying bastard! Bill, he's a right guy, huh?"

Jeanne put out a hand and touched his face.

"Oh, my dear!" she exclaimed. "Do you mean—your eyes—"

"A shell," he said, and laughed. "Never mind. It's nothing. They say it may get better some day. Let me look at you, Jeanne! I've found you, I've found you!"

She stiffened. "Yes, look at me," she said, and turned the right side of her face to him. "Look well at me, and you'll see why you must not be foolish. You must go back to England and not think of me any more, monsieur. It would be very wrong."

Buck just laughed. "Why? You look splendid, Jeanne! More in love than ever."

"This scar!" she shot at him.

"What scar?" He peered again at her and shook his head, mystified. "I don't know what you're talking about. There isn't any scar that I can see. You mean that little red mark near your mouth? No, that isn't a scar."

I saw her begin to tremble. She drew back, incredulous. But just then the old priest moved in between them, put out a hand to each, and spoke upon a dead, strained silence.

"My children, you must explain all this to me," he said quietly. "Monsieur, who are you, if you please?"

BUCK LOOKED at him—no, looked past him, I noticed.

"I was a paratrooper," he said. "I landed behind the German lines on D Day and was injured. Jeanne found me and took care of me, nursed me, finally got me back to my own people. We were in love; I promised to return. And I did, but I've been unable to find Jeanne. My friends have to see for me, you understand. Now we must find a priest at once and get married and go to England—or around the world. Why not? Where can we find a priest, monsieur?"

"I am a priest, my son," said the old man.

Big Michel stirred. He was holding his belly and listening, with an expression of painful amazement. I held down a hand to him and he got to his feet, staring at the scene.

"Oh, you are! Good!" exclaimed Buck. "Listen, Father: She has been saying something about a scar. I do not understand at all. I cannot see what difference it makes if my face is a little bit scarred, do you?"

The old man looked at him, then looked at Jeanne.

"I certainly do not, my son," he replied. But abruptly Jeanne caught his arm and burst into a passionate storm of dialect which I could scarcely follow at all—about Buck being a great man in England, and how shameful it would be if she married him, I gathered; tears were streaming on her cheeks as she spoke. The old man put his arm about her shoulders and made a gesture to the rest of us not to interrupt.

"Dear child Jeanne," he said, "this man loves you and needs your care. Do you not comprehend what he says? He cannot see any scar. Is there any reason why you should not be married—do you not love him?"

He held her against him, her face against his soutane, and we could not hear her reply; but there was no need. Big Michel reached out and grabbed my shoulder.

"By God, monsieur, your friend is a gallant gentleman!" he growled.

I am not certain of what happened next; Buck had Jeanne in his arms, and the priest was telling them that he could make some sort of wartime dispensation and marry them on the spot, and they could arrange the civil formalities later, and the whole crowd began talking at once, with a voluble chatter that would have drowned out a barrage. The main point was that Jeanne was kissing Buck, and he was kissing her scarred cheek. The old priest must have suspected something, because he left them and came striding over to us.

"You are the friends of this gentleman?" he said.

Gondy answered for us, and gave his name and title, and shook hands.

"Ah! Tell me, M. de Gondy," said the priest, eyeing him keenly, "is this Englishman really blind? I may be mistaken, but I seem to recollect having seen such a man recently, driving a small car. I cannot afford to make mistakes in this affair."

Gondy looked at us, then back at the priest, and swallowed hard.

"Upon my honor as a gentleman, *mon père,*" he said, with his grand bow, "I can assure you there is no mistake; it is precisely as Lord Buckleden says. Ultimately, I believe, there is some hope that his sight may be restored—as," he added softly, "there is every hope that plastic surgery will remove the scar in question."

The old priest looked at him for a moment, then his eyes twinkled. He made a gesture to everyone, went back to Jeanne and Buck, and walked them straight back into the church. We all followed.

You can understand, probably, why Murchison and I thought the world of the Vicomte de Gondy.

VIII

VIKING LOOT

In England our treasure-seekers put their mine-detector on a strange quest—and thereby hangs this dramatic tale.

THE THREE of us—I, Bill Carson, and his two pals, Murchison and the Vicomte de Gondy—sat in conference in the sunny land of France, reaching a vital decision.

"I'm fed up with it," snapped Murchison. "Let's go to England."

"There are difficulties," murmured Gondy thoughtfully: "The law and such things."

"Nonsense!" Murch was skinny, opinionated, and at times a stubborn ass. He and I had been pals from boyhood days, all through the war, and still were. He was a good guy. "We've been barging around Europe, and I'm sick of it. We run into trouble everywhere. Let's go back where people talk the same language."

"If you mean England, they don't," I put in with a chuckle. "I seem to remember, when we were billeted there, what a time you had trying to savvy those noncoms—"

Gondy's eyes, dark and brilliant, twinkled at us, but he said nothing.

"Look," went on Murchison: "This gadget of ours will locate buried treasure; we've proved it to the hilt. What happens? First, Gondy's ex-relative Félice tries to murder us all, and keeps after us. She knows what a big thing we have; she wants it herself, also the loot we dig up. And we hit nothing but trouble everywhere. I'm fed up with it. There's more buried treasure in England than in all France put together. Let's go back there."

Gondy nodded brightly. "Oh, that's true enough," he said.

"Some enormous finds have been made. I know this minute of half a dozen possibilities, but—what d'ye say, Carson?"

I puffed at my pipe and considered this question. Murchison and I, through the war, had done laboratory work on mine-detectors, finally evolving a radionic detector that would do the job handily. Since then we had taken up one of our by-products, which was useless against mines, but very useful in finding other things. With the Baby, as we called it, we had been knocking around Europe detecting buried treasure of one kind or another, and with plenty of luck, too. We had taken in Gondy to make a third, partly because we liked him, partly because he served as contact man and was useful in a dozen ways. As Murchison said, however, there were a few drawbacks, and chief among these was the beauti-ful and damned Félice.

"Well," I said at last, "the Continent won't budge, and we can always come back to it if we like. We've half the summer ahead of us; why not spend it in England, which is certainly no winter resort? We could move with the seasons, like the birds, going maybe to Egypt next winter. I'm for it. Anything against it, Gondy?"

"What the devil are you chaps about here?" the man on horseback demanded. He put his horse at me and motioned with his riding-crop.

He spread out his hands and shrugged, then reverted to the matter of the law, saying that we'd practically be outlaws in Egypt, were our errand known, for the Government came down hard on any treasure hunters.

"America is the only land of freedom," he said wistfully. "In England, the law is adamant; all treasure-trove belongs to the Crown, and the Crown insists unmercifully on its rights. So true is this, that even when there exists well-authenticated

information about hidden treasure, the owner of the land usually refuses even to look for it—would do him no good."

Murchison picked up his ears. "Sounds fine," he said hopefully. "I know a guy back home in Boston who put himself through medical school in prohibition days, bootlegging. I bet more than one Britisher noses around and locates stuff and keeps his mouth shut."

Gondy nodded. "I had a friend who found a little and knew where there's a lot more, when I was liaison officer with those British troops," he said. "Alan Cobham, his name was. He has a place in Sussex. However, anyone is free to search; the crime is concealment—"

"Wire him tonight," said Murch, rubbing his hands. "We can take the ferry from Havre to Southampton overnight—the Baby is a scientific invention, and the British customs won't bother us. Eh, Bill? It'll lend spice to the quest, if we have to do it on the quiet! Grow whiskers on the Baby, and pretend we're looking for oil!"

"Your spice will be hot pepper if we rub up against the wrong side of the British law," I said. "But so far as I'm concerned, wire your Sussex friend and let's go!"

Cobham wrote back a hearty invitation to us all, and that is how we came to be in Sussex.

I HARDLY know whether the men or place held more interest. Alan Cobham was sturdy, massive-faced, steady-eyed, a man of deep currents, of unswerving convictions, of slow and implacable nature; if your friend, he was your friend for life. He was not what the old-fashioned call a gentleman; rather, a rural farmer type. He had served in North Africa and Greece. The war had left him a major, with an ugly scar down one cheek. As Murchison put it, he was one grand guy. His place was called Inchgore; the house was several hundred years old, and serviced daily by a couple of women from the village. He was a bachelor. His place grew hops.

From his house on the hill we could see the glint of the sea;

once it had extended up the valley, and where the village now stood had been a deep harbor in Roman days. He indicated the old sea-line to us, and pointed out a rising clump of broken, naked granite at the edge of his hop-field.

"That used to be a sunken reef; it destroyed many a ship," he said, puffing at his big pipe. "Things have been found about there. The year the war started we were digging a drain-ditch past the Beacon, as it's known around here. I suppose a beacon for ships stood there in King Alfred's time. We turned up this."

He pointed to what stood above the fireplace.

This house, Inchgore, was one of the wonderful old things that abound in England. It had been a tithe-barn, whatever that is, in Elizabethan days. It had enormous beams, black with the years, but was a bit of a patchwork—the walls largely of Caen stone from France, yellowed with lichens and sea-winds' weathering. The thing above the fireplace was of a piece with the house.

It was large, curved, shapen piece of wood, another piece projecting from one end and held by a bolt. The wood was worm-holed and rot had thinned the wood to nothing.

"An odd thing, that," said Cobham. He was well educated; his speech held none of the local patois which was past comprehension to American ears. "An archaeologist chap was down from London and saw it. Said it was the prow of a ship, probably a Viking ship wrecked on the Beacon, since the bolt you see is of bronze.... Well, that's one thing. Another is that, almost at the identical spot, old Watt Chodsale struck upon something thirty-odd years ago; he picked up the head of a crosier and got thirty shillings for it from a shopman in Barnsdale. From what I gather, the thing must have been solid gold. And there's the makings of my treasure-trove—at least, I call it mine."

WE LOOKED at the sheltered hop-fields, known locally as the Marsh—odd, how the memory of long-past centuries survives in these local English names! Alan Cobham talked, slowly and steadily unrolling ancient things to us. It was a touchy business, he said, to talk of treasure-trove these days. A man could go to prison, even after the lapse of years, for finding and keeping anything worth while. I got the impression that he had enemies who might well turn him in. It was our first hint that he, even as many another man, might have a past that was like a quagmire under his feet, ready to swallow him up at a false step. He went on about the crosier that had been found.

"It must have belonged to an abbot or bishop. There was a big abbey here in Saxon times, Bosham Abbey; not a stone of it left now. The Danes or Vikings sacked and burned it. Tradition, often more accurate than history, says the Viking ship with its loot ran on the Beacon reef and was lost."

Vikings and loot were gone. The sea had receded during the centuries. An abbot's crosier had been picked up; at the same place had been found the curved prow of a Viking ship—and here we were. Fantastic? Not in England, which has more verified treasure fantasy than any other country on earth. The solid, sensible man sitting there and telling about it, made the thing seem entirely probable.

Cobham had never dug for the ship. Everyone here knew everybody else's business; excavations might be a lengthy business and a ruinous one in the end. He knew the location in general but this did not say the treasure lay there—the ship might have broken in two on the rocks or been carried afar. If

someone knew the exact spot, it would be different; and the exact spot might be found by Murchison & Co.

"Here's my notion," our host concluded. "Next Monday will be Bank Holiday; between Saturday and Tuesday, there'll be no work in the fields. This gives you the better part of a week to grub around with your machine. Locate the spot and leave it until Saturday night; dig it up and have the ground smoothed over by Tuesday—and no work by daylight, mind. To account for your presence, I can say you're taking soil samples for the Hop Marketing Board or any such damned thing. Suppose we have a look over the spot here and now."

We tramped off with him, gladly.

COBHAM KNEW somewhat how we meant to work, but took no interest; he cared only for the result. I believe he regarded us as slightly crazy anyhow; soldiers usually thought us technical experts a bit balmy. In a good-humored, offhand way, he had agreed to an equal division of any spoils among the four of us—a fourth to him.

So we went tramping with him through the fields to the Beacon. As we got there, an elderly workman came plodding along, and saluted him respectfully. Cobham stopped.

"Morning, Humfry. I hear your rascally sheep-growing master has battered down my fences and the lower marsh gate."

"It were the lorry, Maas' Alan," said the man apologetically in broad dialect. "The lorry ta-akin' the tegs up above. What wi' the drythe and heat, there's little grass left down below. The lorry—well, it bumped the gate-posts a bit."

"Aye, and then some," Cobham said angrily. "Tell Greg if the repairs aren't done by the week-end, I'll close the way completely, and he can send his damned tegs to the upper meadows through the air, and himself with them."

The old fellow regarded him with a shake of the head and a rather proud look.

"Maas' Greg won't be loiking that, Maas' Alan—"

"To hell with him and his likes!" snapped Cobham. "Tell him that, too, Humfry."

"An't loikly; queers me, it does, how he do go on, and you too—and her dead and gone these long years! Her wouldn't loike that, and her a-praying—"

Cobham shut him up with an oath, and he went his way. Our host had shown an ugly side of him; but next minute he was drawling and humorous as ever, and pointed out to us a spot here and a spot there, as we stood under the long pile of rocks that had been an ocean reef in the dim dead past. He marked with a hop-pole the exact place he had dug up the ship's prow, and showed where in a little hollow close by the crosier had been found.

It seemed incredible. Here was plain earth, the sea far away; yet under our feet must be the rust and rot of a Viking ship of a thousand years ago. I found it past belief, but not so Murchison and Gondy. They were two of a kind, given to wild dreams. Just before the war Murch had sunk all his savings in a Cape Cod cat-and-rat fur farm—skin the cat and feed the carcass to the rats, and vice versa; and he was still trying to figure out why he was not rich. But he was a great guy, and in radionics a five-star wizard. It was Murch who first figured out how a bat flies by radar principles, and harnessed them.

OUR HOST made it quite plain that, to avoid local gossip

and consequent trouble, we must locate the treasure with due precaution, and then dig like blazes when we dug, and cover up fast; years afterward, if it got a whiff of treasure, the Crown would prosecute. So, for Cobham's sake as well as our own, we had to watch our step.

That evening—it was a Sunday we arrived—Cobham went to the village, to church, being a religious soul; and the three of us went into executive session. The Baby was mounted in a wicker perambulator, hence the name, for greater convenience of operation, but this now promised to have its drawbacks.

"Pushing a pram around those fields will draw attention," said Gondy.

"I'll say!" assented Murchison. "Imagine, Bill, the gossip in a New England village if strange guys turned up and began shoving a baby carriage around Abel Smith's cornfield! Still, that's the easiest way to do our job. Looks like we must work at night."

"That won't be so tough," I said. "We've got good weather. It's all clear and open under those rocks; the spot doesn't lie out in the field, but close to the Beacon."

"With a time limit on the job for best results," added Murchison. "Well, we can work all night if we want, so we'd better go at it tomorrow night after dark, when the two women have gone back to the village and the coast is clear. We'll have to install those new batteries in the Baby and put the thing together. Might do that now."

We set about it, having the place to ourselves. The Baby had been taken apart and packed in the back of our old but sturdy Fiat, and by the time Cobham returned we had it put together and in good working order. Cobham suggested that we keep the gadget in our car, with a cloth thrown over it, since workmen or the two servants might otherwise get to wondering what we were doing with a perambulator.

Next afternoon—early, because of the English closing hours—we three walked to the village, half a mile away, for a

look around. We found the pub and settled down, found the
local beer to be excellent, and listened to the wholly unintel-
ligible Sussex talk of those around, which amused us.

After a bit in came an odd little old chap who got a mug of
half-and-half, looked around, and brought his mug to our table.
He had wild gray hair, a bright and kindly eye, and a face like
a wizened apple.

"D'you mind if I sit with you?" he said in excellent English.

*"A buzz-bomb killed my
wife, and I've hardly
been the same man since,"
said the old chap.*

"I'm Alf Meghorn and a bit of an antiquary, and I like to tell
strangers about our local antiquities."

We gave our names, shook hands, and made him welcome.
I saw the barmaid catch Gondy's eye—they always did—and
tap her temple significantly in warning. Our new friend made
some brisk talk about Americans.

"You're the chaps staying with Alan Cobham, eh?" he went

on. "Interesting, very. I saw you looking over the honeypools with him yesterday."

"Honeypools?" repeated Murchison blankly. "I don't get it."

"That's what the bit of the marsh under the Beacon used to be called," Meghorn explained. "Interesting bit of tradition there. After a heavy rain that bit of ground is still a big honey-pool; but it's been a dry year. I did know some odd things about there, but they've gone out of my head. One of those bloody buzz-bombs, during the trouble, hit my cottage and killed my wife, and I've hardly been the same man since."

"Honeypools?" Murchison stuck to it in his stubborn way. "What may that mean?"

The bright little eyes twinkled at us, merrily enough.

"That's local speech. Mud-puddles, by way of translation. Strangers always like the sound of it. I used to be up at the Beacon a good deal. I still slip up there now and then, on watch, but so far I've never had any luck."

"On what kind of watch?" I asked.

"Well, you know tradition, in this country, is usually based on fact," he said very seriously. "For hundreds of years tradition has said that the Beacon is haunted by the ghosts of people drowned there when the sea was up around the rocks. I've kept on the lookout a many nights, but never saw a ghost. Greg Cobham laid his bull-whip to me once," he added, a sudden deadly flash in his eye, "but Alan doesn't mind. If Greg hated to have me prying around of nights, as he put it, that would make Alan give me permission."

In the next twenty minutes we learned a lot of surprising things.

COBHAM HAD a younger brother, Greg. They had been enemies from youth, when Greg had married Alan's girl. The Cobham inheritance had been split, causing further ill-will; an unusual thing in England, for Alan should have inherited all. The two brothers had staged some elegant battles, we gathered, until the war came along with a bigger one. Greg's wife had died during the war. According to our informant, Greg was a slippery rascal.

Pub closing-time ended our talk. I rather liked this Meghorn chap; there was something quite gentle and kindly about him, cracked or not. At that, many a crackpot has better sense than some of the normals around him. Under his wrecked life, Meghorn had a lot of basically sound stuff. However, we had more important matters on hand than confabbing with a village nitwit, and Alan Cobham's family affairs were none of our business, so we dismissed the whole affair from mind—or at least, I did.

That night after the two servants went home, we got down to work. Cobham, who made no great company of us and regarded our work with an amused tolerance, went off to a political meeting—one of those granges or rural boards that keep English farmers regimented.

An old moon hung in the sky as we trundled the Baby down the path and through the field and to the Beacon. Murchison, who was a little moon-mad anyhow, pointed to the jagged line of rocks.

"There's something you can't see by daylight," he chirped. "The old water-line. See it? Part way down the rocks."

Gondy did. I did not.

"You'll be seeing ghosts next, you and Alf Meghorn," I told him. "No sense in all of us staying here all night. We'd better take two-hour shifts, after we get things going, and those not working can stay at the house."

"Not so easy, Mr. Carson, when we work at night," retorted Murch. "You, for instance, need watching. There's a lot of ground to be covered. The guy walking the Baby can't easily determine his own bounds; someone must keep score from the side lines."

"As usual, your maunderings make sense," I conceded.

We had already calculated that treasure possibilities would be confined within a rough triangle. The base would be some two hundred yards along the Beacon rocks, centered on the spots indicated by Cobham; the search, naturally, would begin there. The point of the triangle, a hundred feet away, would fan out to this base line. Within this space ought to lie whatever remains might exist of any ships wrecked on the Beacon.

I could take no stock whatever in the whole business; it was too full of moonshine. For this special reason, Gondy and Murchison were nuts about it. Anything that required strong imagination appealed to them. Gondy even took the notion that the crevices among that long pile of rocks must hold countless objects that had been washed ashore; to hear him talk, one would have thought it was only last week the sea was washing around here. Murchison took up this utterly insane notion and elaborated on it until I lost my temper and we went into a good row.

From boyhood days in South Boston, Murch and I had been pals. We got rid of a lot of combat instinct on each other. Because we never got on each other's nerves, our rows always ended well, provided no one else chipped in. This was a really good one and we worked off a lot of steam, and Gondy had the sense to keep out. So it was pretty near midnight when we actually got down to work, and along came Cobham, his meeting ended, to see what we were at. He laughed immoderately at our squabble and stuck around to see how we operated, and laughed anew to see me rolling a pram along the ground.

To do him justice, he was amazingly quick to catch on. During the war he had picked up some knowledge of radar and of electronics in general, naturally. Murchison's example of how the bat flies, guided by supersonic waves, made clear how such waves could penetrate the solid earth and bounce back upon striking a still more solid obstacle.

As we worked along, I explained to him how, upon encountering any underground substance, the rays would register on the dials, and how we had from these registrations evolved a chart that would show the nature of the object and its depth. He quite comprehended that the force of the kickback would depend on the solidity of the object struck; in fact, without knowing an actual thing about it, he had the principle down pat.

"I can give you a bit of help there," he volunteered. "I know there's a stratum of solid rock at varying distances underground, deepening as you get away from the Beacon. Any ship sinking through the mud in ancient days would lie on it."

"A ship might take a century sinking that way, or might not sink at all," put in Gondy, with reason.

"True; it's all a gamble," said Cobham.

He was interested enough to stay with us, and suggested that we come here by daylight and outline, by means of stones placed for markers, the patch of ground to be covered at night; a good idea. We got the Baby adjusted to work at a depth of from six to twenty feet, and in the immediate vicinity of where the ship's prow had been found, the buzzer indicated strike after strike, but nothing to get excited about—rock or logs. Cobham confirmed this. Huge witch-elms had once grown along here, he said, so long ago that when the logs were dug up they usually turned to powder after reaching the air.

We stayed at it until three in the morning and then knocked off, all of us, after making careful observations of the ground covered, so we would not go over it twice. As we pushed the Baby home, I pointed out that there must have been a current washing along these rocks, and consequently anything sunk there would have been carried far.

"I never saw such a man for relentless logic," grunted Murchison resignedly.

Cobham laughed. "Well, the best answer to that is the ship's prow at the house, what?"

True enough, or so it seemed at the moment.

We turned in and slept until noon. It was hot, dry weather. In the cool of the afternoon we sauntered off to the Beacon and made a mental layout of what ground we had covered and the amount we would cover tonight, and marked it with stones large enough to see later on. While we were at this, we walked into something—rather, it rode into us.

A MAN on horseback, a big brawny man on a fine horse, came along and pulled up. The man was young, under thirty, and well-dressed in a British way.

"What the devil are you chaps about here?" he demanded. His voice had a rasp to it that lifted my hackles. He was good-looking; I should have answered with the politeness becoming a foreigner. Instead, I did not. He put his horse at me and motioned with his riding-crop.

"Careful," I said, seeing Murch on the run. "Any arrogant misconception of what an important person you are, and you'll maybe get a broken neck."

I did not use those exact words, but shorter and less polite ones, being angry. The man drew rein and turned his horse, and waited. I saw Cobham coming out of nowhere—he had not been with us. He strode along at the soldier's double. The visitor barked out at him.

"I heard you had foreigners looking over the land, Alan. Came to see why."

Cobham halted. "No affair of yours, nor the land neither."

"So? And what's this message Humfry brought, about closing the thoroughfare?"

"Apparently you got it diluted," said Cobham. "I said either repair the damages your lorry caused by this week-end, or your damned sheep and you together could go to hell by some farther way."

So this was the younger brother!

"The damage will be repaired," said Greg Cobham. "But not because of your threats, my loving brother! Save them for strangers. Because I prefer to have the property in good repair when it reverts to me, that's why. As it will when the gallows gets its due."

Alan squinted up at his brother. "You're in one of your pleas-ant moods today, Greg."

Greg snarled nastily. "I suppose you set that addlepated Alf Meghorn on me with his blasted prescription?" As he spoke, he balled up a piece of paper in his hand, angrily. "It'd be like your bloody cheek!" He flung the ball at his brother.

"Oh, is that it?" Alan laughed. "Aye, he gave me a copy of it too. Said it'd serve to avert trouble between us if we followed it. Does his nonsense trouble your conscience?"

"You be damned! Nan always said you'd come to a bad end," blared Greg furiously. I saw Alan go dead white. "Pity the war didn't leave you in Africa!"

"We're not alone, Greg," replied our host slowly. "However, these friends of mine are gentlemen—too much so to be introduced to you. I don't care to pull you off your nag and brawl; but if you'll step down, I'll give you a thrashing that'll leave your ugly hulk of a body in the shape it should be!"

The sudden gusty fury breaking through his last words was a revelation. Greg looked down at him, snarled out a grin, and picked up his reins.

"This big lump of clay with an American brogue," he said, indicating me, "hinted at the same thing. He might scalp me. So, not being among friends—"

"Wait just a moment, please," said our host quietly. "Greg, you've just done something. Well, I warn you here and now: Drag her name into it again, and I'll kill you. Do you understand? Kill you like the cur you are."

He was quiet enough, his voice was quiet, but he was shaking, too. There was death in the air that very minute. The man in the saddle felt it and was afraid, and licked his lips; then, with a lusty growling oath, turned his horse and rode away. Alan Cobham stood unmoving, looking after him.

I picked up the balled paper, which was at my feet, and opened it, Gondy and Murch at my elbow.

Cobham turned to us.

"I'm sorry about this; unpleasant scene, very," he said. "Oh, read the damned thing if you like! That poor chap in the village—got buzz-bombed during the war—lost his wits, thinks he's an evangelist or something."

IT WAS a single amazing paragraph scrawled on the paper; harmless, of course, just the sort of harmless nonsense a village nitwit might hand out to avert trouble. It read:

PRESCRIPTION

An ounce of faith, a shake of hope, much charity, well mixed. Season with as much careful thought for others as may fill the mind. Add to this a quantity of precaution never to speak hastily except when speaking kindly. Over all, sprinkle with a suspicion that each word uttered by the mouth of Man reaches the ear of God.

"'Allo!" said Gondy. This was the only English word he could never pronounce. "'Allo! I like this. I'd like to take a copy, Cobham, if you don't mind! It's not half bad, really."

"Keep it if you like." Cobham shrugged. "I must apologize, my friends. That chap is my brother, I regret to say. We've never got along. He wangled a nice cushy berth during the war—oh, to the devil with it! Let's forget it, eh? See here, I'm having Anna leave a cold snack for you in the kitchen tonight. Might slip my mind later, so I mention it now. If you're bloody asses enough to work like you did last night, a bite to eat around midnight will pull the old heart up enormously! And what about coffee?"

"We'll make that ourselves, thanks a lot," I told him, mindful of English coffee. "Come along home; it's time you knocked off, and we might have a rubber of bridge."

None of us forgot that scene, of course, but we eased it for him quite well, and after supper Gondy walked down with him to the village while Murchison and I took the first trick with the Baby.

"I was talking with the cook today," Murch confided to me, as we trundled the Baby toward the Beacon. "Good old soul. She said Master was dead in love with the girl who took the other guy, and the girl loved him, but this Greg worked some shenanigan. And they got word Alan was dead in Africa and it killed her. There's a hell of a lot behind the whole situation, Bill."

"You're getting to understand the English dialect," I said dryly.

He chuckled. "Oh, Cook can talk proper English if she wants! She nearly married a technical sergeant from Brooklyn, during the war, only it turned out he had a couple wives already. You sort of blew off your top today, didn't you? Too bad our host stopped the show."

"Damned good thing for that blighter Greg," I said.

The moon was older and higher. Up and down we walked the Baby, hour after hour. Gondy came back and took his turn. He turned up trees, bedrock, more trees, and never a suspicion of metal. Around midnight we broke off for the waiting snack, then stuck out the rest of the night in starry darkness with the moon sunken and gone. We had no luck whatever.

Wednesday we slept until noon, brunched with Cobham, then spent an hour going over the ground, laying out the night's work and marking it off. We had now covered the likeliest spots, finding nothing. The bedrock lay at uneven depths, and was a nuisance. If we adjusted the machine to work too low, the buzzer would sound all the time, as the rays struck rock and kicked back; if not low enough, we might miss what we sought. As a detector, our gadget had its disadvantages, and we were continually trying to overcome them, because we intended to put the thing on the market for commercial use, in course of time.

Gondy offered the bright suggestion that we might adjust the waves so that they would ignore rock, be immune to it, as it were. A mere matter of adjusting them to rebound from the molecular construction of metal and nothing else, he said. This was so damned fantastic that Murchison admitted it was possible, theoretically. Being a very practical person I put my foot down hard, and for an hour or so we had as hot an argument as ever was. Then, as he usually did, Murch came up with a truly sound idea.

"If bedrock lies all along here, Bill, it would have been well scoured when the tide swept around these rocks. Let's go find Meghorn, the antiquary chap!"

"Why him?" I grunted.

"He knows all this country. He can sketch for us the old shoreline in ancient days. Then we can figure the possible drift and currents—"

THAT WAS really something. I was deputed to the job, so off I went to the village.

Meghorn's house was partly ruins, partly an old British Army hut moved on the lot after the buzz-bombs had hit. Alf was digging in his vegetable garden out back. When he savvied what I was after, he beamed all over to be taken for a real an-

tiquarian. I saw that one side of his face was bruised and swollen, but made no comment.

I got in some beer, he dug up an old Ordnance map of the district, and we settled down in his rather messy place to work. He sketched out where the old shoreline had run, making a very nice job of it, and showed me his antiquities—Roman coins, bits of carved stone, pottery and so forth. I asked how he had hurt his face, and he reddened.

We got the Baby adjusted to work, but found nothing of value.

"By not minding my own business," he said.

"I read that thing you gave Cobham," I told him. "That prescription. It was a good thing in its way, but wasted on those hard-headed chaps. You're something of a poet, eh?"

THIS PLEASED him no end, and he grew confidential.

"I'm not a busybody, really," he told me, "but I've tried hard to keep those two from doing murder; that's what I'm afraid of. Greg is an ugly blighter." He touched his hurt cheek. "He gave me a lesson today, right enough. You see, this is the danger period."

"I don't understand."

"Greg married Nan Evarts; she and Alan were in love, but Greg wangled some sort of a slimy scheme and tricked her. A report came that Alan was killed in Africa, and she didn't survive long after that. Tomorrow is the anniversary of her death. Alan put flowers on her grave last year, and it drove Greg into a fury, and they had a row. If Alan does the same thing tomorrow, anything may happen. 'Twould be no loss if Greg were killed, but I'd be sorry to see Alan Cobham swing for it; he's a fine sort."

"Oh!" I said. "And you've been trying to plant noble sentiments instead of hatred in their hearts, eh?"

"There's not much I can do," he said, and sighed. "I've known 'em since they were little tykes; I can influence Alan, but not Greg. It's a mortal bad situation, Mr. Carson. And I've not been too strong i' the head since that buzz-bomb landed here. If you could keep your eye on Alan in the next day or two, it'd be a good deed."

"Cobham rather goes his own way; we don't see much of him," I responded, and got away before he could inveigle me into any promises. I mind my own business, mostly.

BACK IN the cool room of Inchgore, we figured over the map until it became obvious that there must have been a scouring tide-rip past the Beacon that had dug out a big section of the higher land this way from the Marsh. We deduced that there must have been a huge eddy at this end of the Beacon, making a quiet backwash where all sorts of things might well have been carried and deposited.

Alan Cobham got into the argument, saying our theory was disproved by his finding that ship-prow where he had. Gondy, who had a flood of words that would drown a phonograph, talked our host into a daze. However, we agreed to finish first with the triangle we had laid out at the start of our search.

Just before dark, we went down to look over the ground itself, and it was not hard to pick out the likeliest spot where the supposed backwash might have been. This was an unproductive corner of Cobham's land overgrown with saplings and brambles. Every nook of these Sussex farmlands had its own traditional name; and this bit, according to our host, had formerly been called Hortel's Shaw, now degenerated into Horlshaw, as nearly as we could get it. Probably some wandering minstrel named Hortel had camped there five or six hundred years ago, and ever since it had been Hortel's Shaw or thicket.

This Wednesday night we worked like dogs right up until dawn, going over the remainder of our triangle near the Beacon; we found nothing except an old iron kettle full of holes, indicating that our guess might be right and anything there had been scoured away. So far as I was concerned, that finished it; the whole layout was cockeyed and I would be delighted to chuck it. However, I said nothing.

We were through here; we had Thursday and Friday nights left, the week-end holiday ahead, and Hortel's Shaw to examine; this would finish it. We might have worked in that thicket by daylight, it seemed, but Cobham advised against it; too many village eyes at work, said he, and as it proved he was right.

So we slept most of Thursday, seeing little of Cobham. After supper he disappeared, and when the help had gone home we buckled down to the task ahead.

In that cursed thicket we could not hope to cover the ground thoroughly; we could only blunder around in general. We had been using a flashlight to read the chart upon getting any reaction, but on quitting work at dawn I had left it behind a rock at the base of the Beacon, forgetting it there. So while Murchison was walking the Baby in the thicket, I went to the Beacon for the flashlight. The waning moon was thin and high and bright in the west. After locating the light, I paused to get a cigarette going.

"Hi!" came a voice over my head. I responded. There was a clatter, and down from the rocks came Alf Meghorn.

"Thought you were a ghost, but ghosts don't smoke," said he, chuckling. I gave him a cigarette and asked what he was doing here.

"Oh, watching. Bill Bunthorn came home from Whitby late last night, well liquored. He cut across the marsh and swears he saw ghosts moving around. So I came to watch."

Some drunken villager had spied us at work and had taken us for ghosts.

"There's bad things brewing," went on Meghorn, as we chatted. "Greg Cobham has been drinking hard all day, full o' fire and threats. Where's Alan?"

Not knowing, I said so. "He'd better have a care," said Meghorn, wagging his head. "Greg will be in a fine stew tomorrow; allus is, after a drinking bout. Well, I'm going to watch till midnight. Ghosts come of a fine night like this, by all accounts."

He clambered back among the rocks, and I returned to Hortel's Shaw.

Something around an hour later, I remember, Murchison finished his trick and was going back to the house, and paused to give us a lecture on survival. We need not expect, said he, to find any bones or armor. Iron goes to rust underground, copper corrodes to nothing, wood rots like bone. If we struck the treasure, it would be all silver, which may tarnish but remains intact, or all gold, which is not affected-

Just then the buzzer indicated a find at the edge of some

bramble bushes. Gondy was at the machine. Thinking he had struck a rock, he ran the Baby along for a foot or so—and the buzzer continued sounding. I came with the flashlight, glanced at the gauges, then took another incredulous look.

"Glory be, boys! Metal at four feet down—and a lot of it! Apparently loose metal, for the dials jiggle, instead of registering a distinct level such as a chest or sheet of iron—"

We were excited; we always were, upon making discoveries. The thrill never palled on us; even when the discovery proved worthless, we got a tremendous kick out of it. Murchison proposed, since the night was still early and the find a shallow one, that we dig for it here and now. No one objected. Gondy and I started home with the Baby, to leave it and get shovels, while Murchison marked the spot and stayed with it.

We found Cobham not yet home, got the pick and shovels, and got back to the shaw in a hurry. The moon was too low in the west to reach through the saplings; the ground was dark, and we dared not use the flashlight too much. But we had to go only four feet down—and we felt it before we saw it. Felt it, heard the click-click—a bed of coins lying loose in the dirt. Once they must have been confined in something, perhaps a leather sack, a huge one. Gondy got two jute sacks from the house and we filled them both and dragged them home, figuring that before morning we would return and fill in the ground.

The dining-room opened off the living-room; we dumped the coins on the big table. There were thousands of them, all gold and silver; and among the coins were brooches and rings and crosses and chains, all of gold. It was the sort of thing you dream about. The silver was blackened, of course; the gold glinted yellow and bright. Gondy picked up a few of the coins and shook his head.

"They look Roman; I can't tell If we— 'Allo!"

COBHAM CAME walking in. He looked tired and old, and had a badly bruised cheek.

"So here you are!" he exclaimed. "I went walking—had a row

on the way; beastly mess all around, I'm afraid. Oh, I say—Good Lord!"

He saw the coins and stood stupefied.

For as much as twenty minutes we all had a hilarious time. He lugged out a cask of beer and broached it, and drank healths and talked big. Alan Cobham became another man, blithe and eager; but once he touched his bruised cheek and his face darkened ominously. We played like boys with the treasure, then started to separate the gold from the silver. While we were at this, the knocker on the big front door began to hammer. We gasped, looked at one another guiltily, and I grabbed a sack and flung it over the table.

Our host walked out into the living-room, and we followed, just in time to see the front door burst inward. Across the threshold flung Greg Cobham, a shotgun over his arm. He looked like a madman. Blood was on his face, and his hair flew wild. He was not drunk nor sober, but in the aftermath of heavy drinking, and at the brink of insanity with sheer blind fury. He stopped short, glaring at Alan.

"I've come for you!" he blurted out.

"Easy on, old fellow," said Alan. "Just because I had to knock you down doesn't call for a gun, Greg. Put it down, and I'll give you another knockdown if you like—"

"You bloody mucker, what business have you putting flowers on her grave?" cried Greg furiously. "I've told you to leave her alone. She was my wife, not yours. I've had enough, and this is the end. I'll do for you now if I swing for it!"

ALAN WALKED toward him calmly.

"You're out of your head, Greg," he said steadily. "I've had enough of your drunken ways, too, but murder is murder, you know—"

Greg threw up the gun, and the hammer clicked as he cocked it.

"You lie! You threatened to kill me. You'd like to do it, so Cobham Farm could all be yours and me out o' the way. You'll not do it! I'm the one' that'll inherit the whole place, damn you!"

"Stop your raving." Alan continued his approach. "There'll be no murder done here. Put up the gun. We settled it with our fists once tonight, and if you want to do it again, I suppose we must."

"Aye, and I went home for the gun, and I'll settle you once and for all, damn you!" raved Greg, his eyes blazing. Murchison and I had begun to circle around him, and he saw us and swung the muzzle toward us. "Look out, you damned Americans! Keep your distance, or you'll get a dose of the same—"

Alan jumped at Greg, striking the gun aside.

One shell exploded with a tremendous roar, but harmlessly, the shot peppering the big rafters. Then the two men were reeling, locked together, fighting for the gun, and doing it with such insensate ferocity that neither Murchison nor I, hoping to disarm the drunken fool, could intervene.

Suddenly I saw an opening, and dived in. Murchison acted at the same instant. Our combined weight sent the two of them crashing into a chair, and we all came down in one mad tangle. But the crash had a terrific echo, as the other barrel of the shotgun exploded. And the charge tore out Greg Cobham's throat....

There was a phone in the house, and Alan called the local constable, who came along and brought a Sir John somebody, the local magistrate, and a dozen more people came trooping in. Meantime, Gondy had rammed the coins into the sacks again and stuck them into a corner of the dining-room out of sight—unluckily missing a few that rolled on the floor.

The corpse of Greg still had the gun clenched in his hands, and this saved the day for Alan. An hour or so later the county coroner came along. Our testimony had been taken down in detail. There was a powwow, and Sir John came over and clapped Alan on the shoulder, cordially, and told him to cheer up, that the verdict was certain to be either "accidentally shot" or "by his own hand," and Alan would be held blameless.

Then I saw the constable beckon Sir John out into the dining-room and knew the worst must have happened.

Cobham only stifled a groan when I told him.

"What does it matter, Carson? The dug-up ground would be discovered anyhow. We can't hope to hide the find. Hand it over, and devil take it. The main thing is to protect you three chaps; that can be managed."

Sir John came back, presently, looking grave.

"Sorry, Cobham—deuced amazing thing, 'pon my word!" he said. "These coins in yonder: It means a charge of concealing treasure-trove—they'll have to be impounded for the Crown till we can get a Treasury man down from London—"

We explained that we had only located the treasure this same night, and cooked up a plausible yarn about accidentally happening on it and so forth. The magistrate shook his head. There it had been in the dining-room, concealed; and the Crown was damned set on making examples, in order to frighten everyone else into turning in whatever they found.

So the crowd was cleared out, the body removed, and Sir John departed with our find packed into his car. He had examined some of the coins, knew quite a bit about them, and said that all were very old, Roman or Saxon in origin; a most valuable find.

The four of us sat drinking beer, Cobham trying to console us, and we trying to hearten him. The poor fellow was pretty low, and no wonder; however, he was lucky that there would be no murder charge—this had been made plain. While we were talking, came a knock at the door and here was old Alf Meghorn, drawn by the lights and commotion.

Cobham brought him in and set a mug of beer for him. We had to tell about the treasure, of course; I had some loose coins in my pocket and he fingered them. Suddenly his bright little eyes struck up at us.

"Cobham! You need a lawyer. Get Clarke, over at Whitby— he's a K.C.!"

"Lawyer be damned," growled Cobham. "He can't help us."

"But he can!" cried Meghorn excitedly. "These are all very old coins, Saxon or Roman! They were found in Hortel's Shaw, and that was under water until about the year 1200 or later."

"What's that got to do with it?" I demanded.

"Everything! The Crown can not touch these coins! I've got a book at home that tells about it. In 1897 there was a case of the Crown against the British Museum over the Limavary treasure.[1] It proved not to be treasure-trove, technically, because the land where it was found had once been under the sea—the treasure had actually not been concealed there but had been lost beneath the sea! The precedent will hold true here—see if it doesn't!"

And be damned if the old chap wasn't dead right, as events proved! We got back our sacks of coin, and there was no case against Alan Cobham, and everything was lovely.

Still, I have often wondered at the curious old fellow sticking around the Beacon watching for ghosts when they were in front of his eyes all the time—the ghosts haunting that story whose details we never learned. The story of a woman who had married the wrong man, the woman on whose grave Alan Cobham had put flowers; and of everything that lay behind the savage hatred between these two brothers.

"And yet we can imagine the romantic details," said Murchison, who was an incurable romanticist. "The details of heartbreak, of sly deviltry on Greg's part, of Alan going off to Africa in the army—"

"Spare us," I broke in. "You can't conjure up anything more downright romantic than that of picking up a Viking's loot where the seacoast hasn't run for a thousand years or so! Oh, that you, Gondy? What's up?"

GONDY CAME breaking in upon us, excitedly waving a letter.

---

1 *Fact.*

"My friends, here is really a marvel! Think of it—a royal treasure! What is it you say in English—busted? Yes. The busted nobleman and the ugly barmaid, and our chance at the crown jewels, ours for the mere picking up— 'Allo! What?"

"Okay," I sighed resignedly. "I'm a hard-headed guy. Tell us, and I'll pick holes in it fast enough."

But, as it proved, I could not. There were the crown jewels of England, no less, waiting for us—but that is another story.

IX

THE NOBLEMAN AND
THE UGLY BARMAID

*Our treasure-seekers turn their mine-detector
on the gold supposed to have been lost from
the baggage-train of King John of England—
and find more than they'd bargained for.*

S IR ERIC POYNTER, BART., was one of those hard-grained men with a lean face, cropped mustache, steely eye and masculine presence, who have knocked about the world. The type is not rare; usually endowed with a certain charming *savoir faire,* it meets every eye with level challenge which, warming into affability, increases the charm.

Thus I thought as I watched Sir Eric. He had spent some years in Canada and in New York, and was far from insular. He made no secret of the fact that he was now broke. Thanks to the war and the political upsets, he had lost everything except Poynter Hall. He would have lost that if he could, but it was entailed—a liability pinned to his coat-tails, as he put it. Sir Eric looked to be about thirty years old. His laughter was a short, harsh explosion that held no mirth....

The three of us—Gondy, Murchison and I, Bill Carson—were stopping at the Rose & Crown, a picturesque but uncomfortable old tavern in Spalding: and Sir Eric had come to meet us and discuss his proposition. He had done well as a tank-corps officer during the war; but ribbons butter no parsnips.

Pointing to the map spread out on the table, he put his finger on the Wash, that deep coastal indentation between Norfolk and Lincolnshire. Into it had emptied the rivers of the fen-country before the English marshes were drained.

Spalding was a tiny river-port on the Nane, one of these rivers.

"THE FACTS," said Sir Eric, "are historic and well verified. In the autumn of 1216, King John started to march across
the Wash. He was at war with his barons, as usual, and had with
him all the royal treasures, plate and crown jewels. His enormous baggage-train was caught by the rising tide, and over-
whelmed at a spot near the present Sutton Bridge, junction of
the branch railroad line to Peterboro. Everything was lost. Since
then the Wash has been heavily silted up by riverine detritus;
the exact spot is now marked by huge sand dunes. Poynter Hall
lies three miles from there. From here to Sutton Bridge is fifteen
miles. All clear, so far?"

We nodded. A treasure seven centuries old? Nuts, I thought.
Gondy fingered his mustache, his handsome aquiline features
thoughtful. Murchison, my pal since boyhood days in South
Boston, had a flush in his skinny cheeks, and his dark eyes were
bright; he was always ready to jump at any plausible story. I was
not.

"I have the best of reasons for believing that I can point to
the exact spot, within a limited radius, where some of that
treasure lies," went on Sir Eric. "That's why I communicated
with you gentlemen."

"Then why—" I blurted.

He looked at me, shrewdly, amusedly. "If I were positive,
perhaps I would, Mr. Carson. First, the area of search is too
great for one pair of hands. Second, the thought of prison is a
deterrent. I trust you—ah—get the point?"

We did. In doing any treasure-hunting in England, as we
well knew, we were taking our lives in our hand. A rigid law,
rigidly enforced, is that treasure-trove belongs to the Crown;
and whoever ignores this, belongs in jail. There are no outs.
England holds the greatest hidden treasure of any country on
earth, is well aware of it, and anyone who monkeys with the
law is playing with dynamite.

THIS WE were doing, in a literal sense. Murchison and I
had spent most of the war in English laboratories, evolving

various forms of mine-detectors for the Allied forces. The war ended, we were turned loose and took with us one of our electronic pets which was quite useless as a detector of mines, but useful in finding other things. We cut in Gondy, who was a great guy, and went to work unearthing buried treasure. It paid.

Vicomte de Gondy was no scientist, but we liked him, and he earned his share of the loot. He knew everyone in and out of society, and also his way around. We had run into a fine mess with his ex-sister-in-law Félice, which only served to draw us closer together. Here in England, Gondy could promote business for us; it was he who had pulled Sir Eric into the game, or so we supposed at the time....

"This is a ticklish business. We can't afford to fluff it any more than you can," Murchison said, his eyes eager. "Why do you think you know just where to find the stuff?"

"Not so fast!" Sir Eric said pleasantly. "I'd best go into that on the ground, if you decide to have a try at it. I can guarantee that you'll be satisfied. Poynter Hall was built in Tudor days, and apparently none of its owners has spent a farthing on repairs since then. It may be a gem of architecture, but it's a damned beastly residence. Only three or four rooms are habitable. I might put up one of you three chaps; the others had best stop at the Cat & Garters in Walpole, seven miles from the Hall. Sorry; I'm thinking only of your convenience. They know me there, and I can secure you comfortable quarters. I've an old couple at the Hall who do for me; but I'm frank to say you'd not like it. No more would I, if I could live anywhere else. But, with the country going to the dogs as it is—"

His grimace was expressive. He looked at us for our answer....

Sir Eric had no car; he drove a dog-cart and cob, making no secret of his poverty. Nor was Poynter Hall a lordly estate. It was a desolate old ruin off to itself amid sand and pines and Norway spruce. The big trees, like everything else of value on the place, had long since been sold off.

I did not half cotton to Sir Eric, but Murchison looked

pleadingly at me, and I read eagerness in Gondy's face, so I nodded.

"Suppose we come over tomorrow, then, to Walpole?"

"Very well," said Sir Eric. "I'll stop there on my way home and arrange for your rooms."

"If they can put me up for the night." said Gondy, "might I go with you?"

"Rather!" Sir Eric brightened. "I'll be glad of your company on the road. Meet all three of you there for lunch tomorrow, eh? And if you don't mind, I'll assuage local curiosity with the story that Americans may lease the place and are looking at it with repairs in mind. Likely story, and all that."

He clattered away, and Gondy went with him; Murchison and I knew the reason. Gondy wanted a chance to buzz about on his own. He had a positive genius for learning things; people

talked to him freely, and he could pick up more information in an hour than others could in a week's time.

"You don't seem so hot about this venture," Murchison said to me later.

"I smell a rat." I told him. "Our busted nobleman didn't ring true in his talk about the risks. There's no law against hunting for treasure; concealing it is the joker. We're steering close to the wind, sure, which lends it spice; but I wouldn't trust this guy any farther than I can spit."

He scoffed. "We can handle him if there's any trouble. All that would make me lose sleep, would be if Félice were in the picture. She's not."

"No; that's a relief," I admitted. "The detectives Gondy put on her trail have lost track of her; in Paris, at last reports. I know there's no ground for any suspicion with Sir Eric; I just don't fancy his type, that's all."

WITH MORNING, we ambled to Walpole, in our ancient but honorable Fiat. In the back end, disassembled for travel, was the gadget we called the Baby. It was no discovery of epochal proportions. Indeed, it was no discovery at all, being merely an adaptation of electronic principles, used in radar and elsewhere, to our present aims. For that matter, every modern steamship takes soundings precisely as we plumbed old Mother Earth for treasure, except that we had harnessed supersonic waves of incredible delicacy, and further split them up to suit our purposes. The tubes were the unique controlling feature. These we had made ourselves, and their secret was ours alone; without them, the Baby was nothing at all.

About mid-morning we reached Walpole, or Long Walpole as it was locally called for some unknown reason, and readily located the Cat & Garters. This was a better tavern than the Rose 8c Crown, boasting flush toilets instead of the usual British thundermugs. Sir Eric had been as good as his word, and we took possession of two excellent rooms equipped with feather-beds and bell-pulls and tiny fireplaces.

Gondy was on hand to meet us.

I WENT around the car to unlock the back end and get the bags, and made an unpleasant discovery: the lock was an intricate Italian one, and somebody had been at it, completely ruining it for further use. It looked and shut all right, but would never lock again. However, nothing had been stolen. The job must have been done at Spalding, we figured out, but there was nothing to show who had done it.

"We've an hour before Sir Eric shows up," Gondy said. "Let's settle down in the bar, and I'll show you Exhibit A. Which of us, by the way, stops at Poynter Hall?"

"Let's toss coins for it," I suggested. "Odd man gets the bad luck."

We took a table in the ordinary room, ordered drinks and made the toss. I was the odd man. Gondy chuckled.

"What do you think of the barmaid?" he asked softly. "Observe her well."

We did so. She was rosy-cheeked, heavy-browed, had a big mouth and buxom fittings; she could not be called handsome, certainly, but she was extremely neat in hair and person. I noted that the barflies treated her with great respect.

"A pippin," said Murchison carelessly. "Smart gal, I'd say. Not so young."

"Ugly as sin with a heart of gold," I commented. "I like her looks. Who is she, Gondy?"

Gondy grinned and loosed his bomb.

"Lady Poynter," said he.

We looked at him hard. "Come on, no kidding," I said.

He shook his head. "Fact—or so I'm led to conclude. There's a good old word that seems to fit our Eric; *raffish*. He's been a bit of a blade in his day. The general social upset due to the war did not help matters. This barmaid, Rose, owns the whole place. Her father was killed in the Dunkirk debacle, her brother was torpedoed, and she inherited. It is supposed that Sir Eric married her, during the war, secretly.... Merely gossip. He would not dare acknowledge her as his wife, here in England. But when he comes, just watch them—their faces!"

"I'd put her down as a damned exceptional woman," I said. "So Eric's a cad?"

"No, no, I don't mean that," Gondy said hurriedly. "A gambler, a heavy plunger always, perhaps a potential rascal—but so far, he's kept up his end of respectability, socially speaking. He's no crook, if you get me; but I fancy he's amoral, like many a better man—unscrupulous. We'll do well to keep an eye on him if we find anything."

"What else have you swept up from backstairs gossip?" I inquired. That hurt him; and it was an unfair thrust. I said so and apologized, and next minute he was grinning again. He began to bubble over, in his eager way:

"There's no question about the loss of the treasure, of course.

That's history, and the exact spot was long ago worked out. It seems, however, that shifting sands and scouring tides might have carried it anywhere; no use looking for it where the loss happened, any more than you could look for Pharaoh's army in the Red Sea. As for Poynter Hall, it was built long after King John's day, of course. There are local traditions about treasure in connection with the place—not King John's gold, just treasure. All very vague, but Sir Eric may have something definite to go on. Local tradition is often surprisingly right."

He gulped his drink and hurried along.

"Now comes trouble: Eric is heavily in debt, of course. And lately he's been paying some attention to another lady—"

"Wait!" said Murchison. "You just intimated that he's in love with his supposed wife, yonder!"

Gondy nodded. "Or she's in love with him. What he means by love, is something else again—that sort of man loves anything in skirts. Anyhow, there's another woman in the picture; no one knows just who she is, which makes the gossip keener. I'm just giving you general gossip, by way of getting you *au courant* with the situation," he added apologetically, for as a rule he detested such loose talk. "It's vitally important that we know everything possible about our man."

We were still chatting when the tall form of Sir Eric entered. I looked at his fine athletic figure with envy, for I am heavily built, and since my discharge had paid scant attention to diet.

"In the autumn of 1216, King John started to march across the Wash.

He joined us with a hearty greeting. Rose came over to our table, and we arranged about something to eat. I saw what Gondy meant, when Rose looked at him: she had the look a woman wears only for the man who means the whole world to her.

BUT I saw, or fancied, something else—a vivid but concealed resentment. This woman had character plus. She was keenly intelligent and had a pride all her own. Within her somewhat ungainly shell she had everything that was lacking beneath Sir Eric's superficial show of gentility. I liked her quiet poise and innate dignity. She was worth a dozen of him.

Sir Eric had walked over from the Hall; a few miles were nothing to him, of course. Some of these chaps in England walk twenty or thirty miles a day and like it. When he found I was to be his guest, he shook hands, commiserated with me, and enjoyed a cheery laugh. He excused us to have a wash, before luncheon; perhaps it was coincidence, but Rose was gone at the same time, another barmaid taking her place..... None of our business, of course.

The meal ended, we all piled into the Fiat, which Murchison and Gondy would keep; and Sir Eric directed us on our way. He took us by a roundabout route, in order to point out how the topography along this side of the Wash had been altered by the river-silt that had built it up in the old days, when this district of England was all marshland, and tides flowed in where

*He had with him all the royal
treasures and crown jewels."*

now lay solid ground. Murchison was the first to get what he was driving at.

"Oh, I see! You mean anything here would have been carried along to that grove of beeches you were talking about!"

"Precisely. It was like a weir along the shore then. Men, animals, anything washed away back yonder, would be caught and held and—sunk. Now, when Poynter Hall was built in the Tudor days, it stood among huge beeches, then on solid ground. I've some of the family papers to prove this," Sir Eric replied. "There's the Hall ahead. The beeches vanished centuries ago and were replaced by pines, of which even the largest are gone now."

We turned at a ruined gateway to a neglected drive and unkempt grounds covered with pine and spruce saplings, and came to the dilapidated and overgrown Hall. Most of it was roofless desolation; one small wing, with a portion of the nearby stables, was sound and habitable, though by no means inviting. "Much patched about," as our host said truly.

Giles and Bradshaw stood waiting to receive us. Male and female created He them, and I have seldom seen less inviting specimens of the creation. Giles was a tottering old boy with a straggly gray thatch and a cleft palate; not a word that he said did I ever comprehend. Bradshaw was, by dress, a female; equally old, her chin nearly met her nose, and both sprouted an abundance of gray hairs. They were the Hall servitors. Giles could not handle my suitcase; he had all he could do to get about, so I hefted it into the house.

Inside we found five huddled little rooms—two bedrooms, small, with broken window-panes, parlor, dining-room and what the English call offices; in this case a kitchen, the best room in the house. The bed in my room caused me a sigh at thought of entrusting my two-hundred-twenty pounds to its mercies, but Sir Eric shepherded us outside in no time.

"NOW LET us look at the best thing about the place, and you'll comprehend my optimism," he said cheerfully, and led us around to the side away from the drive. No doubt a stairway had once been there. Now it was just a hole in the ruined walls, with a ramp leading down to the cellars.

But what cellars they were! The plural was used with justice here. Except for one end heaped with rubble and branching forth saplings to the sky, they ran under the whole place. The ceiling and floor above was upheld by massive stone pillars three feet thick. Underfoot was beaten earth. Wreckage of old winebins, broken furniture, junk of all kinds, strewed the place. A flashlight provided the only illumination, even in mid-afternoon. The ceiling was a good eight feet high.

"Among the title deeds and other estate papers," said Sir Eric, "is an account of the building of the Hall. The foundations were put in down through sand to a solid clay substratum, and somewhere in the course ot the work, trouble was encountered. Bones of men and horses were dug up; the workmen sickened, some of them died; superstitious fancies were wakened. One man declared that he saw the devil in person grinning out of the hole; another related that he uncovered several great chests, and that gibbering ghosts pulled the earth back on top of his discovery. This man was among those who died.

"Whatever the truth may be, undoubtedly something was discovered of a nature that caused much terror; in panic, the excavation was abandoned and the foundations were put down as they now are. The legend was started that a curse lay on the spot. You'll still hear told that the Hall is haunted."

HE TRACED what he considered a logical connection between these happenings and the beechwood that had stood here in previous centuries, trapping and burying anything swept down this bank of the Wash. What was more to the point, he took us upstairs to the parlor and opened a cupboard to display a number of objects that had been dug up by the builders and preserved—sadly rusted remnants of weapons, and bits of iron, which archaeologists had identified as being of Angevin types— that is, of King John's day. The iron fragments were what he called "horse furniture."

He was deadly serious about it all, the conclusion being that part at least of King John's treasure was to be found under the cellar floor. Where treasure was concerned, Murchison would believe anything, and became quite lit up over the possibilities. Gondy, too, was all for it, being equally flighty in his imagination.

I said nothing. When a man is obsessed with a fixed idea, sane talk is wasted time. My old lab chief was the ultimate whiz on electronics, but he had a firm belief that the whole English language would have to be rewritten and based on the hep-cat jargon of pre-war days, and would argue you black in the face if you objected. Same with Sir Eric. This delusion of his was

arrant nonsense, of course, but I figured it would not take us long to explore these cellars—and we might always find something or other. That is one nice thing about treasure-hunting in England; you're almost sure to turn up something.

He talked for a solid hour about his belief without saying anything new, then dug out a couple of old lanterns and took them down the hole, while we got the Baby unpacked and put together. This gadget of ours was very light, being made of a magnesium alloy. We had mounted it in a wicker baby-buggy, which held the batteries compactly and covered ground with ease. Like a radio, it should ideally have been hooked up to a 110-volt current, but that was out of the question here, and the batteries would do the work.

The north end of the cellars was the point toward the Wash, whose waters now ran at a considerable distance from the Hall. We began there, working for an hour just to get in running order and let Sir Eric see how the Baby strutted its stuff. He refused to believe it. He could quite comprehend that the rays, or waves, would kick back from any solid substance they encountered, and would register on the dials; but that we could tell the depth and nature of that substance was too stiff for him.

The earthen floor presented no difficulty, of course. There was little junk in the north cellar, and for twenty minutes we worked nicely, until the buzzer sounded. I consulted the chart, on which we had mapped all combinations of the dials and gauges, and which gave us at a glance the nature of any strike.

"Wood, four feet down," I said. "Apparently a stump, not a log."

Sir Eric went off and came back with a pick and shovel, took off his coat, and buckled down to hard work in spite of our attempts to dissuade him. It was a job, for the floor was solidly packed down, but at length he reached his objective. Sure enough, it was an old stump, and a big one—beech, he thought. While I filled in the hole, he rested. We knocked off and went up into the fading afternoon daylight.

"Wonderful!" cried Sir Eric. "What did I tell you about the beechwood? This proves it. How deep does the bally thing probe?"

We had adjusted it to a depth of fifteen feet, which was plenty. We were not anxious to sweat digging up relics of the flood. Having thoughtfully fetched along a bottle of Scotch, we laid out the campaign. I was to stay here and work when the spirit moved me; Murchison and Gondy would return to the Cat & Garters, and come back in the morning, bringing a lunch hamper, to put in the full day. It was impossible, said Sir Eric, to get anyone except Giles to do any digging; no one else could be trusted. Giles being what he was, we voted him out and made up our minds to pick-and-shovel work.

My pals got off. Sir Eric and I bathed in the good old English fashion—little tin tub and sponge—and dined. It was a good dinner of roast pheasant; if old Giles could trap birds, Bradshaw could certainly cook them to the king's taste. After dinner, my host said he was going for a walk, and would I come along? I declined, and fancied that he looked a shade relieved. He told me to make myself at home, and went striding away.

I pottered around the sad mess of a house, inspected the cob and dog-cart in the unruined corner of the stables, above which the two servants lived, and finally turned in, disgusted with the whole business. The Baby was safe in the cellar.

WE PUT in two cheerless days of wearying labor. Sir Eric did his share, but each afternoon he borrowed the car and went off on his own errands. But on Saturday morning we turned up a slab of stone and he insisted on going after it. Eight feet down, it was. Instead of a slab, we found it to be a stone chest containing the bones of an ancient British warrior, with some bronze implements, and a sword and pottery. Magnificent, said Sir Eric; we did not agree. Filling in on top of that chest was a job in itself. I got it done after lunch; he went off in the car, and I sat outside smoking and resting before taking my trick at the Baby. I walked down to the gate to stretch my legs, and was just in time to get all but run over by one of these miniature British cars as it swung in from the road.

The thing swerved to avoid hitting me—I had already jumped clear—and slammed into a sapling and stopped. The shock threw the driver forward; she hit her head against the wheel and slumped over it, knocked silly, but not before I had recognized Rose, the ugly barmaid.

I ran to her and pulled her out from under the wheel, letting her down flat on the ground. In repose, her features were equally resolute but more pleasant; they had a rather charming freshness and youth. She wore little makeup, was neat and trim as a pin, and I was surprised by her hands—long and slender, beauti-

*She came close to me—and slapped me twice across the
face. "That's for old times, Mr. Carson!" she cried.*

fully formed, though roughened by her daily work. A red mark
on her forehead was rapidly becoming a bump.

The truest kindness was to let her come around by herself,
so I did. In getting her out of the car, I had dislodged some
papers and letters lying on the seat. Those I picked up and
replaced, then sat beside her, lit a fresh cigarette, and waited.
No rings were on either hand; the one lying by me had a beautiful and costly watch, set with brilliants, on the wrist. It was
her only ornament.

My cigarette was half finished when she sighed, stirred, and opened her eyes.

"Don't move," I advised her quietly. "You're all right now; relax and rest. You hit your head against the wheel, and it knocked you out."

She lay looking at me; I had pillowed her head on my coat.

"I know you," she said calmly. "You're one of Sir Eric's friends—the Americans."

"Two Americans, one Frenchman," I said. "Yes. You're Rose; I know. How did that inn ever get its queer title of the Cat & Garters?"

"It's been that for ever so long." Her tongue held no trace of country brogue. She had education, obviously. "A gentleman from London said once that it must have been a French name originally—meaning the Four Carters, he thought…. French!" A shadow crossed her face. "There's no good bodes to us from anything French—anything! Naught but ill. That reminds me—I came to see Sir Eric."

I failed to get her association of ideas. "He's not here, so relax," I said. "He borrowed our car and went out, I don't know where."

"But I can guess," she said bitterly. She kept watching me steadily. "You are Mr. Carson. Your friends at the inn have spoken of you. Is there no one else here at the Hall?"

"You mean visitors? No."

She sat up. "I'm all right; I'd better be going. Tell him, if you will, that I came over to see him in regard to Denemere; he'll understand."

I helped her up, then got the little car into the road for her, and she twisted herself under the wheel. As I closed the door, she showed a trace of the usual brusque independence of the average Englishwoman.

"Sorry I was such a rotten driver and made myself a nuisance." She gave me a sudden flashing smile. "I wish I could help you, really; but I don't know just what to warn you against. You will keep your eyes open, won't you? Good-by."

She sent the car away fast, leaving me astonished. Warn me? That was an odd thing to say. I turned, and then saw a paper on the ground where the car had stood—one of her papers, no doubt, that had slid under the car in falling. I picked it up, saw that it was simply a folded sheet bearing writing, and pocketed it. Regaining the house, I put it on the dresser in my room, intending to send it back to her by Murchison and Gondy. Then I went back down cellar—and what I found there put everything else out of mind.

Murch was hacking away with the pick; Gondy was shoveling; and both were in high excitement. Metal at four feet down—solid metal, six feet long and four wide—might be an enormous chest of some kind! As usual, I bit. Their fever infected me, and I got busy with the pick; and sure enough, the Baby had told the truth. What we brought to light was a huge sheet of lead, part of the original roof-covering which had been stripped off. We left one corner bare for our host to see, and I took my spell at the machine while Gondy and Murchison went topside to clean up and rest.

Working down in that gloomy vault by flickering lantern-light was depressing; it was a ghostly and rather ominous place and in time got on the nerves. I plugged along for quite a while, and felt thankful that we had covered most of the north cellar. When the buzzer sounded, I jumped; it was like getting a big strike after trolling idly for an hour.

Another sheet of lead, I thought, and flashed my light on the dials. No! To my surprise, the gauges did not hold steady but flickered. Apparently something had been struck at a depth of ten feet. I was consulting the chart, trying to find the nature of the object, when Murchison and Gondy returned.

"That's an extraordinary thing!" cried out Murch. "Where on earth did you get it?"

"What are you talking about?" I demanded.

"That letter or message on your dresser. Haven't you read it?"

"Certainly not," I began.

Gondy cut me short. He was waving the folded paper.

"Then listen to this, Bill!" he exclaimed excitedly. "Looks as though some anonymous friend were tipping somebody off!" He read over the writing:

"*For your own good, you had better know that E. P. spends part of each day with the foreign lady at Denemere; they do seem most intimate.*"

Denemere! I remembered all of a sudden what Rose had said.

"You two chumps are reading a lady's private correspondence," I said. "Forgot to tell you about Rose."

I RELATED what had happened, and how I came to have the letter. It was plain that somebody was trying to warn the barmaid with word of Sir Eric's philanderings: she had come to the Hall to have things out with him. Gondy swore ruefully; the idea of having thus surprised the secret irked him.

While we discussed it, we heard old Bradshaw squawking at us, and we emerged from the cellar, to find her and a strange man there. The man touched his cap and said Sir Eric had sent him back with our car, and wanted him to bring the dog-cart; our host was detained and would not be back until later in the evening.

"Decent of him to send back the car," said Murchison. "You'd better run into town with us for supper, Bill; bring you back afterward."

THE MAN departed toward the stables, and I told the old witch we would not be on her hands for dinner. She grinned and cackled something about Denemere, and Gondy asked her where that was. She waved her skinny hand vaguely, and said it was a place that had been let for the season to furriners, and shuffled away.

"She means the shooting season, which is on," Gondy explained, as we started back toward the lower regions. With that, I remembered.

"Having thus settled important matters," I said, "suppose you guys join me in trying to learn whether we've unearthed King John's treasure."

We settled down around the Baby, gripped by the thrill that came every time we made a strike, whether worth while or not. As nearly as we could figure, metal had been encountered ten feet down; the kickback registered iron one minute, gold the next, as though unable to make up its mind. The reaction was entirely different from that occasioned by the lead sheet, but this substance was of approximately the same size, as we determined by running the Baby over the ground, back and forth, making soundings. Excitement took hold of us as we marked out the spot in the hard-packed floor, getting the same reaction from all of it; because, whatever it might be, gold was assuredly a part of the substance.

"Ten feet down—that'll be one hell of a dig," said Murchison. "See here; it's getting late, so why not run in to town now for supper, and restore that letter to our friend Rose, then come back here and make a night of it? Sir Eric ought to be back, and we'll let him share the glory of wielding that shovel. Earth wouldn't be so bad, but the sand under this floor is the very devil to scoop out."

"All right," I said. "And if we can get to town before closing hours, let's get a bottle of whisky to help with tonight's job. I think we're going to have something to celebrate."

This was true enough, but not as I thought.

We were bundling into the car when Bradshaw and old Giles begged a ride into town, since it was Saturday night and they were for the cinema and a bit of a holiday with the master's permission. They had relatives in Long Walpole and would return on the morrow. So we crowded them in, and found the gas-tank low, thanks to Sir Eric's lady-chasings.

Getting to town, we dropped the precious pair. I landed at

the inn to give back the letter, and the other two went off to find petrol and whisky, since there was no off-sale at the tavern.

Rose was not in sight. I asked for her and found that she was in her own "parlor" at the back, and was taken there. Here were two rooms, beautifully furnished; and the ugly barmaid had become a gracious young woman, who invited me to have tea from a Sheffield urn that would have made any collector's heart turn over with envy.

"Thanks; you're very kind," I assented. "We ran into town to get dinner, and are returning later to the Hall; some work has come up."

"Sir Eric has returned?"

"No." I produced the folded paper. "I stopped in to give you this. It must have fallen out of sight under your car. I'm glad to see, by the way, that the bump on your forehead has left no mark to speak of."

I was trying to pass off the matter casually; but no soap—as she took the paper, her eyes rested on mine. Perhaps I was blushing.

"You read it?" she asked, in her queer direct fashion, as though we were old friends.

"Sorry. My friends found it—didn't know that you must have dropped it—"

A telephone was on the wall. Its jangling ring interrupted my stammerings, to my quick relief. A word of apology, and she went to it.

"Oh, it's you!" she said. "I drove out to see you today, but found you gone as usual. What about? You'd scarcely like it said over the telephone, would you? Besides, I have visitors."

She paused, listening. When she spoke again, there was a bite in her voice that made me sit up.

"Never mind all that, Eric. Keep your pretty falsities for the Frenchwoman. I've warned you, and for the last time.... I'm wearing it now, do you understand? And I intend to wear it in future. I'm afraid you'll have to face the music, my dear.... Oh,

I say! Don't get ugly, old chap. Two can play at that game, you know; and I happen to hold all the cards. No doubt you're calling from Denemere? Not very well done, my dear Eric. Good-by."

As she hung up, I could hear the explosive mutter of oaths over the wire. Sir Eric must certainly have received a headful, I thought. That quiet, forceful delivery of hers carried a punch, and it amused me. Wearing—what was she wearing?

She came back to the table and poured from the silver urn. With my cup, she gave me a quick, frank little smile, dropping all pretense.

"Sorry, Mr. Carson. I expect you've heard no end of gossip."

Then I noticed the wedding-ring on her left hand. The meaning of her phrases over the wire struck me abruptly. Nor did I make any pretense.

"You English people," I rejoined, "assuredly have the knack of understatement down to fine art! Yes, I think I understand. I'd hate to be in his shoes when you really cut loose on him!"

"Afraid I'll have to. May run out to see him tonight. I've been a patient Griselda too long." She folded her hands and looked at me thoughtfully. "I know you're here on business of some kind. As I told you today, please be careful! He has great charm, ability, every talent. He has only one lack, and the man who has this lack is beyond hope. He has no loyalty—either to me or to anyone else."

"I see what you mean, now," I replied, and thanked her for the warning. "In his own interest, I think he's tied to us, though."

"That's precisely what I thought, once," she replied, twisting the ring on her finger. Then she broke into a smile, shifted the subject adroitly, and we had no further mention of personalities. It was a pleasant little visit.

"She's a really charming woman," I said, telling Gondy and Murchison about it while we sat at dinner. "She has the knack of putting you at your ease; I've met great ladies who lacked it."

Gondy nodded. Murchison chided me for a wolf, and said

we had better take her warning seriously. They were both disturbed and uneasy; Sir Eric had lost his appeal so far as we were
concerned, and the idea of getting involved in an ugly domestic tangle was not pleasant....

We talked it over on the way out to the Hall. We were all
dumb nitwits; none of us caught the significant things that
might have pointed up the truth for us. We agreed, however,
on a vague feeling that the quicker we were away, the better. So
we decided to end the search on whatever it was that we had
found, and then pull out for green fields and pastures new.
Gondy said he had already got wind of a most promising
venture.

"All right, boys," I said, as we pulled up at the dark Hall.
"Let's get the Baby packed first thing, then dig. If we've got the
treasure, well and good; if not, quit cold. We're under no obli-
gation to Sir Eric."

This decided, we hustled down cellar and lighted the lanterns.
Disassembling the Baby, we packed it and the carriage in their
cartons and loaded them into the back of the car. The lock on
this had not been repaired; nobody thought of it as an important thing.

Sir Eric had not returned, so we hung up the lanterns and
attacked the job awaiting us, and went at it with a vim. When
we got through the hard-packed earth and clay on top, sinking
a ten-foot shaft through sand was tough work until we be-
thought us to get a couple of buckets of water and wet the sides
of the shaft.

An hour passed, and most of another, before we struck something solid. It proved to be one end of a small box or chest of
some kind. In order to clear this, we had to enlarge the hole
considerably, and took turns grubbing away at the bottom of
the shaft. Five minutes after being helped down to take my
turn. I scraped out a whitish object; it proved to be a skull of
some sort, which turned to dust as I brought it into the light—
all but some teeth. It was the skull of a horse or mule.

We wet down the walls of the shaft anew so there would be no cave-in, got a rope from the stables, and presently had the box cleared. It was surprisingly small but very heavy, and seemed to be of badly rusted iron covered with bull-hide. We hauled it up into the light and freed it of the rope. I gave it one stroke with the pick that shattered it—and such a blaze of excitement gripped us as we had never before known.

O U T   O F   that chest fell all sorts of rotted matter—and amid it a sheen of gold and glitter of jewels that left us dumb. None of us could utter a word. Murchison leaned over and picked up something and shook off the rot—cloth wrappings, no doubt. It was a crown, a rim of gold set with golden spikes, and in the spikes were jewels. Gondy clawed out a necklace, a round of great golden knobs and chains, held it up, then laid it down again and came to his feet.

"I—I'll get a sack," he said hoarsely, and picking up one of the lanterns, went out of the cellars. Murchison looked up at me—we were sitting beside the chest—and his face was white as a sheet, his eyes like saucers.

"Bill!" he said, and licked his lips. "It is! Look at the crown— the King's crown, just like in pictures!"

"That's not all." I stirred the mess before us and brought to light rings, bracelets and other glittering gauds. "King John's treasure, no doubt of it. Won't do us any good, Murch. We're not looters. This will have to go to the British Museum."

"Yeah, I expect so," he assented. "Crown jewels, Bill. It'd be a crime to bootleg this stuff, melt it up." He rubbed the crown with his cuff, brightening the gold, then perched it on his head. It slid over one ear, and he looked like a drunken sailor playing Neptune. "Lordy! Me, wearing King John's crown!"

We played with the stuff, raking out rings and arm-bands and what-not, but realization that in common decency we could not keep it had a chilling effect on our ardor. That crown fascinated Murchison. He rubbed it up some more, put it on his head again, and came to his feet, posturing beside the huge pile of sand and dirt removed from the hole.

"Look, Bill!" he exclaimed. "We might take this stuff back to Boston before turning it in. Look what publicity we'd get—our pictures in all the papers! If we put the Baby on the market commercially, what a break it'd be! Why, it'd be a million dollars' worth of free advertising—"

The crown, which was too small for him, slipped off his head. He made a wild grab for it, lost balance and stepped smack into the hole behind him. He went down, with a smothered yell. The crown rolled across the floor. I caught up the lantern and went to the edge of the hole. There sat Murchison on the bottom—or part of him. His fall had brought down enough sand to cover him to his chest; its weight held him immovable.

"Bill! It's caved in on me!" he gasped. "Any more will bury me—gimme a hand, quick! I can't move!"

There was a step behind me—Gondy, I supposed.

"Come on, Gondy," I said. "You take the light, and—"

"Thanks," said another voice—not that of Gondy. The lantern was taken from my hand. I turned. There was Sir Eric, holding up the lantern in one hand, and in the other a pistol that pointed squarely at me.

"He'll keep, Carson. That hole will make a good grave for you too.... Back off, you fool!" his voice snarled acidly. "D'you want me to blow hell out of you, you blasted American rotter? Put those hands up! Back—move back, I tell you!"

Aghast and incredulous, thinking for a moment that he had gone mad, I obeyed him and moved away from the hole. He followed me, with the light and the gun, backing me until I came to one of the massive columns that upheld the roof. He ordered me to reach my arms out around it. I did so. Something—someone—caught my wrist and knotted a cord around it—Sir Eric was not alone! My wrists were made fast; I stood there, bound to the column, helpless. He looked at the stuff on the floor, and laughed excitedly.

"Here's a rum go as ever was, sure enough!" he cried. "It was here all the while, and me thinking you were a pack of blessed idiots for swallowing my fairytales! Well, live and learn. Kind of you to dig it up for us. Thanks for leaving the machine neatly packed where we could get it, too. Better get the stuff together, my dear—and don't step on that crown."

I WAS still stupefied, unable to account for his attitude. His companion moved, a dark shape in the obscurity; I caught a whiff of perfume—and I knew that odor. It clarified everything, startled me into mental acuity. Félice, by the gods! Gondy's former sister-in-law, our deadly enemy!

She moved into the light, removed a dark cloak she wore, put it on the floor and into it scooped the gold and the crown. She stood up and looked at me, laughing wildly, came close to me, and slapped me twice across the face.

"That for old times, Mr. Carson!" The beauty of her, lighted up by exultation and inner ferocity, was something to see. Sir Eric caught her by the arm and wrested her aside.

"None o' that, my dear." He dominated her with his coldly savage manner. "Get the stuff up to the car and wait for me. And mind, no tricks with Gondy! Leave him as he is. Slip a knife into him, and I'll wring your pretty neck! There'll be no murder done here to get Scotland Yard after us. We've got what we wanted, and far more. Get!"

She-devil as she was, she was afraid of him. Murchison, who had been cursing furiously, had fallen silent. Her golden hair fell about her face as she leaned over, gathered up the cloak with its precious contents, and slipped away into the darkness; she held a flashlight that pierced the road for her. Sir Eric watched her off, picked up the lantern and went to the hole, and looked down. Murchison swore at him luridly. He laughed, came back to me, put the lantern on its ceiling-hook, got out cigarettes and lighted one.

"I'll just have a word with you, since you're a man of some sense," he observed amiably. "Now, take notice: The Frenchman is knocked out and tied up; not hurt bad. I'm off with Félice and a fast car; this time tomorrow we'll be across the Channel, with that machine of yours, and the loot you've so kindly provided us."

"You treacherous rat!" I said. "Think you can get away with it? Not much."

"That's the point, my lad," he replied coolly. "Think, for a minute; think. All you can get after us for is taking the machine. Would the game be worth the candle?"

I could not think at all; I was in a mental riot. The "foreign woman at Denemere"—the broken lock on our car—the way we had walked directly into this trap—

"So she and you together laid the snare for us!" I said.

He nodded cheerfully. "Right. Suppose we're run down for taking your machine? Then your little game will be cooked for good. We'll know nothing about any machine, any gold, and you'll have no proof—all you'll get will be publicity, and you won't relish it by half."

"You forget Lady Poynter," I said.

This staggered him for an instant. "Oh, you know about Rose, eh? Let her be Lady Poynter, and be damned to her, now," he replied. "I'm off for good. I'll get the marriage annulled, quick enough—or she can do it, blast her!" His mirthless, explosive laugh burst forth. "Aye, let her do it! Now, when the servants return tomorrow you'll be freed, and no harm done. So take my advice. If Félice had had her way, you'd be dead. I'm too wise for that sort o' thing; this is no bally cinema, y'know! You're stuck; so accept it. I'll leave the light to keep ghosts from troubling you—"

He swung around, strode away and was gone, leaving the lantern.

"All right, Murch?" I demanded.

"Yeah, but can't move. Heard it all. How about you?"

"Tied to the pillar here."

Shrewd Sir Eric! The more I thought over his advice, the

more sense it made. Félice must have put him up to the whole game. Knowing its value, the Baby was what she was after. He had dreamed up a plausible treasure yarn—what a break for them that we had really found treasure! Now they had it and the Baby to boot.

They had planned the job for tonight, with the servants out of the way, and would probably hide their loot and skip out by air for the Continent. Even if we caught them, we might recover nothing, and the publicity would do us no good at all. They had a car, too. I heard the engine start, speed up, then lessen in the darkness outside.

"I'm afraid he talked sense, Bill," came Murchison's voice, drearily. "She's smart."

"I hate to admit it. I hate to let 'em get away with it," I replied. "After all, the gold would do us no good. We might stop 'em, but would recover nothing. It's losing the Baby that hurts."

"Me too. Though we can always build another. But can you wish that guy any worse luck than being tied up to Félice?"

"I dunno." I tugged vainly at my bonds. "She'll be tied up to him; I imagine that might be worse yet. Maybe we'd better let 'em go and play safe. How are you?"

"Not so hot. More sand is slipping down around me. Say, Bill! Remember that horse-skull? I can feel something hard with my foot at the end of the hole. A horse would maybe have one box on each side to balance the load. If there's another here—"

"Check it!" I halted him. "Who's there? Speak up, you!"

A slight laugh came from behind me. Hands touched wrist and worked with the cords.

"No use; I'll have to cut it," said a voice. "Steady on, now."

The voice was familiar. The long connecting cord between my wrists, around the big pillar, was parted; the speaker came forward into the light, holding a small knife. It was Rose. She worked at the knots about my wrists; a dark raincoat cloaked her.

"Where'd you come from? How long have you been here?"
I demanded.

"Too long. I heard it all," she said, sawing at the knots. "I
came out here to see him—sorry I dared not intervene before.
I had to choose between impulse and common sense. So must
you, I expect. All clear—help Mr. Murchison."

We went to the hole. Murch was buried to his chin but had
one hand free. I reached down with the shovel and got part of
him cleared. We had been using rope and bucket to get the
sand out. I let down the rope; he took a grip and wriggled
himself loose, and we hauled him up. Beyond an excited word,
he scarcely noticed Rose, but caught up the bucket.

"I'll get some water—keep it from caving in—and see to
Gondy," he ejaculated and departed on the run.

Rubbing my chafed wrists, I stood looking at Rose.

"WE OWE you a good deal," I said. "What did you mean
just now—about choosing?"

"It's clear enough. He's gone, with her; I had to let them go,"
she said calmly. "I'm on hand as a witness, if you want to stop
them. You might convict them—of what? Theft? Assault? You
might recover your machine, whatever that is; but would it all
be worth while? They'd have the gold hidden, be sure of that."

"I'm afraid so. Do you want him back?"

She smiled faintly and shook her head.

"As you said, he goes to his worst punishment, a life with
her. Let him go."

Murchison came back, panting, and hurriedly sluiced water
on the sides of the hole.

"Gondy's blacked out. I loosed him. He'll come around," he
gasped. "Bill, get to work! Clear the hole, down there; the other
box—oh, hell!" He blinked at Rose, taken aback by realization
of her presence. "I forgot—"

"Never mind her; she's one of us," I said. "Hurry up, tie the
rope to the bucket."

I lowered myself into the hole and began sending up buckets of sand. Sure enough, a second box was there; one on either side of the horse, as Murchison had said. Presently Gondy came staggering in and sat down, holding his head. He and Rose and Murchison all talked at once. I paid no attention, but worked the box clear of the sand, made the rope fast, and we hauled it up.

I lost no time in attacking the box. This time, no rotted cloth greeted us; instead, it was full to the brim with little rolls of vellum, hard as metal. Gondy snatched one, drove the shovel through it—and out fell a stream of golden coins. The little rolls were wrapped coin, both gold and silver.

EVERYBODY BABBLING in wild excitement, we dumped out rolls until we realized there was no sense in opening more. King John's gold! Here it was, sure enough; yet the edge of our excitement had been taken off by the first find. The only one of us not carried away by the thrill was Rose. She was interested, yes, but quietly so.

"There's no time to lose," she said now, "if you want to reach a telephone and get the police after them."

We looked at one another. Did we? It was a hard choice, sure enough. They had—or we supposed they had—the Baby, and the crown jewels to boot. We had this pile of money, of which we could quietly and easily dispose, and it looked like a lot.

"If we bring 'em back," said Murchison, "the chances are we gain little or nothing. And yet of course King John's gold is museum stuff. We couldn't just spend it, even if the Crown didn't have a prior claim."

"But the Baby, Murch—we've lost it!" I exclaimed.

"I know," he said gloomily. "That hurts, sure."

"You fellows decide," put in Gondy. "The machine is yours, not mine."

"Come on," I said, and rose. We scraped up the loose coins, dumped them in on top of the unopened rolls, and hefted the busted chest out to the open air to where the Fiat stood. The back end stood open and rifled; no mistake—the Baby was gone. We loaded in the chest, extinguished the lantern, and piled into the car—we were taking Rose with us, of course. The actual and visual loss of our machine hit me and Murchison hard.

As we crowded in, my foot struck against something.

"Here, wait—I'm tangled," I said. "What's this on the floor? A box?"

"Oh, yes," Gondy replied. "There was no room in back and I put it in front. It's that small carton of spare parts for the machine—"

"Holy mackerel!" Murchison let out a yip. "Bill! The tubes!"

"What tubes?" I said. "The spare ones?"

"Yes—all of 'em! I took the tubes out of the Baby while we were taking it apart, put 'em all in this one box—hey, you know what it means? We've got all the tubes! They can't use the Baby. We can build another—"

We all began to laugh hilariously until Rose caught the infection without knowing what it was about.

As to getting the police after Sir Eric and Félice—well, it proved a hard job, because at first they thought we were spoofing them. And by the time someone in authority was convinced that we were discussing immediate and important business, Félice and Sir Eric somehow made a get-away or dodged into hiding. So until one of those ancient jewels turns up and offers a new clue, that part of the story must remain unfinished.

X

DEATH-TRAPPED GOLD

Underwater mines still threatening a French
harbor present a tragic problem for even a vastly
improved mine-detector; but they also lead an
American volunteer on a dramatic treasure quest.

MURCHISON AND I, with our pal the Vicomte de Gondy, sat in the lounge of a London hotel, looked at our visitor and tried to appear brisk and cheerful. It was a flat failure. We were utterly miserable. Our visitor was the only cheerful one there, and we knew what he was after. He was a three-star U. S. general—Murphy, I shall here call him, because that was not his name. He turned to me and beamed.

"I'm delighted to meet with you, Mr. Carson," he said. "The work you and Murchison accomplished during the war with mine-detectors was marvelous."

"The war was over a long time ago, General," I said. But he took no hints.

"Yes, but its effects remain. Are you aware how many thousands of people, since the war's end, have been killed by German mines? The French and Holland and Danish coasts are still alive with mines. German-occupied houses and towns are mined and booby-trapped, as well as the shores. Here and there in our base sectors we've been able to do a little de-mining, but it's a slow business for us, for the French, for everyone affected! Are you aware how many—"

"Skip it," said Murchison, his thin features very sour. "What's the bad news?"

"You three gentlemen," and our visitor included Gondy in his sweeping glance, "have been running up and down Europe, very profitably. With the help of an electronic mine detector which you, Mr. Murchison, invented with Mr. Carson while in the service, you've been hunting buried treasure and other things—"

"Just a minute," I put in. "That's no mine-detector. It's one of our failures. It won't work on mines at all, but does work on other things. We had permission to keep it."

"Oh, naturally," said the General amiably. "Now let's take a look at Hauteville harbor, on the French coast, gentlemen. We've been trying to make this into a first-class harbor; we have urgent need of it in redeployment. But in the past month, we've lost two Liberty ships, one tanker, and a dozen French fishing-smacks there. How?"

"I'll bite," said Murch. "By mines that should have been de-mined and weren't."

The General took that one on the chin, and nodded.

"Correct. In their death-rattles, the Nazis spewed out some beautiful big shrapnel mines that squat underwater like giant crabs; some are detonated magnetically by any steel ship close by. Others are Remingtons."

"Remingtons?" queried Gondy.

The General smiled. "Touch system, yes. We can't tell where these damned things are; we've cleared out everything to low-tide mark, but they're below this in deeper water. We've lost a good many men—German prisoners, French de-miners, and our own men. It's got to stop, and one way of stopping it has been suggested."

"I'm wearing a discharge button," I said…. Mines! I had a horror of them.

"Yes. So are the French fishermen; but they must fish to live. They perish almost daily; the sands may spout death at any moment. The French are, of course, in nominal charge of de-mining, but you know how the French do things. The problem is ours as well, particularly at Hauteville."

Murchison was looking stubborn, angry, resentful—precisely as I felt.

"It has nothing to do with us," he said defiantly.

"Just the same, I'm talking to you," rejoined the General with quiet good humor. "You and Carson carried the fine art of mine-detecting to its zenith. You applied electronics to the work; you accomplished great things. The story goes that you two fellows can pick mines out of the air or out of the ground and spin 'em around your fingers. The question is, can you pick 'em out from under the water?

"You see," he went on, blind to our hostility, "ever since V-E Day there's been a mad rush to get home. We've kept our organization, of course, but some of the special services are disrupted all to hell. We've no one who can handle this thing. We can't use mine-sweepers, even if they'd work on these crab-mines, because of the shape of the harbor. Further, a good many of the houses ashore have had to be closed up and left empty because of the danger; some of them are magnificent villas. We've cleared a good many, of course, but—well, we lost too many men doing it, if you want the truth."

We did not want the truth. I knew exactly how Murch felt; the idea of contacting any mines made us crawl inwardly. Scared? Yes; personally, I was too damned scared to think about it.

"So you're drafting us to do the job—is that it?" growled Murchison.

"Not at all, my dear chap," said the General, smiling. "You and Carson are out of the service. I've no authority to do any drafting. I'm merely pointing out that you two men have an unrivaled knowledge of detectors, of electronics, of detecting devices. I'm hoping that you might be able to adapt some device to the purposes in view. Not, essentially as a Government service, but as a human service."

"Human?" I repeated ironically. "Blow ourselves to hell, in human service?"

"Exactly, Carson," said he. "But don't be silly; you'll not blow yourselves up. The human service is both to us and to the French—to these poor devils who depend on the sea for their existence. You, with your skill at mechanical devices, can do this. I might even suggest that you might have been given such skill for just this very purpose."

I EXCHANGED a look with Murchison. We knew each other well; we had been friends and associates for years. I knew what was in his mind. We had worked and worked with our treasure-finder—the Baby, we called it facetiously—until we had carried it far beyond our original concept. We knew now, for example, that although ordinary radar will not work under water, our projected improvements in the use of supersonic waves would make the Baby of some service, at least, in such a job.

"I beg your pardon, *mon général.*" Gondy leaned forward, his pleasant features intent. "May it be permitted me to ask a question?"

"A dozen, if you like."

"At this Hauteville, there is or was a villa of great beauty, belonging to a man named Pappacoulis, a Greek, who was killed during the war. May I asked whether it is now occupied?"

"God forbid!" ejaculated the General. "I know the place—Villa des Mimosas. It's a death-trap. It's been boarded up, until we can get around to de-mining it."

"Oh, thank you." Gondy rose, beaming. "With your permission—"

"Hey, where you going?" shot out Murch. Gondy waved his hand.

"To pack," said he, "and to get off some telegrams."

Shaking hands with our visitor, he departed. Murchison and I exchanged a look. I caught the reluctant twinkle in his eye, and nodded.

"Well, General, I guess it's unanimous," he said. "We'll take the job, dammit—though we can't promise miracles."

General Murphy regarded us gravely.

"I knew you would, and I appreciate your feelings thoroughly. Now, here's the proposition. You'll be civilians, of course, but I'll stand behind you in every way. You'll be our guests. You can requisition any damned thing you want in the way of men, machinery, supplies of every sort."

"We'll have to build a new detector," I said, "having lost that gadget of ours last week. So much the better. It'll give us a chance to tackle the changes and improvements we've thought up, Murch. I was over at the BBC works yesterday, and am getting some tubes made up for me."

Murchison nodded "And if I can get into the lab we used during the war, at Lord Iverleigh's arms works in Kent, I can get hold of a magnesium-alloy framework that'll be just the ticket. We can do the rest of the work right on the spot. We have the wiring and layout in our heads—"

"You can have anything in God's world that you want," said the General. "When can you get away?"

I looked at Murch. "You get that framework tomorrow. I'll hustle up the tubes and other things. Tomorrow night?"

"Okay," he replied. "Tomorrow night it is. But we'll have to get cracking."

"Then we'll leave the morning after," said the General, somewhat taken aback by this prompt action. "I have a few things to finish up tomorrow, myself. Does your friend Gondy go along?"

As the weighted cork went over the side, the Colonel waved, ordering a detonating charge to be dropped.

"He's a jump ahead of us; he's practically there now," I replied. The words held more truth than I realized.

I SUSPECTED by Gondy's query about the Villa des Mimosas that he had something juicy up his sleeve; but from that moment until we got away, there was no time for any get-together. Murch and I were back on the job again; we wore no uniform but had to produce double in consequence. In less time than it takes to tell it, we had to come up with a gadget better than any other gadget going, all out of our heads—and we did it. We did not sleep; we scarcely ate. When we disembarked at Hauteville, we were bug-eyed and staggering, but we had the thing thrown together. It was clumsy—it looked like a Gold-berger; but it would work—at least to some extent. We got

there about noon, told Gondy to call us next morning, and crawled into bed....

As it turned out, we had all next day to ourselves, the General having been called to headquarters of the Normandy Base Section at Deauville. So we fell to work adjusting and tinkering. Gondy plaintively tried to get us into conference with him, and we ignored him. We were one-track guys and no mistake, just then. So he disappeared on his own errands; he had located some old friends from the Maquis, I gathered, and what with his title and all, was a personage of consequence in French army circles.

By evening, we had our detector working—satisfactorily, so we hoped—and mounted on a flat-bottomed boat of good size. The General had sent word that he expected to take part in the trial runs; and since all through the day we had been hearing mine-explosions at half-hour intervals and seeing French de-mining squads running around, the more generals the better. We were frankly nervous.

However, Gondy grabbed us that evening and would not be denied. He took us across town to a disreputable French place where we fed on excellent lobster and Chablis, and could talk. Gondy had plenty to say. He had been working hard, it seemed. He was enthusiastic.

"I commandeered a squad of men, thanks to the kindness of your general," he said, with a grin. "Today, and for the next couple of days, I am at work on the Villa des Mimosas. A couple of expert Boche prisoners have helped a lot."

"Doing what?" I asked.

"Making it livable—by removing booby-traps; searching in the garden for mines. We'll take over that villa as our head-quarters in three days."

"The hell we will!" said Murchison. "That death-trap?"

"*Zut, alors!*" Gondy sniffed disdainfully. "Listen, my friends! The Greek who owned that place, Pappacoulis, was killed there by the Nazis. He was a gambler; he was enormously wealthy, but he left nothing. He married a French woman, who is in Paris. I've been in communication with her, and this is the result."

He spread out a gray-blue telegram on the table; we read it. Madame Pappacoulis had gladly leased him the villa, for the season, at a nominal price.

Gondy winked. "A protection. Both French and Americans are requisitioning villas as fast as they're cleared of traps and mines. Our friend General Murphy will take over from us when we're finished there."

"Finished?" I repeated. "Finished with what? We're comfortable at headquarters—"

"Not prospering, though," said Gondy. "I heard of this Pappacoulis before D Day, when I was with the Resistance, the Maquis. There were stories. He was shot by the Nazis; but they never found his money. A lot of money! He had hidden it somewhere in or about the villa. Eh?"

We got the point. The Nazis had turned the place inside out to find the treasure, in vain. Nor did the widow know of it. Gondy was convinced that it existed. We understood vaguely that the widow was engaged in some relief work in Paris and needed money for her work.

We assented to Gondy's desires without great interest. At the moment, neither Murchison nor I were in any treasure-hunting mood. That afternoon we had seen two men blown apart by a beach mine, and had received a disgustingly cheerful message from General Murphy that he would be back tonight and expected to go to work with us in the morning. Also, inquiries had told us that these underwater crabs, or shrapnel mines, were anti-invasion devices of deadly effect. So we proceeded to have several drinks, fast, and gave but little thought to the Veuve Pappacoulis. The more so, as Kitty came walking in, slid into a chair at our table, and demanded a drink.

The Little Cat—that was all the name he had. We made it Kitty. He was perhaps fifteen, and looked nine or ten: a ragged,

Kitty was perhaps fifteen,
a ragged, wizened boy with
an air of arrogant depravity
and the ethics of an alley cat.

wizened boy with wide gray eyes, a German automatic pistol
at his belt, an air of arrogant depravity, a smile to charm angels,
and the ethics of an alley cat. Gondy introduced him as one of
the Maquis, a Nazi-killer. Inside of half an hour he was one of
us. In fact, he glued himself to us from that moment.

KITTY WAS all a boy should not be. A bad egg, impudent,
obscene and rascally; yet something behind his pinched little
face captivated us. He was a product of Nazi brutality; he had
seen his family butchered, and taking to the brush, had in turn

become a butcher. It was incredible, but true. He now calmly
announced that he would be of great use to us, needing only
food and cigarettes. He was bright as a dollar, and Murchison
promptly took him on.

We did not share Gondy's dreams that night. Our own
dreams were realistic and unpleasant; and next morning they
seemed to be coming true. General Murphy showed up as large
as life. He brought along a French colonel who was in charge
of de-mining operations, and who spoke English. We brought
along Kitty; rather, could not get rid of him. It was a crazy
assortment that moved down to the pier.

We had four rowers in our flat-bottomed boat, which left
no room for ping-pong. The Colonel had another boat with a
French de-mining crew standing by under his orders; also he
had some corks tied to long lines with sinkers at the end.

"Suppose we start with the channel," said General Murphy. The Colonel said no mines were there; they had all been removed. Murphy said we would try it anyhow; he was taking no Frenchman's word for anything. So we headed for the channel.

Our gadget sat in the boat's flat bottom. Kitty watching it with avid eyes. We had connected good strong batteries, and she was humming nicely. In the channel, the oars dipped slowly. Our previous day's tests had given us the general reaction of the gauges. We explained this to our guests, telling how the rays swept the bottom as we moved along and kicked back from any solid objects, registering on the gauges according to the mass of the substance encountered. The gadget was similar to any ship's electronic sounding devices, except that our tubes were infinitely more delicate, and penetrated the bottom instead of registering it. Rock, of course, would cause a kickback, but this was not rocky bottom.

GENERAL MURPHY obviously had his doubts of our detector; the Colonel eyed it with undisguised scorn. The Little Cat kept up a fire of questions under his breath; his adoration of it and of everything American was amusing. For some time we moved about with the other boat trailing us. We picked up a large expanse of metal—a sunken landing barge, said the French colonel. The gadget buzzed again: according to our chart, the figures indicated stone. The Colonel said it was an old hull filled with cement. which his divers had blown up. When, the next time we got a buzz, we pronounced it metal, the French colonel waved his hand and said it was a mistake.

We backed and filled, hovering over the spot. By the figures, I set it down as metal of circular shape, about six feet across, at a thirty-foot depth.

"Mine, by George!" exclaimed Murphy. Quite impossible, the Colonel said loftily. To prove it. he dropped one of his weighted corks over the side for a marker, and waved a hand at his following boat, telling them to drop a detonating charge.

We moved on up the channel and their boat came to the marker. They put down a detonation charge, and we took it for granted that they knew what they were doing. Actually, of course, their idea was to show us up for a pack of fools. I did not realize this, and was tinkering with our gadget when—

WHAM!

The concussion hit us with terrific effect. I looked around to see water and smoke bursting high; the air began to whine all around us. The men in both boats let out frantic yells. General Murphy went down on his nose; Murch and I went down on top of Kitty, and the French colonel hit his head but not his *derrière,* which was large.

WHISTLING OF the shrapnel continued, and the Colonel let out a frightful scream. We had detected and set off one of those damned crabs that rose up above the water and then loosed shrapnel in all directions. The boats were hit repeatedly, and why we were not all killed was a mystery. The only man hurt was the Colonel, and his wound was not mortal. It was highly irritating, however; it would keep him on his feet for a long time to come, and Kitty directed at him a burst of Gallic jokes that shredded what was left of his dignity.

"Let's get the hell out of here quick," said General Murphy. We did! When we got ashore and were off by ourselves, Murphy talked with blistering candor.

"No mines in this channel, huh? Well, he's learned different, blast him! Now I'll take this work in hand myself; I'll know who's handling the detonation charges and how, by God!"

We were in entire agreement. He took us to lunch at headquarters in the old casino. Like every French seaside resort, Hauteville had sported a casino with private baccarat and *chemin* games, and open tables for one-franc pikers. It was now occupied by headquarters, and all the VIPs in the sector, French or American or Hottentot, congregated there. General Murphy had taken a liking to Kitty, who came along with us.

At lunch we met a touring chaplain just from Paris. He was

full of stories, and had gone off the deep end over some woman in the capital who was doing a great and thankless work among children. She had organized several homes, gathering the street gamins and city riffraff and juvenile delinquents together. She had evolved a practical system that really worked, and was doing untold good. I was only mildly interested until he mentioned her name—Pappacoulis.

"She is an angel," said he fervently, "a saint! She has a personality that hits one between the eyes. She has half a dozen homes started, and when not engaged there, travels around France begging help for her work. The most wonderful person I have met over here—"

Just a coincidence, or so I thought at the moment. Presently we forgot about it under the pressure of our own job. An hour later, we were out on the water again with an organization that ticked like clockwork. And before knocking off that day, we located seven of those damned crabs and two ordinary mines. We would mark the spot; then the detonation squad would blow up the mine, with due precaution. When handled efficiently it was a simple matter....

During the next three days we scarcely drew a free breath. We went from the channel to the harbor in general, wasting no time recovering mines, but just blowing them up as rapidly as possible. We got the kinks out of our detector, and picked off mines like nobody's business. Also, we lost our fears. As we handled it, the job was reasonably safe.

In all this Kitty stuck to us like a leech. The young rascal did not inspire affection, but he was keenly interesting and did make himself of great use; we liked him, felt sorry for him, and appreciated his hero-worship. After a couple of days he transferred himself to Gondy, who was busy getting the Pappacoulis villa in shape. It was a mean job.

Friday night we had dinner with Gondy, who wanted us to come see the villa. We refused. Two men had been blown up there during the day. Gondy merely shrugged.

"They were Boche prisoners, and were caught by one of their own booby-traps," he said. "When can you move in, then?"

"Tomorrow night," Murchison replied. "We'll not work over Sunday."

"Fine! We'll be together again, plus the Little Cat. I've engaged two of the Pappacoulis servants to do for us. I'll expect you for dinner Saturday. Leave your things packed, and Kitty can get them moved in. Why not bring the General for dinner? Murphy's a good guy."

So, on Saturday, we gathered about the festive board. It was our chance to establish a new *modus operandi,* and we made the most of it. General Murphy was altogether too enthusiastic about our work and wanted it extended to the land area.

At dinner we worked out a scheme by which we would spend the mornings on the water, and would be off duty for the rest of the day. Nominally, that is; actually, we had to rig up a couple of the regular French detectors, to give them the benefit of our own devices. De-mining, even with Boche prisoners on the job, was a tedious business. Had the Nazis spent half the energy on fighting which they put into mining and booby-trapping, the war would have lasted longer.

It was a grand dinner. Not until it was over and General Murphy gone, did we have a chance to inspect our new quarters. These were amazing. Even after Nazi looting, the rare furniture and rugs and pictures and knick-knacks represented a small fortune. Gondy had put everything in shape. The rooms on the ground floor were half-walled and floored with tile—to do away with fleas, said Kitty practically; but the tiles were glorious bits of color from Tunis. The gardens had been equally sumptuous. Now, alas, they were in sad condition, mere heaps of earth and dead stalks of flowers and shrubs, with some broken bits of statuary. Pappacoulis must have liked statuary. There was a lot of it around the house.

"But be careful!" Gondy warned us, and particularly Kitty, who frisked about the place like a young imp, "We probably haven't found all the booby-traps. The place has been well gone over, but one can't be sure, naturally; so leave things as they are."

Kitty emphasized the warning. "No need to worry about me," said he. "I know all about these Boche traps. I would touch nothing in this house without making sure!"

Next morning, Sunday, we all slept late. Then, getting rid of Kitty the three of us held a treasure conference. There were more bedrooms in the place than we could possibly use, and we wanted a go at the hidden wealth before General Murphy commandeered a few rooms and moved somebody else in on us.

PAPPACOULIS, A terrific plunger and heavy winner at gambling, had sneered at the idea of any trouble from the Nazis. He was a Greek, had many German friends, and would never be molested, said he. To err is human, as he learned.

"It's known that he had a whopping lot of cash on hand," said Gondy. "The Nazis didn't get it; he died cursing them, defying them. The story has become a regular legend around here. They say millions are hidden somewhere about; the place has been ransacked repeatedly, of course."

"We've always had luck with gardens," said Murchison.

"Check it off. That garden is good for mines, nothing else. We've taken out six, and there are more; apparently every stone is booby-trapped. That's where my two Boches got their tickets. Quite a few people have dug there for treasure, with fatal consequences."

"That lets me out," I declared. "Suppose each of us looks over the place today on his own. Tonight we can meet and compare notes, making some plan of operations. What about Kitty? Do we confide in him?"

It was unanimously resolved that we would not. So far as he was concerned, we would merely be fixing up the two detectors for the French de-miners.

All obvious places of concealment in the house had long ago been attacked; even the walls had been ripped open. There was no safe of any sort. There was no cellar, though an alleged "central heating" did exist under the front of the house, in the inadequate French style. A stairs went down from the outside into a little furnace pit eight feet square, room and stairs all carved out of the earth and not even plastered. A toy heater stood there, with pipes to heat the three front rooms. That was all. At best, it would only take the chill off the rooms above. There was no place to store fuel, even. Oddly enough, a niche had been cut out of the earthen wall, and in it stood a small six-inch pottery figure of a woman—a graceful thing, though an arm had been broken off. Just a broken little statuette put here to ornament the furnace room, perhaps in derision.

That afternoon Murchison and I went down to the Recreation Center. Having no dignity of rank to uphold, we got into a G.I. crap game and had fun. We got home late, and walked into a real surprise. An odd little woman dressed in black sat in the parlor, talking with Gondy and Kitty—indeed, she had her arm around the boy. I thought his mother had turned up, until Gondy. beaming and bubbling away in delight, introduced us to our landlady, Madame Pappacoulis, who had come down unexpectedly from Paris for a few days.

What was more, Gondy had installed her in the best front bedroom. The two servants were happy as larks at her presence. Already the place had taken on a different and happier air. To my surprise, that arrogant little devil of a Kitty was a different person in her vicinity—she brought back to him a magic touch of lost boyhood, and his cynical diablerie vanished completely.

MADAME REALLY was something. She was neither young nor pretty. Like so many Frenchwomen, she had a big nose; and like all Frenchwomen these days, her black garments were undistinguished and worn threadbare. She had brown eyes, beautiful hands; and when in repose her features looked sad and empty. But in animation—wow! She became another creature. One realized how the inner self can shine and radiate through the outer shell, and what a lovely thing it can be. Before dinner was over, we were her slaves; nor was it absurd. She had character plus.

She was full of the most amazing sincerities. If she spoke of her work with juvenile delinquents, it was not to recount what had been achieved, but to reveal the human aspect of the thing. She had new ways of looking at any subject, without bias or prejudice, as from some height invisible. Yet she was definitely practical.

"It says gold is back of that earthen wall— quick! Get some tools and bust into it!"

"I really came here to get some linens and other household articles which we need and you don't," she said. "Also some personal belongings, chiefly jewelry. I left hurriedly for Paris, but my husband, poor man, refused to go."

"And did you find any jewelry, after all the looting here?" I asked.

She shook her head. "My husband hid it. He had a safe place; I don't know where."

We exchanged glances. Gondy tactfully broached the subject of the Pappacoulis treasure. She spoke of it openly as a fact, yet had no idea about any hiding-place. Later, she gave us full permission to look for it on a fifty-fifty basis, but could afford us no help whatever.

I noticed a peculiar thing, now and later; she seldom or never smiled. That is, with her lips. All the expression of her countenance lay in those glorious brown eyes. With them she could smile or laugh vivaciously enough, but there her emotions stopped. She was not a bit glum—she could be quite gay, in fact. I suppose she had just lost the art of smiling. It was this, perhaps, which lent her such impressive power, this and her force of character. She could sit and say never a word, and dominate everyone. Yet she was inexpressibly kind and gentle. The two servants loved her. Kitty just sat and watched her, with a rapt expression, by the hour; he absolutely abandoned us for her.

Later that night, after she had retired, Murchison and I and Gondy got together and talked of treasure. Gondy had a notion it might be hidden in the furnace pit. Murch and I were devoid of ideas, particularly after what our visitor had told us. Her jewels were kept in a small carved oak box a foot long. Pappacoulis had owned two little old ikons or paintings which he prized highly, of about the same size. Therefore, she thought, the container of the treasure must be of fair size, and was probably of metal because of fire peril. So our perplexities were perfect, since nothing of such size could well be hidden about the house. Added to which, our own detecting gadget was kept under guard at headquarters.

"We have to work up those two detectors for the French," said Murchison finally. "Why not do it right here, Bill?"

"Sure," I replied. "Of afternoons. Use our own tubes till we get some made. Take our time about it, and combine business with pleasure. Spot mines of mornings, and look around for the hard cash of afternoons."

"You got it," said he. "Kitty won't catch on; we'll just be testing the detectors, so far as he knows. We can jazz up one of those things in a day or so and get cracking."

So we left it at that, and next afternoon brought home one of the French detectors we were to work over, and got busy on it.

By this time, we really liked the set-up. Having Mme. Pappacoulis around was more than a pleasure; we had even prevailed on her to remain for a full week. Gondy wanted to give a dinner or two for her, suggesting that she might as well raise some funds for her work. As for Kitty—the widow had taken a liking to that young devil. I had some doubts whether she could reform him, and suspected he was playing some sort of swindling game with her. We had come to think so much of her, that we meant to protect her at all costs. I tried to warn her against him, and she laughed at me in her quiet, unsmiling way.

"You know so little about children, dear M. Carson!" she said. "The boy has a heart of gold. I shall take him to Paris with me."

"Then watch your pocketbook," I said. "I like the kid too, but I like you more."

This amused her.

THE DAYS passed rapidly. We spotted anti-invasion mines in the mornings, and labored of afternoons on the French detector, really making something super out of it too. When we got it working, we experimented in and around the house, turning up nothing at all. We tried it in the garden with a squad of French de-miners at hand, and discovered three mines within an hour. The thing was working perfectly.

"Try the furnace pit with it now," Gondy begged.

"Tomorrow," Murchison rejoined. "I want to get away from here while they remove those mines. Tomorrow it is!"

I wanted to get away also. We went for a walk and took Mme. Pappacoulis with us. The three mines were removed without incident however, while we were gone.

That evening—it was Friday—General Murphy and three of his staff came to dinner. It was an eventful meal. By the time the entrée arrived, the General had forgotten our existence; he was completely wrapped up in our fair widow, as were his officers. With the coffee and liqueurs, he was planning a subscription list to aid her work, and had invited her to dinner at headquarters next evening. In short, it was a triumph for her.

Saturday morning we worked on the harbor as usual, and came home for lunch. We found Mme. Pappacoulis packing linens and other things, with Kitty aiding her. Since Gondy was insistent that we try out the furnace pit for the treasure, I told him to meet me there in an hour; neither Murchison nor I had any faith in the Pappacoulis hoard, and Murch trotted off downtown on some errands of his own.

At about the appointed time I carried the detector down to the furnace pit and switched on the light there. Gondy came, presently. We got the detector to work and ran it all around the tiny furnace, covering the entire floor, without making a strike of any kind.

Gondy was crestfallen; he'd counted heavily on getting results here in the cellar.

"No soap," I said. "Might as well call it a day—"

I broke off, as steps sounded on the stairs and Mme. Pappacoulis appeared. She nodded brightly to us.

"So you're here, messieurs! I've come for my Tanagra statuette. I want to take it with me."

"Your what?" I asked. She indicated the little image in the wall.

"That. A genuine Tanagra—so delicate, so gentle! My poor husband laughed at me for loving a broken statuette, and put it here, to keep warm as he said. It was his little joke, you see. But I shall take her with me, because I always loved her."

A PATTER of feet, and down came Kitty. He stopped short at sight of us, gawking; then, as Mme. Pappacoulis stepped forward toward the niche, he crowded past me and quickly caught her arm.

"No, no!" he cried sharply. "Don't touch it, madame! It is not safe!"

She patted his cheek. "Don't be absurd, my child," she said. "That little image was made long ago in a Greek city of Asia Minor, and it is a very beautiful thing; even if it is broken, it is still lovely, for scars do not affect true beauty. I got it when I was a girl, and I shall always keep it. So it goes to Paris with us—"

She stooped as she spoke, and reached forward to take the little statue from the niche. We were all squeezed into that tiny space. Kitty fairly flew at Gondy, knocked him aside, flung himself in front of Mme. Pappacoulis, and with a sobbing cry struck her arm away—too late. She had already caught up the statuette....

The flash, the explosion, came together. I was knocked headlong, and Gondy fell on top of me, the clothes half ripped from his body; yet he was unhurt. He yanked me erect. The electric bulb still burned; the ghastly scene stood stark revealed amid the dust and fumes.

We lifted Mme. Pappacoulis and carried her out to the sunlight, shouted for the servants and then plunged back for Kitty. He was covered with blood. We got him outside, taking for granted that he was dead. She, by great good luck, suffered only from shock and a few cuts; Kitty's body had saved hers from the flying death. He had done it deliberately, guessing what would happen. He could smell a booby-trap, as he had often said.

Hauteville had become efficient in mine-disaster work. The Little Cat, with two surgeons already at work on him, was whisked away to a hospital. Mme. Pappacoulis was taken to her room in the villa and put to bed, her few hurts bandaged; she was already conscious, and inquiring about the boy. The little Tanagra statuette was still clutched in her hand.

Murchison came home, bringing word that Kitty was alive but badly chewed up, with seventeen grenade fragments in him; everything possible was being done for him.

"It's a toss-up," said Murch gloomily. "One of those fragments, tore right through him and lodged against his spine. Even if the kid lives it may paralyze him. How you guys came to let it happen, I can't see. Is it true that he sacrificed himself for her?"

"Yes. And she's got a bad cheek-wound herself," Gondy rejoined, with a groan. "Looked like a scratch, but the surgeon who was here says it may have severed the facial nerve."

Presently two more surgeons came. They looked Mme. Pappacoulis over, then joined us downstairs for a drink. Both were savagely profane.

"About her, it is very bad," said one. "Bourguet is the only man in France who could help—no one else dare try that wound of the boy's, either. Bourguet could do it—"

"Hell's bells!" I broke out. "Then get Bourguet! Get him at once!"

THEY LOOKED at me and shook their heads. Bourguet, the great surgeon, had a hospital at Biarritz; he did private practice at huge fees. They went away gloomily and five minutes later General Murphy's car roared up.

The General was all lit up about Kitty's action, but when he heard our report, he just looked at us. Then he jumped to his feet.

"The war's over, is it?" he blurted. "Like hell it is! We've still got phones and airplanes, haven't we? By God, I'll have this fellow Bourguet here by morning!"

He actually went out of the house running, and his car roared away. We looked at one another and mixed another drink.

"Looks promising," said Murch. "Still, at the best it's a bad thing for her. Means that she'll be laid up for a long time, poor old girl! I suppose the explosion blew hell out of the detector, Bill?"

"I don't know," I said. "Never thought about it. Let's go see."

In spite of General Murphy, we were not cheerful. Those surgeons had told us what it means if the facial nerve is severed. I touched Gondy's arm, as the three of us started for the outside cellar entrance.

"Remember what she said, just before the crash? Scars don't affect true beauty, she said. Sounds nice, but think what it means to any woman to have a paralyzed face—"

Gondy let out a groan. "Shut up, Carson! I don't want to think about it."

We got down in the furnace pit. Where the niche and the statuette had been, was just a gaping hole in the earthen wall. Blown against the furnace and lying on its side, was the detector, still attached by wires to the bundle of batteries.

"Listen!" exclaimed Murchison sharply. "What's that noise? Sounds like—"

"The detector!" I cried. "Don't touch it—look at how it's lying... Why, it's working!"

It was, too, though the batteries were nearly run down by this time. As it lay there on its side, it was shooting straight at the curved wall of earth surrounding the furnace, at some distance from where the booby-trap had been. In that confined space, to examine the gauges was difficult. Murchison lay on the floor, looked at them, then drew back and motioned me.

"Look at 'em, Bill. See if you see what I see—or has the gadget gone haywire?"

I stretched out, and looked at the gauges.

"My Lord! If it's not crazy, and I'm not either—we've found something!" I cried. "It says gold is back of that earthen wall—quick! Get some tools and bust into it!"

We dug away six inches of the earth—and found it: A big metal box....

The earth of the wall had simply been hollowed out; after the box was hidden in the hole, wet earth was plastered in against it, leaving no sign of any opening after it was dry. So safe was the hiding-place that the box was not even locked.

After filling in the hole, we sneaked the box up to my room, so no one would know, and examined it. Gondy was jubilant; he had said all along we would find the treasure in the "cave," as the French call a cellar. He had reason to be jubilant; so did we all, in fact.

There were rolls of English sovereigns, and bundles of big flat twenty-pound notes, and even a large amount in United States money. Most of the plunder consisted of French thousand-franc notes. These were now just waste-paper, having been demonetized by the De Gaulle government, but there was plenty without them. The oak box of jewels was there; so were the two little ikons mentioned by Mme. Pappacoulis. So was some loose jewelry.

Scratching the French money, we divided up the rest of the loot on the spot. We were still at it when the dinner-call came, so we threw a blanket over the table and went to dinner. It was a hurried and excited meal, but we could do no talking, because the nurse taking care of Mme. Pappacoulis ate with us. The one thought with us all was what this find would mean to that woman upstairs; it put us into such a fever of repression that the nurse must have thought all three of us demented.

JUST AS soon as we were free, we rushed to my room and finished the job. If the French money had not been worthless, the total amount would have been something to write home about. As it was, after laying aside the ikons and box of jewels, in which we wanted no share, each of us three found himself with a neat little pile of cash totaling close to two thousand dollars.

"Which, converted into current French funds," said Murch happily, "will come to a hell of a lot more! Now let's get the stuff packaged and out of sight. When do we tell her?"

A knock at the door made us jump. As though in reply to his words, the nurse had come to say that her patient had come out from under the opiate given her, and wanted to speak with us before being put to sleep for the night.

We went into the room where the little woman lay with her face bandaged, and Gondy took her hand and kissed it, and whispered the good word at her ear. The brown eyes flashed at us.

"But where is the Little Cat?" was all she said.

"Oh, he'll be around in a day or two," I lied. "He's at the hospital now; he was hurt a bit, but he's all right."

"Thanks to the good God!" she murmured.

Then the nurse put us out. with word that we might see her at more length in the morning. We went back to my room and gathered around the table again.

"Well, I'll be damned!" said Murch. "We tell her about this, and all she can say is to ask after Kitty! Let's get to work."

We did so, making neat packets of our individual loot and a big one of her share. By this time the evening was done, and after a drink of celebration we turned in. Murch had discovered where we could pick up a good used car cheap, Gondy was talking about a jeweled trinket for a girl friend, and I knew a half a dozen ways I could spend my share.

However, I lay awake in the dark thinking about it, and the glamour faded. I could not get away from the memory of the swift, determined manner Kitty had acted that day. He had guessed what was coming, and had taken it; I knew damned well I could never have done the same thing. The thought kept me tossing for a long time; and before I got to sleep, I had a sneaking suspicion about where my Pappacoulis loot ought to go. It would be a job to square it with Murch and Gondy, because Murch was set on getting the car tomorrow and we all had to kick in for it. So I resolved to say nothing about it to them. Might change my mind by morning, anyhow.

WE WERE up in good time, though we were not going to work this morning. While we were at breakfast, a car came roaring up, and in walked General Murphy, looking cheerful and cocky. He sat down with us and demanded a cup of coffee.

"Well?" demanded Murch. "Did you get that guy?"

"Did I get him?" barked Murphy. "Say! The Air Force Command is still cussing me, but I got him. He's here. He's been over at the hospital with the kid for half an hour, and he'll be here later on this morning."

"Swell!" I exclaimed. "And what about Kitty? Can Bourguet pull him through?"

"Yeah." Murphy swigged his coffee. "But he says it'll be a long job, and he's worried about the lady here. He'll have to take 'em both to his hospital. I'm arranging it now by air. With her it'll be one of those delicate, long-drawn-out affairs. Poor woman! I'd like to give that boy a medal, damned if I wouldn't! Well, I must rush off. Got to arrange things with this damned Air Command—I'll do it if it costs me a star! See you later."

I let the others see him off. I went up to my room and got my packet of loot, because my mind had not changed. I met the nurse, and she said I could see Mme. Pappacoulis for a minute or two, so I went in and sat down beside the widow, and held her hand.

"Dr. Bourguet is here, and he says Kitty will be all right, and he's taking charge of you too," I told her. "Also, we've divided up the money and things we found last night."

"Oh, don't talk about that now," she murmured.

I squeezed her hand. "Yes. Got to do it, madame." I got out the packet and shoved it under her pillows. "This is my share. I don't want it. I don't need it at all. You do. Take charge of it, because you and the Little Cat will have lots of expenses ahead.

Don't say anything about it to anyone—just use it and it'll make me happy."

She looked at me for a moment, and those brown eyes of hers said things. Then her fingers drew at my hand and I leaned over, asking what she wanted.

"The Little Cat," she whispered. "He admires you. He says you are *un brave*. Me, I do not know what to say; there are no words. Please—come closer—"

I obeyed. She lifted her bandaged head and kissed me. That was all. But believe me, I wouldn't have swapped that kiss for the Medal of Honor!

Well, before we knew it, the villa was like a madhouse. Bourguet came, with surgeons and nurses fluttering around him; and pretty soon in roared General Murphy with word that a special plane was waiting to take them to Biarritz. There was not a minute to lose, because Bourguet wanted to get to work on his two patients as quickly as possible with his own assistants and nurses and so forth.

We went to the airfield with them and saw them off. We could not speak with Kitty, but Mme. Pappacoulis took our messages for him. Gondy had seen to packing her share of the loot, so everything was settled.

Afterward, the three of us went back to the villa, and sat around a drink. I knew the evil moment had come, and I was right. Murchison came out with with it.

"Now," he began, "about that car—"

"Hold on," I broke in. "Does it have to be settled today?"

"You're damned right it does," he said. "A French officer is taking it if we don't. We lay down six hundred berries, and it's ours. The biggest bargain you ever saw. The only trouble is that I want to borrow my share, two hundred, off of you for a few days—"

"You—what?" I stared at him. "Cough up some of your loot, confound you! Here, Gondy, you kick in with a loan—"

Gondy spread out his hands and looked worried.

"My friends, it is most regrettable," he said, "but I—well, it is impossible. You see, I got into a baccarat game last night, and I must be the one to borrow—"

"Baccarat game? Like hell!" exploded Murch. "You were home in bed all last night!"

There was a silence. We looked at one another. Gondy was rather white, and finally he broke the silence, rather desperately.

"My friends, I can't lie about it. I know what a fool you'll think me, and I know you depended on my share of the price of this automobile. Well, I must disappoint you. I am sorry. I haven't a sou to my name. I—I spent all that money."

HIS STAMMERING words ended, as I met Murchison's eye. Suddenly we both understood.

With a laugh of relief, up I jumped.

"Hurray! This calls for champagne—go get that last bottle, Murch! And I thought you guys would snow me for being a damned fool—why, we're all damned fools together! And I don't know when I've been so happy."

We were all laughing and babbling in unison, as we cracked the bottle to the health of the Little Cat and the widow whose scars did not affect her true loveliness. I would like to say that it ended there; but Gondy was a Frenchman after all. Between champagne and sentiment and enthusiasm, he insisted on embracing us, and his breath was garlicky.

And we did not get the car.

H. BEDFORD-JONES

BEDFORD-JONES IS a Canadian by birth, but not by profession, having removed to the United States at the age of one year. For over twenty years he has been more or less profitably engaged in writing and traveling. As he has seldom resided in one place longer than a year or so and is a person of retiring habits, he is somewhat a man of mystery; more than once he has suffered from unscrupulous gentlemen who impersonated him—one of whom murdered a wife and was subsequently shot by the police, luckily after losing his alias.

The real Bedford-Jones is an elderly man, whose gray hair and precise attire give him rather the appearance of a retired foreign diplomat. His hobby is stamp collecting, and his collection of Japan is said to be one of the finest in existence. At present writing he is en route to Morocco, and when this appears in print he will probably be somewhere on the Mojave Desert in company with Erle Stanley Gardner.

Questioned as to the main facts in his life, he declared there was only one main fact, but it was not for publication; that his life had been uneventful except for numerous financial losses, and that his only adventures lay in evading adventurers. In his younger years he was something of an athlete, but the encroachments of age preclude any active pursuits except that of motoring. He is usually to be found poring over his stamps, working at his typewriter, or laboring in his California rose garden, which is one of the sights of Cathedral Cañon, near Palm Springs.

Bedford-Jones has written stories laid in many corners of the earth, but among his most popular tales were the John Solomon stories which started many years ago in the *Argosy*.

www.ingramcontent.com/pod-product-compliance
Lightning Source LLC
Chambersburg PA
CBHW050123030726
47505CB00007B/2008